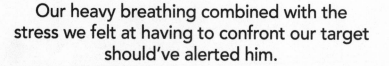

Our heavy breathing combined with the stress we felt at having to confront our target should've alerted him.

But feeding vamps are so immersed in the moment they rarely sense their hunters. Ours had stopped beside an empty donkey cart, a hulking shadow stooping next to the wheel like he was checking its integrity. Except that a man wearing a plain white shirt, wrinkled blue pants, and backless leather shoes that dangled from his toes like dead squirrels lay twitching on the cobblestones beneath him.

Movement at the corner of my eye sent my hand to Grief. But it was just one of the gaunt, raggedy-eared cats that stalked the streets for scraps. This one must be hoping for a feast. It darted away when Cole strode forward, switching off his gun's safety as he said, "That's enough. Drop the guy before you kill him."

The vampire turned. And my heart broke like it had every night I'd been forced to witness this scene. While Cole lifted the cart driver onto his seat and slipped him the wages we'd promised, I watched the creature that had shattered my defenses and made me fall in love lick the man's blood from his lips.

"Madame Berggia," Vayl said to me as he straightened. "Why are you interrupting my meal?"

Praise for the Jaz Parks series

"If you're in the mood for fast-paced supernatural adventure, the Jaz Parks series never fails to deliver."

—sfsite.com on *Bitten to Death*

JAZ PARKS NOVELS

Once Bitten, Twice Shy

Another One Bites the Dust

Biting the Bullet

Bitten to Death

One More Bite

Bite Marks

Bitten in Two

The Deadliest Bite

Bitten in Two

A JAZ PARKS NOVEL

Jennifer Rardin

www.orbitbooks.net

Orbit
Hachette Book Group
237 Park Avenue, New York, NY 10017
www.HachetteBookGroup.com

First Edition: November 2010

Orbit is an imprint of Hachette Book Group, Inc. The Orbit name and logo are trademarks of Little, Brown Book Group Limited.

The characters and events in this book are fictitious. Any similarity to real persons, living or dead, is coincidental and not intended by the author.

Library of Congress Cataloging-in-Publication Data

Rardin, Jennifer.
   Bitten in two / Jennifer Rardin. — 1st ed.
      p. cm.
   Summary: "In their newest urban fantasy adventure, Jaz Parks and the gang are back to take down their most treacherous enemy yet"—Provided by publisher.
   ISBN 978-0-316-04378-6
   1. Parks, Jaz (Fictitious character)—Fiction.   2. Vampires—Fiction.   I. Title.
PS3618.A74B585 2010
813'.6—dc22

                                                                2010011851

10 9 8 7 6 5 4 3 2 1

Printed in the United States of America

This story is for Kirk. My heart is yours, forever.

CHAPTER ONE

"H oly crap, do you smell that?" I asked. I leaned away from the square, sun-bleached building and spat, but the creeping stench of death and rot had already made it down my throat.

Cole didn't answer, just nodded and pulled the collar of his new gray T-shirt up over his nose. Vayl and I had presented it to him as we'd waited to board the endless flight from Australia, the site of our last mission, to Morocco, the scene of our present mess. Our sniper and occasional interpreter had worn the shirt over a fresh white tee every day since, making this the third night in a row I'd read the bright red letters on the front that said THE OTHER GUY GOT THE GIRL. On the back, a black widow perched on her web with her mate's leg dangling out of her mouth while her rejected lover observed the carnage from under a striped beach umbrella as he sipped a fly-tai. The caption read DAMN, THAT WAS CLOSE!

"Promise me you'll wash that tomorrow," I whispered as I peered down the narrow cobblestone street. No room even for breezes here, where the red ochre buildings melded to one another like coffin lids. Every door was shut, locking poverty inside, but each displayed a unique inlaid design that raised even this arid, neglected neighborhood out of squalor. I had bigger distractions than the work of long-dead artists, however.

Where'd you sneak off to, you pain-in-the-ass vampire?

"Washing seems like a waste of time," Cole mumbled, his voice muffled by one hundred percent cotton. "I'm just going to wear it again because, you know, it's only the best shirt ever. I'm not saying you look like a spider, but if you were to cannibalize Vayl, I'm pretty sure that's exactly the picture the tabloids would end up printing." The crinkles beside his bright blue eyes gave away his hidden grin.

"Would you just throw some suds on the thing?" To soften the blow I added, "Make it my birthday present." *Crap! Only he could make me slip like that!*

"Tomorrow's your birthday?"

"Nope."

"Tonight?"

I nodded. Reluctantly.

And here I stand under the rickety metal awning of a building so old I can practically hear the ghosts screaming from behind these stucco walls. I should be lolling on some starlit beach with Vayl, half-naked and—naw, make us all naked; it's already been too long for me to waste time on foreplay. But instead I'm slouching through the back alleys of freaking Marrakech, sniffing what has to be the city's cesspool with an ex–Supernatural PI whose sleuthing skills may only be matched by his passion for red high-tops.

Moving quicker than I'd have given him credit for, Cole pulled me in for a hug so squishy I figured I'd spend the rest of the night with the imprint of my modified Walther PPK outlined on my left boob.

"Happy birthday!" he said. "You're twenty-six on May twenty-sixth. How cool is that? Especially since I didn't miss it. I thought it was earlier this month."

"Why?"

"That's what your file—uh, I mean—"

"You read my file?" I balled his shirt into my fist, forcing his collar past his nose to reveal his gaping mouth. The scent of cherry-flavored bubblegum wafted past, giving my churning stomach a break. Then it was gone and my nose hairs recurled.

"Vayl read it too," Cole reminded me.

As the CIA's top assassin, Vayl had been given full access to my information well before he'd decided to make his solo act a duet and, eventually, a whole band. I said, "That doesn't make it okay!"

Cole plucked his shirt out of my hand and repositioned it as he asked, "Why don't you want anyone to know the real date you were born?"

"Because I hate surprise parties. And I'm not interested in sharing my best secrets with snoops like you." Hoping to head off more questions, I tapped the thin plastic receiver sitting inside my ear, just above the lobe, activating my connection to: "Bergman? He's slipped our tail. Have you got a read on him?"

"Gimme a sec; someone's at the door."

Our technical consultant's clear reply confirmed my suspicion that we were still within two miles of him and the Riad Almoravid where we'd set up temporary headquarters. We'd only left the town square, which locals called the Djemaa el Fna, twenty minutes before. And since the fountain in our riad's courtyard could probably shoot a few sprinkles onto the square's crowds of merchants, performers, and shoppers on a windy day, I'd figured we were within the limits of Bergman's communications gizmo, which Cole had named the Party Line. Nice to be right about that, at least.

Now, instead of using his own transmitter, Cole leaned forward and spoke into the glamorous brown mole I'd stuck just to the left of my upper lip. "Bergman, today is Jaz's birthday. We need cake!"

I glared. "*You* need to use my alias," I reminded Cole. "And, Miles, you can just ignore what's-his-face completely. Just find—" I stopped when the swearing began.

Cole nodded wisely. "See what happens when people hang around you? Poor Bergman probably didn't even know what those words meant before you lived with him."

"Nobody should be blamed for the language they teach their roommates in college. Right, Miles?"

Before my oldest and smartest friend could reply, Cole said, "Your potty mouth is gonna get you in trouble someday." He turned his head, like Bergman was skulking in the shadows next to us. "Right, dude?"

Bergman growled, "Goddammit, she's back! I thought hotel owners had better things to do than annoy their guests every ten minutes!" We heard the door open. "I have plenty of towels—"

"Hello, Monsieur Bergman." It was the 1-900-Fantasy voice of Monique Landry, still accented with Paris despite the decades she'd spent away from home. Contrary to our genius's opinion, she'd been nothing but courteous and helpful. Except to Miles, who'd gotten extra snacks and the fluffy pillows from day one. Her twenty years in the Guests-R-Us biz had definitely honed her into the perfect hostess. And somehow she'd made the fact that she looked fabulous for a widow in her late forties (like Demi Moore with actual meat on her bones and enough past hardships to lace her eyes with compassion) part of the riad's mystique. Unfortunately all Bergman had noticed so far was that she wore brightly flowered dresses and "bothered" him a lot.

We heard her say, "I noticed you were working late so I had Chef Henri fix you a plate of beignets and a cup of green tea."

And Bergman's reply: "I'm kind of busy here, Monique. And I'm still full from—" I heard a smothering sort of sound backed by attempted talking, which I interpreted as Monique stuffing one of the small fried doughnuts into his mouth. "Hey," he said after he'd finally worked his teeth around the dessert. "That's good!"

"Lovely," she purred. "Henri will be delighted. And how is the world's weather today?"

When we'd moved into the riad three days earlier, we'd explained Bergman's mass of electronics by telling Monique that we were studying climate change.

Miles chuckled. Uh-oh. I knew exactly what expression went with that sound. His eyebrow had just gone up. He held his hand out as if a pipe filled it. And now he was shaking his head from side to side as if he'd just been caught inside a bell tower at noon. "Well, the weather waits for no one, my dear. I'd explain, but I'm sure the technical terms would make your head spin. We are, in fact, in the middle of a testing cycle, so I must get back to work. So good of you to come."

Cole and I cringed as we waited for Monique to order him off his high horse—because he looked ridiculous riding sidesaddle—and stop insulting her intelligence. Instead we heard her hand, gently patting his cheek. "You are so adorable! All right, then, I'll leave you to your work. Tomorrow morning we have fresh bread and Berber omelets for breakfast. And just for you, I will ask Chef Henri to make his famous chocolate éclairs!"

"But I don't eat breakfast," Bergman muttered. After the door had clicked shut.

Cole said, "So good of you to come? Dude, who are you, Queen Elizabeth?"

Bergman huffed, "I was trying to get her to leave without pissing her off! What would you have done?"

I said, "I'd have gotten on my knees and thanked her for those éclairs. Be nice, Miles. You need the calories."

Bergman muttered, "Are we working, or what?"

I sighed. "Constantly. So get busy, will ya?"

I imagined him checking his satellite maps and hacked surveillance video, not to mention the tracker he'd attached to our target's right boot heel. While we waited for his pronouncement, Cole reached behind his back and pulled a tranquilizer gun out from under the light brown jacket he wore over his T-shirts. The weapon blended so perfectly with his black jeans that it disappeared when he dropped his hands to his sides.

"That looks...lethal." *Could be, too, if we got the dosage wrong. Which we didn't, because I double-checked it myself. Maybe we won't need it, though. Maybe he'll cooperate.*

I cleared my throat. "Was that thing stuck in your belt?"

"Yeah. But don't worry, the safety was on." He sighted down the long, lean barrel. "Hey, imagine what would've happened if I'd shot myself in the butt. My cheeks would've been numb for a week!"

I took off down the sidewalk, keeping to the shadows, avoiding puddles of brown liquid that I knew weren't water because, according to Monique, who'd been so ecstatic to rent all five of her riad's rooms to us that she gave us random weather reports for free, it hadn't rained in the past two weeks.

Cole jogged after me. "Jaz, where are you going? We don't even know—"

"I'd rather walk aimlessly than discuss your ass, all right?"

"Yeah, but this is my *numb* ass. Do you think my legs would stop working too?"

I was getting ready to grab the gun and perform an experiment that would satisfy both his curiosity and my need to shoot something when Bergman said, "Got him. Two blocks northeast of you. He's stationary."

We turned the corner, moving so quickly we nearly plowed into two men carrying bundles of bath supplies, which meant they were headed for the nearest hammam. They'd just exited a diamond-mosaiced door. Cole hid the tranq gun behind his thigh, mumbled an apology in French, and pulled me around the men, who wore light shirts, long pants, and baseball hats, all of which were blotched with mustard-colored stains. And damn, did they stink! They must work at the dump we'd been smelling.

One of the men, a black-mustached thirtysomething with a scar under his left eye, spoke to Cole, who replied sharply, his hand tightening on my arm. Already I was used to natives offering to guide us anywhere we wanted to go, but these guys didn't have the look of euro-hungry street hustlers. I looked up at Cole. His face had gone blank, a bad sign in a guy who assassinates his country's enemies for a living.

Like the knife in my skirt's hidden pocket, the .38 strapped to my right leg weighed heavier, reminding me of my offensive options if I decided not to pull the gun disguised by my snow white windbreaker. But I didn't want to spill blood knowing a vamp prowled nearby.

"What do they want?" I asked.

"The dude with the scar is demanding a toll for the use of his road, and extra payment for nearly running him and his buddy over."

"What's his name?"

Cole asked, and while the man replied I checked out his friend. He was maybe seventeen, a brown-eyed kid with lashes so long they looked fake. He couldn't bring himself to meet my eyes.

Cole said, "His name is Yousef. The boy's name is Kamal."

"Tell Yousef I'll pay."

"What?"

"Tell him." Cole began to talk.

I swished forward, making my full red skirt swirl around my knees as my boots clicked against the cobblestones, letting my alter ego take the spotlight. Lucille Robinson was a pale, slender, green-eyed sweetie with a white streak in her red curls that might've signified another time when a man had taken advantage of her weakness and bashed her across the head before forcing her to his will. Yousef didn't know I'd earned the streak in hell, or that the Eldhayr who'd taken me there had already brought me back from the dead. Twice. All he could see was that Lucille's curls looked more likely to bounce up and defend her than her fists. Mission accomplished.

I looked up at him like he was the cutest teddy bear I'd ever hoped to squeeze. Even though he couldn't understand the words, I figured he'd get the tone as I reached down the V-neck of my dress with my left hand and said, "Just give me a second, okay? I keep my money in here so I don't have to worry about pickpockets. I understand they can be a problem in Marrakech. Am I right?"

By now I'd come within an arm's length of the reeking man, who was staring at my hand like he wished it was his. He never saw the base of my right palm shoot up. Just grunted with shock as it jammed into his jaw and knocked his head backward. He staggered. Cole aimed the tranq gun at Kamal to make sure he stayed peaceful as I followed Yousef down the sidewalk, throwing a side kick that landed on his chest with the thump of a bongo drum. He landed flat on his back in the street.

I watched him struggle to breathe as I said, "We go where we please."

Cole translated. To my surprise Yousef smiled. I looked over my shoulder at Kamal. He was staring around nervously, making me think he didn't savor a conversation with any authorities that might show to investigate the noise. He didn't seem concerned about Yousef. Maybe girls hit him a lot.

"Feel better?" Cole asked me.

I backed off before the bully's blech could stick to my sunny-day outfit. "Yeah. Let's go."

We headed down the street, keeping our eyes and Cole's gun on the mini gang until we reached the end of the block and turned north. Yousef called after us.

"Unbelievable," said Cole as he shook his head.

"What did he say?" I asked.

"He wants to know if he can see you again. He says his uncle's friend owns a good restaurant above the Djemaa el Fna."

"You're shitting me."

"No." Cole's wild blond hair danced at the suggestion. "I think he liked what you did to him. In fact, I think he liked you. Do you think he'll try to follow us?"

"Move fast," I urged, pulling him into the next alley. It would mean doubling back, but Yousef was one freak worth losing. At the same time I asked, "Bergman, is our mark still there?"

"He hasn't moved." *Finally, good news.*

At the end of the alley we turned into another neglected street. This one didn't even have sidewalks to separate the painstakingly carved apartment doors from the hit-and-run lanes. A single light at midblock threw a weak glow onto the run-down two-stories, allowing for multiple hidden spaces where people could do their worst to each other without ever being witnessed.

Our heavy breathing combined with the stress we felt at having to confront our target should've alerted him. But feeding vamps are so immersed in the moment they rarely sense their hunters. Ours had stopped beside an empty donkey cart, a hulking shadow stooping next to the wheel like he was checking its integrity. Except that a man wearing a plain white shirt, wrinkled blue pants, and backless leather shoes that dangled from his toes like dead squirrels lay twitching on the cobblestones beneath him.

Movement at the corner of my eye sent my hand to Grief. But it was just one of the gaunt, raggedy-eared cats that stalked the streets for scraps. This one must be hoping for a feast. It darted away when Cole strode forward, switching off his gun's safety as he said, "That's enough. Drop the guy before you kill him."

The vampire turned. And my heart broke like it had every night I'd been forced to witness this scene. While Cole lifted the cart driver onto his seat and slipped him the wages we'd promised, I watched the creature that had shattered my defenses and made me fall in love lick the man's blood from his lips.

"Madame Berggia," Vayl said to me as he straightened. "Why are you interrupting my meal?"

Madame Berggia. I think that hurts the most, Vayl. That you were calling out my name like I'd invented sex three days ago, now you don't even remember it, and we can't figure out why. Do you know how much I'd give to hear you call me Jasmine that special way you do, like a song (Yazmeena), right this second?

"You could've killed the poor guy," I said dully.

"You saw him in the Djemaa el Fna," he replied. "He shoved his wife. He was shouting at his children."

Because we paid him to. So we could set up your hunt tonight and make sure your victim didn't end up dead. Like the first one nearly did, before we realized what had happened the night we arrived in Marrakech when you went missing and we had to hunt you for real. The night you woke with such a bizarre case of amnesia that you thought you were still a Rogue, still outside of your vow never to take human blood, and so deep in this brain-blip of yours that you'd mistaken all of us for people who shared your life over two hundred and thirty years ago!

I wanted to slap him with those words like a dueling glove. But he'd just look confused, and I'd be extra miserable. So I said, "The man's family would starve without him."

Vayl lowered his eyebrows. "I did not hire you to remind me of such things."

I shoved my hands into the pockets of my sundress. It was one of his favorites, and I'd hoped seeing it would snap him out of his past. But he still believed that I was his frumpy middle-aged housekeeper. He also thought Cole was my husband, his valet, who he simply called Berggia. In his mind we'd just traveled to Morocco from his estate in England along with his beloved ward, Helena, whose part was played—grumpily—by Bergman.

My hands closed around the items most likely to console me. In my right pocket sat the long knife my great-great-grandpa, Samuel Parks, had used during his stint as a machine-gun operator in World War I. Mistress Kiss My Ass (my loudly suffering seamstress) had skillfully made a place for the sheath in all my clothes. My left pocket held eight poker chips that rang like bells in my ear when I shuffled them. And on a silver hoop attached to the material so it wouldn't get lost: my engagement ring. I hadn't worn it long. But I cherished it now more than ever, because I was sure the man who'd slipped the pear-shaped emerald on my finger eighteen months ago would never forget me, no matter where he ended up. *Right, Matt?*

It's not like you've slipped Vayl's mind. Not Matt's voice. He'd kept a steady silence since the vampire Aidyn Strait had murdered him two weeks after our engagement. On the other hand, my Granny May, who ruled my frontal lobe, couldn't wait to comment. *He believes he's living over two hundred and thirty years before he met you,* she reminded me.

Exactly! The way he looks at it, Jaz Parks doesn't exist at all!

So quit whining and figure out why! Granny May had taken up needlepoint. She sat in her tree-filled backyard in the old metal chair she left out year-round (paint flecks hinted that it had once been red) alternately watching the cardinals fight over the sunflower seeds at her gazebo feeder and taking long, smooth stitches in a piece of fabric the size of a pillowcase.

I watched her manipulate the needle with one hand while the other steadied the hoop that framed her workspace. Why did I suddenly think she would've been just as precise with a throwing knife? I shook my head.

I'm not whining!... Okay, I am. It's such sucktacular timing, that's all! I mean, I may have control of the demon in my head. But I think you need reminding that Brude is still a Domytr. Which means Satan's go-to guy is not going to give up without a fight. Especially when he was so close to succeeding at his own coup. And there's Vayl, out of his right mind just when I need him to be the sharpest!

Granny May snapped, *You still have Cole, Bergman—and Kyphas—whether you want her or not.*

We should've deep-fried that hellspawn permanently, I huffed. *Not cut her a deal that keeps her in our back pockets like a Chicago politician.*

Of course, Gran knew what I was really worried about. *Cassandra's soul is safe from Kyphas, you saw to that. She's an ocean away, secure behind her locks and wards in her colorful little apartment in Miami. You're lucky to have a friend like her. A psychic who's willing to dog-sit and research a cause for Vayl's amnesia is practically a walking miracle. Just remember what she said last time you talked. You're standing in the city where you believe the tool that you need to end Brude's possession of you is located. So find it!*

It sounds easy the way you put it. But I'm *not convinced Kyphas is done with Cassandra. And until we know what caused Vayl's amnesia—*

You're a girl. Multitask!

I sighed and scratched my head, wishing for the thousandth time that Lucifer's gofer hadn't infested my synapses. Then I could just concentrate on finding the bottom-feeder that had slapped Vayl into a virtual time machine and strapped a pair of 1777-tinted goggles over his eyes. Unless he was just plain sick. In which case I'd be on my own with Brude.

Who I couldn't stop obsessing about. The Domytr who wanted to create a whole new hell was still stomping around in my mind. And although I had him contained in a place where he couldn't control me anymore, I'd begun to show physical strain from keeping him imprisoned. Mainly nosebleeds. But also headaches that started behind one of my eyes and spread across my skull like I'd cracked it on an iron post. Even without consulting experts, I knew those were bad signs. If Brude broke free of the room where I'd imprisoned him, he'd destroy more than virtual walls. Which was why failed exorcisms often ended with a coroner writing the word "aneurism" on the victim's death certificate.

We had to complete our original mission. The one Vayl had set us on before he'd lost his way. My life depended on finding the Rocenz, a demon-forged hammer and chisel that had been supernaturally welded together. Once we had the tool and figured out a way to separate the parts, we could engrave Brude's name on the gates of hell. At which time the power of the Rocenz to reduce everything to its most basic elements would transform the Domytr in my head to dust.

Proving once again how utterly useless Vayl would be for this aspect of our operation, he asked, "Has your husband's cough eased now that we have spent a few days in the dry air?"

"Who? I don't—" *Oh, he's asking about Cole.* "Yeah, yeah."

His lips tightened and I thought I was about to get another lecture on my presumptuous behavior. Which would've been fine with me. Another chance to zone out, try to formulate some sort of plan. Plus, okay, I'll admit it. Despite the fact that it had only been three days since I'd held him in my arms, I was already hunting excuses to stand and stare at my magnificent *sverhamin*, imagine my fingers brushing across his broad brow, sinking into his soft black curls. Pretend I was standing on the invited side of that come-love-me look in his emerald eyes.

I watched his lips part, wind around the words. My mouth went dry as he said, "I can tell you have something on your mind, Madame Berggia."

If you only knew! "Uh, well, sure I do. That is, there's something I've been wanting to ask you since . . . we got here."

"Yes?"

"I have a hard time believing Co—I mean my husband—was the real reason you left England." I waited. He liked it when I did that. Freaking elitist.

"You are a very astute woman." Vayl turned so all I could see was his profile, the proud bridge of his nose, the hard planes of his cheeks and jaw reminding me of pictures I'd seen of Roman generals. Until I realized he was watching his breakfast drive away in the creaking old donkey cart with a look of hunger that made *my* stomach clench.

"So what's the deal?" I demanded. "Why are we really here?"

He turned his head, spoke sharply enough that I probably should've felt put in my place. But at least he explained. An entire story in a single word. "Helena."

Chapter Two

While the cart driver urged his donkey to speeds it hadn't attempted since it was a yearling, Vayl dug one of the evil-smelling cigars he'd begun smoking after his "transition" out of the breast pocket of his black duster. His lighting routine was so elaborate I was surprised he didn't have to sacrifice a goat too. Cole took advantage of the pause to needle Bergman through the Party Line.

"I don't think Lord Brâncoveanu's ward has the right kind of dresses for this climate, do you, dear?" he asked, turning his head so Vayl couldn't see him crossing his eyes at me the way we did every time we had to use his title along with his tongue-tripping surname. "Maybe we should take Helena shopping tonight."

Bergman growled so loud we both had to adjust our earpieces. He said, "I'm only pretending to be that girl because Cassandra said Vayl could be permanently damaged if I didn't. But if you make me try on dresses I will happily vegetize him."

"You're the one who got your hair all permed and dyed to match mine," Cole whispered. "Can I help it if it makes you look like Uma Thurman?"

"Who is Uma Thurman?" asked Vayl.

While Cole tried to explain, I urged them both to get moving. The less time we spent dawdling in the medina's mean streets, the better. Not that the criminals who hung out in Marrakech's old city were any worse than the ones who preferred the modern section. Just that I'd have relaxed more back at the riad, where I wouldn't have had to watch our backs while I recalled the moment when Bergman realized Vayl thought he was an eighteen-year-old girl whose interests revolved around painting and playing the piano-forte. But let's face it. Even if a whole gang of thugs jumps out of the shadows, a moment that priceless is going to loop in your head until your inner bimbo stops trading howls of hilarity with the bartender and resumes her drunken dance with the coatrack. So I let the memory reel roll.

We'd been gathered in the courtyard that filled the center of the riad, giving the building the shape of a grater that went straight at the top. The eye-catcher in the whole outdoor garden was the fountain rising out of the rectangular wading pool, a gracefully crafted urn that made it hard to look away. But then, there was so much more to see.

The pool was surrounded by wooden chairs and tables with such ornate arms and legs you'd almost believe fairies had done the crafting. These sat on sand-colored tiles, two-foot-square sections of which had been removed in choice spots around the courtyard to make room for plantings of banana trees. Copper planters full of ferns, palms, and lemon trees took turns with hanging lanterns to line the courtyard's pink walls, providing some relief for the eye when the sun beat down during the brightest part of the day. Escape also came in the form of two corner-built gazebos hung with raspberry-colored curtains that could be closed for extra privacy. Inside, Monique had placed two couches framed in metal that was bent to reflect the shovel-shaped arches that showed up in so much of Marrakech's architecture. The burgundy cushions topped with enough pillows to satisfy an entire legion of interior decorators cozified them.

I'd been admiring those gazebos for days, thinking about what

Vayl and I might have gotten away with behind their thick curtains if he hadn't been brain-fried. Now I shared them with my crew, watching the sky darken, waiting for the moment when—there. Cirilai sent a shot of warmth into the palm of my hand. The ring Vayl's grandfather had made to protect his soul had warned me he was waking. Which meant it was time to prepare the troops.

I looked at Bergman, sitting with his hands in his lap. Across a glass-topped table framed in exotically carved wood and covered with flickering candles sat Kyphas. I kept my eyes on her couch because, honestly? I could still barely look at her without reaching for the gun strapped to my shoulder. So what if she'd promised Cole to stop trying to corrupt souls for the Great Taker. My reaction?

Sure, and my belly ring's set with moon rocks.

What I hoped was that she'd keep her paws off Cassandra now that we'd promised her Brude and a shot at the Oversight Committee in our psychic's place. *Four souls for one? Come on, that's like a damn clearance sale, even if the soul you're giving up* had *promised herself to you over five hundred years before.* In return she'd agreed to help us find the Rocenz, which, because it had been demon-crafted, was more likely to be rediscovered by a demon. She'd even signed on to helping us carve Brude's name onto hell's gates. What a gal.

The problem was, Kyphas didn't believe in generosity. In fact, greed tended to ooze out of her like hangover sweat. Cole might not recognize the stench. But he tended to get distracted as soon as boobs starting bouncing within his line of sight. *I* knew that for Kyphas, the more souls she took back to hell with her when this was all over, the higher she'd rise up the hierarchy, so she'd be looking for any loophole she could find in her contract with us. No Cassandra? Okay. Cole's soul probably looked as juicy as a medium rare T-bone to her.

And she did look like she could gobble him whole as she eyed him from under her lashes. Which caused me to growl a little louder than I'd intended to when I said, "We can't put Vayl off any longer. He keeps asking for a girl named Helena. We think that must be you, Kyphas. Play the part or—"

"Or what?" The demon's perfectly pink lips quirked in amusement. "Go ahead, threaten me some more, Jaz."

"He calls me *Madame* Berggia. You should too," I snapped, reaching for Grief.

"You know, Kyphas, you are probably the most beautiful woman I have ever fantasized about," Cole said as he laid his arm across my shoulders. She sat forward, giving him full access to her halter-topped, tight-jeaned magazine-cover bod. He took his time with the view. Then he said, "Why do you have to be such a bitch all the time?"

She sat up straight, crossing her arms as he went on, almost casually, like he was discussing the price of lawn mowers this season. "I've killed snakes that were cuddlier than you. Well"—he glanced at me—"those inland taipans you offed during that Scidairan witch mission were pretty gnarly. But I remember this pygmy rattlesnake I had to shoot during a case in Miami when I was still a PI. It was actually pretty—"

"All right!" Kyphas slapped her hand against the armrest. "I'll cooperate!" She glared at Bergman. "Am I that bad?"

He shook his head, but the shake slowly turned to a nod. The motion made his hair bounce, which activated Cole's AGR (automatic giggle response). Because, despite my daily suggestions to dye it back to brown, Bergman insisted that if he modeled his look after Cole's he might have the same luck with women. So far he'd gotten two imaginary cell numbers and an outright, "Are you kidding me?" Personally I thought his head was too big and his frame too skeletal to pull it off. He needed a girl who was into unwrapped mummies.

Or, maybe, one who enjoyed feeding people. Monique had come out with a tray full of cookies and tea just in time to say to Cole,

"Lord Brâncoveanu is calling for you." She smiled sympathetically, still buying our loony-but-lovable uncle story. Which is why nice people are always getting suckered.

I reminded myself to leave her a big tip as I followed Cole out of the courtyard, motioning for the others, especially Kyphas/Helena, to follow us to Vayl's door. Where we waited while Cole went in to do valet crap. Ten minutes later he invited us into the suite.

I felt a familiar pang of regret as I glanced at Vayl's bed, its white spread resembling a cast-off wedding dress. Except the mesh canopy that draped overhead and tied at each corner of its black metal support was a rich chocolaty brown. And the black-domed sleeping tent perched underneath that veil seemed less like a vampire's shield from stray rays of light than a tunnel into another universe.

Cole said, "He's changing. Thank God I talked him out of needing assistance with that yesterday! Have a seat."

Bergman and Kyphas moved into the conversation area, which contained a fireplace, a couch, and matching armchairs upholstered in bright green satin. I took the round white ottoman that stood between them, ignoring the couch because, frankly, I needed Bergman's moral support.

Vayl swung open the bathroom door and strode out, the deep line between his red-rimmed eyes announcing his hunger. He wore a black button-down shirt with purple pin stripes and tailored slacks that kissed the tops of his shiny black boots. Cole handed him his duster and he shrugged it on as if he was chilly. In fact, he'd informed "Berggia" that he felt naked without it.

Bergman leaned next to my ear, since nothing had happened to injure Vayl's hearing, and whispered, "How does he pull that off? It's hot enough for shirtsleeves but I guarantee you nobody will harass him about his outfit. I'd probably get the crap kicked out of me if I tried to pull that off. But *he's* so manly strangers will probably stop him on the street to ask where they can tour his castle."

I sighed. Vayl's vibe was working on me, as well, but in more of an oh-baby-let's-play-doctor kind of way. Before I could pull myself together, Vayl held out his arms. His smile, while it kept the fang-reveal to a minimum, was so gentle that for a second I thought he'd come back to himself. My heart jumped, making an utter fool of itself, when he followed the gesture by saying, "Madame Berggia. You have brought my little Helena to see me. What a fine way to greet the new day!"

"Oh. Yeah, well, you insisted—" I jerked my thumb at Kyphas so she'd get the lead out and stand up already. She shot to her feet, but with a full-faced pout that revealed just how much Cole's comment had hurt her.

Damn. Maybe she has a heart after all.

Kyphas raised her arms to return his hug, her hands hanging limply as if she'd inherited some zombie traits from her mom's side of the family. Vayl raked his eyes over her. "It would help if my walking stick was balanced on those," he snapped. "But I will forgive you since you are, in fact, *Helena's* maid." And then he engulfed Bergman in a hug so enthusiastic I was pretty sure I heard some Russian tourists cheering in the streets.

"How are you, my dear?" Vayl asked, patting Bergman on his fluffy head when the hug had ended. "I missed you. I had not realized our travels tired you so greatly. Here, let us be seated while you tell me everything."

"Uh." Bergman shot a look of pure panic over his shoulder as Vayl took him by the hand and began to lead him toward the couch. *I'm not a girl!* he mouthed.

Suck it up. I'm not a fat Italian housekeeper either! I mouthed right back.

Cole was making a helluva racket taking down Vayl's bed tent. Normally it collapsed very quietly. Then I realized he was punctuating the folding of the poles with swallowed snorts of laughter.

Which made me smile. When I thought about it, I could see how it was kind of—

"It's not funny, *Berggia*!" Bergman said.

"That's me!" Cole hooted. "I'm Berggia. And *you're* Helena!" He pointed at Kyphas. "And you are a maid. How do you like that, Ky—"

Vayl interrupted. "I assume you all have better things to do than stand around exchanging names? Madame Berggia, that ensemble you are wearing is completely inappropriate for a woman of your age and girth. And you have, once again, worn your hair down around your shoulders like a common strumpet. Must we have this conversation twice, or shall I just sack you and leave you in Morocco without a means of transportation back to England?"

I reached for the lamp on the table but Kyphas intercepted my hand. "You'll regret it later," she murmured.

"What do you know about regret?" I snapped.

"More than you can imagine." I caught her glancing toward Cole, but was too busy glaring at Vayl to give it much thought. Naturally, he remained totally oblivious to me. All his attention focused on Bergman, who he thought was the little girl he'd saved from a werewolf attack seven years earlier. Since my newest blood-borne skill seemed to be reliving his past, I'd been in Vayl's body for a replay of that battle. So I knew he'd risked his life for her. But I thought he'd given her money when it was over and told her to leave. Until the previous day I'd had no idea he'd gone after her and promised to take care of her until she became independent.

1777-Vayl is a coldhearted shit, I thought. *Unless your name is Helena.*

I toyed with the idea of changing my name to something Vayl would respond to with as much love and kindness as he showed her. But it couldn't be a tag you'd hang on your favorite great-aunt. Would people want to call if I answered the phone by saying, "You've reached Myrtle!"

Then I realized someone was repeating my real name into my ear.

"Jasmine? Yoo-hoo!"

I touched the receiver, waking to the full crapality of my present life when I saw Vayl walking ahead of me, still smoking that stinking cigar.

"Jaz! What are you waiting for?" Bergman demanded. "Find out why Vayl's so worried about Helena. Maybe you can convince him to lock her in her room for her own safety."

"Bad idea," I replied.

"Come on! I've been so busy playing Vayl's favorite teenager I haven't had time to set up the security system properly. And don't tell me to relax because the riad's already got an alarm. You know it's outdated," Bergman snapped. Meaning he hadn't invented it.

Vayl, responding to my comment as well, said, "I know you hate my cigars, Madame Berggia, but they help me think. And you did ask about Helena."

"Yes, I did."

I tried to focus all my attention on the vampire strolling through Marrakech's old city like he was the damn mayor, but Cole was still interested in the security system issue. He said, "I don't get the paranoia. We left Astral there."

Vayl frowned. "How is Helena's kitten going to protect her from werewolves?"

At the same time Bergman's snort rattled my eardrums. "A robotic cat who can shoot a couple of grenades out her butt is no comfort when you have a demon sleeping in the next room!"

Cole whispered, "Bergman! Kyphas told me personally that she's not interested in your soul. It's probably only wired for space travel anyway."

Vayl said, "What?"

I said, "You know Berggia, Vay—I mean, Lord Brâncoveanu." Cole and I crossed our eyes at each other. "He has such a strange sense of humor sometimes. Now, about Helena and the werewolves—"

But Bergman wasn't done with his side of our bizarre conversation. He said, "Even if I believed you, Cole, which I don't, that doesn't change what happened to...your supervisor."

Ouch. We paused, none of us even able yet to say Pete's name, his murder was still such an open wound. And it wasn't healing any faster in light of the fact that we felt we'd triply betrayed him.

Because we still didn't know who'd killed him. Therefore—

We couldn't avenge his death, plus—

We'd missed his funeral.

It didn't help that Pete would've understood that we had to find the Rocenz pronto. And that Vayl in his present state would've been impossible to explain to the grieving widow. But I preferred imagining that Pete would've been überpissed to find out we'd skipped the final ceremony of his life. That would've been a more comforting feeling. Familiar. Like all the times he'd yelled at me for wrecking rental cars during the course of my assignments. Not that they'd—all—been my fault.

Wah, wah, wah, my God, you're a bigger whiner than Mom. It was my inner adolescent. Teen Me lay on her stomach on Evie's bed because, of course, hers wasn't made. She was reading a comic book she'd stolen from Dave's stash while she listened to her fave radio station, WFAT, play Casey Kasem's American Top Forty. While Matchbox Twenty sang, "She says, baby, it's 3 a.m. I must be lonely," Teen Me said, *Remember all that bitching she used to do?* Teen Me launched into a great imitation of Stella's smoke-roughened voice. *"Gawd, working at night sucks. You kids should try it sometime. Maybe then you'll be a little more grateful for the food I put on this table."* She snorted. *As if Albert didn't always have his check sent to the house! Oh, do you remember this one?* *"What the hell, you mean I have to go to the Laundromat again? Why can't you kids wear a pair of jeans more than once? What are we, the Rockefellers?"*

I said, *I sound nothing like her!* Wait, that did have something of a whiny undertone.

Teen Me sat up and carefully laid the comic on Evie's pink, lace-rimmed pillow. If Dave detected a single new wrinkle in the pages she knew there'd be hell to pay. She said, *Losing Pete, I get it. That's gonna suck a long time. I dunno, maybe forever. But all this mental grinding you're putting yourself through about him understanding your motives or not? Lookit, he was your boss and you were lucky that he cared about you. Also vice versa. Now he's dead. Be sad, but quit torturing yourself! That's all.*

I didn't realize I'd stopped in the middle of the street until I saw Vayl and Cole coming back to get me.

"Madame Berggia, are you quite all right?" asked Vayl.

"No. Are you?"

He took a big puff of that obnoxious cigar and, thank God, blew the smoke into the night sky. When he looked back down at me his eyes were the dark blue of drowning waters. "Not at all," he said. "I am rarely afraid. But you know how Helena came to be in my care. In all this time, the werewolf who brought us together has not forgotten. He has watched from afar as she has grown in grace and beauty."

Cole snickered, and then coughed. "Uh, sorry," he said.

Vayl patted him on the shoulder. "Never fear, my man. This dry air should do wonders for your lungs."

"What about the Were?" I asked.

"His name is Roldan. And he has marked her."

"You mean, like, as part of his territory?" I imagined a werewolf peeing on a wigged and long-skirted Bergman. I slapped a hand over my mouth. Really, this was no laughing matter.

Vayl paused. "I realize you have very little knowledge in this area, so I must explain. And I do apologize if I upset you unduly. But werewolves know when they have met their life's partner. Roldan wants to change Helena, Madame Berggia. He has, in fact, become obsessed with the idea ever since I cheated him of the satisfaction. And her rejection of his every advance has merely emboldened him." Vayl lowered his head. "No, it has crazed him," he corrected himself grimly.

I remembered. I stood absolutely still so I could clearly recall the moments when I'd discovered that donating blood to Vayl had given me the power to walk in his memories. I'd *seen* Roldan's first attack on Helena. Defending her had felt so real that even now I wanted to bury my fists in the wolf who hadn't died in that first battle but had, evidently, stalked the girl for years after. And who, unlike any other Were I'd ever heard of, had survived long past the 150-year mark to put himself at the top of the our Most Likely to Vaporize the World list.

I said, "Even if Roldan wasn't after Helena, could he still be jonesing for revenge on you?" *Even after all these decades?*

Vayl nodded. "I do not believe his surname is Jones"—puzzled glance at Cole as his "valet" slapped himself on both cheeks to maintain his composure—"but given our history, I think it entirely possible that he and his pack are hatching plans to kill me even as we speak. All they need is my location. Which, I assure you, madame, is an absolute secret."

On the other end of our receivers, Bergman emitted what could've qualified as a silent scream, except we heard a sort of echo, like a kid's attempt to make crowd noises into a microphone. Then he said, "Astral? Here, kitty. Let's check those grenades, okay, girl?"

Chapter Three

C ole and I followed Vayl back toward the riad, walking a couple of steps behind him like the obedient servants he expected us to be. The closer we got to the Djemaa el Fna, the more people we met. Black-haired, brown-eyed men dressed in colorful caps and the choir-robish jellabas that Vayl had insisted on wearing as pajamas, smiled and wished us a good evening. Tourists with one hand on their wallets and the other clicking pictures either nodded or ignored us completely. Maybe they couldn't be bothered with socializing when Marrakech demanded so much attention, its original builders somehow infusing an exotic beauty into everything from mosque minarets to bathhouse floors. Its current citizens added to the color with displays of intricately woven rugs, mounds of ripe fruits, and materials dyed in vibrant colors that dared the sun to fade them. The variety, volume, and availability all increased the closer we got to the square. Which, considering how much Vayl went for hunting nowadays, we'd be smart to avoid.

Another quiet evening inside. Sigh.

Maybe I'd call Cassandra and check on Jack. (By now maybe he'd forgiven me for putting him on yet another airplane and, even worse, sending him away from all the action. Because demons get their kicks infesting canines, and I couldn't risk my favorite malamute around Kyphas any longer).

Cassandra would probably bring me up to speed on her and my brother, Dave's, wedding plans. And then I'd ask the inevitable question. "Still clueless?" And she'd say, "I'm sorry, Jaz," because by now I didn't expect her to hit anything but dead ends in her search for the cause of Vayl's massive memory lapse.

I tried to cheer myself with the sight of Riad Almoravid, its walls rising out of the street like a mini fort coated in cotton candy. A former villa remodeled for tourist stays, it contrasted starkly with the neglected homes we'd left behind. Here an elegant awning offered us instant shade so we could more comfortably admire the white molding that hung like lace from the double arches that formed its entrance, or rest our sun-blasted eyes on the cool beauty of the small garden that filled the area between riad and sidewalk. Like the courtyard, it was packed with greenery, huge pots full of starlike blooms, and a fountain that always reminded me to hit the bathroom ASAP.

Vayl hardly noticed. He glanced at the double doors, the arch above which had been filled with triangles of green glass, and said, "The two of you go on in. I will catch up later." He picked up his pace.

I grabbed Cole's arm so hard that he jumped. "Uh, Lord Brâncoveanu?" he said. Pause for eye roll. "We'd be happy to do that but, er, you know how Helena worries when you're out on your own. What do you say we all stay together tonight? You know, do something as a family?" By now we were nearly jogging to keep up with him.

"That would be fine, except I am planning to find a woman who—"

I lost the rest of Vayl's sentence in a mental whiteout. The sensation was close to the feeling (or lack of) that I reach just before my finger squeezes the trigger. But it was misleading. Because before a kill I go to a place very close to peace. This was the indrawn breath before a battle cry.

Cole lunged forward to yank on Vayl's coat sleeve, managing to stop his progress. At the same time he shoved his body in front of mine. He said, "I'm afraid Madame Berggia doesn't understand. At all."

Vayl didn't even spare me a look. "She does not need to." His voice was hard as the eyes of the children who suggested we use them as our guides every afternoon when we went to the Djemaa el Fna to search for the answers we couldn't find in Cassandra's books or at Bergman's keyboards. Only Cole kept me from shoving my face into Vayl's, wrecking our relationship and maybe his mind by demanding that he remember the only woman who should matter to him anymore.

Cole turned and put both his hands on my shoulders. Leaning down so our noses were nearly touching he murmured, "Get it together."

I glared over his shoulder at the vampire who was tapping his foot impatiently. "I hate that son of a bitch!"

"I know."

That stepped me back. "But... I love him."

"Which is why you hate him right now. I get it. Don't you think I've felt the same way about you practically every day since we met?"

I looked into his eyes and, for the first time, truly understood. "Jesus. I'm sorry. I really wish—"

He shook his head, his smile so small it resembled Vayl's least readable expression. "My mom used to tell me that we can't help how we feel. It's what we choose to do about those feelings that makes us shits or saints." His hands slid down my arms until they fell to his sides. "I guess I finally understand what she meant."

I dropped my head.

I love you, Cole. So much that I wish you could find the perfect girl. Someone who wants to wrap herself around you the same way I do Vayl. With a mind-blowing passion that keeps making me forget to breathe. The downside is that it can tear your heart out. Slowly, so that you feel yourself bleeding, dying inside, every time he looks at you, past you, not seeing, not remembering. And if he never comes back? Another kind of living death that zombies are glad they never have to experience. And still I can say I've held the world in my hands.

But you're not content, are you, Jazzy? Granny May peered at me from around the blouse she was hanging on the clothesline. *You're still going to fight to get him back?*

Damn straight, I am. Because in the end, I may be greedier than Kyphas. I've had it all. But I want more.

Even so changed, Vayl hadn't lost his ability to move like one of the tigers that had been carved into the cane he no longer carried. Despite my Sensitivity to his presence, I was still surprised to find him standing at my shoulder when I finally looked up.

"I am sorry to remind you of your sorrows, Madame Berggia," he said, his fine black brows drawn down in a frown of, geez, could that actually be concern? "Let me assure you, the woman I seek is nothing like the Seer who led me to your home in the first place."

"I...uh—"

His lip quirked, reminding me so strongly of my old lover that I had to grab a handful of skirt to prevent myself from wrapping my arms around his waist. He said, "I have forgotten myself again."

"No kidding."

He reached out as if to touch me. I stepped back. If I had felt those fingers brush my hand I'd have lost it completely. His chin tipped. "You *are* angry."

I shrugged. "You know what happened before." *So tell me!*

He put his hand to his heart. "My life on it, this Seer is virtuous and ethical. She is part of a guild called the Sisters of the Second Sight, which strictly forbids its members from sending vampires like me into homes like yours, expecting to find their reincarnated sons..."

Aha! I said, "But they weren't there, were they?" Even I knew the reunion was supposed to happen in America.

"No. You and Berggia were. Mourning over your young men. It

is still a wonder to me that you did not burn me alive, considering how they had been killed."

The real Berggias' boys were slain by vampires, then. *Damn.*

I nodded. That must've been the expected response, because Vayl went on. "I always wondered...did it ease your mind that I found the Rogue who took their lives? That he is now little more than vapor and a few specks of dust?"

I thought about how Vayl had killed Aidyn Strait. That moment of knowing that my fiancé's murderer would never laugh again. "There was a need in me. I don't exactly know what to call it. I'm— it's right that he's gone. There's a balance restored. But it's bitter."

"Yes. Revenge." He sent me a look full of fire and blood. "I thought it would be satisfying enough to give me rest for eternity. And yet here I am, still seeking what I have lost." He stopped suddenly. Glanced at Cole. "You never speak of my search. I suppose you think it insane?"

"It's not my place to judge," Cole said. A good valet's response. But Vayl wasn't satisfied. He turned on Cole so quickly that I reached back, touched the hair I'd woven into a knot before we left the riad. And not just because Vayl had bitched about my choice of dos. When I twisted it up, it looked natural holding the bright blue Japanese hairpins whose true use had been disguised by the CIA's most creative artists. Each needle tip released a full dose of vamp tranquilizer when properly, uh, shoved into place.

I relaxed when Vayl's only violent movement was to fling the cigar into the street. "How do you do it?" he demanded.

Cole ran a hand through his hair, glancing past Vayl to show me what-the-hell eyes. I rolled my hands. *Just go with the flow.*

"How do I do what?" he asked.

"I have been without my sons for twenty-six years now. It has been only five for you. How is it that you manage to function as though life still has some meaning? As if you occasionally see beauty among all this horror?" Had he meant to gesture at the mottled walls of the buildings that had closed in on us again as soon as we left Zitoun el Kattabi Street?

Cole looked at the toes of his high-tops. I felt myself go tense. Tried to think of some way to deflect the smart-ass comment he was about to fling at Vayl, which would be followed quickly by a huge bubble and a suggestion to me that if the Seer was pretty, you know, since he and I were a temporary couple, maybe we could make it a threesome. But when he looked up I saw depths in his eyes that made me take a quick breath. As if I'd just met the real man behind the fun pal for the first time.

He said, "People deal with pain in different ways. And I can promise you that sometimes what seems like coping to the rest of the world is really just hanging on by your fingernails. You want to know how I survive?" He took Vayl by the arms and turned him until he was fully facing me. "There she is. And here's another promise. Someday you'll find somebody just like her. When you do, don't fuck it up. Because you will never find anyone like her again."

Vayl nodded. "You are a lucky man, Berggia. To find such a partner is rare. My wife was…" Vayl trailed off, and after a while we realized he didn't intend to finish that thought. Not out loud anyway.

We stared at one another, an island of silence surrounded by vividly dressed socializers, all headed anywhere but here. They didn't mind our blockage. Walked around us without comment, like we'd become part of the city's hardscape despite the fact that we stood in a stone-paved thoroughfare so narrow that even a couple of cyclists might brush shoulders if they weren't careful how they passed each other.

Somebody accidentally bumped Cole, apologized in French, and that was all we needed to get us moving. Vayl led. Cole came next. I followed, feeling like I'd betrayed him without ever meaning to.

Raoul? Come on, give me something to cling to here. Tell me Cole's got somebody out there waiting. A woman who'll make him look at me later and laugh.

I didn't expect a reply. My Spirit Guide hated the feeling that he was on 24-7 Jaz-call. But within a few minutes I felt the buzz of his presence, so big I clapped my hands over my ears and fought to clear my vision. And then his voice, like a boxing match announcer with his microphone maxed out in my head, said, *COLE'S MATE IS CHOSEN. BUT THEIR TIME IS STILL DISTANT.*

Thanks. Oh, man, I can't tell you what a relief—okay. That's something at least. I caught Cole's gaze. As soon as he felt my eyes on him he stuck out his tongue, tinted red from his bubblegum.

I grinned as he pointed to Vayl. *More information*, he mouthed.

I nodded and said, "So, Lord Brâncoveanu, you want to visit a Seer. That's an excellent idea, actually. But, uh, we really should go with you." Which was what we were doing at the moment, of course. But Vayl could ditch us whenever he wanted, and we all knew that.

"Why?" he asked.

That's an excellent question. Anybody have a clue? Shit! Not one of my inner girls was up to the challenge. In fact, most of them were still out of breath from doing the Cole-will-finally-get-his-girl jig.

Once again, my coworker and former recruit came to the rescue. "Considering what you said about Roldan wanting to change Helena, maybe she'd be safer in your care for the night." Before Vayl could object again Cole added, "I've heard bad things about this Were. He has connections far beyond England. If he knows we left the country, he can trace us here. Wouldn't we all be safer if we stayed together?"

Vayl pinched his bottom lip between his thumb and forefinger, a gesture I'd never seen before. Maybe he'd dropped it after he'd gotten the cane and could spin it between his hands instead. But he'd rejected it, along with me, the night he woke with most of his life missing.

He said, "All right. We will go back for her. But none of you are allowed into the Seer's chambers while she reads for me. I must insist on privacy in this matter."

"Oh, sure." Cole nodded at me.

I raised my hands. "That's your business," I said.

"Good." Vayl cleared his throat.

I waited. Then I prodded him. "Isn't this where you apologize for threatening to strand me here earlier?"

He glanced at me from the corners of his eyes. "Do you mean like I left you in the middle of Cornwall last autumn?"

"He's done it before?" I murmured. "What a son of a bitch! And she came back? Why?"

His tone went all Dennis Miller on me, so cutting I was surprised droplets of blood didn't fly off my skin. "I do not understand why you continue to speak of yourself in the third person, madame. Have you suddenly discovered a familial link to King George?"

I clenched a fist and shook it under his nose. "I'll give *you* a familial link—"

Cole shoved my arm down. "Relax, woman. It's 1777, remember? You don't even get to vote yet."

"Yeah! Because of pigheaded brutes like him!" I yelled.

"If I am such a brute, why *did* you return to my service after our last dispute?" Vayl demanded, his voice closer to a roar than I'd ever heard it. I'd have screamed right back at him but for the note of desperation I heard threading under the anger, brightening his eyes to the color of flames.

I thought about it. Why would a woman who'd pissed off her employer enough that he'd abandoned—but not fired—her, come trudging back to his door? She probably needed the work. And there was her husband's job to consider. Plus maybe she felt loyal to

Helena. More likely it was a combination of all of those reasons plus a few others I could name. But there was only one that really mattered.

I looked into the face of the man an old Italian housekeeper had stared at over two hundred years ago, and before thought could move me I was standing so close to him I could've felt his chest rise into mine if he'd chosen that moment to sigh. I looked down, momentarily fascinated by the sight of my slender white fingers, not hanging empty at my side, but instead wrapped around his broad, workingman's hand.

I said, "Until this moment I never completely understood why my Granny May sat by my Gramps Lew in those last days of his life, when he couldn't talk anymore and she knew he wouldn't wake up. Why every single morning she rejoiced that he was still there with her. To hold hands with. It was enough for her. You know?"

That line between his brows—how can you love a man's frown? But I saw it and was glad. It meant he was tuned in—to me. I went on. "Some people, yeah, you catch the first coach outta there and you never look back. But some…" I paused to lock on to his gaze. "You can somehow see past all the bullshit to a soul that shines so bright it brings tears to your eyes. And that's why you stay." I dropped my eyes to our interlocked fingers. "Even if all you have left is holding hands."

Because I knew it would break my heart when he pulled away, I slid free first. When I looked up again, Vayl had stepped back, made his face into the mask he'd worn constantly in the first months of our partnership.

But I could hear a new thoughtfulness in his voice when he said, "You must understand that I was angry because you are Helena's sole model of virtue and genteel behavior. If I cannot count on you to provide a proper example for her I fear this whole facade I have built for her will crumble on her head and she may never recover.

We must teach her how to survive in this society. How to be strong and flourish." He emphasized his words with pumps of his fist, like he'd beat down anyone who came against his ward, even if it was a sharp-tongued socialite with a reticule full of invitations and the power to withhold them all from Helena.

I said, "She means a lot to you, doesn't she?"

His shrug barely creased the seams of his coat. It seemed like none of us could purely explain our feelings anymore. But we could still make concrete gestures. Which he did now, by turning back toward our hotel.

We walked in silence until, again, we stood in front of Riad Almoravid. Vayl's golden eyes climbed walls so old that, if they could, they'd double over and chuckle at his immaturity. He took a quick breath as a shadow passed in front of the drawn curtains of Bergman's room. Miles wouldn't leave his den willingly, which was why Cole and I were now signing to each other, arguing silently about which one of us would be the loser who had to go drag him out. We shoved our hands into our pockets when Vayl turned to us suddenly and said, "I never thought to have another child. Not just because I am a vampire. But because I performed so poorly as a father with my first two. If I fail with Helena, I will never forgive myself."

I hadn't heard the girl's story before. And the fact that he'd never mentioned her didn't leave me much hope for a happy ending. So instead of reassuring him I said, "We all know you're doing your best by her."

"It will mean nothing if Roldan takes her."

As if I needed another reason to pull Vayl back to the present. But now I just had to know what had happened to Helena. And the Berggias. I decided to call Cassandra as soon as we got inside. And if her first words were "I'm stumped!" I was going to swallow my pride—and a big spurt of fear—and bring in Sterling. Since our department had been shut down he couldn't be that busy, unless his band had lined up a bunch of gigs to fill his free time, in which case I'd just have to convince (bribe) him to cancel. I wondered if our resident warlock still favored the Tullamore Dew. And if so, how was I supposed to get my hands on a case of Irish whiskey in the middle of a teetotaling country like Morocco?

Chapter Four

Though I'd done it at least a dozen times already, I still wasn't used to the transition. Stepping from the dusty, crowded streets of the old city into the quiet elegance of Monique Landry's traditional Moroccan villa, with its blue and white tiled floors, their pattern so intricate I stood in awe at the time and care that had gone into the job. Smaller tiles in brighter shades of green, red, yellow, and white climbed a third of the way up the ground floor's walls and lined the stairways on either side of the main entrance. Above the tile, pink or gold stucco was decoration unto itself, though here and there an original painting hung, usually signed by a local artist who had managed to capture the radiant soul that moved within every corner of the city.

Everywhere we went in the riad—whether it was the big lounge in the front of the place, the formal dining room down the south hall, the kitchen at the west end of the house, up the stairs to the rooms we'd rented, or out to the courtyard where our after-dark meetings occurred—scalloped archways marked the passages, as if the doorways themselves wore lace scarves out of respect for Allah.

Monique had managed an atmosphere of elegant warmth throughout her home. Except for this moment when, stepping into the lounge, I felt the sinister aura of conspiracy tainting the air. My first clue was that Bergman had not only beaten us downstairs, but was willingly sharing space with our hostess and Kyphas. Astral looked far too innocent sitting in the doorway with her tail curled around her paws like an actual cat. And Cole was shoving me into the room like he was afraid I meant to make a run for it.

Then I saw the cake.

And Bergman started singing.

And Cole handed me his phone—which I put to my ear—only to hear my sister harmonizing from thousands of miles away.

I waited for the rush of pain that I'd been trying to avoid all day, now that I'd been forcefully reminded that this was the second birthday I'd spent without Matt. That the mind-blowing celebration I'd been planning with Vayl had melted into a nightmare.

It didn't come.

Instead I saw my old roommate, his ridiculous Cole-perm flying out from his head like Einstein Jr.'s, holding a flaming dessert out in front of him. Which meant Monique had rushed out in the middle of the evening just for me. At my right, the man who loved me and would never be more than my dearest companion had made it all happen. At my left, the vampire I'd become so entwined with that I couldn't tell anymore where I stopped and he began was trying to comprehend how everyone knew the words to a song he was sure he'd never heard before. But he still had a smile for me. In a dark wicker chair with palm-printed cushions, separate from us all but struggling to understand how we fit so well together, a demon managed not to stain the moment. And in my ear, my kid sister belted like a Broadway star.

When they were done I said, "Thanks. This is so cool of you guys. I'd say you shouldn't have, but it turns out I'm glad you did."

Cole gave me a gentle shove toward the courtyard. "Go on. Talk to Evie. We'll wait."

As I walked out I heard Vayl say, "What is that contraption Madame Berggia is holding to her ear? Has she gone partially deaf?"

Ignoring Cole's attempt to explain his cell, I spoke to my sister for the first time since Vayl's...accident. "Yo, Evie, thanks for checking in!"

"As if I'd miss this day," she replied. "Have you found any rad new medicinal plants out there in the middle of nowhere?"

I took half a beat to sink into my research scientist Evie-cover. "Morocco's amazingly cosmopolitan," I informed her. "Especially in the new section of the city. But to answer your question, no, nothing major. We're going out into the countryside again tomorrow. Don't worry, if I have anything to do with it, Demlock Pharmaceuticals will find at least five or six cancer cures in our lifetimes."

"Well, hurry it up. E.J.'s grown about a foot since you saw her!"

"That's physically impossible. Put her on the phone." I waited until I could hear my infant niece gnawing on the receiver. "E.J.? This is your auntie Jaz. Are you being a good girl?"

I heard a gurgle. Or maybe a burp. And imagined the phone covered in regurgitated breast milk. Gross.

"Child, you're what, almost four months old now? Stop being so cooperative and tell Mommy you want your own phone. Make sure you get texting. I hear that's the new craze among babies your age."

Evie said, "Are you corrupting my kid?"

"It's my job. Look up Auntly Duties online. The description's on Wikipedia."

Evie laughed. "Okay, now cut the BS and tell me what's wrong."

"I—nothing. I'm having a fabulous birthday."

"It's only four o'clock here. That means I have a full hour until Tim gets home. E.J.'s just discovered her hands, so all I have to do is make sure she finds them again after she's lost them and I can nag you until you break."

"I think Congress considers that torture."

"Spill."

I sighed and looked around the courtyard. It was empty. Which meant Chef Henri, who liked to savor a glass of wine after work, had probably already gone home for the night. I stepped into the gazebo farthest from the front of the house and curled up on the couch. "I've been dating a guy at work."

Amazing. Thousands of miles from home and my sister's squeal still forced me to pull the phone away from my ear.

I said, "See, this is why I don't tell you things. Now my eardrum is bleeding."

"It is not! Tell me all about him."

Ha! Like I want you jumping a plane to Marrakech so you can shake your finger under Vayl's nose and make him promise to keep his fangs to himself!

"He's, ah, older than me." *But only by a few hundred years.*

"Is he hot?"

Why did I suddenly feel like we were teenagers again? First day at our new school, trading stories about the cute guys in our math classes. I said, "Smoldering."

"Oh my God, I gotta sit down. Wait, I'm already sitting down. Okay, go on."

"Would you rein it in? It's not like that. Well, it was. But now, I don't know. He's...changed."

"Aw, Jazzy, tell me he's not married."

"No. He was, but she's dead." *In fact, I killed the evil bitch, but I'll edit that one out of our little talk too, 'kay? Dammit, why did I start this in the first place? I hate lying to you.*

Granny May spoke up from behind a bridge hand that, from the sparkle in her eyes, looked to be a winner. *Maybe you needed to talk to somebody real for once,* she said. *One of the few people you know who's in a good relationship.*

Could be. I tipped my mental hat to her, acknowledging a spurt of joy at seeing her seated at the table near the front of my mind again, no longer concerned about whether or not Brude was going to swing by and chop off her head. As if to celebrate the occasion, she'd chosen some real winners to play cards with too. Winston Churchill and Woody Woodpecker were partnered against her and Amelia Earhart. It was shaping up to be a helluva game.

"Jaz? Are you still there?"

"Yeah, I'm sorry, what'd I miss?"

"I was just wondering why you think he's different now."

"He's kind of...living in the past. I really lo—like him. But this is starting to get to me. What if, you know, what if he never—"

"Everybody changes, Jaz. Every day. All the time. How important is this relationship to you?"

I cleared my throat. "It's up there."

"Well, I'd tell you to be patient, but I'm not sure you ever learned that one." We both laughed. "In which case, just don't kick his ass so hard you put him in the hospital, okay?"

I visualized me attempting to do just that. It ended up with me on the ground. Bleeding. "I can pretty much guarantee that's not gonna happen."

"Well, I hope you hang in there with this guy, then. He's the first one you've told me about since Matt. And I have to think that's a good thing. Really, really good." I heard the hope in her voice and felt warmed that it was all for me. I knew some people had crowds of relatives cheering them on all through their lives. I had two. Maybe three, but I still hadn't decided about Albert. Which was when Evie said, "Dad called today."

"Yeah?"

"Now that you've told me about your new boyfriend, I think I understand why."

"Really."

She paused. "Um, he wanted to know, theoretically speaking, how I'd have reacted if he had forbidden me from marrying Tim.

So, of course, I asked him what was wrong with Tim, and he said nothing, it wasn't about him. It was you. Which must mean he's met this guy you're dating. And he disapproves."

I thought back to our mission in Scotland, the one he'd dropped in on unexpectedly. Though we'd tried to hide Vayl's true identity, we couldn't have fooled Albert during that last battle, when he'd caused sleet to fall from a clear sky and blown a hole the size of an elevator in the side of a burial cairn. So the old fart didn't like it that I'd hooked up with a vampire. I'd worried about the ramifications of that for a while. But the fact that he'd called Evie first? I felt a smile slide onto my face. "Cool."

"Yeah, I figured that would make you happy. You can have the rest of your present when you get back home. Party at my house next weekend. Be there."

"Okay." *I hope.* "Love you."

"Same here. Buy me something extravagant while you're in Morocco."

"It's *my* frigging birthday!"

"Okay, buy yourself something too."

She was still laughing when we hung up.

Chapter Five

I'd heard from Dave earlier in the day, a short text reminding me that although I'd been born a few minutes before him, he was still bigger and therefore deserved more gifts. Also Cassandra had confessed that she'd let their engagement news slip, and because he knew I'd bullied the information from her, I owed them dinner. That he'd left Kyphas out of the message meant Cassandra still hadn't told him the rest of the story—that the demon had come after her because the holy contract she and Dave had entered nullified all the protections she'd used to successfully duck their deal for over five hundred years. At least he knew about that. But *she* should know that any guy who'll marry somebody who once traded her soul for the death of the slaver who raped her will also roll with the follow-up punches.

I wondered if Albert would approve of her if he knew what she'd done. And then I decided it didn't matter, because *I* sure as hell wasn't going to tell him. And if he was pissed at *me*, that meant he wouldn't call at all, so I'd never even have the chance. It also meant I could leave the cool, dark corner of the gazebo and rejoin my crew in the lounge.

The room was dominated by a brown wicker couch upholstered with the same dark green palm-dotted material as Kyphas's chair.

In front of it sat matching square coffee tables that usually held vases of fresh roses. Fat forest-green floor pillows sat at their bases. Overlooking the whole scene was a painting of kestrels, six of them flying in a background so black it reminded me of the maw of a ravenous monster.

The painting looked less ominous when Cole joined Bergman and Monique beneath it, wiggling his butt between theirs, his easy grin making even Bergman's shoulders relax enough that I was fairly certain the blades weren't meeting at his spine anymore. He still kept picking nervously at his jeans, a new pair without the rips or bleach stains that made him happiest. He'd stepped even farther out of his comfort zone by changing from his typical pullover to a shirt in gray and white plaid with only one missing button near the tuck, which Monique probably thought was cute. Maybe she even liked the pocket protector, which contained a pen in each color, a tire gauge, and a calculator that folded to the size of a paper clip.

But she might as well give up hoping that he wasn't so distracted by his dress-up clothes that he'd notice her wardrobe change. Instead of the white dress with lavender flowers she'd worn all day, she'd chosen a low-cut strappy number with an ivory background covered in amber vines. Faceted amber gems surrounded by black beads dangled from her ears, and the same gems sparkled along the straps of her sandals. The whole outfit complemented her smooth skin and silky black hair, which Kyphas seemed more interested in than Bergman. Probably because Cole had just taken the time to tell her how pretty she looked before nudging Bergman, hard, with his elbow.

"Uh, yeah, you look great," Miles agreed. He pulled at his collar.

When the silence got awkward Monique stepped in. "I think Kyphas looks lovely as well, don't you, Cole?" As Cole murmured an agreement, she turned to the demon. "Where in the world did you get that lovely dress? I have never seen such a pattern!"

I hadn't either. She'd worn a little black number with bell-shaped sleeves and a scoop neck. Splashed onto that background were huge white flowers. At least that's what they looked like at first. But if you let your eyes go blurry the flowers began to resemble skulls.

Kyphas said, "My mother's a designer. She put it together for me."

Vayl said, "I thought your mother was a scullery maid."

Oh. Shit.

He stood near the edge of the room like the shy kid who knows he doesn't belong and has no idea how to make it better. As if the warmth of the room didn't affect him, he still wore his duster over a white silk shirt tucked into black trousers. Where he'd found suspenders to replace his belt I had no clue, but they suited him, as did the walking stick he'd picked up in the Djemaa el Fna.

Unfortunately his view on us didn't fit nearly as well. After a brief, strained silence, Cole was the first to recover. He laughed and said, "Oh, you know how it is, sir. Daughters say a lot of things when they're angry. Monique! Should we light the birthday candles?"

Huge uproar as we all loudly agreed that we should start a small, controlled fire. I kept my eye on Vayl as Monique went to the cake, which she'd set on the coffee table closest to the wall. He got over our weirdness with astounding speed, but that may have been due to the fact that he'd found a better area for his focus. The confection fascinated him. And why not? Vayl had probably never seen a dessert quite so...loud...in 1777.

Three layers of chocolaty roundness covered in hot-pink icing and silver sprinkles, my cake was decorated with silver and neon-blue flourishes shaped like banana peppers. In the middle the baker had written *Joyeux Anniversaire!* in big blue letters. My enhanced vision, an ability I'd developed the first time I'd donated blood to

Vayl, usually added extra colors to the mix. In this case it caused the red and silver dots of icing between the peppers to glow. Like they were radioactive. I started to grin.

"This has to be the most obnoxious birthday cake anyone has ever gotten for me." I looked at Monique, whose soft brown eyes had gone the size of lightbulbs.

She looked at Bergman hesitantly. "Obnoxious is good?"

He nodded. "Oh, yeah. Cole, for instance, is one of the most obnoxious guys I know and women can't get enough of him."

Her laugh was so sultry I expected the couch to unfold into a bed right then and there. Bergman, on the other hand, couldn't seem to stop obsessing about his dress-up clothes. He said, "Cole could probably get a date wearing prison stripes. But he tells me I have to raise my game if I want any action." He pulled his shirt away from his chest. "My game is itchy!"

I'm gonna nickname him Clueless McGee, I thought as Cole tried to get Bergman to shut the hell up and Kyphas laughed out loud.

Luckily Monique's humor was as long as her patience, and she just chuckled along with Kyphas as she said, "But it was so kind of you to do this for your friend. Come, help me serve the cake. It will take your mind off your discomfort."

She'd put all the necessary accessories on the second table, which sat at Bergman's knees, running him out of lame excuses before he could even begin. And when Monique sent Cole to the kitchen for the coffeepot, Miles had no choice but to let her snuggle a little closer as she cut the cake.

I accepted my honorary first piece from *Clueless McGee*, who whispered, "Eat fast, I need to get back to my computer," without telling him what an idiot he was. I was, however, forced to turn my head so he wouldn't see me rolling my eyes. Which was when I noticed Vayl frowning. As I went to him, Kyphas leaned over and murmured, "How's the romance brewing between you two? Is

Vayl into older women? Or does he get all snooty about banging the hired help?"

I considered stomping the demon's foot and playing it off as a tripping incident, but nobody who mattered would buy it and I'd just end up looking petty. Which, okay, maybe I was a little. But this time I decided to rise above and settle for quiet disdain. Ignoring Kyphas as if she was no more important to me than a wiggly white maggot, I marched past her and up to my boss. Whose orders I had regularly ignored for the past few days. But still.

"What's wrong?" I asked.

He couldn't seem to take his eyes off the dessert. "I did not realize it was your birthday. I apologize. I have nothing for you."

"That's fine. I'm used to it."

When he looked at me, his eyes were that hurricane blue that let me know he was genuinely disturbed. "That is the problem. Somehow I knew your birthdays were never special. And I meant to make this year different, but I failed you."

I watched him struggle to understand.

Come on, Vayl. Work it out!

When he looked at me again his eyes had darkened to everyday brown. "Ah well, perhaps we will find you something pretty in the souk when we go back out tonight, yes?"

My throat tightened so much I had to swallow before I could say, "Sure. That would be great."

Kyphas chuckling behind me dropped my mood to the gutter, so when Vayl said, "Monique, I wonder if you can tell us where we might find a Sister of the Second Sight?" I wanted to inform him just what the vision of his future was going to hold if he didn't pull his head out of his ass and start seeing *me* straight!

I shoved a huge bite of cake into my mouth so I wouldn't say anything I'd regret later and nodded at our hostess, winking to let her know it tasted great as she gaped at me. Then she remembered that at least she had manners and replied, "In fact, yes, Monsieur

Brâncoveanu. A Sister named Hafeza Ghoumari lives just north-west of the Djemaa el Fna. You can visit her tomorrow if you like. Her souk opens at nine o'clock."

The line between Vayl's eyes deepened. "You mean, she does not do readings at night?"

"Only by appointment. You could call and leave a message."

"Then that is what we will do."

Monique went back to mutilating my cake and sending Bergman around the room with the pieces.

Vayl turned to me. "You must pay a call on Madame Ghoumari first thing tomorrow and make an appointment. I want to see her as soon after I wake as possible."

I put my hand on the phone in my jacket pocket. "But I could just—" Then I stopped. When people said "call" Vayl's mind went to putting your feet on the welcome mat, because to him phones didn't exist yet. "Okay. I'll make the arrangements."

What a colossal pain in the ass this whole deal is turning out to be. If this isn't some sort of vampiric disease, but an actual attack on him, and I someday come face-to-face with the person responsible? We're talking some meticulous, well-orchestrated torture before we ever get down to the killing.

Now that he was finished with me, Vayl ignored me like I was an embarrassing relative. I stood on the other side of the doorframe and jammed a whole day's worth of calories into my mouth, wishing it didn't taste so good because now I wanted to eat the whole cake. With my hands. I could just see myself at the end, sitting on a crumb-covered pillow, my face smeared with fuchsia icing, bawling because I'd just consumed a week's worth of meals in one sitting and I *still* wanted to punch my lover in the face!

Okay, this is pathetic. Go to your room. Get a grip. Call Cassandra. Call Sterling if you have to. Get some sleep. In the morning you'll have a better idea what to do.

I was on the landing, heading up the second set of steps when Kyphas caught me.

"Are you insane?" she asked. My adrenaline surged as her eyes flashed yellow in the light of the glittering glass chandelier that hung from the ceiling.

I spun, facing her completely, as if she'd pulled on me and we were about to do battle. But she stood still at the bottom of the stairs, her hands at her sides, one of them clutching a *tahruyt*, which anyone else would've thought she'd bought on her latest shopping trip. Of Berber weave, the scarf's gold and ochre stripes brought out the repetitive black designs tooled on top of them, one of which resembled intertwined sickles, while the other reminded me of dagger-impaled hearts. But I knew the *tahruyt* was more than it seemed. Just like I knew Kyphas couldn't be shrugged off as an exceptionally beautiful American girl whose braid shone like ripe wheat on her shoulder.

I kept a wary eye on the *tahruyt* as I said, "The last time I checked, Vayl was the one having trouble with reality."

"That's exactly my point." She came to stand on the same tread as me. I moved toward the wall, glad that we'd rented a place where even the stairs were wide enough to grab personal space.

I said, "What, that *I'm* crazy because *Vayl* can't figure out what year it is?"

She shook her head. "I'm standing here looking at you, thinking you're nuts for still hanging around. I mean, you and Vayl have been together as a couple for what, two weeks?"

"More like eleven days," I mumbled.

Her mouth drooped, like I'd just rescinded all her vacation time. "You don't have that much invested in this relationship. And you're looking at eternity with a man who can't remember one single moment of the time you spent together as a couple. Why aren't you and Cole on a plane to Cleveland right now? I mean, there's a guy who knows your real name." She raised her fingers to tick off the advantages as she listed them. "He loves you; I've heard him say so. He's not a vampire, so you could have children. He's funny. He's sweet. Where's the downside?"

She forgot to say he's yummy. It was my Inner Bimbo, staying home for once. It must've been Monday in my mind. Which made a lot of sense, considering. She lounged in a black negligee and transparent robe on a round bed covered with a faux tiger-skin spread. *I'm imagining Cole in a pair of skimpy black shorts, all oiled up like one of those calendar models. Yup. He'd be way more fun than—*

Shut up, I told her. *Anyone who'd do it in the back of a '79 Pinto doesn't get a vote.*

But Kyphas sure thought *she* had a say. "Vayl is only going to become a bigger burden to you. Cut him loose before his enemies realize he's become vulnerable and you spend what's left of your life fighting for a brief interlude that will never happen again."

I leaned in to the wall, feeling the knife in my pocket slide back as my balance changed. "I could have Cole anytime I wanted. I don't need your help, if it comes to that. So why are you really here?"

She nodded, giving me a good-on-you look that reminded me of all the times I'd passed Vayl's little tests. The bitch. "I knew you were a quick study. Of course, if you really wanted Cole, I could smooth the road for the rest of your lives. But you and I both know he's not your true desire."

"No?"

She shook her head. "You want Vayl back? I could give him to you. Along with your job. Just like it was before your boss went and got his throat slashed."

"Who did it?" I demanded.

She wagged a finger in front of my face, which I had a juvenile desire to bite. "Information is expensive, Jasmine. Are you willing to pay for the name of Pete's killer?"

I realized I'd pushed forward, letting her know how eager I

was for any facts I could gather related to his case. I let my shoulder blades fall against the wall.

"All right, then," said Kyphas. "For Vayl? What would you give to have your greatest love back? How much do you miss Vayl right this minute? Or Matt? I could give you either one, just like this." She snapped her fingers. Was it just me, or did I see a spark light the air along with the sound? I felt something move inside my chest. Vayl. Matt. The two best things that had ever happened to me. Both lost by the age of twenty-six. Boy, could I pick 'em, or what?

I peered toward the lounge, where Cole's laughter, Bergman's staccato comments, and Monique's soft tones offset the rumble of Vayl's voice. Even from here his presence made me feel a little less like feeding Kyphas a couple of bullets. So what if I could have him back? Or Matt? What if I could close my eyes, turn around, and see him standing there, smiling, just like he'd been the morning before he died. Saying, "I love you, Jazzer. After we get married, let's dump this gig, build a big house, and fill it with dogs and kids and bowls of fruit salad!" And I'd laugh and throw a pillow at him, and maybe we wouldn't leave the bedroom right away after all.

I slid my hand into my pocket, said, "So this is how you do it, huh?"

"Do what?"

"Corrupt decent people. You start talking to them about the gravel-road stuff they're pondering. Because everybody has thoughts like that. It's just part of the shit your brain churns up every day. Demons, though, they take that shit and make it seem like a newly sealed interstate."

"It's not?"

"Not when you factor in the price."

"But you're tempted."

"I *am* human." *I'm human. After all this time and all that's happened, I'm still ...* I began to smile.

"You've got no reason to show your teeth," Kyphas snapped. "You're more miserable than you've been in nearly two years."

"Nope. Maybe you have to strip the meat off a relationship to understand what its bindings are made of. And that's why Vayl could never tell me full out what it meant to be the *avhar* to his *sverhamin*. He just had to slip his ring on my finger and hope someday I'd figure it out for myself." I held Cirilai up to the light coming from the hall. The red facets reflecting on Kyphas's face made her look diseased.

"Oh, right," she scoffed. "Your lover thinks you're a fat old lady and suddenly you understand why you can't leave him?"

I shrugged. "Ten days. Ten years. Time stops counting when you've found somebody you can't live without for the second time in your life. He's mine, Kyphas. I'm not leaving him. And I'm going to bring him back. He deserves that from me."

I didn't react when I caught the movement of her hand out of the corner of my eye. She'd banged the *tahruyt* against her thigh hard enough to transform it into a sword whose shape I recognized immediately. Straight at the top, curved and tapered at its razor-sharp bottom, the flyssa was a local creation, especially beautiful because of the brass design inlaid along its spine. The pommel of Kyphas's blade, shaped like a bird of prey, flashed its ruby eye at me as she raised her hand.

"I can alter your prediction," she said. "See what I know?" she drawled as I watched the blade approach my throat. "You can die now, even if you are Eldhayr. One short stroke and I can send you straight to hell."

"Yeah, I've only got one life left. But neither of us believes you could Pit me. Besides, I've already escaped once. Don't think you could keep me there, even if you tricked me into dropping in temporarily."

My smile widened as I saw her eyes flash toward my white curl, winding among its red neighbors along the right side of my face, providing evidence that I hadn't just filled her full of crap. Not that hell gets much in-and-out traffic, but those of us who do go in and then receive the touch of a family member come back with a memento that no brand of hair dye can disguise.

She dropped the sword. Her smile gave her face a beauty-queen shine. She said, "I had to try. No offense?"

I shrugged. "It's who you are."

"You weren't afraid I would cut you?"

"You've already signed a contract agreeing not to hurt anyone in Vayl's Trust. I know how demons are bound."

"You understand us, do you?"

"It's part of my job."

She smiled again, sisterly, like her next move might be to hug me. I shoved my other hand into my pocket in case she decided to follow through. Instead she jerked her head toward the chandelier and the light sputtered out, leaving us in almost total darkness. I yanked out my bolo, but it wasn't necessary. All she did was lean forward and whisper, "Then you'll appreciate why I set you up for this next bit." She kissed me, peck, on the cheek, and ran up the stairs.

I stood with my back against the stairway wall, its tiles so cool I could feel them through the thin material of my dress. *That's why I'm chilled*, I told myself as Cole and Vayl walked out of the lounge and came to stand at the bottom of the stairs.

"Berggia," Vayl said, his smooth baritone more hesitant than I'd heard it the nearly ten months we'd worked together. "I did have a favor to ask of you now that your wife has gone up for the night."

"Yes, sir?"

"Do you remember the first evening we arrived here?"

Droll humor in Cole's voice as he replied, "That'll be tough to forget."

"Yes, you and Madame Berggia seemed quite confused at first. Of course, long periods of travel will do that to anyone. But then you insisted we play that game with the small portraits. Remember? You showed me several and asked me to respond if I recognized any of them."

I remembered. The panic. Near desperation. Bergman's idea to show Vayl familiar photos, every face we could find online, from vampires he'd lived with in the Grecian Trust, to mass murderers he'd disposed of in the thirties, to members of our present crew.

Cole said, "Yeah. Did you want to play the game again? Do you think—"

"No." Impatient. Almost like, *Get with the program, dammit. In fact, I'd be ecstatic if you could read my mind so I wouldn't have to say this out loud.* Vayl rubbed the back of his neck. Stretched his shoulders. Finally blurted it out. "I am interested in meeting a woman."

I stopped breathing.

Cole said, "Madame Berggia is making your appointment with the Seer in the morning—"

"No!" Deep breath. "I want an entirely different sort of woman." Long pause.

Cole: "Oh."

Vayl: "One of the small paintings you showed me ... I was captivated. I have been unable to turn my mind from her in these days since."

Me: *You fucker. I'm going to kill you. Right here. Right now.*

Granny May: *He doesn't know about you yet. You'd be murdering an innocent man.*

Me: *Like hell! Kyphas was right.* I turned to go upstairs. *Maybe I will just—*

Cole: "Which one was it?"

Vayl: "I cannot remember her name. She was a green-eyed beauty with flaming red hair. You told me she was biding in Marrakech with her lover, a vampire named Vayl."

I shoved my palm against my mouth. Two fat tears tracked down my cheeks.

Cole said, "Her name is Jasmine." Bless him, he pronounced it just like Vayl would have.

I turned back. My *sverhamin* stood on the balls of his feet, his entire body tight with anticipation. "Yes! Can you arrange a rendezvous?"

"Sir." Cole pushed his hands into his hair, pulled his palms down his face. "Although I'm fairly sure she's unhappy with her current situation, uh, I don't think a face-to-face is going to be that easy. Vayl is the jealous type."

"We shall start with a letter, then. I will dictate and you will pen and deliver it, yes?"

Cole nodded, but slowly, like he couldn't quite believe the conversation. "I guess I could."

"Excellent!" Vayl clapped him on the shoulder. Which was when I realized his next move would probably be to bound up the steps and rush to his room on the third floor, next to mine, where he could have the privacy he needed to write his fantasy girl a love letter.

I grabbed my skirt, hiked it up to my thighs, and ran toward my room. My mouth was open the whole way, pulling in big breaths of air to fuel my race, pushing out gusts of silent laughter. Because 1777 Vayl wanted me too. *Yeehaw!*

CHAPTER SIX

Vayl never talked much about his childhood. But I always suspected it included lots of hand-me-downs and skipped meals. Because he'd reached the end of his second century with a well-developed appreciation for the finest clothes, food, and accommodations.

I could see instances where spending extra dough got you better quality, but to me a room was pretty much just a place to crash unless you lost so many stars you began to see mold and bugs. Yeah, I appreciated my sunset-striped king-size with its wall-length headboard and the silk-cushioned bench at its foot. But Vayl would've wanted me to ooh and aah over my yellow and red bathroom (egad, was there no end to the tile?) and the metalwork decorating the windows and the door that led to my balcony. No dice. I saved that kind of reaction for, say, people who could eat entire lemons without puckering. Now, that's impressive!

For lack of a better place to put it, I'd set my trunk against the wall between the bench and the bathroom. I opened the lid, dug through a couple weeks' worth of clothing, most of which Monique had sent out to be cleaned for me the day before. Vayl's cane nestled between a pair of jeans and a pile of silky lingerie that threatened to depress me all over again. So I concentrated on the item that had been his companion so long that he'd added a metal tip to its base and then replaced that twice. Even if he hadn't recognized me, he should've known his cane. But even it had gotten a REJECT stamp.

Which was, maybe, why I spent time with it every day, curled up on the bench with the cane across my knees, my fingers trailing along the whole length of the black wooden sheath that held a sword Vayl had once wielded like it was part of his arm. Now I wasn't sure he knew how. I turned the cane on my lap, watching the carved tigers spiral down its length while the blue gem at the top glittered in the light of my wall sconces.

Maybe he'll ask for it tomorrow, I told myself, as I had every night since we'd arrived. My new mantra. The one I repeated right before I called Cassandra.

Who, once again, had nothing new to tell me. Except that she wanted to put Jack on the phone.

"Cassandra, I'm not talking to a dog on the—"

"Here he is!"

I heard panting. Echoes of my conversation with E.J., only Jack had enough control of his slobbers that Cassandra wouldn't need to decontaminate her mouthpiece when we hung up.

"Uh, hello, Jack. This would be Jaz. Talking to you on the phone." I dropped my forehead into my hands, knowing Cassandra could blackmail me until the end of time now. Because I would pay, yes, raid my savings regularly to make sure nobody ever heard about this. Even so, I said, "I don't know how you dogs deal with disembodied voices. My guess? You're wondering why I haven't walked out of Cassandra's bathroom by now. Anyway, be a gentleman and do your business outside, okay, buddy? See you soon."

Cassandra said, "He's smiling. Huh. I wonder why he's checking out the toilet?"

"No idea. So we're still stuck on what happened to Vayl?"

"I'm sorry, Jaz. I haven't found any mention of this kind of memory loss in the Enkyklios or my books so far, so I don't think it's a natural occurrence for vampires."

"Yeah, Astral hasn't come up with anything either."

Which sucked. Cassandra could research hundreds of supernatural sources. Astral, the wundercat Bergman had invented for me, also contained an Enkyklios, along with every government database I cared to access. Problem was, only a small number of vamps had ever made it into the records. Most of them lived highly secretive lives, and of those who'd shared info, none had experienced Vayl's current malady.

I took a deep breath. "All right, then. I'm bringing in Sterling."

Silence.

"Cassandra?"

"I've heard of him."

"Who hasn't?"

"Do you think—that is—maybe someone else would do just as well?"

"We've worked together before."

"And how did that turn out?"

I cleared my throat. "I believe the city was going to have that house torn down anyway—"

"Jaz—"

"He's the best. Nobody else will do."

"Okay."

"So, uh, could you call him?"

I didn't actually hear her gulp. But the long pause led me to believe she went through a hard swallow or two before she said, "Me?"

"Yeah. Well." I pulled my poker chips out of my pocket. Set them down on the bench and began to shuffle them. When I'd calmed down enough to talk again I said, "The last time I saw him, he told me that if I ever spoke to him again he was going to turn my hair purple and put a permanent knot in my tongue. He's good enough to pull that off, you know."

"What did you *do*?"

I sighed. If she was going to be my emissary, maybe she should have some background. "It was about three months before I started working with Vayl. I was chasing down a mage who'd been hired by some lobbying group to give the first lady a disease. I can't even remember the name of it now. But it was rare enough that the government wasn't providing any research funding. They figured if the president's wife came down with it, the money would come pouring in. I'd cornered the mage once, but when he nearly dropped a bank sign on me, Pete decided I needed some hocus-pocus in my back pocket."

"So he sent in Sterling."

"Who is, I kid you not, the most annoying man on earth. We're only on the case for two weeks, but the entire time he never stops bitching about all the gigs he's missing and how his band is probably just falling apart having to play with this dude from St. Louis. Like they've never heard of jazz in Missouri."

I shook my head, realized Cassandra couldn't see me, and went on. "So we're searching through this abandoned house in the worst neighborhood in D.C., where we've heard the mage has holed up. There's trash everywhere. It stinks like rotten potatoes and I'm pretty sure rats are living inside the furniture, so at least Sterling's wearing shoes this time out. But I can't figure why he's dressed the rest of himself like a house painter. If his T-shirt was any whiter it would glow, making him a prime target. This, of course, makes me realize my black-on-black ensemble has probably qualified us to star in the next series of Good vs. Evil videos on YouTube. But I'm not interested in becoming a cartoon. I just want to kill the mage and run before I catch whatever he's got cooking for Mrs. President. However, Sterling's not in the *mood*. He's just had a call from his drummer, who's enchanted with his St. Louis sit-in. Dumbass just can't stop complimenting the guy whose name is, I kid you not, Doobie. We're in the kitchen, I've got Grief off safety, and Sterling should be ready with a kickass spell. But instead he starts muttering the same old complaints."

"Fucking Doobie, stealing my gigs, no doubt fucking everything up."

"Hello?" I say. "Potential target behind the fridge. Or in the closet. And you don't even have your wand ready!"

He looks down at his empty hands. His fingers are long and pale. Great for weaving spells or playing the piano. I can't imagine why his chosen instrument is the trumpet. "You can't just carry wands around like cocked guns," he says, frowning at me like I should have intimate knowledge of warlock lore. As if they don't have it all guarded closer than nuclear material.

"Why not?" I ask.

"It's dangerous, Chill." That's what he calls me, I think just to piss me off. He shakes his head to emphasize his point. His hair falls straight to his shoulders. It's so black I'd suspect a bad dye job if he wasn't a Power. He's saved from utter geekdom by two factors. The hair sweeps directly back from his forehead, so there's no part to reveal the freakish white of his skull. And he walks and talks with a rhythm that comes from somewhere deep underground, like he's locked into the music of the earth itself.

We move on to the dining room, which may contain a table, but we can't be sure because all we see are moldy boxes packed with old newspapers. I think we're back on track until he says, "If this assignment goes on for more than a couple of days I'm gonna have to split. I gotta get back to my band."

"Are you nuts?" I'm so mad I'm hissing. "We're about to confront a disease-carrying mage and all you can think about is your stupid band? Would you like me to tell you what matters least to me right now? I mean even less than clipping my toenails? Your band. The fact that some dude named Doobie is getting his ass germs all over your chair. And that he's probably playing better than you do."

"Where do you get off talking tunes?" he spits. "You don't know shit about jazz. Hell, you're not even black."

Anybody else might've laughed until they blew snot. But Matt and my Helsingers have only been dead for four months. I still feel like I'm walking around with no skin, just bleeding through my clothes like they should be bandages. So if you scratch me, I don't bleed harder. I scream:

"You're not black either, you bigoted twat! You're whiter than me, and I'm a pasty-ass redhead! All you do is sit around and whine about how you'd be better-looking if you were black, you'd get more dates if you were black, you'd be a better musician if you were black. Because you know that's the one thing even the most powerful warlock on earth can't change. So it's the one excuse you can make that nobody can throw back in your face as your own failure. How about you shower more than twice a week? Shave some thorns off that ego of yours, and get some damn trumpet lessons? Work at it day and night the way you have your magic. Oh, wait, it actually matters to you whether you fail at music so you're not going to put the sweat into it just in case it all comes to nothing. Right?"

"Enough!" Sterling's voice spikes in my ears, so full of venom and jagged edges that I cover them with my hands. Well, I try. Grief is still in my grip. Should I take aim?

As I consider my options, he slaps the palms of his hands against the carved bone bracelets on the opposite wrists. He slides them off his fingers, and they seem to reach toward each other, as if they know *they belong together. They link with a sound like searing steak.*

I have time to think, Oh shit, that's his wand, *before he raises the gnarled weapon and traces an intricate pattern in the air. As the wand buzzes and he chants, I charge.*

Warlocks don't do much hand-to-hand fighting, and Sterling's ego won't admit that anyone like me would dare to attack in the face of his might. In a sense he's right. No way would I shoot a fellow spy. But I sure as hell would head-butt him.

Our skulls crack with the force of a couple of rams. For a couple of seconds everything goes gray.

Cassandra stopped me with a gasp. "You head-butted Sterling Nicodemus? You. Head-butted? The most powerful warlock in the world?"

"Well, that was before Paolo Grittoli died, so technically he was number two at the time. In retrospect, it *was* a stupid move, though. Too much risk for too little gain. But as I stood back and my eyes cleared, I gotta say I grinned when the blood gushed from the gash I'd opened up on his forehead. Within seconds it had blinded him. One point for me, right? But my lead disappeared when he hauled off and punched me. Not literally. Dude doesn't have to. Just waves that wand of his and all the *oomph* he's stored up goes zapping through his special little conduit. Looks like a damn blue claw coming at you."

"What did you do?"

"I flew through a wall. It was a flimsy wall, which is why I'm still alive today. Luckily that put out the flames, so my clothes were only smoking when I got up and ran. He came after me, which led to a five-minute attack/escape/something-gets-blown-to-bits chase that finally caused the place to collapse. Unfortunately, the mage we'd been after had never been there in the first place, so we still had to neutralize him before we could ditch each other. We managed a temporary truce. Did the job. He threatened to rearrange my reflection and we went our separate ways."

I knew Cassandra was shaking her head because I could hear her earrings clicking together. "Does Vayl know about this?"

"No."

Sigh. "All right. I'll call him. But you have to promise to behave."

"Cassandra. I'm a totally different person now. It'll be no problem. You can promise him that. And, you know, make a deal if you have to. Tell him I'll buy him a new trumpet or something."

"You think he's still that angry that he's going to have to be bribed?"

"I don't know. I mean, Vayl did request his help when we went to Scotland and nothing came of it. At the time he thought the Oversight Committee was responsible. I never corrected him because we were finally going somewhere with our relationship, and the last thing I wanted to say was, 'Oh, by the way, can I tell you about the time I was a complete ass to a sensitive artist?'"

Cassandra said, "He was out of line too."

"See, that's why my brother loves you. Is he home yet?"

New excitement in her voice as she said, "I'm meeting his plane tomorrow. I can't wait! Is it okay if I take Jack with me?"

"Sure. Just tell him he doesn't have to get *on* the plane this time, okay? Otherwise he'll take off in the opposite direction."

"Okay. And, um, I'll call Sterling now."

"You are the best future sister-in-law ever." I had to sit there for a minute after I hung up before I could identify the strange new feeling making me want to jump up and pace around the room.

Huh. I think it's called hope. But don't quote me on that. I've been wrong before.

Nothing makes me hungrier than a gut full of optimism. So I took Vayl's cane in one hand and let the other brush back the sienna-tinted curtains that spanned my balcony door. Across the courtyard, through the doors that exited the lounge, I could see people moving around inside the room. Which meant cake could still be snatched from under their noses if I was cunning, bold, or charming, all of which I felt were suddenly within my skill set. But just in case I needed help, I pulled a compact from my battered black weapons bag and, from it, peeled off two fake eyelashes. Besides making me resemble Trixie the Velcro-uniformed nurse at the Silver Spurs Saloon, they gave me access to any video feeds our friendly neighborhood robokitty might want to send me.

I ran down to the second floor and knocked on Bergman's door.

He didn't answer. I knew better than to barge in. He probably had a rocket launcher set to fire as soon as the knob turned the wrong way. So I knelt by the crack between the embellished wood and the floor.

"Come on out, Astral," I coaxed. "I know you're in there. I can hear your gears purring."

Without another noise she slid out to me, her sleek black coat in blob-array to allow her to pass through the thumb-sized opening. "Thatta girl," I said as we both took our typical stances. I only popped a couple of times at the knee. She sounded like a bag of Orville Redenbacher's, and kinda resembled one too, her parts reinflating to catly proportions with remarkable speed. I waited. When her claws didn't appear I said, "Aren't you going to recalibrate?"

She regarded me with golden eyes that seemed to cross slightly the longer we stared at each other. Then she said, "Hello!" Eerie how her lips made just the right shapes. Bergman must've spent six months on her mouth controls alone.

"I'll take that as a 'No.' Now remember not to talk in front of Monique. You're barely believable as it is."

I headed for the next set of stairs, glancing down at Astral as she trotted beside me. I knew if I touched her she'd feel like one of those metallic silver sleeping bags that insulate to forty below. Which was why we'd told Monique that Astral was a weather cat. We'd unraveled this huge yarn about her already having predicted three tornadoes and a volcanic eruption. So now part of our research (specifically mine) was to see if she could foresee sandstorms. Or flash floods. But it all had to do with her unique coat, so we'd asked Monique never to touch her, because to do so could ruin all our data.

"You know, I'd worry about there being a special place for liars in hell," I whispered to her. "But I'm pretty sure the assassins' level is so much worse, it's not even worth my time to stress over it anymore."

Her only reply was a twitch of her inky ears to let me know

she'd heard. At least she hadn't spoken, or worse, sung out a reply. And once we got to the lounge I realized I hadn't needed to freak about Monique at all. She'd taken off for the night, leaving Cole and Kyphas to play a game of backgammon. Well, that seemed to have been the original idea, because the game board and pieces were all set up on the table where the cake had been. Which meant Monique had probably taken it back to the—

Kitchen raid! shrieked Teen Me. She'd been lounging in a hammock she'd strung between Granny May's clothesline poles. Now she rolled off with such an utter lack of grace you'd have laughed out loud to learn her track coaches occasionally referred to her as an "athlete." *I want the icing! That's all I want! Just the icing! You eat the cake part!* she said, glancing over her shoulder at Gran, who had just begun to hang a sheet on the line.

Granny May looked over the tops of her glasses at me. *You see what I had to put up with?*

I shushed them both. Because though I'd thought Cole and Kyphas were bent over the instructions to the game at first, I knew differently when he pulled the sheet of paper they'd both been holding out of the demon's hands.

As he studied the paper I backed to the stairs, leaving Astral in the room to send the signal that played out like a holograph three feet in front of my eyes. I sat on the bottom step, turning Vayl's cane between my fingers as I watched Cole slide the paper in his, giving Astral enough of a view to show a hammer with a double-thick handle that ended in a sharp point.

"So this is the Rocenz," he said, sitting back on the couch and shoving his feet out in front of him until the toes of his shoes hit the table.

"Yes." Kyphas leaned toward him, resting her elbows on her knees to show off the remarkableness of her cleavage. And, of course, his eyes tracked to them like radar. Smiling wickedly, she said, "I thought you'd already seen it."

He shook his head. "Vayl told me about it, but I missed the slide show. So it's two tools that are, what, magically joined at the hip?"

"You could say that."

"And how do you separate the hammer from the chisel?"

She scooted closer to him. "I have no idea."

"Sure you do. It was forged by a demon, right?"

She nodded. "Lord Torledge created it." She looked down at the picture. When she looked up again I thought I saw her eyes flash bright yellow. But I could've been mistaken. A second later they were back to hazel.

Cole let the picture rest on his thigh and laid his arm across the back of the couch. He seemed so relaxed that I wouldn't have been surprised to see his eyes flutter shut. "Is he still around? Pounding out new weapons for hell to lose track of?"

Kyphas sat back. Now it was as if Cole had his arm around her shoulders. She said, "He's still working. And I know where you're going with this. He does know how to separate the parts." She turned toward him, pressing the side of her breast into his chest. "I can find out for you. If..."

"If?" He dropped his free hand to the expanse of tanned skin between her neck and shoulder. Watched his fingers push her sleeve down her arm, then move across the dangerously low neckline of her blouse.

She gasped. Reached up for his face and pulled him to her. Their kiss was so fiery that I turned away. My stomach rolled. Everything about this moment was wrong. But I couldn't do anything to make it better. I stepped back.

Then I heard Kyphas say, "I can give you everything you want, Cole. You have only to ask. The Rocenz. The key to unlock it. You can save Jasmine. You can have me."

"I want that. But I'm not as convinced as everybody else is that this tool is going to work."

I recalled the playback *I'd* seen of the Hart Ranch hand, Zell

Culver, using the hammer and chisel to carve the name of the earthbane, Thraole-Lulid, into the gates of hell. The tool had performed as promised, diminishing the monster to a pile of gore.

Kyphas's next words pulled me back into the conversation. "I don't make agreements I can't keep, Cole. Jasmine can defeat Brude with the Rocenz."

"All you want in return is my soul, right?"

Yellow lit her eyes. "I could take it without your permission. The Rocenz is more than just a primitive demon-killer, after all. It was designed to do much more intricate carving." She smiled as her eyes darkened. "But I'm not that kind of girl. I like my souls freely given. And when you think of it, it's a small price to pay for eternal ecstasy."

Cole transferred his hand to the back of the couch. "I don't think so."

"Why not?" No, I wasn't wrong. That was real pain in her voice.

His voice was hard as flint as he said, "Jaz would never forgive me if I sold my soul for her. And I couldn't live with that. In fact, I couldn't live with you. Yeah, you're the most beautiful woman I've ever kissed. But you're not her."

"I *could* be." Was she ... begging ... a little now?

"No. Jaz may cross the line once in a while, but at least she knows where the line is."

"Line?"

Cole rose, bringing Kyphas up with him. My cue to backpedal. "Exactly."

"You should reconsider." Harshness now, clear warning in that hellborn tone.

"What're you going to do to me, Kyphas? And before you answer, let me just remind you how many burn wards would've written you off the last time you came after a member of Vayl's Trust."

She snorted. "Vayl is no threat in his current state."

"But Jaz is. I'm not saying I know a whole lot about Vampere politics. But as his *avhar*, she's gotta be perfectly capable of stepping in and kicking your ass out the door. Or, to be more specific, enforcing the contract you signed promising you wouldn't hurt anybody under Vayl's protection."

I could only see her profile in the silence that followed, but it was enough to show the frustrated color that had risen in her cheeks. Even though Astral picked up minute sounds, I had to lean forward to hear her whisper, "You have to know I would never willingly hurt you."

His laugh was so sharp it should've drawn blood. "You're a demon. That's who you are."

She stepped toward him. Her eyes were wide, intense on his as she said, "It's not who I want to be. Not when I'm with you."

She reached forward. Pressed her hands against his chest. "You confuse me. You enrage me. But I'm tired of pretending that you're nothing but meat to me. I'll do anything. I'll be anyone you like. If you only kiss me again."

Anticipation curled the corners of my mouth. *And now for the final cut.*

I nearly gasped out loud when he pulled her into his arms. Their lips met in a kiss so fiery I was surprised their clothes didn't melt off. When Cole grabbed her by the hips and her legs wrapped around his back I tore off the fake lashes, Astral's cue to get the hell out.

She joined me on the steps, sitting beside me while I tried to think what to do next. Thump from the lounge as the couch rammed back into the wall. That did it. My buddy, one of the most cheerful, hilarious dudes I'd ever met, was screwing an unrepentant demon. No good could come of it, especially for him. As soon as Kyphas became expendable I was going to kill her.

CHAPTER SEVEN

So much for cake. I gripped Vayl's cane tight and sped up to my room, Astral a rocketing shadow at my heels. The run did me good. By the time I collapsed on my gigantic bed with the cat curled up beside me I could think again. As I stroked her smooth head I decided to have a real face-to-face with Raoul. Fighting demons was his gig after all. If anybody could help me take Kyphas down, it would be him. And in the meantime?

I had to think of some stellar babe to fix Cole up with. But I didn't really know any nice girls besides Evie. Hey! That was it! She had a lot of friends who spent their whole lives in Normalville. She could easily find Cole a fabulous woman. Somebody who wouldn't flip out if he traveled some. A woman who liked guys with sun-bleached hair and...

I didn't realize I'd nodded off until I heard a tapping at my window. I sat up in bed, pulling Grief from its holster before my feet hit the floor. Again the taps, four or five, hitting almost, but not quite, at the same time. The window was the one that faced the street.

"What is it, Astral?" I whispered.

The cat didn't reply, just hopped off the bed and went to the curtains, where she waited patiently for me to pull them open. I stood by the wall. Peering between the material and the glass, I could see down to the street, where a man wearing a gray button-down shirt and white pants stood, his hand full of pebbles, his upturned face clear in the streetlights.

"Oh, for chrissake!" I flipped the curtains aside and lifted the window. "Aren't you the guy I kicked the crap out of before?"

He smiled and slapped himself on the chest. "Yousef!" he announced happily.

"How did you find me?"

He glanced over his shoulder and his young translator slunk guiltily out of the shadows. After a brief conference the teenager said, "Yousef says it is not difficult to place you, as you may be the only red-haired woman in Marrakech."

Dammit! Why didn't I dye my hair before we came here? "What do you want?" I demanded. I checked the watch Bergman had made me, wishing it shot lightning bolts or laser beams. Holy crap! "And why are you here at four thirty in the morning?"

"We are on our way to work, lady," said the boy.

"Where do you work?" I asked.

"In the tannery."

That explained the stench on the men and in the part of the medina where we'd been following Vayl the night before. Transforming animal skins into supple leathers was a laborious and revolting job, but I wouldn't look down my nose at these guys for the work they'd chosen. At least they were trying to make an honest buck.

I said, "Isn't this out of your way?"

Another discussion between Yousef and the boy. What was his name? Oh yeah, Kamal. He wiped his hand across his lips, clearly wishing he didn't have to say, "Yousef would like you to know that he is falling"—he made a diving motion with his hands—"into the love with you. And you would do well to marry him before you leave the country."

I felt my jaw drop. "Are you insane?" I slashed my hand at Kamal before he could translate, stomped back to my weapons bag, grabbed my silencer, and screwed it onto Grief's barrel. Just as I got back to the window a handful of pebbles flew through.

Shit!

I dodged aside, waited a beat to make sure Yousef wasn't launching a second handful, then whipped my Walther PPK into position.

Kamal squealed as soon as he saw the gun clear the windowsill. He dove into the bushes that belonged to the two-story house across the street. Yousef, on the other hand, spread his arms like we were about to do big reunion hugs. He started speaking rapid Arabic, shaking his head back and forth to emphasize his words and closing his eyes blissfully as he talked.

"Kamal! Tell your buddy to go away!"

Kamal translated. When it was time for him to relay Yousef's message to me he was nearly weeping. "Yousef says he must stay until all the birds of Morocco have sung your name. Please do not shoot him, lady. He is not a bad man. He is just a little crazy."

I took aim. Squeezed the trigger. *Ping!* The cobblestones in front of Yousef's feet flew apart as the bullet impacted them.

Kamal screamed and jumped out from behind the bushes. Yousef laughed and did a little soft-shoe.

What the hell?

Kamal grabbed his friend's arm and tried to pull him away. They argued vehemently for about thirty seconds. Finally the boy's head dropped and he yelled up to me, "Yousef says he will only leave if you give him your name. I apologize, but it was the only way I could secure his agreement."

I shrugged. "It's Madame Berggia."

Kamal sighed as Yousef talked some more. Then he said, "Yousef wishes me to say these words: 'All right, I leave, my wondrous one. But while we are apart my heart will beat with the sound of your name. Until we meet in our dreams!'" The tanners walked away, leaving me free to go back into my room, dropping the window and the curtain.

"Ow!" I picked up the pebble I'd stepped on. "You know what, Astral?" The cat looked up inquiringly. "No matter how I look at it lately, love hurts."

"Love is a battlefield," she sang softly, making me wonder how many of Pat Benatar's hits Bergman had downloaded into her memory.

I flopped back down into bed, so tired that I didn't have a single conscious thought before the dreams began. And they made no sense. It was like one of my inner girls had commandeered the remote and decided to channel flip her way through the night. I relived the poker game I'd played with Dave's unit, after which Cam, his right-hand man, had given me my precious chips. Stella screamed at me again as the dogs dragged her back into hell. And just as I turned away, the blizzard-swept cairn dissolved into a Hawaiian pier, and Matt stood before me, his hands outstretched. "Dance with me, Jazzy."

Every fear lifted. All my worries dissolved as I felt his arms close around me. I laid my head against his shoulder and took a deep breath. The scent of cedar and freshly mown grass that was uniquely Matt filled my lungs, and for one moment I felt whole again. I smiled against the rough cloth of his jacket. And then realized.

"You should be wearing a cotton shirt. One of those ridiculous Hawaiian numbers with huge pink flowers."

"Jasmine. It's me."

I shoved him away. My blue-eyed Navy Seal had been replaced by a uniformed Ranger with a soft Spanish accent. "Raoul? What the—I mean, really? Here? Now?" *When I was finally feeling good? I'd shove you again, but that's probably a major sin and I am so stocked on those.*

He ran his hand through his dark brown crew cut. "I am sorry, but jumping into your dreams is like parachuting into an active volcano. Do you realize how unpredictable they are? I'm lucky not to hit when you're under a barrage of gunfire!"

"Are they that real?"

Raoul led me to the table at the end of the pier. It was still set for two. Hell, even the candles were still burning. He said, "Not until I arrive. And then they become something more...that makes me want to avoid blades and bullets."

"Well, couldn't you time your drops a little better? What if I'd been having a really hot dream about Vayl? That would've ended our relationship right then and there!"

"I would *never*—"

"Good!"

We sat down and I grabbed a breadstick from the woven basket. "Do you want some?" I held the basket out so he could reach it easier.

"No, thank you."

I put it down. Started breaking little pieces off my breadstick and tossing them into the water. We sat there until Raoul decided I'd calmed down enough for us to talk like reasonable human— uh—Eldhayr. I jacked my arm back and threw the rest of the breadstick into the ocean.

"Are you all right?" he asked.

What kind of question is that for somebody whose broken neck you once repaired as easily as if it was pieced together with buttercream icing? I mean, Raoul, every time you and I meet I have to face the fact that we have our own classification. You could at least avoid reminding me that I was the only one who agreed to come back to fight. That Matt preferred paradise—or whatever—to me.

I said, "I'll be okay." I badly wanted to shuffle through my poker chips. When I found them in my dream pocket I nearly cheered, but since Raoul knew what that was all about I satisfied myself with grabbing one and holding it tight between my fingers while I faked a relaxed expression. "It's so great that you showed. I wanted to ask you about—"

"I need a favor."

"Oh?" I looked at him a little closer. He seemed as controlled as ever. But I realized his knee was bobbing up and down under the table like he was trying to run one of those treadle sewing machines you occasionally see in antique stores. And every once in a while he would tap the base of his water glass with his forefinger, until he caught himself and made himself stop.

He said, "I wonder if I could borrow Astral."

I felt my eyebrows shoot up. If I let the cat go I wouldn't just temporarily lose access to all the information she stored. I'd be loaning out my scout and backup arsenal. "How long do you need her?" I asked.

He looked over his shoulder. I did too. If he thought somebody else could follow him into my dreams I sure as hell wanted to know who.

He said, "I'll tell you. If you promise to keep it to yourself."

I said, "Okay." He waited. "Oh! I promise not to tell anyone," I finished.

He lowered his voice. "Remember the woman we discussed a few days ago? The one with the shiny lips?"

"Yeah. What was her name? Tina? Thea?"

"Nia," he said.

I nodded. "Right. Nia with the intimidating lip gloss. Did you make with the chitchat?"

"She's coming over for lunch." He slid toward the edge of his chair, like I was about to send him off on a vital errand.

"You smooth talker, you!"

"Yes. Well, no. I wrote everything down first and memorized it." He took a breath through his nose and blew it out his mouth. I could see the stress drop away as the corners of his mouth lifted. "Spending my life in the military did not prepare me to converse with women."

"You're talking to me."

"You're different."

Okay, we'll stop before you tell me I'm just another guy, okay? That way I won't have to club you over the head with this flower vase. I asked, "So where does Astral come in?"

"Nia mentioned that of everything in life she had to leave, she missed her cat the most. So I thought…" Mischievous smirk. Gosh, it seemed that even higher beings needed props to get to second base.

So I guessed the question was, should I steer Raoul away from the shiny-lipped cat lady or get comfortable with a Diet Coke and a bowl of popcorn? Well, he had interrupted one of my favorite dreams. "Astral will make the trip okay?"

"She's a robot."

I'll take that as a "yes." "Then you can have her. But—" I raised my hand before he could shower me with thanks. "I'm going to need some payback."

"Anything."

Oh, no, Raoul. Tell me you haven't got it this bad. I said, "Kyphas is going to betray us."

"Naturally."

"Can you find out what she can do with the Rocenz if she gets her hands on it? I mean, beyond the obvious political gain she'd receive by returning it to hell? We know what it'll do for humans. But she hinted that it works differently for demons, and I'm worried that someone's gonna lose his soul if we don't head her off quick."

Raoul nodded. "You make an excellent point. I'll get busy with that."

"Okay. And next time I wake up, I'll send Astral through the portal. I should warn you, she's developed some funky habits since Jack accidentally blew her head off."

Raoul nodded. "Good. That will be a great icebreaker." He leaned over and took my hand. "Thanks, Jaz. I really appreciate this." I looked down at his fingers, long and bronzed by endless days in the sun. And watched them change into shorter, broader digits that wrapped around my own with familiar strength.

"I think it's time for bed, Jazzy. How about you?" I raised my eyes to Matt's. Such a clear blue I could imagine sailing around the world in them.

"Okay," I whispered.

He pulled me to my feet. Slid his arm around my waist, slipped his fingers under my shirt so he could brush them along the sides of my ribs. I shivered with anticipation. "Let's get married right away," he said. "Can we get the whole thing planned in a month?"

I caught my breath. "Why are you in such a rush?"

He pulled me closer. "I've always wanted to be a dad. What do you think? Soon?"

I smiled up into his eyes, part of me dancing as I imagined the future unfolding ahead of us. But even deep into sleep I couldn't push away the voice that said, *Hold tight to this moment, Jaz. Because two weeks from tonight the dreams die with him.*

I woke feeling more exhausted than I had when I'd fallen asleep. My hand went to my face, trying to brush away the drool that must've dried on my chin while I was out. But it was too thick for spit and too smooth for upchuck. Then I realized it was on my upper lip too. I sat up and looked down at the T-shirt I was wearing. It was one of Vayl's. Plain white cotton that made him look like a bodybuilder but hung to my knees. I'd bled all over the front of it. I checked the pillowcase. Soaked. Geez, how do you sleep through a gushing nosebleed like that?

Maybe when you spend the whole time dreaming backward instead of looking forward.

I ignored Granny May, who was staring at me with uncharacteristic concern from behind her embroidery hoop. Because I still had to deal with the aftermath. Not as big a deal as you might expect, because I'd already done cleanup twice before, and I was starting to develop a process.

I showered and then spent another half hour in the tileriffic bathroom. With gallons of cold water, a little soap, and some scrubbing, I got all the blood out. I hung everything but the pillow over the shower's curtain rod, and that I just set on the toilet lid. At the end of that time I finally admitted to myself that the race was on now. If I couldn't carve Brude's name on the gates of hell before he blew my circuits for good, it wouldn't matter much what century Vayl thought we were living in. Because he'd be trudging through the rest of it without me.

I returned his cane to my trunk and motioned to Astral. "Time for breakfast, girl. What do you eat, like, bolts and oil or something?" She looked up at me and blinked a couple of times. "No patience for stupid questions, huh? See, that's why you're a sucky pet. Now, Jack? He thinks everything I say is brilliant. You can tell by the way he wags his tail. Have I told you lately how much it bites that he's gone? And so, pretty much, is Vayl?" I stopped, shoved my palm against my chest. Amazing how it literally hurt from time to time. Maybe people really could die of broken hearts.

"But not in this getup, right, Astral?" I looked down at my sun-colored T-shirt and couldn't help but feel cheered by the grinning superhero posing on the front, who was pretty much all straight white teeth, pointy-edged face mask, and flowing red cape. He had his hands on his hips as he gazed bravely off into the wild blue. The caption read IMAGINE WHAT I COULD DO IF MY TIGHTS WEREN'T STUCK UP MY CRACK!

I'd found it in a package outside my door just before going downstairs and had immediately decided to change clothes. It had come with a note: *You're the best. Happy Birthday!* ♥ *Cole*

I also wore a pair of denim cutoffs that hit me just above the knee and black running shoes. I left my hair down and shoved the yellow-framed sunglasses Cole had also bought me on top of my head for later. Grief needed a place to hide, which wasn't a big deal now that the temperature hovered in the mid-sixties. I threw on my white jacket from yesterday, made exclusively for gun-toting babes like me. Lined to hide the dark contours of my holster and gun, it was still made of material that breathed like cotton. It might begin to look slightly awkward when the temperature rose to eighty-five or so. But that was where my country of origin saved me. People just seemed to accept weirdness from Americans.

Walking downstairs for the fourth day in a row didn't feel any more habitual. I still marveled at the exotic feel of Monique's riad, a house so old that even the dirt lodged in the carved curlicues of the stair balusters had become valuable. While we stepped in and out of the rays of sunshine slanting through classically arched windows, Astral played a song she'd overheard in the Djemaa el Fna the day before, one that a group of musicians with flutes, drums, and a couple of brass instruments had been belting out with more enthusiasm than talent. It felt like a fanfare as I reached the front door.

"So you know where you're going?" I asked her. She looked up at me. I slapped my chest. "Jump up here." She sprang into my arms. "I'm sending you to spend some time with my Spirit Guide, Raoul. Be a good girl."

She launched into a terrific cover of Cyndi Lauper's hit "Girls Just Wanna Have Fun." Which made walking her to the end of the block where a plane portal stood between a fruit seller's souk and a shoe repair shop somewhat awkward—because I had to pretend to be belting out the words as she sang, "Oh, Mother, dear, we're not the fortunate ones. And girls, they wanna have fu-un." By the time we were done with the song, we'd gathered a small crowd, who clapped politely and gave me a handful of euros for our performance.

"Thanks," I said, waving goodbye to them as they moved on down the street. I glared down at the cat. "You are a pain in the ass, you know that?" I held my finger under her nose as she opened her mouth. "Don't. Sing. Don't talk. Just act like a damn cat for a second."

I stood watching the portal, the flames that framed its rectangular entry flickering from blue to orange and back again as I waited for Raoul to open it from his side. A car slowed down and a grinning old man with hair sprouting from his ears leaned out the passenger door. "Hello, pretty lady!"

"Get lost!" I yelled.

Come on, Raoul. I have now done a cappella karaoke and convinced the natives I'm a prostitute, all so you can get a date. Open the damn door!

The shadowed entryway swirled and then cleared. I looked straight into his penthouse, a tidy black-and-white-themed bachelor pad located high above the rooftops of Sin City. He stepped into view, his boots polished to a gleam, his trousers and jacket creased so sharply if you looked at them too long they'd give your eyeballs paper cuts. He held out his hands and I stepped forward just far enough to set Astral into them.

"She's in a musical mood today."

He nodded, his clear blue eyes busy taking in my T-shirt. When he laughed out loud I nearly fell off the curb. Relaxed Raoul was a whole different guy. Like somebody you'd want to go bowling with, because between frames you knew he'd have you rolling with stories about when he and his buddies had once hung a gigantic sign lined with old-lady bloomers from the high school roof that said NOW WE KNOW WHY NOBODY BAKES LIKE GRANDMA!

I said, "One thing."

"What's that?"

"I still haven't figured out quite what you are, but I know you deserve the best. If she doesn't treat you right, move on."

Still smiling, he said, "I'll go one better. If she breaks my heart, I'll sic *you* on her."

I nodded. "Works for me."

He lifted Astral, who'd been rubbing her paws against his buttons, as if she was fascinated by their shape and texture. "Thanks for this."

"You're welcome."

He looked over both shoulders. Touched Astral on the forehead and whispered, "Some celestial interference, if you please."

Astral yawned widely, but her mouth didn't close again. If any sound was coming from it, I couldn't hear. But suddenly I felt... tense. "Raoul?"

"My scouts have discovered information that not everyone thinks you should be privy to. They fear, if you knew, you would throw this mission and run back to America. They don't know you as well as I do, but they have more power." His voice went even lower. "So listen closely and be careful who you repeat this to. What you asked me about before? About the...tool and what the demons could do with it?"

I swallowed past the sudden dryness in my throat. "Yeah?"

"Don't allow the demon in your party to get ahold of it. If she did, she could turn any one of you into spawn as well."

"How?"

"They're still questioning the informant, so I can't be sure. I only know she'd have to use her own blood and another item, the source of which we haven't pinpointed yet." He looked around again. "You'll be careful?"

"Of course. And thanks. For everything. But I should really go. Because I'm sure it looks like I'm talking to myself in the middle of the sidewalk in Morocco. And I think I've pulled all the weird stunts this neighborhood can handle for one day."

He nodded. "I'll be in touch." The image of his place grayed out, and I turned back to the riad before I was, once again, staring into a black hole. It just felt like I was doing too much of that lately.

Chapter Eight

Monique Landry had probably been born smiling. In fact, I'd never met a person I believed more when she said, "I'm delighted to know you!" This was a lady who ran a hotel because she'd be lost without company.

She almost never talked about herself, but Bergman liked to know as much as he could about the people inside his comfort zone. So he'd fast discovered that our hostess had been born in Paris to a family with money so old it reeked of mildew and rotten grapes.

Similar story with her husband, who'd spent most of his youth jumping off cliffs and out of airplanes because, apparently, the guy couldn't get enough thrills driving his Jaguar at full throttle. When he finally landed badly and broke his pelvis he met Monique, who'd decided to fill her boring days with a career in physical therapy. They had two kids, now in college. And he'd died less than two years ago while attempting to relive his youth. Turned out the guy who'd packed his parachute had been drunk at the time.

Monique rarely mentioned Franck, though she did say he was the one who'd hired Chef Henri. And good on him for finding such an excellent cook. Every morning he spoiled us with a bounty of home-baked breads, herb butters, freshly squeezed orange juice, and mint tea. Which was probably why I'd gained a couple of pounds despite the stress related to my current mission.

In fact, as I stood at the door where the lounge entered the courtyard, my mouth was already watering from the smells Henri had risen early to tempt us with. But as soon as my foot hit the tiles I lost my appetite. Because laced with the aroma of homemade goodness was the psychic scent of a newcomer. Wouldn't Vayl just ride the smug all around the block to know his always-be-prepared lessons had saved me yet again?

The source of my change in breakfast plans sat in the shade of the gazebo. He was tapping his fingers against his thigh to a rhythm only he could hear while he watched Monique put the finishing touches to the breakfast buffet. She lined up the elegantly folded napkins, futzed with flowers so yellow they made me blink, then poured a couple of glasses of juice and joined him.

I should too. I knew that. Casually, like my heart wasn't trying to make a break for the street. Instead I stepped through the open door, silent as Astral on her best day. Five quick steps took me to an enormous banana plant, one leaf of which could've wrapped all the way around me. Which wasn't a bad idea. Because despite what I'd told Cassandra, I wasn't ready to see Sterling, much less talk to him.

But by the way he sat, long legs stretched out in front of him, his bare feet crossed at the ankles, it looked like I couldn't count on him leaving anytime soon. He set his glass on the table and linked his fingers over his flat stomach. His piercing black eyes moved from Monique's to the serenity of the pool and back again as they talked quietly and waited for me to show.

Part of me (one guess which) blew out a sigh of admiration. Something had altered in him since last time. Though his hair was just as black, long, and flowing as I remembered, he looked... grown up. His heather-green shirt was unbuttoned far enough to reveal a silver chain holding a black onyx amulet that looked like dozens of midnight-tinted lightning bolts had fused at a single point. At their center a silver sphere glittered so brilliantly it gave the illusion of rotation. He still wore the wide bone bracelets that had made him famous. Their color complemented his khaki cargo pants, which hugged hips and thighs with the long, slender shape reserved for an endurance runner. My old adversary might spend his weekends jamming with his buds, but it looked to me like Monday morning found him pounding down the miles at his local track.

I couldn't even get my feet to move. Because, you know, what if I pissed him off? Again? I knew exactly what he was capable of pulling off these days. And I hadn't lied to Cassandra when I said I'd changed. Now it did matter what happened if he decided to reach into one of his pockets, pull out a pinch of *shawackem* dust, and wait for me to turn my back before sprinkling it on my toast.

He rose from his seat, slow and lazy, just another guy who's ready to nap after a good meal. But I knew he was a cheetah. If the mood took him he could tear territorial intruders into pieces so small even the vultures would snub them.

Monique stood too, looking confused. He put her at ease with his let's-share-stories grin. "We have company," he said.

"We do?"

"She's cowering behind the banana plant."

Oh! Well, that's just—I am not! I stomped right up to him, trying to glare the smirk off his face. It didn't work.

Monique rushed into the awkward silence with the grace of a born party planner. "Your friend arrived early this morning," she told me. "He said you were expecting him?" She raised her eyebrow just enough to let me know that under the civilized veneer lurked a she-bear fully capable of throwing the guy into the gutter if he turned out to be an asshole.

"Yeah, I...yes, I invited him. I was thinking he could room with Mr. Berggia. I'm just surprised to see him so soon." So how do you greet a guy who—*aw shit, really?*—wore a small white scar on his forehead because of you? I said, "Thanks for coming, Sterling."

He's goddamn Harry Potter. Which makes me Voldemort. I am, officially, the most evil bastard on earth. And I don't even have a mini me to pawn off the guilt on! Grannyyy!

Sterling said, "It's been a while…Madame Berggia."

"Yup." I held out my hand. "Thanks for coming." I waited. When he shook it, I felt an extra slap on top of the jolt that always hit me when I touched him, which I'd only done this time to show my genuine appreciation. I looked at our linked hands and noticed his pinky ring. Nothing fancy, just a silver band with some deep black engraving. But my Sensitivity told me it was just as powerful as the amulet and bracelets. The hairs on the back of my neck only began to lie down after I pulled my hand away. Which was when I felt like I could breathe again. So, apparently, could Monique. Her sigh actually left a mist on my cheek.

Sterling said, "Cassandra told me you're offering to pony up a new trumpet."

I couldn't hide my surprise. "I figured you'd put me on a hunt for your favorite whiskey instead."

"Naw." He pointed to the pocket where he knew I kept my cash. "This job's gonna cost you more than booze, Chill." So he hadn't forgotten my nickname.

"Fine, you want a trumpet? You got one."

"I've changed instruments. It's all part of my ten-year plan. Now you're going to have to buy me a guitar."

"Deal."

"I'm not finished negotiating."

"Oh?" *Shit! I should've bartered. Then he wouldn't have realized how desperate I was for his help.*

Granny May, back in her outdoor sewing chair, stabbed her needle into the material like she wanted to draw blood. *He already knows you're dangling off the bottom rung of a helicopter's rescue ladder, girl. The way you two parted—what else could he think? All you have to decide is how much pride you can swallow before you've met your limit.*

I said, "What else do you want?"

He smiled, ducking his head so we could stare straight into each other's eyes. "*You* know."

Aw, fuck.

"How long?"

"Twenty-four hours."

"Are you out of your goddamn mind? How am I gonna—"

He backed away, his hips twisting slightly, as if he was moving to tango music played too low for uninitiated ears like mine. He said, "Not my problem. You want my help, those are my terms. Your move, Chill."

Monique's eyes moved from Sterling to me as if she was watching a slow-motion Ping-Pong match. Her hand had stolen to her lips, where she gnawed a fingernail, waiting for my reply. Geez, what would she have been chewing on if she'd actually known what was at stake?

I closed my eyes. What sucked more than anything had so far was that I hadn't even approached the pride line yet. What did that say about the lengths I'd go to for Vayl? In a word—terrifying.

I said, "Done." Patter of applause as Monique clapped her hands. I glared at her. "I wonder if you could give us a moment."

Sterling shook his head. "You know this kind of deal needs a neutral witness. Now seal it," Sterling demanded.

"Oh, for—okay." I crossed my hands, one over the other, and pressed them against my chest. "I swear on my heart's blood that I will give you a guitar and twenty-four hours of uninterrupted time with you and your Wii playing any damn game you want—"

"I'm going to kick your ass in tennis—"

I gave him my like-hell-you-will stare as I finished. "—in return for your help in solving my partner's current problem."

He'd made the same gesture. Now he said, "I swear on my heart's blood I will aid you to the end of my abilities until"—he hesitated, glancing at Monique, so I put in—"Vasil Brâncoveanu"—since Vayl no longer answered to his modern name and Sterling didn't know him by any other.

The warlock nodded gratefully. "Until Vasil Brâncoveanu is restored or until you release me of my duties." We clasped hands, my right in his left, his right engulfing my left. I felt, not a zap exactly. More of a slow-dizzy, the kind that falls over you when you've looked in a fun house mirror way too long. It came from his bracelets, making our agreement official. And from his *pull*.

Warlocks borrowed energy from other people to fuel their powers so they didn't have to sleep sixteen hours a day. Sterling was so good that his was mostly reflex, as much a part of his character as his eye color. I also knew he could crank it up when he wanted to, which was why I enjoyed touching him about as much as I liked slapping skin with psychics. I took my hands back as soon as I could. His eyes dropped to Cirilai. "Your ring…"

"Is none of your business."

He let it drop. But I could see the regret in his eyes. His look said, *If only I'd known it wasn't just a hunk of metal when I was wheeling and dealing.*

I slipped my hands into my pockets. *What have I done?* I watched Sterling touch Monique between the eyes, saw the jolt of blue move from his ring down his finger into our hostess's skull, and knew the memory of our contract would now be locked away where she could only access it if either of us welshed. Her foggy expression, followed by a trip to the buffet to fix the same flowers she'd been working on when I'd entered the courtyard, convinced me it had worked. And brought on the guilt.

We shouldn't be here. Monique's place should be full of vacationing families. Moms and dads planning shopping excursions or trips to see the Koutoubia Mosque and the Bahia Palace. We belong in an empty plain, surrounded by the ruins of long-dead buildings where we can't destroy anything that isn't already rubble.

I felt something trickle down my lip.

Sterling frowned. "Your nose is bleeding."

"Oh." I looked around, but Monique was already beside me holding a tissue, her kind brown eyes big with concern.

"Thanks." I took it and shoved it against my nostrils. "Don't worry, I'm fine." I glanced around the courtyard so I wouldn't have to deal with her sympathy or Sterling's curiosity. I said, "You know what? I think Sterling and I will eat in the gazebo this morning. We have some business to discuss."

"Of course. I'll find Shada and tell her you're ready for her to clean your room."

I nodded, reminding myself to leave the quiet little maid a big tip before we left for keeping her mouth shut about all my hand-rinsed bedclothes. "Thanks."

"I'll be working on accounts most of the morning, so if you need me please feel free to knock on my office door." Monique nodded to Sterling. "Nice to have met you," she said, then she left through the kitchen doors.

Sterling waved her away, the twist of his wrist and curve of his last three fingers making me wonder if he'd just hexed our hostess until he said, "A small blessing to follow our witness for the rest of the day. It's the least I can do, don't you think?" While he tore a generous piece of bread off the loaf and scooped a spoonful of butter onto his plate, I mopped myself up. Again. Fearing that chewing motions would just reconvene the bleeder's convention, I settled for a glass of juice and followed him into the gazebo. I spent as much time as I could arranging myself on the couch, the cushions at my back, my cup just so on the table. Sterling watched me for what seemed like hours. Finally he'd had enough.

"Chill. I'm not gonna jump you," Sterling said, his voice as smooth as icing.

"Oh. Good."

"Although an apology would be cool."

I stared.

He said, "You know, there's nothing wrong with wanting to be black."

"I never said there was!"

"You said—"

"I'm sorry, okay?" I pressed my lips together before they spat out something that would aggravate him all over again. "I need you on *this* mission. I need you to concentrate on what's happening now, not on the past. Is that possible?"

"I'm here." Some irritation in the way his teeth ripped into the khobz. But I'd take it.

"You got here quick. I appreciate that."

His eyebrows went up. "You *have* changed. Well, me too." He leaned toward me. "I'm better. At magic. At music. You want to know why?"

"Um—"

"Because at their core they're the same. I'm making my way to the source now. And when I get there?" He paused, his amulet swinging hypnotically, his eyes glittering like I should prepare for hefty news. "I'll be a Bard."

I sat back. "Dude. There hasn't been a Bard roaming since..." I thought back. What had my History professor said? "I dunno, 1715?"

"Olfric the Hand was the last Bard, and he was murdered by Calico Jack Rackham and his pirate crew in 1718." We both looked over our shoulders at the mention of pirates, who had strongholds in North Africa guarded, so it was said, by badass magic and wicked beasts. They'd never been a national security threat, so we hadn't dealt with them directly. But we'd heard horror stories, and I sure as hell didn't want to take any of them on. Especially when they'd made it part of their code to exterminate the Bardish from the face of the earth.

I whispered, "Why would you want to be a Bard?"

"As a warlock I'm at the top of my game. Musically I'm finally pulling it together." He lowered his voice. "Sometimes when I'm playing, I think I can hear the universe singing back to me." He made a pillar of his fists on the table and rested his chin on them. Staring at the grouping of purple candles at its center he said, "That's really why I'm here. Because I couldn't have done it without you."

"What?"

He turned his head, letting his cheek rest on his hand. I watched his dark lashes sweep against his cheeks as he closed his eyes, wincing against the admission. "Nobody ever stood up to me before. For obvious reasons. I mean, we destroyed a fucking house."

I nodded. "I was just thinking that we should probably be banned from property that has any value. At all."

Tiny smile that dropped right off his lips as he said, "You were right. I needed to stop whining and start working." He sat up and glared. "I still think I'd have been a better man if I'd been born black." His eyes softened. "But that's probably because the only people who showed any kindness to me when I was a kid were a Jamaican named Teller Keene and Skinny Day, who was African American."

I nodded. "Where'd you grow up?"

He looked through the curtain-framed opening to the sparkling blue of the fountain, then up to the ornate metal-worked balconies. "Louisiana. First in a Catholic home for orphans. Then I spent a couple of years in juvie." He glanced at me. "I may have been a killer even longer than you."

What do you say to that? Especially when the guy revealing all these intimate details once tried to collapse a roof on your head?

"Why are you telling me this?" I asked.

He shrugged. "I've got a pretty thick skull. Skinny always said I was so hardheaded that I could drive nails with my eyebrows.

But I'm not fool enough to turn my back on the few people brave enough to throw an honest opinion under my feet." Again with the smile. "Especially when it comes with the offer of a new instrument."

"Never let it be said that I'm above bribery."

He swung his legs onto the couch, crossing them in front of him so he could face me as he spoke. "Cassandra said Vayl's got a pretty serious problem."

My bottom lip started to tremble, so I bit it. "Yeah. About that. We haven't been able to discover what could've caused it."

He nodded. "During my flight I thought about all the dead ends you've been trying to make into highways. And then I realized there was one road you hadn't considered." He draped an arm across the couch's metal backrest. "Maybe this is a curse."

I shook my head. "Curses are personal. My understanding is that you need the victim's hair and clothing, stuff like that, to pull it off."

Sterling said, "That's true. They're also all about timing, meaning they can only be cast in special circumstances. For instance, has Vayl been in New Orleans in the past three months?"

"No."

"Has he killed an innocent or cursed someone else recently?"

"No to both."

"Has he—"

"Wait a minute! Wait, wait, wait…" I rubbed my forehead, trying to pull a scene I'd wanted to forget forever back into focus. "About two weeks ago we were in Scotland. My mom escaped from hell to—well, it doesn't really matter what she wanted with me. But before the dogs dragged her back down, Vayl whispered something in her ear that really flipped her out. And then Satan's Enforcer"—*who's trapped in my head right now, but I'm sure as hell not admitting that to you*—"he said, 'So it shall be.' And he took her away. Does that sound like it might've been a curse to you?"

Sterling had started to straighten up and sit forward halfway through my story. He nodded and said, "When someone lays down a curse, they leave themselves vulnerable to the same kind of attack. It's not a wide window. In fact, it starts to close right away, and by the time the moon changes again they're safe. But if an enemy can attack that person within the month, they can do massive damage."

I stared at the candles. Was it just my imagination, or had they begun to melt in the heat of my gaze? "The only person who knew about that curse before today was the Enforcer. Brude. Who, we just discovered on our last mission, has ties with the Sol of the Valencian Weres. Have you heard of him?"

"Just through office memos. His name's Roldan, right?"

"Yeah, but he's not just some superalpha who's in the mood to throw his weight around. He's so old that he met Vayl for the first time *during the same era his mind is currently stuck in.*" I looked up at Sterling. "Do you believe in coincidences?"

"Not when they click like a seat belt. How does Roldan feel about Vayl?"

"A week ago I'd have said he was just some creeper who'd backed a bunch of fanatical gnomes that were trying to gut NASA. I never knew about Vayl's history with him until the end of the mission. And even then I'd have guessed Roldan was only after what he got when we were able to stop the Australian gnomes— you know, a major reputation boost among the moon-changers. But now I'd guess he's probably hating like a reality-show reject, and it's all to do with this ward Vayl had in the late 1700s named Helena."

Sterling raised a finger. "We also know he killed Ethan Mreck."

Ethan had been one of us, a Were assassin assigned to infiltrate Roldan's pack. News of his death had reached us shortly before Pete was killed. Sterling must've been thinking along the same lines because he went on. "Pete's killer was clawed too."

I shivered, almost like I could feel the tips of those razor-sharp spikes brush against my neck. "That's enough for me. You want to know what I think?"

Sterling's eyes had begun to blaze. "Hit me."

"I'm glad you don't mean that literally. There's this guy named Yousef—never mind." I took a deep breath. "I think Roldan was moving to fill the power void that was left when we took out the Raptor and Floraidh Halsey lost her coven. He killed Ethan and Pete in a largely successful bid to bring down our department, which was the biggest threat to his safety. Take us out, he hamstrings his worst enemies. In addition, somewhere along the way, he learned that Vayl was working for Pete. I don't know how or when. The chronology doesn't really matter. The point is that he's created this perfectly geometric plan, which probably has him bouncing like a kid on a trampoline, where he gains power over all Weres by taking his revenge on Vayl."

Sterling shoved his plate away from the edge of the table so he could tap at its top, almost as if he was playing the notes of a song as he spoke. "But this kind of curse? It's mondo magic. Only a few people can pull off the kind of mind-fuck Vayl's experiencing right now."

"Meaning?"

"I'd bet big money that Roldan's hired himself a mage. I can't give you a name. They keep their identities closer to their chests than poker cards. But if you get close enough to him, you'll be able to sense him."

I jumped off the couch. If the mage felt anything like Sterling, my hair would probably fly straight off the nape of my neck the second I hit his neighborhood. "Let's go get him."

He raised a hand. "I'm not wasting my energy looking for a guy who's probably guarded his home better than a super-max prison."

"So how are we going to find him?"

Sterling flicked his hand like I'd just presented him with a simple math problem. "He'll be where the crowds are thickest."

Right. A parasitic pickpocket, feeding off mass energy so nobody in particular would notice what he was stealing. Sterling had probably done it hundreds of times himself. I said, "That'll be the Djemaa el Fna after dark. It's rolling with people."

"So we know *where* he'll be." But Sterling didn't seem satisfied. He ran a hand through his hair, pulling it back far enough to reveal an earring that hung halfway to his shoulder. Shaped like a boat oar, it was inscribed with runes that made me feel a little sick when I stared too long. I concentrated on his straight black eyebrows as he said, "But I'm not positive I'm right. No mage could have pulled off the curse without using some of Vayl's personal things. I looked it up. He'd need something from the year he wanted to stick Vayl's mind in. Something with his blood on it. Something related to a habit he'd had in—what year was it?"

"1777," I said.

"Okay, so let's say he drank a glass of port every night before he went to bed in 1777. The mage would need a bottle of port of the same brand Vayl liked. How would he have gotten hold of something like that?"

I shook my head. "It couldn't have been from his house. Bergman designed his security system so nobody's broken in. And he would've mentioned stuff going missing from our hotel."

"What about other places Vayl's lived?"

I thought about it. I knew he'd spent his early days as a Rogue, wandering Europe and parts of Asia. Then he'd settled into a Trust in Greece before moving to America. With his kind of power and pull, Roldan could've easily stolen, or even bought, a few of Vayl's old possessions. In fact, as soon as he'd found out Vayl had left the country in 1777, he could've robbed him blind, stomped his valuables to bits, and then thought, *But I'm keeping this box of foul little cigars just to remind me of how I got one over on the bastard.*

"It's conceivable," I said.

Sterling nodded. "So let's assume it's a curse and move forward from there."

"Then we're hunting a mage tonight?"

"Shit, yeah."

Chapter Nine

I was suddenly ravenous. Tearing into the bread on my plate, I tucked both my feet under my legs and munched happily, wondering what kind of preparations Sterling would need to make for our showdown tonight. I was hoping for an explosion. Somehow I felt that only splattage would make up for what I'd been through the past few days.

Sterling leaned toward me, his hair sweeping forward like an axe to cut the air for him. He shoved it back as he smiled, blinking sleepily as he gave me a good long look.

"What?" I asked through a wad of half-chewed carbs.

He rolled his head toward the door that led to the lounge. "Someone's coming. I've got a little ward up that he's making tingle in all the right places. Tell him I'm available."

"I thought you had a girlfriend."

He shrugged a shoulder, his look telling me his tastes in love were about as flexible as his spell range.

I said, "My guys are straight, Sterling. Although maybe I could hook you up with this dude I just met named Yousef. You never know what he might be interested in."

We turned our heads as Sterling's lost love interest strolled into the courtyard. He wore his black widow T-shirt, military-green

Bermudas, and neon-pink flip-flops. Which he called thongs, because that was the word for them in Australia, where he'd bought them. But mostly because he thought it was hilarious. And he carried a briefcase. It clashed with the outfit so badly that if they were people they'd have been throwing rocks at each other, but somehow Cole managed to pull it off.

He also looked remarkably refreshed for a guy who'd just spent the night boffing a demon. I waited for the spurt of anger. Jealousy. Whatever. Nothing happened. Which was when I realized I trusted my buddy to make the right choice in the end. And if he didn't, it wouldn't matter, because I was still going to kill her.

In fact, the idea cheered me up so much that I ran to meet him halfway. "Cole! You'll never guess what I just found out!" He looked curiously over my shoulder at Sterling a couple of times as I told him about the mage and the curse.

"That dude needs to go poof," he pronounced when I was done.

"That's just what *I* was thinking!"

"Then we're set. Who's your buddy?"

"Oh. That's Sterling."

Cole ducked a little. "The warlock?" he whispered. "Wow. I don't know whether to ask for an autograph or go buy a talisman." When I raised my eyebrows he added, "The analysts say he's moody."

"Oh. Well, he hasn't tried to hex any of his partners since—" I stopped. Hid a wince. "I'm sure you'll be fine."

I introduced them. Cole, at least, knew enough not to shake Sterling's hand. He gave the warlock a lazy sort of salute and sat opposite him inside the gazebo, laying his briefcase on the table.

"I thought you were done with the office accessories," I told him as he went for breakfast.

"Oh, no. You always gotta think progress," he told me, nodding sagely. "I'm liking the shirt by the way," he said, pointing at my chest as he stuffed half a roll into his mouth. Around the flying crumbs he added, "Glad it fit. Got something else for you too."

He cracked the case and slipped out a folded sheet of paper. "What is it?" I asked.

He just smiled and rolled one hand toward me so I'd open it and give it a read. As soon as I saw the signature I walked away from the table. It was from Vayl. The letter he'd written to me last night thinking I was an eighteenth-century damsel who could be wooed away from her badass vamp lover. *Well, let's see what old-timey Vayl has to say to Jaz-in-the-picture.*

My Dearest Jasmine,

Please forgive my boldness, but your beauty captivated me from the moment I beheld your portrait, a work of artistry so intriguing I felt as if I could reach out and touch your soul.

Can a man fall in love with a woman simply by viewing her image? Perhaps not. But I am no man. I am Vampere. I have looked into your eyes, and what I see makes my heart race as never before. That, itself, is a miracle. For I thought it had been broken forever, a ruin no creature could rebuild after the deaths of my sons. Perhaps you are the one who could make me whole again, my Jasmine. If I could but touch your hand, taste your lips, I would know. I must see you tonight. Say yes.

Yours alone,
Vasil Brâncoveanu

Whew, baby! I folded the letter and fanned myself.

"Dude knows how to put words together, doesn't he?" asked Cole.

I spun around. "You *read* it?"

He shrugged, sharing one of those guy-smiles with Sterling that made me want to knock their heads together. "Lord

Brâncoveanu"—we rolled our eyes—"can't read or write. So Berggia had to do a little secretarying last night."

I came back to sit with them. "It's fine. I'll write him back later this morning." When Cole's smile widened I added hastily, "It's just to keep him from running off into the city looking for some tramp that I'm going to have to end up beating the crap out of sooner or later." I paused to think. "Probably sooner."

Sterling began to laugh.

"What?" I demanded.

"Only you could get yourself into this kind of jam. Tied to a cursed vampire who's hot for your bod—only he can't see it."

"And that's only half of the story," Cole claimed as he cracked open the briefcase and pulled out a plastic, G.I. Joe–sized doll.

"What's the other half?" asked Sterling.

"That's on a need-to-know—and you don't," I snapped.

He held up his hands. I pulled back, an instinct that doubled Sterling's grin. The jerk. Luckily his attention wandered before he could piss me off so much that I repeated history and ended up ribbiting and snagging flies out of midair. He'd become fascinated with Cole's new project, which involved lathering his doll's bald head with superglue and then sticking tufts of platinum embroidery thread on top. Afterward he pulled some scissors from his case and began to trim the doll's do. Sterling couldn't hold back any longer.

"Is there a purpose to this hobby or do you just enjoy playing beautician?" he asked.

Cole snipped and fluffed as he spoke. "This is just a prototype. I figure to make millions when I sell this to Mattel." He thought a second. "Or maybe Hasbro."

"And why should they buy it from you?"

"Because it's the Cole Bemont action figure."

I slumped in my seat. But Teen Me sat forward. *I don't know, it could be kinda cute.*

Shut up; you're too old to play with dolls.

She nodded toward Bergman as he shuffled into the courtyard.

He's older than you and he has a bookcase full of them.

Those are called collectibles, I informed her.

Not if you talk to them when nobody else is in the room.

I ignored her—because what we were doing wasn't a whole lot more mature—and waited for Bergman's greeting. It didn't happen. Which meant the record was still intact. Someday he'd make it into the Guinness Book for number of mornings waking up grouchy. Because until our techxpert had downed at least two cups of coffee, he wasn't even fit company for a room full of assassins. His mood did promise to improve later on, however, because he'd worn jeans that were ripped in *both* knees *and* he'd put on his gray pullover right side out this morning.

"See that dude?" Cole whispered to Sterling. He waved toward Bergman, who was scratching his unruly mop as he yawned so big that for a second I thought I could see his lungs. "He did his hair just like mine on purpose because he thought it would get him more girls."

"Has it?"

"No, but that's only because he keeps forgetting to ask. I'm telling you, this action figure is going to earn me my way into—" Cole stopped when he realized Sterling wasn't listening anymore. He was staring at the woman who'd followed Bergman into the courtyard. Well, actually two had come out. Monique had brought a pitcher to refill the orange juice. And Kyphas had strolled in.

What a contrast. The human, her hair pulled back in an elegant French twist, looked cool and sweet in a light blue sundress covered with embroidered daisies. Bergman didn't even growl at her when she patted his shoulder and asked if he'd hand her the half-empty carafe. How could he? That smile had been made for him.

The demon, on the other hand, had let her hair fly free, and it seemed like no layer was quite the same shade as the next, giving it the flow and glow of a lion's mane. Her bright red capris hugged her curves like they'd only just met, and her black tank had the word "angel" written across the chest in shiny red rhinestones. She skipped the buffet completely and strode toward the gazebo, her eyes glued to Cole, who seemed determined to pretend she didn't exist.

Sterling hadn't hidden the fact that he was well aware of her presence. His eyes hadn't left her since she entered the courtyard. Both his hands rested easily in his lap, but his fingers were touching the bracelets, his equivalent of cocking a gun.

Shit! Knowing what it would cost me, I put my hand on the warlock's arm. Hard not to gasp at the sudden drop in energy, like I'd just been dumped into the aftermath of a 10K run. His fingers hadn't moved, so I kept my hand in place.

Sweating now, I said, "Kyphas is with us. She signed a no-harm contract. You're included under that umbrella now."

When his hands dropped to his thighs I pulled away. So tired that I knew it would be a major undertaking to drag my sorry ass up the stairs, I turned to Kyphas. She'd finally gotten Cole's message, backed off whatever open display she'd intended, and decided to be social instead. Which was when she realized we had a visitor. If I hadn't been exhausted I'd have gotten big hairy kicks out of the bug-eyed terror on her face. She yanked off her scarf.

"Stow it!" I snapped. "He's with us!"

She shook her head. "No. No, this is too much. I will not hold to my vow to protect the likes of *him*!"

"Jaz." Bergman nodded at Monique, who was looking at Kyphas curiously. I jerked my head, motioning for him to get her out before all hell literally broke loose. He shoved his plate in her hands, picked up his coffee, and slipped his arm around her waist so he could guide her to the door. "You were telling me before about the ramparts that were built around the medina. I looked some of it up online. Really fascinating stuff. Could you explain what you were saying about some of the old legends relating to the gates?"

"Of course!"

The rest of us remained frozen in place until Bergman had escorted Monique from the courtyard. And then Sterling rose to his feet. Slowly, like a monk beginning evening prayers, he said, "I thought I threw you back into the pit once already." His pupils had dilated so drastically I couldn't tell where they stopped and his irises began. Bolts of black lightning flew within the amulet he wore, and I could feel the power building kind of like Vayl's did, only this was a sense of bottomless wells of fire preparing to explode.

Kyphas snapped her *tahruyt* in the air, transforming it into the ruby-hilted flyssa she'd threatened me with before.

"Stop!" I stepped between them, holding out my arms, too aware of how my hands were shaking. I dropped them before it showed, pissed that Sterling's shining power was partially fueled by me.

I said, "Kyphas, you know exactly what will happen to you if you break your contract. So go stuff your face with some damn eggs until you've calmed down enough to pretend you're normal. And you—" I turned to Sterling. "Get it through your thick skull that I need her, at least for now."

"Why?" Such a reasonable question. But my eyes were drooping so badly now that even if I wanted to tell him I thought she would be the one to find the Rocenz for us, I'd probably be asleep before I could make any sense of it for him. So I said, "Cole, tell him everything you think he needs to know. I'm going back to bed. You're in charge of Vayl's safety until I wake up again."

"Okay," Cole said. "Just remember, he's going to want a reply to that letter."

"Fine. I'll do one before my nap."

Which turned out to be a good thing. Because the person who woke me up, with a tooth-clicking shoulder shake that made me feel somewhat queasy, was Vayl.

Chapter Ten

adame Berggia, how can you be sleeping at a time like this!" I opened my eyes. Vayl's face, hovering inches above my own, had locked down so tight I could see the muscles jumping in his jaws.

I shot up in bed, pulling Grief out from under my pillow as I did so. "What's wrong?"

"Your husband says you have a note for me from the Lady Jasmine. Why did you not bring it to me the instant I rose?"

I loosened my grip on the gun. "What time is it?"

"Eight in the evening. Why are you abed? Are you ill? It matters not. Where is the letter? I must have it!"

Just remember, eventually he stopped being an asshole, I told myself as I swung my feet onto the floor. I would've glared at him, but why waste a perfectly good expression on the broad back of a clueless vampire? He'd turned away from me, so anxious to read the letter that he'd begun to search for it himself.

"Hey!" I yelled. "Get outta my trunk!"

He rose to his full height, holding his cane in one hand and a pair of black pantyhose in the other. "What are these?" he asked, hefting the hose. "They seem not to stop where garters would be required."

I put my hand to my chest because, seriously, I thought my heart might've skipped a couple of beats. It was the first time he'd seen my clothing as something not straight out of a museum. "They're a new invention," I said. "They stay up all by themselves."

He dropped the cane, not even noticing as it clattered against the rug, and used both hands to stretch the waistband. "Fascinating."

"Yeah. Uh, how did you...sleep?"

He shrugged. "As usual."

"And when you woke up? How did you feel?"

He dropped the hose. "I could think of nothing but the woman whose portrait Berggia showed me yesterday. Her face has begun to haunt me. Come, where is the letter? I cannot wait for it a moment longer."

"Geez, quit being such a freaking Romeo before I have to gag or something. Here." I trudged over to the bed table. I couldn't remember half of what I'd written, I'd been so tired at the time. *That's the last time I touch you, Sterling, you damn leech!*

Vayl was so excited to read it that he rushed to the table before me, and for a few moments we stood together, two people sharing space meant for one. He was bent over, fully involved in the message I'd left, his hands flat on either side of the ivory stationery as if to keep it from flying off and leaving him stranded there.

He'd turned the lamp on. He didn't need it, but he'd probably done it for my sake, so as not to freak out the old gal during her rude awakening. I was glad of the light, though. It gave me the chance to follow the dance of his short, dark curls across his head and down to the strong expanse of his neck. My fingers ached to glide down that path, to slide under the collar of his dark almond shirt and feel the muscles of his back move under my hands. He still wore suspenders, which I found oddly charming, and tonight they held up a pair of gray pinstriped trousers that made it really hard to look away from his ass. But I managed it when he shoved the paper into my face.

"The words look lovely, almost as if she painted them. Tell me what they say."

I tried to back up, but the bed got in my way, so I ended up bouncing on my butt a couple of times as he moved toward the bench. I watched him get comfortable. "You want me to...read it out loud?"

"Yes."

"Won't you be embarrassed?"

"Not unless you run out and tell everyone in the street what you have just read." He stared me down, and I discovered a spectacular reserve of happiness saved just for this moment when I rejoiced not to have ever been one of his victims.

"No. I wouldn't."

"That is what I thought." He nodded. "Proceed."

I held up the paper, tried to ignore the pain behind my eye that signaled the beginning of a nasty headache, and began reading.

My Own Vasil,

Can you imagine how happy your letter made me? Before it came I was falling into the worst kind of despair. But now I have hope. Maybe heroes exist after all, and you are mine. But the way will not be easy. Because you cannot see me, my love. If I stood next to you and whispered, "I love you," into your ear, you would not hear it. Some prisons are so hard to break free from that it seems nearly impossible to think that we could ever be together. But I believe in miracles, Vasil. So come if you can. Try your hardest to see me, and I believe you will.

Your own love,
Jasmine

I'd dropped my head into my hand at the last line. Embarrassed to have to read it out loud, but also feeling every word to my core, I knew my knees just wouldn't hold me anymore. When I looked up, Vayl was gone.

I scrambled to my trunk, pulled out the Party Line, and stuck the pieces into place. "Bergman! Vayl's gone! I mean, I don't know where he is, but I'm assuming he went out to hunt or something. Have you got him?"

"Hang on." I heard the tapping of keys. Bergman said, "Yeah. Looks like he's heading to the Djemaa el Fna."

I grabbed Grief, my holster, and the jacket that hid both. "He's headed to that Seer's place. Find the address for me, then tell Cole and Sterling to meet me there."

"Okay, but . . . okay."

I weaponed up, threw on the jacket, and ran down the stairs. Each step felt like a nail in my skull. Ignoring the pain, I slammed out the doors, gasping a little at the change between the cool, air-conditioned riad and hot, dry Marrakech.

People filled the sidewalks, and as I moved toward the old city's central square, I passed an equal number of gaping tourists, bright-eyed immigrants, and smiling natives. Some of the last bunch felt I couldn't live another day without their services, but I turned them all down and, miraculously, they moved on, probably uninterested in keeping up with my pace, which was nearing a run.

Bergman said, "I just got done talking to Monique. She says Sister Hafeza Ghoumari lives just off the Rue El Koutoubia. I can guide you most of the way just watching Vayl's blip. But when you need the right door, you'll be able to find it easily. She says it's really distinct, with dots like brown rivets in a flowery pattern at the top, and then more dots going down the front that are in more of a triangular pattern. Also the doorframe is set with a mosaic of white and yellow tile."

"Okay. I'm entering the Djemaa el Fna right now. Where's Vayl?"

"He's on the north edge. Looks like he's just leaving. Uh-oh."

"What?"

"He's moving kind of slow. Like he does when he's hunting. You'd better hurry, Jaz. I think he means to get a bite to eat before he visits the Sister."

Shit!

At night the Djemaa el Fna is like a city unto itself. And negotiating the crowds without getting your pocket picked or punching a butt-groper in the face was a feat unto itself. I skirted audiences gaping at the amazing feats of Tazeroualti acrobats and ordered myself not to get caught up in the wonder of their twisting, leaping tricks. I strode past circles of men roaring at the rambling tales of storytellers whose nimble fingers mixed herbs and fire to make moving illustrations in the air above their handwoven baskets. I shouldered past tourists bartering over silver jewelry or standing in line to have their fortunes told. And all the time I talked to the ring on my finger. Out loud. Like a crazy woman.

"Tell him," I whispered. "Tell him I'm coming. He doesn't need to do this. He doesn't *want* to do this. Deep down, he knows it's wrong. Don't let him tear up his own soul...or...whatever it is that makes him so...Vayl."

As if in response to my pleas, Cirilai warmed my hand. But it wasn't much of a comfort. I could feel him, just beyond my reach, his powers rising like a winter storm. And in my own pounding head, an echo to the pain drumming through my brain, *Hurry! Hurry! Hurry!*

"Bergman! I'm through. I'm on the Rue El Koutoubia now."

"Okay, turn left. Do you see the police station?"

I looked at the building. Funny. No matter where you are in the world, you can tell cops work inside the place just from the way it holds itself. No frills. With just enough bars and cement in the picture to bring prison to the minds of those who walked through its doors. But I read the sign to make sure. COMMISSARIAT DE POLICE. "I'm in the right place," I told him.

"Vayl's about two blocks past that. And Sister Hafeza is another couple of blocks west. Got it?"

"Yeah." I pocketed my Party Line. No sense in Bergman hearing what I was about to say. And I really didn't want him to know what I was planning.

As soon as I left sight of the police station I broke into a run. Cirilai and my Sensitivity took me straight to Vayl. He was still on the street, his attention wholly focused on a man who'd stopped halfway up the block to talk to a group of three friends. They all wore light gray jellabas and mustaches so heavy that their lips had given up the attempt to dig out from the avalanche.

"Lord Brâncoveanu! Whew, you're a fast walker. I thought I'd never catch up to you!"

Vayl whirled, so pissed to be interrupted that he was actually snarling. Oddly, that put me in a great mood. I shook my finger at him and grinned. "You went off without your supper. And here I'd prepared something especially luscious for you."

His eyebrows shot up. "You did?"

"Absolutely!" I strode up to him and slapped him on the back. "Big fella like you needs his nourishment, right? We can't have you staggering around Marrakech like one of those forty-day fasters, now, can we?" I linked my arm through his and drew him into a side street. "Here, let me take you to the feast, okay?"

Halfway down the block he stopped. "I am nearly at my destination. To backtrack now would waste time I do not have. Sister Hafeza—"

"Can wait a damn minute," I growled. "Look. You promised yourself to stop hunting."

"I did no such thing."

"Yes, you did."

"Not at all."

"Vasil, you made a solemn vow—"

"Poppycock."

I stared up at him. "Oh. My. God. You're a pompous dick *and* an asshole. You're a pockhole!"

His nostrils flared so wide I'd have sworn he'd just gotten a good whiff of Yousef and Kamal. "Your services are no longer necessary. Gather your things and—"

I waved him off. "Even in your current state you know I'm good for you. In fact, I'm probably the only thing standing between you and a permanent gig in Vampere hell. So listen up. I know you. I know what you're going to do to yourself if you start hunting again, and I promised myself to help you. Which is why Berggia and I arranged willing donors for you these last three days who agreed to make it look like they were victims. But today I overslept, and obviously Berggia got sidetracked too." *Probably by the demon bitch. I can see this whole mess being one of her underhanded schemes.* I went on. "I can see you're hungry."

Red flared in his eyes. "Starving."

"So do me."

We stood in a wide street lined with pink and brown buildings, some of which had rickety awnings attached above their tall doorways. These displayed small lights that did little more than beam down, laserlike, on their museum-quality doors. The buildings were souks whose owners, during the day, would set out huge plaid bags full of herbs and spices, or hang hand-spun skeins of wool from long white poles. Pleasant shopping even at noon, because swaths of material had been stretched across the street from roof to roof to cut the glare so that people could stand and haggle. At night, however, that meant deep shadows filled the alleyways.

Vayl pulled me into the darkest spot, where part of a wall had crumbled away and no one had bothered to repair it. I don't know why I thought he'd argue against my plan. He wasn't the vampire I knew. He was a prequel. Like the Statue of Liberty must've looked when we first got her. Kind of obnoxious and brassy until she developed that eye-pleasing veneer that only the pounding of the elements and surviving to a ripe old age will get you.

Still, when he wrapped one arm around my waist, when my hands flattened against his chest, I couldn't help the anticipation. And when his fangs sank into my throat, my gasp wasn't purely pain. I closed my eyes and held him, falling into the rush of emotion like I'd just come off a water slide. Except when I surfaced I only had a second to gasp for air. Because it was already time for another ride.

Just like I had on the tower in Australia, I reached for Vayl through Cirilai. But this time, understanding the power he'd given me then to walk in his past, I visualized the specific time I needed to relive. And as my blood and Vayl's powers danced, I opened my eyes. Over my *sverhamin's* shoulder I focused on a window, its bars as black as the snakes that had once killed his beloved dog.

No, I don't want to go to his childhood. Take me to 1777. Show me why Vayl really left England.

Yeah, I'd mostly bought his story that he'd taken Helena away for her own safety. Except for the part of me that didn't buy the idea of Vayl running. From anybody.

Like hard edges will when you've stared at them too long, the bars blurred. Then they started to bend. I blinked. And when my vision cleared I realized I'd been gazing out of my carriage, leaning forward because mud from the large back wheel had splattered up onto the glass. I looked closer. Yes, there it was staring back at me. The reflection I'd hoped for.

A dark-eyed Rom whose curls were long enough to tie with a velvet bow at my neck. I wore a white shirt with a straight, stiff collar. It was covered by a superbly tailored black suitcoat unbuttoned to reveal my gold waistcoat. I could feel the quality of my matching breeches beneath my hands. One clutched my thighs so tightly I might have given myself bruises had I not supped of immortality. The other held a black walking stick that matched the shoes whose gold buckles twinkled up at me as if to remind me of the event I had just deserted. The accessories whispered, Opera, *while my white knuckles shouted,* Danger!

My home filled the frame of my window like a painting. So unreal, those three lovingly crafted floors of redbrick and mortar fronted by a broad brick stair. The door had been whitewashed, as had the window frames. Pink roses arched over the entryway. I found that strange, even though I had lived in the house all these seven years. It seemed to me that somewhere the home I had taken from a dead man should show black, like the corruption that oozed from my heart, filling my lungs with such vile hatred that sometimes the desire to maim, to murder, overcame all other thought.

But the brightness of the people within those walls stole all the shadows away. I did not deserve them. Not Berggia, nor his kindly wife. And never my dearest Helena, whom I would have chosen as a daughter even had she not been a helpless orphan when I found her begging on the streets the night after I vanquished the wolf who had tried to destroy her.

"Father!" Her scream, too faint for any but my ears, pulled me out of the moving carriage. Later I would castigate myself. Self-pity had blocked my senses from detecting her fear and pain. Else I would have leaped to her rescue sooner, would have burst through the door before Roldan could have done more than startle her as she sat in our flower-filled drawing room, reading from one of the many books she could never convince me to touch.

By the time I reached her, Helena was lying on the floor beneath the wolf, the bloody gashes on her arms and long rips in her skirts raising in me a fury such as I had not experienced since the deaths of my sons.

I knew, deep in my mind, that if I had been a human father I would have roared my rage, and perhaps even the chandelier would have shaken in response. But I had traded fire for ice, and now I was glad of the cold wind that swept through my murderous thoughts, forcing them into order, adding a thread of calculation that would make Roldan's death more likely and infinitely more painful.

I strode forward and, grabbing the wolf by both his ears, yanked backward. His scream, high-pitched as Helena's, brought a smile to my lips.

I took stock of my daughter. Shock had distanced her. The hands that held her torn bodice closed shook like leaves in a storm.

"Helena!" I snapped. Her eyes came to mine, hurt that I would speak to her so given her terrifying circumstance. I steadied my tone, willing her to respond in kind. "My flintlock is in my desk. It is loaded with silver."

She nodded.

"Lock yourself in the study with it and shoot anything that tries to get in. Either Berggia or I will come for you when this is over. Do you remember the secret knock?"

Her head bobbed again, but this time she seemed more self-assured.

"Then go."

She rushed from the room, shoving the door closed behind her as if it were the gate to hell itself. Perhaps a real lady would have swooned, or at the least begged to stay under my direct protection. I had certainly tried to raise her in that vein, knowing full well the misery that accompanied a life led outside Society. But my ward had learned early that her world rotated on two axes, and if she meant to survive she must develop a backbone strong enough to hold her steady no matter which way it tilted. My grandmother had been such a woman. But I had never told Helena how my heart swelled when I saw her jaw jut and her shoulders lift, reminding me of the tiny woman who had fought bullies, bandits, and corrupt sheriffs to ensure my survival.

I lifted the wolf by his ears, forcing another squeal from him as I flung him against the wall. He recovered quickly, pulling himself up onto his enormous paws, growling so deeply that I felt the rumble shake the back of my chest.

He charged, the weight of his massive body making the floor quake under my shoes. I yanked my silver dagger, a constant companion since

Helena had entered my care, from its cradle in the hollow leg of my walking stick. And then he was on me.

We toppled into Helena's favorite Louis XIV settee, our impact throwing it backward, sending my dagger flying. My head slammed into the floor with a force that might have stunned another man. A real man. I did not even feel it.

Hooked fangs longer than my fingers slavered at my throat. I shoved my fist into the maw that they surrounded, gaining another yelp for my collection. Roldan gagged and jerked his head back. But he was no green street fighter. Even on the defensive, he kept his wits clear enough to rake his enormous black claws down my sides, scoring me so deeply that I suspected bone now showed between flaps of flayed skin.

I cried out, but still and all, not for myself. For my girl, whom this monster had bled and bitten, whom he had attempted to defile.

I kicked, a sharp jab to his soft underbelly that compromised Roldan's balance even further. As he staggered off of me I kept hold with one hand and rolled with him to the wall. When I had him pinned, I shoved my fangs deep into his throat, pouring the ice of my cantrantia *into his blood, knowing now that my core power would not slay, but only slow him.*

His tongue drooped from his gaping mouth, stray flecks of saliva freezing in midair. I released my grip and lunged for the dagger, which had dropped onto the hearth of our empty fireplace. My body screamed, tortured by the stretch as much as if the Church had laid me on its altar. I felt dampness on my cheeks and realized two bloody tears had escaped my narrowed eyes. And in that moment I felt the separateness of my selves. One half weeping in protest for the anguish the other half must eternally push it through.

My fingers wrapped around the dagger's hilt, a fine leather-wrapped handle that fit snug as a tailor's tuck in my hand. I slid free of the wolf's snapping jaws and staggered to my feet. Blood soaked what was left of my shirt and suit coat. I had knocked over Helena's reading table, shattering a lamp, which had soaked her books with whale oil. My sitting room was in shambles—and for the first time since I had crossed its threshold I could finally relax. This *was* my territory. Roldan must pay the price for crossing its boundaries.

He charged me again. I looked into his fiery yellow eyes. And laughed. When he leaped, I spun, shoving the dagger deep into his side. It was not a killing blow, nor did I mean it to be. Silver takes Weres slowly, painfully. That was how I wanted Roldan to die. That was how the men who hurt my children would always go.

I hauled him up by the scruff of his neck, dragged him to the front doorway, and threw him into the street, my dagger still hilt-deep in his flank. My satisfaction at seeing him tumble into the gutter where he would die like a beggar snapped as a shot rang out from inside the house.

I spun, running so quickly to the study that the wind of my passage blew the window draperies midway up the parlor wall. Parts of the shattered door cracked beneath my feet as I swept into the room, one glance telling me all that I needed to know. A Were lay dead on the floor, his features already melting back to human. Another, still in his man's form, had dealt Helena such a bruising blow that she lay unconscious over his shoulder. He could take her through the window, but we both knew how badly the shattered glass would cut her.

He stared at me from the center of the room, surrounded by thrown papers and the items that the gentleman who had built the home felt he needed for his comfort. A tall, hickory desk full of cubbyholes and drawers. Two ladder-back chairs to sit on either side of it. A chaise on which Helena occasionally lounged, regaling me with stories of her tutors (less often their amazing revelations regarding history or mathematics than how she tricked them into spending entire afternoons roaming the park, listing the names of flora and fauna she had known since her toddling days). Beside it, a table holding a vase full of flowers she had picked from the garden only that morning, and two half-burned tapers held aloft by matching silver candlesticks.

"Put her down," I ordered.

He hesitated, staring toward the door as if measuring his chances of escaping me with Helena weighing him down.

"*Make me a deal first.*" *He spoke with a broad cockney accent, tossing the limp patch of hair blocking his sight out of his way as he spoke. I smelled the greasy sweetness of his unkempt locks from across the room, and my stomach turned that Helena should have to bear his touch.*

"*What?*" *I snapped.*

"*My freedom for her neck.*"

I inclined my head. "*Done.*"

The Were deposited Helena on the chaise and moved toward the door. My next question made him hesitate with his hand on the latch. "*I must ask. Why would you take the word of a vampire?*"

He glanced back at me. "*Aw, now, yer being modest. Yer not just any vamp. All hoity-toity, living in this house here, surrounded by humans. Kinda like a Trust, as it were,*" *he said, his grin revealing an overabundance of brown teeth dominated by sharp, yellow incisors.* "*Which means yer Vampere. Which means you put a whole lotta store in contracts.*"

"*I am impressed at your knowledge of the inner workings of the Trust. And yet you have somehow managed to miss the most important rule.*"

"*What's that?*"

"*That Trust members must be protected at any cost. Even if that means breaking a solemn vow.*" *Before the scoundrel could do more than widen his eyes, I strode forward and seized him by the throat. At the same moment a short but immensely broad-shouldered olive-skinned man burst through the door. He brandished a sword, while the white-aproned woman behind him held an iron skillet aloft with both hands.*

"*Berggia, does that weapon contain any silver?*" *I asked.*

"*Not that I know of, sir.*"

"*Did that monster hurt my baby?*" *asked the woman. Her hips were even broader than the man's shoulders.*

"*I am afraid so, Madame Berggia. Unfortunately, he——*" *But that was enough for her. She swung her frying pan down over her husband's shoulder and smashed it into the Were's head. He fell limp in my hands.*

"That'll teach 'im," she announced. Dropping the pan on the floor, she rushed to the chaise to tend to Helena.

"Call the bobbies," I told Berggia. "We shall treat this as a human matter. Which means we must first remove the wolf that lies in the gutter outside the door."

"Excuse me, sir, but they came and took it away already."

"You saw?"

"Yes. That was what sent me and the wife running inside from the errand you sent us on." I did not bother to tell him that the chore had been a ruse of the wolves to remove them from the premises. I could tell from the haunted look in his eyes that his story would not bear interruption. He said, "It was strange enough that two people were loading a bleeding wolf into a carriage. But even more bizarre that one of them, well, seems like I saw the same lady during the war. She was a'leaning over one of the dying chaps. And after it was over, they both stood up and walked away."

"How did you recognize her again?" I asked, a ring of ice encasing my heart. Berggia, who had never stepped away from a task in all the years I had known him, blanched. "Come, now, man. I must know."

"Hu…her dress belt looked like it were made from snakes. Like living, moving ones that intertwined at the clasp. And this gel had the selfsame belt on." And now, surely, my heart had stopped altogether. For Berggia must have witnessed one of the cubs of Medusa herself. "What was it, sir? What did I see?"

I strode to the desk and began pulling out papers. Though I could not read their contents, their seals told me enough. Only the ones most vital to our travels would be packed. The others must stay to make it look as if we meant to return. Because the Berggias had to understand our plight, I said, "That werewolf wanted Helena for his own. He is obsessed with her. And now he is in the hands of a Gorgon." I tried to speak as clearly as I could despite the necessity for speed and my growing fear for my daughter. "Gorgons can eat death."

I waited for the Berggias to recover from the initial shock. They had seen enough in their time with me that it did not take long. I continued.

"I will not describe to you the nature of this consumption. It is"—I looked up to find them both staring at me from pale, still faces—"quite ghastly. But you must understand that once Roldan—the wolf—agrees to the Gorgon's terms, he will become beholden."

"What do you mean by that?" asked Madame Berggia. She had maneuvered Helena's head onto her prodigious lap, and was now smoothing back her shining brown hair.

I had emptied the drawers and now moved to the safe that was hidden behind a series of books on the occult. Turning my back to them (Not because it is difficult to face the fearful eyes of those completely dependent on me, I whispered to myself) *I said, "The Gorgon will return when Roldan's life has run its natural course. And every night thereafter she will eat Roldan's death until the Were's soul shatters." I heard Madame Berggia gasp, but did not turn around. Reaching into the safe, I pulled out all of my earthly goods.*

"How long do you suppose that will take?" asked my valet.

I deposited the small trunk in which I kept my cash and valuables onto the desk. "It depends on the wolf. But I doubt that Helena will survive him. So we must take her out of the country. And we must leave tonight." Opening the trunk, I began to load it with papers.

Berggia said, "What do you want us to do?"

"Take Helena upstairs and tend to her. I wish we had time to call a surgeon around, but we must trust that she will wake soon and make a complete recovery. While she sleeps, pack as if we are simply taking a short trip. But take everything we cannot do without. I shall go and book tickets on the first steamer out of port." (And then we will board the second. Perhaps that will throw Roldan off long enough for me to devise a better plan.)

Sharp pain, beginning at my neck and shooting around to my spine, ending at the backs of my knees. Which had begun a fine tremble. I felt Vayl's former reality melt away and reached out for it, as if I could give it enough support to find out what happened to Helena. "No, no," I heard myself murmur. "Where'd she go?"

I felt something impeding my hand, which wanted badly to reconstruct the picture in my head, and realized it was a broad, hard chest. I rolled my head straight, letting the wall behind me provide support for a heaviness I was pretty sure my neck couldn't yet handle, and peered up at my *sverhamin*. He stared down at me, his eyes dark as a forest path. I watched him lick my blood from his lips. Felt him press his handkerchief against my wound, his fingers so warm I could feel each one of them through the linen.

"You are too generous with me, my Jasmine, you always have been."

"What?" I slapped my hand against his so he couldn't back away. "What did you call me?"

His eyebrows twitched. "Are you quite all right?"

"What is my name?" I demanded.

"Madame Berggia, of course. It always has—"

"You just called me Jasmine."

He pulled his hand away, leaving me to hold the temporary bandage. Even if I hadn't been able to read irritation in the lines between his forehead and beside his lips, I'd have sensed his withdrawal from a mile away. No wonder Wraiths were often found encased in the ice of their own breath. Eventually you get so cold nobody wants to touch you.

He said, "If I did, which I am certain I did not, it was no doubt a slip of the tongue engendered by the fact that I have been corresponding with a lovely woman from this city who goes by that name."

"You're so fulla shit," I muttered.

"Excuse me?"

"I said I need to learn to knit." I began trudging in the direction of Sister Hafeza's shop. I was really trying to feel like crap. It seemed like the appropriate moment and all. But my postdonation high had kicked in, big-time. And I had to think Vayl whispering my name was a hopeful sign. An unbreakable curse showed no weak seams to begin with. I'd just found one. Which meant this state Vayl had found himself didn't have to be permanent after all.

If I skipped down the street, would he pull out the pockhole and try to fire me again? It might be fun to tell him to shove the snooty. Only then I wouldn't get to read any more hot love letters. *Oh! No, I didn't...yup. Just shower me with confetti now, girls. Because I've just dreamed up the best note motivator ever!*

I said, "Speaking of that Jasmine chick. She didn't just have a courier drop her letter by. She brought it herself. While you were, uh, sleeping."

"What? I missed her?" I didn't dare look at him; he'd pick up on my barely disguised glee. "Did she resemble the portrait?"

"Why wouldn't she?"

"Oh. You know how artists take liberties."

Aw, man, don't tell me 1777 Vayl is shallow too! "Would it matter?" I asked.

"Not the least," he said. "But now I know the face I envision every time I close my eyes is genuinely hers."

"Oh, okay. Well, uh, then you could understand why she wanted to take a look at you too."

"She...wanted to see me? During my day-sleep?"

"Well, we said no. But this girl, she's very strong-willed. Just insisted. Said things like she couldn't go another day without gazing upon your manly visage or some such thing. And we couldn't be responsible for her jumping off a parapet, could we? So, you know, we gave her a peek."

Now I just had to look. Vayl was staring down the street we'd turned onto, past the crowds of pedestrians, into a world that looked like it kinda freaked him out. "What did she say?" he whispered.

"She was concerned that you sleep with your mouth open. Because, you know, bugs and dust can get in."

"Oh." Destitute. What, had he forgotten the note already? I decided to let him off the hook.

"And she liked your butt."

He jerked his eyes to mine. "What?"

"Of course, being a lady, she couldn't say it out loud. But you were lying on your side, so there it was, all outlined by your, um, that thing you wear to bed. And I could just tell."

His chest swelled with the breath he took. "I will write her tonight. I will demand to meet her." His hands clenched. I could tell he was imagining what he wanted to do to her...me...with them. It took my breath away.

When I finally managed to gulp myself back to reality, I said, "What about the vamp she's with? Aren't you worried about him at all?"

Vayl's voice dropped into the sexy growl that set parts of me on fire. "She will leave him willingly once we have...spoken. I am sure of it."

Me too. "Um, Lord Brâncoveanu?"

"Yes, Madame Berggia."

"If you don't mind my asking, how many women have you... you know...since you became a vampire?"

He shrugged. "I have lost count. For a time *all* I knew were women, as if only they could keep me from completely destroying myself."

I imagined Vayl rolling in a virtual sea of naked bimbos and felt sick. "Oh."

"I have tried many avenues of excess, Madame Berggia. None of them have given me the reward which I seek. But somehow, looking at this portrait of Jasmine, I feel she may be the key."

"Uh." *Me? The key? More likely the nitro that blows the key to bits.*

"Perhaps Madame Hafeza can confirm my suspicions."

"Well, there's her shop." I pointed to a two-story building in the middle of the block, the door of which had been left open to allow the night breezes in. Above it hung a sign bearing the international symbol for psychic, a pentagram with the Seeing Eye at its center.

We stepped inside, the smells of incense and dried herbs covering the scents of the street behind us. All we could see was a single room, as broad and deep as a bus station, with light wooden shelves lined up to form three wide aisles halfway to the back. Finely woven carpets covered every inch of the floor, and the walls were tiled, not in some typical geometric pattern, but on one side to depict a woman with flying blue hair riding a stallion across the desert. On the other side litter bearers carried a queenly figure down a palm-lined street.

The shelves were packed with books. Small plaques on the edges organized them into categories—if you spoke Arabic or French. I did see a few titles in English. But nothing I'd ever heard of.

Vayl whistled. "Sister Hafeza must be immensely wealthy to have collected so many tomes in one location."

As if she'd heard her name, a woman nearly six feet tall threw open the beads that curtained off the back room and strode up behind the blue-tiled counter that held a cash register, credit card machine, matching black containers for office supplies, and a pack of tarot cards.

"You're here!" she announced in a deep alto. I took in her heavily shaded eyelids and cheekbones, perfectly outlined lips, and long red nails. She wore an ankle-length dress in pink satin that, along with her strappy heels and curly brunette updo, screamed nineties prom. The Adam's apple sealed the deal.

"Sister Hafeza?" I said.

Vayl pointed at her. "That is a man!"

Aw, shit.

Chapter Eleven

I wanted to smack myself in the forehead. Or club Vayl in the back of his. I forced a smile, the kind only Lucille Robinson can shine on impossible situations. "He's sick," I told Hafeza.

"I am not!"

I ignored him. "He thinks it's 1777."

"It is!"

"See?" I looked at him. "Tell me you're not this big of a schmuck about transgender people in the twenty-first century." I turned back to Hafeza. "Or do I misunderstand? Are you just into the clothes or—"

"No," she confirmed. "I was born in the wrong body."

"There is no such thing!" Vayl bellowed.

"See there?" I pointed at my boss. "He never yells. Or swears. But lately that's all I get."

Vayl stepped forward, his brows a straight line, his eyes nearly black. "I have had it with the both of you! Now, tell me how it is that you are masquerading here as a Sister of the Second Sight before I tear you limb from limb."

Sister Hafeza's hand fluttered to her massive, well-constructed breasts. "You are a forceful one, aren't you? Well, basically, I went to the initiation. And Sister Lizia, that's the Highness right now, well, she touched me and, of course, she knew right away who I was and where I belonged. Because I am a Seer. Only"—Hafeza gestured at her large frame—"somewhat unique among women."

"And not even Moroccan," Vayl said bitterly.

"Nope. I'd place your accent at, um, Atlanta?" I asked.

Hafeza nodded, her broad smile letting me know how pleased she was that I'd recognized her roots. "But you didn't come here to discuss me," she told Vayl, laying her red-nailed hands gently on the countertop.

He stood stubbornly silent, his fists clenched at his sides.

Hafeza nodded at me, though she kept her eyes on my currently questionable prize. "I see you've tasted recently of your companion here," she told Vayl.

My hand stole to my neck, my fingers brushing the wounds that he'd reopened over the old scars. They wouldn't be easy to hide from the rest of the crew. Should I get a scarf like Kyphas's? And if I did, would I somehow manage to accidentally decapitate myself with it?

Vayl said, "Who I feed upon is none of your business."

Hafeza fluttered her lashes at him, like they both knew he was joshing. "What did you feel when you bit her?" she asked.

His lips pressed into one another. For a second I thought he wasn't going to respond. And then he whispered, "Power."

"That should prove to you she's not who you think she is," Hafeza told him. "But you *can* trust her. And for the same reason that you can trust me, even though I'm not who you thought I'd be." She turned her hands over and let him see her empty palms. *No weapon here.*

He finally nodded and dropped his hands onto hers.

She closed her eyes. Nothing happened for so long that I started to get bored. I picked up a book and read the title. *How to Make Love to a Man* by Alexandra Penney. Really? People needed directions? And if so, did that mean I was doing something wrong?

Vayl blew out a quick breath. I looked over to see Hafeza clutching at his fingers, her nails digging into his skin until drops of blood rose from the wounds. Her lips drew back and through her snarl I could see her molars grinding, as if she was trying to chew through ropes.

As quickly as it started it ended. She jerked her hands away and pressed them against her stomach. "You are in some deep shit, my friend."

Vayl didn't even glance at me. "I know."

"No, you don't. But I understand why, so I'll try to make this as clear as I can. You haven't escaped Roldan yet, all right? The only way to make that happen is to accept the help of a warlock named Sterling."

Vayl jerked, the blood from his hands splattering onto the counter tiles as he moved. "Warlocks are evil."

"You should know better than to believe everything you hear," said Hafeza.

Vayl dropped his eyes to his hands. "All right, then, what about my sons? Did you... See anything about them?"

Hafeza cocked her head sideways. "You're something of a legend among my Sisters, Vasil. According to the Enkyklios files, this search of yours has been persistent, to say the least. And we've always given you the same answer. But you've changed. You're more alive than dead now." She glanced at me. "I think I know who to credit for that. And maybe that's why the vision has changed."

Vayl's fingers arched, the tips digging into the countertop so intensely they turned white.

"Um, Lord Brâncoveanu?" I said. "You've already broken one of those in the past few weeks. Here." I handed him the book. "Maybe you could work on this instead."

He curled his hands around the binding without replying or even looking at me. It was like, if he let his eyes waver from Hafeza, maybe she'd disappear, and then he'd never find out what she had to say. And then he'd surely die. He said, "What did you See?"

"You will meet your sons again. Only this time the three of you won't die together." Vayl let out a breath I didn't even realize he was holding. Hafeza went on. "But I still see death stalking all of you. Whatever surrounds your reunion could still destroy your line forever."

"Thank you for the warning." Vayl hesitated. Then he got that determined look you see on people right before they jump into extra-cold water. "One last question, if you would. I need to find a woman named Jasmine." He pulled out the note I'd written him earlier and handed it to her. "Can you tell me where she is?"

Hafeza took the paper and, without even blinking, handed it to me. "This woman will lead you to her." She leaned forward, making sure Vayl got the drift. "So stop threatening to dump her. It's bad for your karma."

"If you insist." Vayl pulled out a wad of bills.

Hafeza held up a hand. Topaz jewels glittered on every finger. She said, "I couldn't take payment from you. Especially when I have one more piece of bad news."

Vayl's hand dropped back to his side. "What is it?"

She pointed to me. "Your companion here is in deeper trouble than you can understand right now."

Vayl smirked at me. "Is Madame Berggia in some sort of gambling debt?"

Hafeza pounded her hand on the counter and a tile cracked. I winced. Even once-removed we were hell on furniture. She said, "Save her and you save the woman you love. Remember that."

Vayl and I stared at each other. Suddenly I understood how the Beast felt every time Beauty cringed at the dinner table. I wanted to pound my chest and yell, "I'm *inside* here, dammit!" Maybe if I burst into song. Hey, it worked in the movies.

As we left the store I said, "Lord Brâncoveanu?"

"Yes?"

"Do you like music?"

"Yes."

"Would you…like for me to sing to you?"

You could've planted beans in those eyebrows they furrowed so deeply. "No."

"I figured. You know, even when I was little I couldn't pull off the fairy-tale princess bit."

"Oh?"

Though he couldn't care less, I explained. "I kept fighting off the dragons when I was supposed to be clapping myself on the cheeks and screaming, 'Prince Chahming, come saaaave me!' You know what happens when you battle dragons, right?"

"What?"

"Your tiara falls off and the monster stomps it into pieces. After which your mother refuses to buy you another one because they're too damn expensive, even though you know she got the first one at a yard sale because you saw her peel off the masking tape."

Vayl patted me on the shoulder. "Madam Berggia, I know you must be worried after what Sister Hafeza said to you, but please let me assure you that I will protect you with my very life." In other words, *Stop acting crazy, lady. You're starting to scare the natives.*

I sighed. "Okay."

Chapter Twelve

Our cease-fire lasted exactly ninety seconds. And then we began to argue. Ignoring the balmy night, the crowds of people out for a stroll, the ancient residences with their towering walls and exotic gardens loaded with palms and lemon trees, we hissed at each other like a couple of pissed-off geese.

"Hafeza said to use *Sterling*," I reminded him, really warming to my lie now that he'd annoyed me. "*I* told you he's an old acquaintance that Berggia called in when he realized Roldan might catch up to Helena after all. But he's not going to do us much good in a fight if he has to worry about protecting *her* ass at the same time!"

"I must ask you to please refrain from using such language! What if Helena—never mind, you clearly do not care anymore!" he repeated, like he, too, thought I'd gone deaf. "I cannot, in good conscience, leave Helena unguarded in the riad while we men go chasing after some mystery mage. That is why you and her maid, Kyphas, must join us as well. I am thankful Berggia taught you how to shoot."

"Oh, yeah, that'll come in so handy against a mage! Vay—I mean, Lord Brâncoveanu! We—"

"I will hear no more on the subject. Helena will remain under my watch because I am the only one qualified to protect her!"

"You say that, but you react just like any other guy when you get kicked in the nads!"

Silence until we stepped up to the riad's doorway. And then Vayl asked, just as he opened the door, "What are nads?"

Cole stood in the foyer, staring, having heard Vayl's question. His expression caused a smile to sneak onto my face. Waving at Cole I said, "Have Berggia tell you. I'm going to get Helena ready to go."

But before I did that I had my own preparations to make.

I stepped into my room and raided the worn black pack I used to tote weapons in. Ten pounds of gear later I whispered to myself, "Okay, so am I ready to move?"

I touched Grief, still holstered at my shoulder. Practiced pulling the bolo that had saved my ass enough times I'd begun to consider giving it a name. Because holy water would only piss the mage off, I'd unstrapped the syringe that contained my mobile supply from my right wrist and belted on a longer contraption that held what looked like a chrome pipe. Spring-loaded just like my syringe, it was built to telescope from each end when the hilt hit my hand, so that within seconds of activation I held a stainless-steel staff almost exactly my height. Usually it rolled around in the bottom of the bag, used only on hand-to-hand workout days because it was great for bashing if you had to fight in close. But girls my size tend to avoid those situations like we skip closing time at seedy bars. So I only brought it out when I needed to defend against spells from men whose magic hated the taste of refined metal. As soon as I spun the staff, the protective runes along its length added even more oomph to the shield, allowing me time to activate my second line of defense.

On my left forearm I'd wrapped a guard that ran from elbow to wrist. Stainless steel wrapped by leather, it provided practical protection against weapon strikes and fanged or clawed attacks. Upon a specific set of hand signals, it also sent a suggestion to my attacker that he should back off before I separated his head from his shoulders. Since Sterling had designed the piece, I trusted that it worked, though I'd never needed to activate it before.

Knowing Cole, Sterling, and Kyphas were also preparing to go up against the mage, I took my time deciding whether or not Vayl's cane should make the trip with us. It still lay inside my trunk like a lost treasure. Finally I nodded. "Might as well assume we're going to succeed," I said as I picked it up.

Holding the cane in the middle so that its blue jewel seemed to light the way, I ran to Bergman's room and pounded on the door. "Miles! Get off your fat ass and lemme in! Work to do!"

Nothing for maybe a full minute, during which I made intermittent loud sounds and escalating threats. And then, shuffling and whispers. Who was he talking to? Had Raoul returned Astral already? The door opened a crack. His eyeball said, "I'll be right down."

"Okay."

The door closed. I backed up, leaning against the wall, crossing my ankles and arms until I was comfy for the wait. When the door opened again Monique came out, so busy rearranging dishes on her tray that she didn't notice me. But Bergman did. He jumped and yelped, slamming the door behind them so hard that I heard a picture fall off the wall inside his room.

Bergman and Monique looked guiltily into my grinning face.

I said, "This place has excellent room service."

They replied at the same time.

Bergman: "We were just talking! About winter, because it's been so long since Monique has seen snow. And sheet—I mean sleet! Not sheets! No sheets were discussed in there!"

Monique: "He is so thin! I just wanted to offer him nourishment!"

I laughed. "Bergman, we gotta go."

"Okay, then." He waved at Monique like she was boarding a bus. And, hilariously, she waved back before heading downstairs.

Deciding it was time to let him off the hook, I changed the subject. "Vayl's waiting for us. I still have to get Kyphas and Sterling." I glanced through the hall window into the courtyard. Our warlock was back at the gazebo. Which meant Kyphas was probably hiding from him. "C'mon," I ordered.

His shoulders slumped. "All right."

Her room was just down the hall from Bergman's. I patted him on the shoulder when we got there. "Cheer up, Miles. Didn't anyone ever tell you that guys are supposed to be happy when they're getting some?"

"I'm not getting any!" Bergman shouted just as Kyphas opened the door.

She arched her eyebrows at our sci-guy, who looked to be searching for handy trapdoors in the floor.

I beamed. "This night just gets better and better."

CHAPTER THIRTEEN

Sterling and Cole sat waiting for me in the riad's romantically lit courtyard.

Cole wore a calf-length overcoat whose lining had been removed as a nod to the weather. He'd still look weird strolling around Marrakech dressed in gangsta duds, but it was better than walking down the street with his rifle flapping. And what a weapon. Before his death, Pete had caved to Cole's nagging and bought him a Heckler & Koch PSG1, which was arguably the most accurate sniper rifle in the world. With it he could strike multiple targets with very little lag time in between. Ideal if the mage turned out to be less of a loner than we'd anticipated.

As I settled in across from the men, Sterling growled, "Where's the demon? You didn't leave her alone with that defenseless little stick boy of yours, did you?"

"He's more skilled than he looks," I said. "Besides, she's still under contract. Anyway, she was right behind me." I looked. Nope. No Kyphas. Squelching the uneasy feeling that she'd followed Bergman, not to kill, but maybe to try a little torture like she'd done with me, I went on. "Miles said he'd get Vayl."

No need to explain that I needed five more minutes away from the Madame Berggia persona he'd forced on me. I knew they could see it in the way I pounded his cane onto the floor tile.

Cole patted me on the shoulder. "Don't worry. We'll find the perfect target for your frustrations tonight." He turned to Sterling. "Unless you're planning on blasting the bad guy with something menacing from your pocket-o'-doom?"

The warlock had been hiding his hands behind his back, which made me more nervous than I liked to let on. Now he brought out an antique teapot.

"I was expecting something a little more…penis shaped," said Cole.

Sterling smirked. "My best stuff is designed to put the victim completely at ease before it strikes." He tipped up the lid so Cole and I could look inside. It already contained half a cup of dried leaves and some dehydrated berries. "When this is boiled, it'll fill the air with an odor that'll deeply relax anyone who smells it. I have a special wax to plug our noses, which will protect us from the other effects."

"Which are?" Cole asked.

Sterling said, "They vary. But overall people find it hard to concentrate on a fight. It begins to seem pointless and silly to them. So at one end of the spectrum they'll be less aggressive during battle. And at the other they'll give up all their secrets, because suddenly they love everybody."

Cole clapped him on the shoulder. "I like having you along. We should work together more often."

Sterling's smile leaned closer to sly than I felt comfortable with. "That may have already been arranged."

I began to say, "What do you mean by that?" But somewhere around the word "do" Bergman jogged into the courtyard, completely winded from his previous run down two flights of stairs and a couple of short hallways. Have I mentioned that he sits too much?

He gasped, "Vayl's gone."

"Again?" *Goddammit! Suddenly he's harder to keep track of than a pissed-off teenager.* "Are you sure?" I asked.

His reply was to point over his shoulder, where Kyphas had just joined us carrying an open note and a closed envelope. I went over and snatched the riad's stationery from her hand. Out loud, I read,

My Friends,

I cannot, in good conscience, ask you to risk your lives in a cause which began—and should end—with me. My tiff with Madame Berggia before was, I fear, a ruse designed to distract you from my true intent.

I would never forgive myself if any of you ladies were harmed in the coming battle. Therefore, I am going to face the mage alone. Please make sure Helena reaches a safe haven. When the war in the Colonies has ended, I think perhaps she should sail there, but until then, my dear Berggias, I leave the choice in your capable hands.

Please accept my deepest gratitude. And a final boon, if you will? The delivery of my second note to Lady Jasmine.

—Lord Brâncoveanu

Kyphas curtsied with a mocking grin, saying, "It's such fun being Vasil's secretary. I like it a lot better than the maid gig," as she handed me the envelope. Since I didn't trust myself to hide my reactions, I took it into the gazebo and sat down on the couch with it, only then realizing that my legs had begun a fine tremble.

What if he dies before we can get to him?

Nonsense! Granny May set down her embroidery and stood, moving to the clothesline to take down her dry laundry. *Vayl may be a little off-balance right now, but that hasn't dumbed him down any. You know he didn't leave without some idea of how he was going to succeed.*

So do I have time to read this, or should we just go?

Give it a look. Granny May couldn't hide the curiosity sparkling behind her bifocals. *Maybe it'll help.*

I tore open the envelope. The thick paper felt like a ten-pound weight in my hand as I opened it.

My Dearest Jasmine,

I think that I shall not survive this evening. Perhaps it is for the best. I chose this existence out of rage. But vengeance only carried me through its first year. And since then, no direction has restored to me that which I squandered on the day I became Vampere.

When I saw your lovely eyes, staring solemnly at me from your portrait, I felt as if I had known you since my soul's creation. My only desire has been to set myself before you in the hope that you will see in me something for which I have given up looking. But it is not to be. Perhaps we will meet again when time has ended and you and I are no longer bound by any tie that love cannot break.

Yours,
Vayl

I want to cry. And hug this damn note like it's my old teddy bear. But I don't see anything in it that could help—
Read it again! demanded Granny May.

And that was when I saw that he'd signed it, not with the name he'd used in his old life, but with the one I'd always known him by. I sprang to my feet.

"He signed it *Vayl!*" I came out of the gazebo with the note high in my hand. "He signed it with his modern name!"

Cole let me take his hands and even jump up and down with him a few times. Then he said, "I have no idea what that means."

"The curse is beginning to break, I think because we keep hammering at it. And our Vayl is waving at us through the cracks. *He* wants us to find him tonight because *he* has no problem with women fighting alongside men. And *he* really wants to survive. So we will find more clues to where he's gone and what he's up to. We just have to look for them!"

Sterling, lounging on one of the padded chairs with one bare foot swinging over its arm, held up a finger. "And what do we do when we find him? We're all about stealth, remember? What if Vayl and this mage are fighting in the middle of the street?"

"We improvise. We're good at that, aren't we, Cole?"

Cole pulled back his jacket so he could brush his hand down the rifle he held at his side. "We usually figure out pretty quick where to point and shoot."

"I'm prepared," Bergman bragged. He looked over his shoulder. Seeing that Monique had chosen to give us privacy, he raised the sleeve of his baggy pullover.

"Miles!" I came forward to make sure I'd seen right. "What are you doing with those rockets strapped to your wrist?"

He gave me *that look*. The one smart people save for stupid questions. "I'm a terrible shot with a gun. With these, all I have to do is look at what I want to hit and I can count on a bull's-eye."

"You did read my report on the Patras mission? The last thing we need is for you to shoot somebody full of miniature robots and have their head explode, like, two weeks later!"

Bergman shoved his hands into his hips so hard that if he'd been an eighty-year-old man he'd have dislocated them. "You are *completely* exaggerating!"

"Not by much!"

Cole jumped between us, massaging our shoulders like a boxing coach as he said, "Come on, guys, is this any way to start a rescue operation?" He looked at each of us until we shook our heads. "Good," he said. "Now I suggest we kiss and make up. Jaz, you start with me, then we can work our way around the circle—ow!" He laughed, rubbing his chest where my punch had landed.

I said, "You're supposed to be falling *out* of love with me, remember?"

"Already done," he announced. "Remember? That was my goal for our NASA job. Which I aced. So any sex I have with you from this day forward will be purely platonic. Even medicinal. You know, like California pot."

I narrowed my eyes. "Ah. So afterward you're going to forget where you parked your car and experience a mounting craving for cocaine?"

He laughed again. "Exactly."

Kyphas made a sound that landed somewhere between fingers-in-the-car-door and lioness-guarding-her-kill. It gave me chills. Which pissed me off.

"Come on," I said, looking at her but directing my words to the courtyard in general. "We've finally got a bankable reason to kick some ass." I strode past the demon, purposely brushing her shoulder with mine. "Oh, and Kyphas?" I smiled into her flushed face. "Bring your li'l scarfy-thing." With no other choice, she fell into line behind me, walking beside Cole with the watchful air of a bodyguard. Or jealous lover. Either way, the look he gave her said their time together was already running to the bottom of the hourglass.

I hid my smile by directing it at Bergman, making it encouraging. He'd rolled his sleeve back down to cover his secret weapon, and now followed Kyphas at his safe-distance pace. Only because I was watching did I see him send Kyphas a glare that she responded to with a smirk. If she'd known my old roomie the way I did, she wouldn't have been so happy to have pissed him off. Because Bergman only jutted his jaw like that when he'd decided to do something extreme. Usually those decisions resulted in rad new inventions that made people like me squeal with delight. I suspected this didn't qualify as one of those times.

As I began to calculate our chances of successfully intervening in a Vampere/mage battle, I knew I didn't have time to go proactive on Bergman's ass. Vayl's predicament and my race against death took priority. So I told myself, *Wait and watch. Miles isn't likely to try anything stupid until, well, ever. Now, since Sterling is on my side, is he going to be affected by my staff? Damned Wielders, their rules are even more confusing than the Vampere.*

Chapter Fourteen

Entering the Djemaa el Fna at night is like joining a huge party. The noise sucks you in. Not just crowd murmur but laughter and shouts and everywhere the music promising entertainment, fascination, maybe a great hookup that could turn into something more permanent down the line. And then the smells. My stomach rumbled, reminding me I'd missed supper and possibly lunch as well. Because Morocco's most famous square held culinary delights that could've kept me munching for months. We passed stalls lit by strings of bare lightbulbs where white-shirted men grilled kebabs stacked with lamb and fresh veggies for customers lined up three and four deep. Other restaurants displayed long buffets offering fresh figs, shrimp, chicken, olives, and sausages. At their edges small wooden tables and benches filled with chattering natives and gawking tourists were tended by white-uniformed waiters who knew so well how to dance among the crowds that they never bumped a shoulder or dropped a dish. All of it had my mouth watering so badly I actually had to lick my lips and swallow.

I might have seemed to be wandering, awestruck, among the food vendors and street performers. But by now I was used to the silk-costumed musicians playing upbeat tunes on instruments ranging from handmade drums to three-stringed guembri. Even the pyramids of red-shirted acrobats barely distracted me. Because Cirilai had stirred when we'd entered the square, the exact kind of clue I'd hoped Vayl would provide. Unfortunately the feeling was so vague I had to force my hit-and-split nature to sit still and listen. It felt like another step back, to the time when he'd tried to train me to track vampires, starting with him. But I counted it as progress. Because it led me to a middle-aged man who looked like all the moisture had been sucked from his skin sometime in the last decade.

He wore a forest-green jellaba over tan work pants and a white dress shirt. He sat inside a circle of people pressed against one another like mosh-pitters doing a practice run. And he smelled of unwashed soul. His audience zeroed in with a fascination born as much of his parasitic pull as his craft, the tools of which surrounded him. A faded rug under his knees. A flute held in one gnarled, brown hand. A round container the color of a canvas sail that reminded me of Granny May's old hatboxes, only it was half the height. Because the creature inside didn't need much of a ceiling. It uncoiled slowly as the man set the roof of its mobile home aside, his head already swaying in a rhythm the shiny black cobra found riveting.

"Who is it?" Sterling asked me, noting the attention I was paying to the snake charmer.

A slope-shouldered guy with a thick brown mustache overheard him and said, in German-accented English, "That's Ahmed. You should stay for the whole show. I can assure you it's like nothing you've ever seen."

No doubt. I motioned to Cole, who walked right up behind Ahmed, while Kyphas followed close behind. Proximity gave our crew's backup Sensitive the chance to sniff him out. A sharp nod confirmed my suspicions. "He's the mage," I said, using our Party Line to get my point across quick. "Vayl found him too, but he's clearly gone now and I don't see any signs of violence. Be alert."

Ahmed slowly brought the flute to his lips, dancing it to the music in the same way he wanted the cobra to respond. It stared at him through pupils so opaque they seemed to hide the secrets to hell as it slid out of the box onto the sole-smoothed bricks of the square. I had to admit the song was sort of hypnotic. Or maybe it was Ahmed's sinuous dance, all done through movements of his torso and head, which the serpent followed with intense fascination.

Even while I watched the cobra recoil its lower half and raise its head nearly a foot off the ground I knew Vayl wouldn't have bolted. Something more than his fear of snakes had changed his plans, and we had to find out what. So I backed away from Ahmed's inner circle, nodding for Cole and Kyphas to join me. Cole paused long enough to drop a bill into Ahmed's bowl, which he held at the corners and only unfolded at the last minute. Like the ones Miles had given each of us, it contained a tracking device that would allow us to find Ahmed again even if he spent it, because the receptors rubbed onto the fingers of the next person who handled the bill.

Bergman and Sterling, standing at each of my shoulders, pretended they hadn't seen the drop as they backed away with me. But they couldn't hold on to the casual front when Ahmed's cobra began to levitate. The crowd gasped, moving with us as the snake swayed in midair, now truly dancing with its master.

"Hey, mister, you take a picture with Ahmed, the snake charmer?" someone asked Bergman. I glanced to my right at a deeply tanned man wearing western clothes. His twelve-year-old son nodded encouragingly at us as his pop said, "Only thirty euros. Great deal for once-in-a-lifetime souvenir!" The photo peddler peered at Miles from the corners of his eyes, which were nearly hidden behind a mass of dark brown hair. I stared at his calloused hand, already open as if Bergman couldn't possibly consider denying him the outrageous fee, then I looked to Cole for verification.

Barely a nod that he'd also scented wolf howling behind the man's shadowed eyes, and something even more foreign sliding under his son's skin. Ahmed had allies after all. And one of them wasn't even supposed to exist.

Oh. Fuck.

Chapter Fifteen

I'll say this about my crew. We figured out quickly how to communicate without making a sound. Within seconds eyebrows, hand signals, and a couple of mouthed words had confirmed our worst suspicions.

Roldan hadn't just hired a mage to curse Vayl. He'd sent part of his own pack to guard the Wielder in case we figured out what was going on and tried to reverse the spell. The wolf's-head tattoo just beneath his ear instantly confirmed the photo seller's affiliation. But it got worse. Because the kid twitching under his hand had actually been grown up for a while. Which had to mean he was a Luureken.

I thought Luureken were just myths. Teen Me glared at Granny May, who didn't say a word, but concentrated on her stitching. So she appealed to me instead. *Gran used to read stories about them to us—fairy tales!* she insisted.

Yeah, I badly wanted to deny reality too. But I'd just smelled one. And all the psychic bells and whistles clanging in my head now made me wonder how much of Granny May's big, leather-bound book of "fairy tales" had actually been original stories written by my mother's mother. I wished she was alive so I could get in her face and demand an answer. Especially now, when all I could remember about the Luureken were the basic details.

Luureken are the runts of the litter. They usually die unless one of their siblings bonds with and protects them. In that case they survive, but they look like kids forever. Which is, maybe, part of the reason they become so savage. They fight from the back of that same brother or sister using a badass weapon called a raes. Which I'd hoped was also a Mother Goose tale.

It's no story. Granny May finally looked up from her embroidery. *Weres can't carry full-grown humans into battle, but they have no problem with Luureken. And you're right, they are brutal. As soon as a fight begins they turn into little spike-skulled berserkers who are happiest when they're biting your ear off as they spill your guts.*

I sighed. Why do I never get to face an enemy whose OCD is all about lining up the handles on his coffee mugs?

Only moments had passed since the photo seller had propositioned Bergman. But now that our technical consultant knew he was facing a couple of man-form Weres he had no clue how to deal with the situation. So he fell back to dictionary definitions. "Cobras are poisonous," he said.

The Were replied, "Ahmed keeps his snakes calm. Very tame. How about a nice picture for twenty euros?" He gestured to the boy, who seemed too thin for health. A ragged scar jigged down his cheek, reminding me of torn paper that never glues back quite right. "My son is an excellent photographer."

I thought, *Really? Then would you like to tell me why he's carrying a raes under his shirt?* I'd only seen drawings of the Luureken's chosen weapon. But they exactly matched the modified ice pick that I'd seen when he'd bowed to me. According to legend, any solid contact with the tip would set off a charge that buried it inside the opponent's body. The Luureken tried to hit their enemies midchest, because upon total immersion, a hook the size of a Brazilian tarantula jutted from the pick's tip. One massive jerk and the Luureken could yank out an enemy's heart. After which he or she generally ate it.

Bergman looked at me, panic squeezing his lips into a straw-sucking pucker as the Luureken's big brother pushed him to make a deal.

Say "no," I mouthed.

"Not today, thanks." He tried to move away with me, but found himself trapped by a man who'd come up behind him to shake his fist at the Were.

"These are my friends!" he announced through the boy he'd brought along to translate so we'd know what a big favor he was doing us. "How dare you try to charge such outrageous prices for a photograph!"

I slapped myself on the cheeks, biting my lips so they wouldn't drop the obscenity that had tripped off my tongue when I'd seen who was shouting over Bergman's shoulder. But I couldn't stop myself from saying, "Yousef! What are you doing here?"

Kamal looked at me sadly. "We followed you."

"That's called 'stalking' in America. It's wrong." *I should know. I've done it enough times.*

Kamal shrugged, about as disinterested as a kid in history class until his eyes wandered to the beauty now standing at my shoulder. His jaw dropped.

"Oh, no," I said, shaking my head like that was the cure for stunned admiration. "This woman is way out of your league." I pointed at Kyphas, who was looking at him the same way a choco-holic views a pan full of fudge. "Don't even—"

Yousef interrupted, bursting into broken English, which he'd obviously been practicing ever since our last confrontation. "You arrre pretty!"

I held up both hands. "Wow, you're rolling those R's like a lum-berjack on a wet log. Good on you, dude. But I'm married," I lied. "So you're SOL. Go away."

Yousef waited for Kamal to finish translating. Then he gave me the universal prove-it gesture. I waved Cirilai under his nose. He threw up his hands and said, "Pah!"

I pleaded with Kamal. "Tell your buddy he's going to get hurt if he keeps coming around me."

Kamal spoke my words to Yousef, who grinned broadly.

"No!" I snapped. "I mean *really* hurt!"

Yousef reached out to hug me. I shoved Vayl's cane into his diaphragm and, with a simple leg sweep, knocked his feet out from under him, sending his butt to the bricks. Before he could react I darted into the crowd, using all my training plus a black scarf I hastily traded a lady my sunglasses for to disappear.

As my would-be lover's delighted gasp faded behind me I murmured into the Party Line, "Okay, here's my idea. Cole, is that you giggling?"

"No! Never! Although now I really wish I'd bought you a whip and some leathers for your birthday . . . Mistress Berggia."

"Hey! Masochistic stalkers are not funny. I mean, I'm contemplating killing the man, and all I can think about is how much that would turn him on!" Roar of laughter from my entire crew. "Thanks for your support," I drawled. "Can we get back to business now?"

"We're all ears," Bergman said loyally. Then he added, "And cameras."

"No!" Cole exclaimed.

"Yup. I got a primo shot of that guy Yousef's face after she pushed him down."

"Madame B.!" Cole said. "You *have* to let me put that one up on my Facebook page!"

"You are an assassin for the United States government!" I hissed, covering my mouth to make sure no one could overhear. "What the hell are you doing on Facebook?"

"Don't worry, I go by my alias. You know, Thor Longfellow?"

"I do know Thor Longfellow, and if he doesn't get his shit together pretty soon, parts of him are going to be a lot shorter!"

Cole did his rejected-beauty-queen huff. Then he said, "Your sense of humor has shriveled like an old spinster since Vayl forgot what time it was."

I thought about slapping myself in the face again in the hope that some sense of reality would return in which I would not be forced to discuss my stalker and social networking while I tried to save the man I loved in the middle of goddamn Marrakech! I took a deep breath. It didn't help. So I went to a fresh juice stall. Bought five oranges. Took them to the nearest open trash can and hurled them into it as hard as I could. By the time I got to number four I felt my balance begin to return. So the last one felt like a bonus squishy. While I was gazing into the garbage, pondering the dead fruits and ignoring the fact that people had begun to give me extra space when they passed by, Cole spoke again.

"Um, Madame B.? Are you still there? You know we were only kidding around, right? Just trying to lighten the mood a little since it now looks like we're about to go against some badass Weres who might just tear us all into tiny pieces considering we probably have an ounce of silver between the five of us. That is, unless they feel their pack is too small. In which case, I don't really wanna become a part-time wolf."

"The moon is barely a fingernail tonight. Maybe they won't be able to transform," came the voice of Kyphas. Such a strange, positive note among all the gloom and doom of the past few minutes that I felt my focus begin to fragment again.

Then Sterling said, "Not likely. They're guarding a mage, after all. You can bet the day he found out they were coming he dusted, washed the sheets, and cooked up a potion that would force their change."

I rolled the kinks out of my neck. Sighed. "Which just reinforces Cole's point that silver would come in handy right about now. Anybody?"

Cole said, "My ammo will take them down, even tear pieces off them, but it won't kill them."

Kyphas said, "My blade contains silver," just as Bergman noted, "There's some silver in your bolo, Jaz. I don't know if it's enough to fatally poison a Were, but I'd bet it'll make them sick for a while."

And if we could count on his rockets taking a head or two, that would even up our odds a lot more, but that invention of his was notoriously unreliable. At killing, anyway.

"All right, then, here's the plan," I said. "I'm betting Vayl took off because he suspected Ahmed had more than two Weres guarding his back. I do too. So, since Cole and I are Sensitives, we'll each have to take a search party around this square so we can find the rest of the guard detail and either take them out or disable them. Hopefully we'll also cross Vayl's trail."

Sterling said, "I'm carrying a supply of the Shining Shadows."

"Well, we may survive this night after all," I said.

"What's Shining Shadows?" asked Kyphas.

Sterling said, "It's a powder that glows in the dark. Not only that, once the lights have been killed, whatever it's touched will freeze for approximately five seconds."

I could hear the hunger in her voice as she said, "You're good."

He drawled, "I'm also saved."

"Kyphas!" I snapped. "Quit being such a soul whore and get with the gang! Okay, slight change of plan now that we can light up the Weres. Cole, I'm going to want you to pick them off, though the rest of you need to understand he'll just be slowing them down. Only a dose of silver or decapitation will kill them. And even Cole's not gonna be successful if we can't figure out how to cut the electricity, so Bergman, total darkness is your job. Cole, can you make your part of the plan work?"

He said, "If I can find a rooftop that isn't teeming with people." I looked around. He had a point. A distressing number of those surrounding the square were covered with outdoor restaurants.

I said, "Make that your priority. Everybody else meet up here. I'm standing near the southeast corner of the square. You'll know the place because the dancers are dressed in blue satin tunics and red caps." While I watched the men whirl in circles so fast it was a wonder they didn't stagger off into the crowd, I kept up a running commentary. It helped keep me from entertaining the slimy suspicion that when we found Vayl, the Weres would've already shredded him to the bone.

I said, "When everybody gets here Sterling can hand out the Shining Shadows and then we'll treat this square like it's actually round and we're the hands of a clock with Ahmed at the center. Half of us will move clockwise. The other half will go the opposite direction, starting at the edges and working our way inward. We'll mark the Weres we find, and whoever sees Vayl first will alert the others. At which point we'll meet up again on him."

Before I'd finished talking my crew had found me. I expected more teasing about Yousef the Spankmeister, but they'd all pulled on their work masks. And since Cole was away scouting sniping spots, nobody thought to make a crack about the Shining Shadows' remarkable resemblance to guinea pig wangs as our warlock handed out the cinnamon stick–sized tubes. They were full of colorless powder held in place by plain paper glued to each end of the tube.

"Puncture the paper just before you're ready to use the blowtube," Sterling instructed. "Aim and exhale hard, just as if it was a dart gun. The powder will do the rest."

I said, "Remember, we're just working the powder until we've made sure all the Weres glow. Nobody makes an aggressive move until we're a full group and Cole's found a likely spot for sniping. That means you, Kyphas."

The demon didn't even try to defend herself. Just said, "Who's my partner for this party?" Brightly. Like she wasn't aware of how deep Bergman's hate ran or how Sterling itched to zap her back to hell.

My heart sank. I knew I had to pair with her. Neither of them would make it ten steps before all-out war broke out. Then Sterling said, "I'll do it."

I turned to him. "Are you sure?"

He leaned his head, just a tick, toward Miles. Whose face had gone bright red with suppressed emotion as Kyphas smiled invitingly at him. "You can scent Weres," he said. "I have my own ways of finding them. It'll be faster like this."

But no safer, I thought as I watched him stride past Kyphas, not even waiting to see whether or not she'd follow him into the crowd. She gave us a mocking salute before turning to trot after him.

"That demon..." Bergman growled.

"Isn't worth your dried scabs," I finished. I tugged at his sleeve. "Come on." We walked away from the dancing Berbers and their clapping audience, letting ourselves be swallowed by the human tide that ebbed and flowed around the Djemaa el Fna.

Three minutes of searching yielded our first targets, standing among another mob of spectators. They were listening to a toothless old storyteller weave a tale of how the spirit of a spring named Amina once chased an old widower named Khalid straight into his hut, and wouldn't allow him to haul water to his garden until he promised to let his son marry her.

As the storyteller spoke, he threw glittering salts into the boiling pot at his feet. Out of the smoke danced an image of Amina, her blue-skinned body as fluid as water, her silver eyes flashing as she ran after Khalid waving an oar-shaped fish that looked just as alarmed as the old man at the violence she threatened. Meanwhile Khalid's son, who the storyteller identified as an innocent youth named Saïd, stood beside the hut's door like a potted shrub, so paralyzed by the conflict he didn't know who to cheer for.

While the storyteller captivated his audience with a chase scene that included fish slapping and clotheslining, I walked right up behind the Were, whose arm rested on the shoulders of what looked like an eight-year-old boy who was trembling all over. But the

Luureken was neither a kid nor scared. He was just barely containing a constant, maddening rage.

I opened my psyche—took a big sniff just to be sure. When I nearly puked from the scent of burning flesh and blood, I signaled to Bergman. He pulled the stick from his pocket, broke open the wrapping, and pretended to cough. Sterling's spelled powder shot out of its container and onto our marks' backs, leaving a splatter I could see only because lately I found it harder not to.

We'd just turned away from the crowd and begun a new search when Sterling's report came into our earpieces. "We've got two over here. Shining them up right now."

I said, "Excellent. We've just done a pair and I'm sensing more ahead of us."

I signaled Bergman to hand me a powder stick and step back, because we were approaching one of the tent restaurants. I'd spotted two male Weres standing together beside a half-size picnic table while their Luureken tore into bowls of, well, it sure as hell looked liked sheep's heads from here. "Two pairs on our end," I told Sterling as Bergman and I maneuvered toward the counter.

My heart threw itself against the wall of my chest as Cole said, "I'm in position on a roof at the eastern edge of the square. I've been scouting the area through my scope"—pause for a metallic-sounding adjustment—"and I've found Vayl. Looks like he's tracking somebody."

"Where is he?" I asked, scratching my nose to hide my demand.

"Almost underneath me at booth number eleven. I'll keep an eye on him."

No! I want to be the one to— "Excellent work, Cole. We have found eight, repeat, eight targets for you so far."

I nodded to Bergman, who nailed his two, then bumped into the guy behind him and made loud with the apologies when the Were turned to see what the fuss was about.

That caught the attention of the Luureken, who stopped eating for a hopeful check on the kill-order. Which put the other Were on edge. He leaned forward to calm his rider, at which point I marked them both.

Bergman had already begun to move east. I caught up to him within a minute, and I asked, "Cole, can you give us a landmark for Vayl's location?"

He said, "Make for the twelve green patio umbrellas."

Suddenly I felt Cirilai go dead on my finger. Eerie. Scary. Like standing in the middle of the woods when even the crickets stop singing. I wanted to turn around. Go back to the riad and lock myself in my room until Bergman invented a reliable time machine. Or better yet, call Kyphas from her place by Sterling's side. Snatch up her offer like it was a half-legal land deal. But the reason I survive is deeper than whim, and it reminded me now. *Keep moving*, it whispered, and I obeyed.

I only knew we'd reached the rendezvous point when Bergman's hand, firm on my wrist, brought my eyes up to his. He pushed me onto a bench at yet another fill-your-face place, and said, "Madame B."

"Yeah?"

He sank down beside me. "You keep forgetting to breathe."

I forced myself to inhale. "Better?"

He searched my face. "Jesus, how bad do you have it for this guy?" I shrugged, shook my head. Even if I had eloquence, I still wouldn't have been able to put the words together. He nodded. "All right. I'm sorry to do this to you, but it's for the best." He leaned back, the table hitting him halfway up the spine as he said harshly, "Remember after Matt died?"

I felt my eyes widen. *You son of a bitch! You bring up the worst moment of my life now? At the worst moment of my life? How dare you!* Gluing my lips together, willing the tears back, I jerked my head forward.

He said, "Wall off your heart like you did then. You can't save Vayl if you can't *think*." He pulled a handkerchief out of his pocket and dabbed at my nose. Showed me the blood he'd mopped up. "Whatever's doing this to you isn't helping either."

I took another breath. Pulled off my Party Line and nodded for him to do the same. No reason for Kyphas to get an extra thrill off my misfortune. "It's Brude. I don't want Sterling to know. But it's getting—physical—now."

"I'm not going to let that fucker take you down."

I let out a chuckle. Couldn't help it. The image of bony little Bergman spinning Brude over his head before throwing him out of a WWE ring cheered me. "You are the best friend I could ever hope for."

He leaned back. "You're not going to hug me or anything?"

"Nope."

"Good. Now come on, show me that cold bitch who makes bad guys want to push her off the sides of mountains."

I took another breath, this one not nearly as forced. "Okay, let's go."

He helped me up. Not that he thought I needed it. Just that he wanted to preserve that moment, when I'd inevitably look up into his eyes, so he could show me the love he'd always be too shy or stuck in his own gears to be able to voice. I slapped him on the back, letting my own feelings shine right back at him. And, strengthened by my best, most loyal buddy at my side, I strode toward the vampire I did not want to survive without.

Chapter Sixteen

When I saw Vayl, whole and vital, leaning so casually against one of the carts whose owner sold ginseng and cinnamon tea along with big hunks of spice cake I felt... nothing. I'd been certain as tornadoes and prostate cancer that he was already gone. Because I had no illusions about myself. Somebody like me, a hired killer whose best legacy was a niece she saw mostly in pictures, didn't deserve the love of a man who could shatter bone in his fist and transform blood to ice. Wraiths like him were the legends of their kind. *I* didn't even know my neighbors. So, logically, I should've found his remains. But I hadn't. And that made me...

I put my hand over my heart. Felt it beating, leaping almost, against my palm. But the void was still there inside me. As if I couldn't decode my own internal messages anymore.

Anytime you want to stop this bullshit you go right ahead. Granny May was sitting in her lawn chair, French-braiding Teen Me's hair. She spoke from around the comb she stuck in her mouth when she needed both hands for plaiting.

I don't know what you mean.

Admit it. You hate loving Vayl this much. Wearing his ring. Walking in his past—he's becoming a part of you now. You can say all the pretty, noble things you want to, but this closeness terrifies you. Because you know what it is to lose. To be alone.

My throat went hot. *Okay, since it's just us, I'll admit I haven't felt this vulnerable since Matt died. But I want to grab life. I want to grab Vayl, preferably by that luscious ass. But there's this—fear—worse than anything I've experienced on the job. I could face a hundred Weres tonight and it wouldn't shake me the way the thought of losing Vayl forever does.*

You're in love, Granny May said.

Why does it have to suck so much?

Because it's so precious.

What do I do?

Leave him. I felt my heart stop under my hand. *Or stay, and celebrate each moment you have with him. Taste the laughter and drink the kisses and inhale the caresses because that's why you're here.*

Oh. So it's not to make Albert yell until he's hoarse?

Granny May chuckled. *We'll talk about your father another day. Now go on. I believe you have a job to do, you slacker.*

I glared at Teen Me. *Stop teaching the old woman slang. It'll go straight to her head and the next thing you know she'll want to go buy herself an iPod and a pair of Jimmy Choos.*

We took a second to ponder Gran's plain brown loafers, then we burst into laughter. It was like emptying a submarine's ballast tanks. I felt myself begin to lift, and my whole attitude toward the coming fight and the vampire who had no idea what part we meant to play in it began to transform.

Another quick look to set my bearings. The green umbrellas belonged to a parade of carts selling the same kind of tea out of copper pots and the same kind of cake in white flowered bowls that filled the wheeled wagon Vayl had chosen. Bergman and I stood at the edge of a crowd near number seven. Vayl's cart had a line of eight patient snackers being waited on by a white-capped gent whose matching jacket made him look more like a hospital orderly than a food salesman. But what he did, he did well and with a friendly attitude that allowed for Vayl's uncamouflaged presence. Then I saw that my *sverhamin* held a glass of tea in his hand and the merchant's patience made even more sense.

Before I could figure out who was commanding Vayl's attention, Sterling sauntered up to me. "Chill, you are a long way gone for somebody who's got work to do right here." Kyphas's laugh was meant to snap my last nerve. But I'd finally hit my groove, and nothing was going to fling me out now.

I said, "Don't worry about me. I'm just thinking a few steps ahead like Vayl would want me to. Which, now that we've found him and marked the Weres, I don't see any point in delaying, do you?"

He spread his hands. "I'm ready for the next step."

Bergman said, "So I guess you're going to want the lights to go out pretty soon."

I nodded. "Yeah. As soon as Cole gives the okay, we're set."

Cole's voice came through our earpieces, calmer and more level than usual. "I'm in position. Ready to go when the lights fail."

"I've been talking to Sterling," Bergman told me.

I turned to him. "And?"

He said, "We have a plan. I could tell you, but I'd rather just show you."

I raised my eyebrows. "You've come a long way from the old magic-is-evil days, you know that, Miles?" I said quietly.

He shrugged. "What is it they say? If you're not growing, you're rotting? I don't want to rot."

"Good. I'd still love you if you were a zombie, but it's more fun not having to bury parts of you in the garden." I gave him the go-ahead gesture and half watched him help Sterling set up. But the rest of my concentration centered on Vayl. You wouldn't think there'd be much to see. Kinda like viewing one of the time-worn angels hovering over Michelangelo's grave. But then most people didn't know what to look for.

Though he stood as still as one of those lamenting saints, he was so close to losing control I wished I could pull a fire alarm and clear the place before innocent people got burned. His eyes, dark as unforgiven souls, lit with occasional bursts of red like exploding stars. His fingers, resting on the cloth-covered counter, had dug in deep enough to leave permanent indentations the blue material couldn't quite disguise. And, this was new—or maybe really, really old—he was biting the inside of his mouth, his lips, his cheeks, bleeding himself to keep the monster on its leash.

I looked in the direction he'd glued to and instantly picked up on a muscle-bound Were with a hiker's tan and sun-bleached pony-tail. He sat at the edge of one of the rooftop eateries that surrounded the Djemaa el Fna, a spot Monique had recommended for its exqui-site food and excellent views of the glittering, smoke-blanketed square.

As I sized up Vayl's target I decided he had to be the one lead-ing this pack. His size alone would've convinced me. But it was also the way his eyes moved across the crowds, measuring, considering, never stopping. No surprise, then, that his Luureken looked more like an imp than a child, with huge ears framing a pockmarked face and orangey-red tufts of hair sticking out from beneath his skullcap.

I jumped when Kyphas spoke. *Why do I keep forgetting she's here? I should ask Sterling if she's toting some sort of I'm-no-threat sachet.*

She said, "Are you really just going to stand here and watch while the rest of your crew saves the day?" she asked. "Let Berg-man and Sterling deal with the lights? Allow Cole to pick off the Weres? Watch Vayl make a fool of himself? I didn't realize you were such a passive little slave."

I stared into the demon's eyes. When I smiled she pulled away from me. "You're sweating. Why is that when the evening is cool? Don't you want us to break the curse?"

She shrugged. "I don't care *when* Vayl thinks he is. He's nothing to me."

"Sure. But the Rocenz does matter to you. And the fact that we're about to restore the mind of the one guy who can not only find it, but keep it out of your hands permanently, must be making you nutso."

"Not at all."

Nobody can lie like hellspawn. They learn it in the cradle. But, then, so had I.

I started to say something, then I changed my mind. Instead, "Kyphas, do you ever stop with the manipulating?"

"I have no idea—"

"We're about to massacre a bunch of werewolves and their riders. Do you think you could manage to cut the bullshit for three seconds?"

Finally, a thread of humor in those hazel eyes. "Yes."

"I'm going to ask you a question and I want you to answer it fast, without even thinking. Can you at least do that?"

Slight frown at the challenge. "Of course."

I motioned for her to take a break from the Party Line, and I did the same. Then I asked, "What do you want, just for yourself?"

"Cole."

I laughed.

Her hands curled into fists. She said, "It's not funny!"

"I'm not laughing at you. I'm laughing because, deep down, you are such a girl. I mean, of course you want Cole. Everybody does. He's adorable."

"You don't."

"I'm not a girl."

She stared at me. "No. You're Eldhayr."

"Did you have to stoop to name-calling?"

She smirked. But the half smile vanished almost instantly as she scanned the rooftop where Cole had settled. "He'll never have me."

"You mean for good."

Hurt in those eyes when they came back to mine, which surprised me. I hadn't realized she felt so deeply for him already. Damn, but he had a way. She said, "Your honesty is no virtue."

I shrugged. "My dad used to love telling us that the biggest obstacle on any course is the one sitting between your shoulders."

"What is that supposed to mean?"

Obviously Kyphas's digs weren't heavily populated with military men or she'd have totally run with the reference. I said, "You'll never snag Cole because you don't believe you can."

"I am hellspawn."

"Yup."

"He wants me. Yet he despises me."

"Oh, yeah."

She threw up her hands. "What else is there to say?"

I shrugged. "I guess nothing. I mean, you and I both agree that you could never, ever become the kind of woman he could love. So just keep on yanking our strings and throwing temptation in our paths. Maybe one of these days you'll have us all in hell with you. And that'll be even better. Right?"

She nodded. Doubtfully.

I turned to Bergman and Sterling just as they were emptying their pockets. They reminded me of a couple of fifth graders comparing treasures. I could almost hear the discussion.

"I've beaten this Pokémon game so many times I'm dreaming about it now. I'll trade it to you for that Snickers bar, your free pass to the basketball game, and the combination to Heidi Neyedmeyer's locker."

"Okay, but the Snickers bar's kinda melty. It's been in my pocket for, like, three days."

"No problem."

"Deal."

I replaced my Party Line so I could snoop. Their conversation wasn't nearly as fun as the one I'd imagined. Bergman was saying, "...still think the hardest part will be distracting everybody from what we're doing. There's"—Bergman gestured around helplessly—"no privacy."

Sterling said, "Stickman, if you're that worried about it, I can toss the ingredients for my special tea into this dude's pot instead of using mine." He nudged his elbow toward seller number seven. "In thirty seconds nobody within a hundred feet will care if we're dancing naked on the tables."

Bergman frowned down at himself. "*Are* we going to want to dance naked...anywhere?"

Sterling chuckled. "I hope not, for my sake. You're too damn skinny to turn streaker!"

"Everybody stays dressed," I ordered. "Sterling, keep the goodies stowed. We may need them later. Bergman, relax. Nobody gives a crap what you're doing as long as you act normal; they're too busy having their own lives."

Muttering something that sounded like, "If you say so," Bergman watched Sterling unpack, well, it looked like a wooden dandelion. A late-phase one, after the bloom has gone to the spunky white seed that reminded me strongly of my landlady's Sunday-go-to-meeting wig. Except where the hair made me want to pile drive her into a frozen pond to see if the spikes were as sharp as they looked, the carving was so intricate I wondered if its artist had studied under the guy who'd done Vayl's cane. Or maybe taught him.

I slapped the cane against my leg, wondering idly if the sword it covered contained any silver, as Sterling nodded at Bergman. "Just like we discussed, now," he said.

Miles eyed the junction box nearest our position. He took a breath so deep that for a second I could detect his ribs straining against the material of his shirt. "Okay, I'm ready."

Sterling caught my eye. "Okay, Chill. Whenever you give the word."

I checked on Vayl. No movement from him or the roofbound Were. "Cole, are you ready?"

"I'm set. Should I take out restaurant boy first?"

I considered our options. "Yeah," I decided. "Do it right before the lights go out. I figure Vayl will move on him as soon as the funkiness begins, and I don't want any friendly fire casualties tonight."

"But..." Bergman lowered his voice. "Can Vayl handle him in his present condition? Especially if he doesn't know what we're up to?"

"It doesn't matter what year Vayl thinks it is," I said. "He's still the baddest fighter in this square. Probably on the whole damn continent. He'll be fine."

Bergman shrugged. I looked from him to Sterling to Kyphas. "Ready?" Each of them nodded.

"Okay," I said. "Cole downs the Weres. Remember they'll be wounded, not dead, so we may have to deal with a couple of them before we can move in and grab the mage. Sterling, you're going to be able to immobilize Ahmed before he can put the whammy on us?"

"It's what I do."

"Kyphas, are you prepared?"

She pulled the *tahruyt* off her head and slid it lovingly through her hands. "Oh, yes."

I pulled out my bolo, slipped it into Bergman's belt, and covered it with his shirt. "Just in case," I whispered as he pulled up his sleeve. He glanced down. "Oh!" He went so pale I put out an arm to steady him. He jerked away. "I'm fine!"

I shoved my hand back in my pocket, contacting the poker chips I kept there, imagining that I'd piled them on a green felt table where I could hear the *click clack* as they slid through my shuffling fingers, constantly revising their positions but never losing their integrity.

I said, "Miles, you and Sterling begin as soon as the Were goes down. Cole?"

"Yes, dear?"

"When you're ready."

CHAPTER SEVENTEEN

Cole's shot cracked across the square like the signal for a set of kickass fireworks. The pack leader fell back in his chair, his Luureken and the people at the surrounding tables staring dumbly as they tried to figure out what had happened.

At ground level, a few people looked for fire in the sky. And they got it. Bergman released four of his missiles at the junction box. They didn't want to go up, however. They were made to seek the warmth of bodies, and the street below was packed with them. Which was where Sterling's wooden seedpod came into play.

He whirled it above his head, chanting, "Up draft. Up breeze. Up current. Fly!" The seedpods broke off the stem, formed a carpet of white that sped after the missiles, caught them, carried them high over the heads of the crowd, and slammed them straight into their target.

Sparks flew. Blue threads exploded from them, reached over the screaming crowd and slammed into two more junction boxes, throwing the square into darkness.

Panic, both in the restaurant, where they'd just figured out the man on the floor was bleeding from a massive head wound and his "kid" had been shot as well, and on the ground, where a fire had started in one of the mobile food stalls when someone accidentally tipped over a pot full of boiling oil.

I saw Vayl cast his eyes around at the rising chaos before separating himself from cart eleven and heading toward the downed Were. I wanted to follow him. But his memory still rested back with Ahmed.

"Cole?" I asked. In my earpiece I heard another shot. Then another. He didn't speak until he'd taken six altogether.

"Three pairs down," he said professionally. "I've got men moving on my position. I'm relocating. If I can, I'll do the rest after I lose these chasers."

"Roger that," I replied. We both knew he'd try like hell to even our odds, but time was not our friend.

I tossed Vayl's cane to my left hand, jerked my right wrist, and felt my staff slide into my palm, its cool handle reminding me to take deeper breaths as it stretched to full length. Following my lead, Bergman pulled my knife. He stared at it doubtfully, like he thought it might leap out of his hand and stab him while he wasn't looking. In the end he took a tighter grip and checked his missiles. Four still nestled in the sheath he'd created for them. Encouraged, he pulled out the wallet-sized tracking unit that would allow us to find Ahmed again.

Sterling watched Kyphas transform her scarf into the flyssa that would, hopefully, stick to Weres this evening. But he didn't prepare anything extra for our trip back to the mage. Just followed at his easy pace as Bergman led us back to the bill Cole had left with Ahmed earlier.

We shoved our way through the yelling, panicked crowd toward one of the streets that led away from the square and finally found Ahmed trying to make his escape with his arms full of half-hat boxes. He hadn't waited long for an escort, but then maybe he'd realized they were indisposed. We'd passed two of them on our way to intercept the mage. One had been lying across a picnic table trying to hold its intestines inside its body cavity while its Luureken lay in a pool of blood at its feet. The other Were had toppled into a juice seller's cart, burying itself in mounds of ripe, orange fruit. Its rider had disappeared, leaving a blood trail we didn't have time to follow.

"Ahmed," I said as we surrounded him. "We have some business with you. Leave the snakes." Kyphas took the boxes and put them down as Sterling grabbed the mage by the wrists and forced his hands into a clapping position. Sterling banged their foreheads together as he whispered, "Bound to me now." His bracelets *reached out*, clasped onto Ahmed's wrists, and then twisted into one another until they seemed to be made from one single line of bone.

I traded amazed looks with Bergman, our specialized contact lenses making our awed faces look even greener with envy as we watched Ahmed try desperately to twist his hands free. But the shackles had become so tight he could barely wiggle his fingers.

"What—" he began, but Sterling held up a finger.

"You can talk—later. Now follow me." Just words to Bergman. But I felt the magic behind them, like the thickness in the air before a storm. My whole body tightened as it surrounded me, and I took a second to congratulate myself that Sterling was on my side. It must feel to Ahmed like being bitten all at once by a thousand mosquitoes.

Our warlock took us back toward Vayl. But before we got there the lights flickered on in the west half of the square. And we were attacked.

We did have some warning. A flash of neon. The scent of wolf. I yelled, "Sterling, guard the mage!" Then a white-furred form took me to the ground, its snapping jaws so close to my jugular I could feel snippets of skin come away in its teeth.

It had seen the staff in my right hand and managed to pin that wrist to the ground. The other I rammed into its mouth. The scrape of my metal gauntlet against fangs made me shiver as I brought both knees up and smashed them into the wolf's ribs. Its claws raked down my right arm, but then they lifted and I was free.

I swung the staff like I meant to ski down a mountain. It hit square, bruising flesh, splintering bone, making the Were scream in agony.

It staggered one way, I rolled the other, abandoning the staff for Grief. But not soon enough. The Were's Luureken, a flame-eyed girl with such deep facial scars that parts of her cheek flapped independently as she screamed, launched herself at me. Though spikes had emerged from her head and her body had grown a hard, outer shell, I figured bullets could still penetrate at close range. If I could only grab my gun.

The Luureken had every advantage. Position. Speed. Madness. And a nightmare weapon. The raes was so close I could already feel it piercing my skin. For a split second I knew that nothing I did or said was going to prevent the claw inside it from ripping out my heart.

I felt a moment of relief that my whole life didn't flash before my eyes. Some things you just never want to rehash. But I did see Vayl as he'd been the night before he forgot me. His eyes flashing like a gemstone, green on green under green until I knew if I dived into them all day I'd never find their ultimate source.

He'd whispered in my ear, "Woman, you make me want to shout."

And I'd said, "Go ahead."

To which he'd replied, "I am too busy listening. Did you know the world was singing?"

"You're such a softie."

He'd kissed me. On the belly button. "Tell no one. If news gets out they will not even hire me to curl the poodles' hair at Le Puppeez Salon."

Regret. So enormous that I suspected it would swallow the world. The raes speeded toward my chest. And then a blur, coming from my right. The whine of metal cleaving air, changing tones as it met skin and bone. Instant blindness as blood spurted into my eyes. And I knew, somehow, I was saved.

I felt a cloth hit my face. Used it to wipe my sight back as I regained my feet. The Luureken lay dead at my side, the spot between its forehead and mouth a mass of gore and brain tissue. The Were had toppled over next to it, panting heavily from its original wound and the secondary smashing I'd given it.

Around us people screamed and ran, flapping their arms like spooked chickens. I felt about that connected to them as I released Vayl's sword from its sheath and, in one smooth motion, decapitated the wolf that had just nearly ended me.

Kyphas stood next to me, wiping her sword on a second piece of cloth that she'd cut from the Luureken's shirt. I used the one she'd thrown me to clean Vayl's blade and then threw it down, aiming it to cover the oozing mass of grossness that was the Luureken's former face.

"Thanks," I said.

"You owe me," she said, nodding to our second pair of attackers. The Were lay, headless, near Sterling's feet, and neither he nor the mage seemed to be able to look away from the carnage. It hadn't returned to man-form yet, but I recognized the Luureken sprawled next to it, my bolo buried in its chest. It was the scar-faced "kid" who'd been hanging out with the snake-photo scammer.

"I said thanks," I told her. But my eyes were on Miles. Who was staring at his bloody hands and starting to shake. I retrieved the knife, wiped it clean, and went to him. "Bergman!" I snapped.

His head came up like I'd kicked him.

I shoved the hilt into his hand. Blew out a sigh of relief when he took it. "Your crisis can wait. In fact, that's the great thing about them. They're like the IRS. They know where you live, and as soon as you've decided you're going to survive the most horrible experience of your life after all, they're knocking at your door to make sure you pay for it."

When he gave me a small smile I said, "Now let's find Vayl and get the hell outta here."

I'd like to say my extra sense led us right to him. But the big crowd surrounding the snarling creatures pretty much gave it away.

Cole found us just as we'd muscled our way to the front. "Should we call this progress?" he asked

I wasn't sure how to answer. Did a word like that fit on a street that had heard the screams of invaders and absorbed the blood of defenders so often in its history that the battle waging across its bricks now wouldn't even make the footnotes of its autobiography? I watched Vayl confront the leader of Ahmed's guard pack, his wound already nothing more than a pink puckered spot mostly hidden by his thick black fur and the fall of drying blood on his head and neck, and understood how little the world would ever care about what happened in the next five minutes. Hell, even finding out that Luureken weren't just fairy tales wouldn't make them blink. Most of the crowd around us were seeing the leader's froth-mouthed little berserker with their own eyes, and all they could think about was what an awesome story it would make when they finally found a computer café so they could post it to their travelogues. But for me and my crew, Vayl's victory here meant everything.

We watched like guest surgeons at an operation while amateur bookies took bets and the people with money on the fighters screamed all around us. We'd already missed the first few moves, so we could only guess what had happened from existing injuries. The Were, bleeding from new wounds across his shoulders and flanks, was going after Vayl like my *sverhamin* had just drowned his latest litter. And it showed. Vayl's coat hung in shreds from shoulders to wrists. Blood trickled steadily down his arms and the back of one leg. I saw claw marks on his thighs as well as a bite on the face that had just missed his eye.

The Luureken, whose shoulder still slumped from the slug Cole had shot through it, hadn't escaped the sharp edge of Vayl's weapon, a butcher's cleaver he must have stolen from Chef Henri. Because he'd sliced four spikes off the Luureken's head, leaving behind freely bleeding stumps.

I called from the front of the crowd, "Lord Brâncoveanu, it's us. We need to get moving. We have Ahmed."

He ignored me. I understood. This was his battle now. It should've been over a lot sooner. Except Vayl was…savoring…the violence. His eyes bright red with bloodlust, he repeatedly wounded when he could've killed. And all I could do was admire him. Because no one had forced him to become the vampire Pete had partnered me with. The quiet, controlled creature who never hunted, and killed only for his adopted country. He'd pulled himself out of the mire without help. That took guts. And strength. And honesty. I couldn't remember when I loved him more.

But there was such a thing as overkill. And the longer we waited, the more likely it would be that the other two Luureken-mounted Weres would show up to swing the odds.

I murmured, "Keep a sharp eye out. The other guards could be—"

A scream and a thump on the back stopped me. I turned around, raising Vayl's cane like a club. What I saw was Bergman being dragged away, gaping members of the crowd leaning in to get a good look and maybe a camera-phone shot of whatever had hooked him through his side.

"Miles!" I bolted after him, shouldering past muttering bystand-ers who'd only now begun to realize that they weren't watching a performance set up just for them. In my favor was the fact that the wolf was slowed by the crowd as well. Plus he had a rider and dead weight to drag. I caught up with them less than a minute later when he tried to swing around orange juice cart number twenty-seven and collided with a red-robed water seller, sending the man, his enormous tasseled hat, and all five of his shiny golden cups crash-ing to the ground.

I threw myself at the Luureken, so keyed on vengeance for

Bergman that no amount of cute could veer me off, not even the lumpy-headed-pup look this one wore. I brought the rider off its mount, our impact making it drop the raes and sending Vayl's sheath flying. Bergman screamed again as the hook jarred inside him.

"Miles! The bolo! For chrissake, use it!" I yelled.

Losing its rider had staggered the wolf. But it recovered fast. And its chest wound wouldn't keep it from turning on my friend. I prayed that he wasn't too deep in shock to react as I jammed the sword into the Luureken's neck, felt muscle give, and then bone. It fell to the street like an abandoned doll.

A scream, more animal than human, and yet I wasn't sure whose mouth it came from until I saw Bergman trying to shove the limp Were off his chest. I ran over to help, and together we slid it aside, still breathing, but not for much longer.

Bergman gazed up at me, his face so bloodless I've seen pinker corpses. "How bad is it?" he gasped.

My eyes did not want to drop to that wound, to take in the torn and bleeding flesh. But we both needed to know. I froze my face into an unreadable mask. Leaned over him and pulled up his shirt.

My relief put me on my ass.

"What is it?"

I looked up at him, smiled at his bravery. My good Miles, not even crying like he would've been only a few months ago. "I don't know how you did it. Probably all those hours you spent sitting in front of computer screens. But your limited amount of body fat has all commuted to your love handles. And that's what the Were snagged. It's going to hurt like a muther for a long time. And we still have to worry about infection. But I think you're going to make it."

We grinned at each other. I'd have hugged him, but I figured he'd had enough shocks for one day. Then his smile vanished. "What about Ahmed?"

"The others can take care of him."

"Not with the rest of the wolves on the loose!"

"Dude. I'm not leaving you bleeding on the ground in freaking Marrakech! Besides, there's only one or two left that we really have to worry about, and they've both been shot—"

He shook his head. "You're not thinking straight. Vayl might never come back to you if you're not there tonight. Monique gave me her number. I'll call her. She'll help me get to a hospital."

I couldn't speak. Miles had been around before Vayl. Before Matt, even. I suddenly realized he'd been the first person after Dave and Evie to really *be there*, day after day. Even later, somehow he'd remained a presence. And now, with a goddamn claw shoved through his side, he wanted me to leave?

He reached up and squeezed my hand. "I still want you to be my partner. You and Vayl both. But how can that happen if he spends the rest of *our* lives in a history book? Go get him back. *Please*." He tightened his fingers until it hurt. For once, the shutters that closed off every mystery behind his eyes opened wide, and I could see how much this meant to him.

But my father had been a Marine. I knew what he'd say if I left a man behind. I knew what I'd think of myself. I sat on my heels, so torn by this decision I couldn't bear to look at him. Then it hit me.

I glared into the gathering crowd and shouted, "Yousef! I know you're out there, you mangy little perve! Yousef! Where—that's better!" I said as my stalker squeezed himself between a couple of Japanese tourists and knelt down beside me.

"You arrrre—"

"I know, I'm pretty. Is Kamal with you?"

He jerked his thumb over his shoulder. A beat later the boy worked his way into our circle, apologizing to the people he'd had to displace as he went. As soon as he saw Miles he did one of those girlie screams that made you wonder if his voice really had changed, and his eyes began to roll up in their sockets. I slapped him hard on the thigh, which got a giggle from Yousef.

"Kamal! Don't pass out, dammit, I need you to speak for me!"

He turned around, holding his hand behind his back as if I needed to be fended off. "Don't make me look!"

"For chrissake, Kamal, just tell Yousef I need him to stay with my friend, here, until the woman who owns our riad shows. Her name's Monique Landry. I'm betting she'll be here in less than three minutes, four if she decides to call in a rescue helicopter."

Kamal translated. Yousef shook his head.

Kamal said, "He wants to go with you. To follow. Always to follow."

I grabbed Yousef by the collar and twisted until his face began to turn red. "You tell this son of a bitch if he doesn't watch over my friend I will never, ever choke the shit out of him again. You got that?"

Kamal talked. Fast. Yousef's vigorous nod was all I needed to see. I slapped him across the face. Twice. He kissed my hand. Can I pick 'em, or what?

Chapter Eighteen

Returning to Vayl's battle felt like watching an überlong chase scene. *Oh look! The cars are a little more dented and I'm pretty sure that tire is going to go flying off the rim before it's over, but they're still driving!*

As I caught Cole's eyes and gave him a reassuring nod, I tried to swallow that Vayl's-enjoying-the-shit-kicking-way-too-much feeling and concentrate on what to do next. But I couldn't. It was the fact that even Marrakech has authorities, who I didn't want to piss with if I didn't have to. And though our whole operation hadn't taken more than a few minutes, they were certainly on their way by now. Plus, blood was every-damn-where. Vayl's worst wound seemed to be on his calf. Hard to assess from where I stood, spinning his cane in my hand, debating my next move. Except that I could tell he was favoring it, and every step he took left a bloody imprint on the street.

I went to stand by Sterling, who had Ahmed by the arm. Kyphas held the other. She'd been studying the mage like a biologist dissects a frog. She noted my presence with a shrug of one shoulder and went back to her thoughts. I reminded myself not to leave her alone with the Wielder. My life could depend on it.

Sterling glanced away from the snarling Were with its

blood-streaked fur and shrieking rider battling a scarily silent vampire to ask, "How's the genius?"

"He'll be okay." I didn't think I could say more without bawling, so I stopped.

"You're hurt," he said, his eyes acknowledging the gashes on my arms.

I shrugged. "I'll heal. But we've gotta get Ahmed outta here before we get shredded by whatever remains of this pack. Any ideas?"

Cole drew his PSG1 out from under his coat. "Yup." The people standing closest to him gasped and drew away as he took careful aim at the snarling fighters. He went so still that for a few moments he seemed to have left his own body. No sparkle in his eyes. No breath.

Vayl slashed at the Luureken, causing it and its Were to rear back.

Cole squeezed the trigger.

Vayl's opponent roared with pain as chunks of its chest blew away. The bullet traveled through its back and into the Luureken's belly, throwing it from its mount.

"That'll work," I said.

Cole restashed his rifle and moved forward, grabbing Vayl by the elbow. "Helena's in trouble," he said. "The only way to save her is to get the mage out of here now." He jerked his head backward at Ahmed, whose lips had begun to tremble. "Come on."

More than anything, Vayl's decision to cooperate was based on his trust in his valet. At least that's what I decided as we double-timed it down the street, leaving the crowd behind us in chaos. He didn't question Cole's sources or wonder aloud how a servant could generate a rescue plan. He just came along.

Our plan had been to haul Ahmed back to the riad and force a reversal spell from him. But that was before we found out about his shaggy friends, none of which did we want within scenting distance of Monique. We couldn't go to the city's safe house, because we weren't on official business. Which left another hotel—also putting innocents at risk—or Ahmed's place.

I picked the mage's pocket with a sweet little move I'd learned from a prostitute in Thailand, one that Sterling found so disturbing he pulled his own wallet out and stuffed it down the front of his pants.

"Like I'd try anything like that with you," I said as I checked out Ahmed's ID.

"You won't now," he said defiantly.

"That's for sure." I flipped the long black case closed and slipped it back into the mage's pocket. "Turn right at the end of the block," I said. "He owns a music shop about five minutes from here."

The knowledge would drive me a little crazy if I dwelled on it. I'd probably passed the place twice during my scouting trips around Marrakech, never realizing who owned it or what he was doing to Vayl. I turned to my partner, looking for the kind of comfort he hadn't given me in days. "You look pretty toasty," I told him.

Vayl swept a lily-white hanky from his breast pocket and dabbed at his face. I couldn't decide if I was more floored by the fact that it had totally missed being spattered by blood in the first place, or that he even had a pocket left after that melee. "If, by that, you mean I am nearly done in, you may be right. This life has left me soft, just when I most need battle hardening."

"Well, sir, most vamps I've met would've been smoke within a couple of seconds of meeting those Weres back there."

He glanced down at me, the bite on his face already completely healed. "I could have finished them quickly," he said. Not bragging. Just telling it like it was. "At first I did not because I knew the best way to infuriate Roldan would be to kill them slowly. But then I began to think that I should only kill for the right reasons. And the very idea confused me. In fact, it infuriated me. Why would I think such a thing?"

I hid a triumphant smile. "Maybe you're changing."

He pounded himself on the chest. "I am eternal!"

I laughed. "You're such a gorilla."

"I am no such thing. Why do you persist in—"

I cut him off with a wave toward his leg. "Your pants are so bloody they're sticking to your skin. Do we need to bandage it right away?"

He wrinkled his nose. "The Luureken bit me."

"How...doesn't matter. Come on, we've got a lot to do before the rest of the Weres regroup, and first aid for you is at the top of the list."

We entered a neighborhood that was, once again, filled with stores whose roofs had been used as anchors for swaths of sun-shading material. None of the souks were open for business at this hour, but the signs above the doors showed even the illiterate what to expect inside. Pottery. Rugs. Jewelry. Musical instruments so numerous you could barely see the walls beneath them. When it was open. Tonight the door was locked, making it resemble a dark brown Hitler mustache against the pink skin of the building's outer wall. Which went straight up, as if it had been built to imprison whoever wandered inside.

Sterling glanced over his shoulder. "Look, Chill, it's like a third-world band closet. What do you say we go shopping for that guitar?"

I didn't ask Sterling how he knew the address matched our mage's ID. Sooner or later I'd figure it out, and it wouldn't do to look ignorant in front of the captive. So I said, "Sounds like a plan," and watched him pull Ahmed toward the shop, his hips and shoulders moving to that internal rhythm that marked him as surely as a tattoo. At the mage's other shoulder, Kyphas seemed more like an attachment, built for the ride, but not committed to it.

She was, however, willing to hold on to the mage while Sterling dealt with the Wielder's lock. In fact, she seemed fascinated by

Sterling's amulet, watching with the greed of a jewel thief as he pulled it out from beneath his shirt and held it between his cupped hands. When his fingers began to glow red, I shouldn't have been surprised at my own reaction. My Sensitivity had jumped a few notches since I'd last rubbed against Sterling's powers. But this was eerie. Like breathing air from a hot oven.

I glanced at Cole, but he didn't seem to be as bothered by the warlock's rising powers as I was. He'd pulled his Beretta and was watching Kyphas do her *tahruyt*-to-sword trick. So I unleashed Grief and said to Vayl, "This could get hairy. Here." I handed him the cane. "If you twist the blue jewel at the top, the sheath will shoot away from the sword that's hidden inside."

Vayl eyed it carefully before taking it firmly in his hand. When his eyebrows lifted a notch I felt another spurt of excitement. He'd recognized it, at least subconsciously. Minuscule progress, but still enough to make me want to hug him. I managed to control myself, but only because Sterling was moving his amulet across the lines of the doorway.

He murmured, *"Evendium."* When the lines glowed yellow he backed up. "It's protected," he said. He blew out his breath, fast and hard, as if he could release every ounce of tension that way. And maybe it worked, because his face settled and his shoulders relaxed. He reached into one of the pockets of his cargo pants and dug out a plastic zip-close bag containing a substance that resembled grape jelly. But when he pressed it against the top right-hand corner of the door it stuck like chewing gum. Circling the amulet over the spot like he meant to hypnotize it, Sterling began to hum. It wasn't a tune exactly. But I could feel the music thrum through my feet, and, weirdly, I wanted to dance.

Cole was already waltzing with Kyphas. Spinning her around the shadowed, dusty street like they'd been partners for years. She threw back her head and laughed, her hair flying behind her like the tail of a racehorse. As she smiled up into his sparkling eyes she seemed to shed all her layers of treachery and deceit. For those few moments she wasn't übergorgeous or evil. She was just a pretty girl with her arms around a boy she couldn't resist. Except the hand that was wrapped around his shoulder held a sword that could easily slit his throat.

Who was I to judge? I held a lethal weapon too, and I couldn't wait to swing my partner. I reached out to Vayl, but the demon had already shoved Ahmed into his hands, so it was Sterling who two-stepped me down the block. We flew past the other dancers, skating over the cobblestones like they were coated in bowling-lane wood, the air whistling past our ears as if cheering us on.

"The door." Vayl sounded surprised. "It has unlatched itself."

We stopped.

"Excellent," said Sterling.

I shuffled toward the entrance after him, my elation deflating like a post-birthday balloon as I realized he'd sucked us into his spell. Cole and Kyphas held hands all the way to the door, then Cole looked at her, shook his head remorsefully, and jerked away.

As I shouldered past Sterling I said, "What you did was out of line. Making us dance like puppets just so you could pull off some minor magic."

"You wanted inside. I assumed that meant—"

I tossed my head, slapping him with my braid. "You haven't changed. It's still all about how people can help you manipulate—"

Sterling interrupted me. "But *I'm* helping *you*!"

"Tell me that wasn't a Bardish spell." Silence. I nodded grimly. "You're already into the change, aren't you?" Even less response this time. "And how do you figure you're going to help us when pirates hear a Bard is operating in Marrakech?"

"Well, *I'm* sure as hell not gonna tell them!" He looked around the circle of people who'd become fascinated by our exchange. "And neither are you." The threat, sung softly, still raised the hair on the back of my neck. Vayl barely reacted. Cole went so pale for a second his hair was actually darker than his skin. Kyphas raised her hands as if to say it was beyond her realm of interest. And Ahmed looked like he wanted to throw up.

I turned my back to him. We both knew his threat probably wasn't necessary. Until he took the oath, and all that went along with it, it was unlikely that anybody would be interested in dicing him up so they could squeeze the magic into an elixir so treasured only the mega-rich could afford it. Still, I was pissed. And that gave me an excuse. To ignore my disappointment that the joy hadn't been real. And that coming down had reminded me so forcefully of how little was good in my life right now. I switched Grief into firing mode and prepared to enter Ahmed's souk. But I couldn't bury the thought that, considering Vayl had just bitten me, the reaction might've lasted longer if Sterling hadn't stuck his nose in. Normally it wouldn't bother me. But I had so little of him left to hold on to. That our warlock had cut the moment short stuck in my throat like a chicken bone.

Feeling frustrated and raw, I kicked the door open, half hoping that I'd find the remaining Weres standing on the other side ready for some hand-to-hand ass kicking. The door slammed into the wall, then sprang shut again. I heard Cole snort behind me.

Vayl said, "I must say, Madame Berggia, I have never seen a lady deliver quite so brutal a blow to an entryway before. Perhaps next time you might simply walk through?"

As I looked up into his bright brown eyes, five different responses occurred to me, most of them containing some form of obscenity that would, no doubt, get the poor housekeeper fired again. Then my sense of humor returned from vacation wearing an exoskeleton T-shirt and carrying a bag full of exploding cigars. I smiled.

And I said, "Where I come from, this is just how we enter a strange building, Lord Brâncoveanu. You should see what we do with suspicious packages."

He sighed. "You make very little sense to me. I suppose I must assume this has something to do with Sister Hafeza's prediction. However, where I come from, ladies do not risk unpredictable situations before gentlemen. Or, in fact, at all." He stood, waiting for me to let him pass. When his eyebrows rose a whole centimeter I fluttered my lashes like a real girl and waved him in.

Because I refused to budge, he had to slide past me to get through the narrow door, his whole body rubbing slowly against mine as he made sure he wasn't stepping into an ambush. I closed my eyes and relished the moment. The smell of Vayl, so unique that it made me feel as cozy as hot chocolate. The feel of his chest pressing against mine, his tight, flat stomach brushing just close enough to make my belly ring jingle against my skin. Our thighs met, and I licked my lips, remembering all the times nothing had separated our bodies and we'd tried desperately to hold off, to take one more minute for exploration, but the passion had stolen our senses and all we could do was try to breathe while it rode us.

"Madame Berggia?" The low rumble of his voice, sweet and dark as brown sugar, glided straight down my throat.

Which I had to clear before I said, "Yeah?"

"Are you quite all right?"

"Um."

"Good. Follow me."

Gladly. Because your ass is a work of art, my dear. I could watch it all day and—probably get my head blown off if I don't pay attention now.

We'd entered a shop that was like the evil twin of Sister Hafeza's place. Small and dark, it was impossible to view in one sweep because at the squat service counter just a few steps in, it swerved and ducked, its countless cubicles each containing enough instruments to supply a small, North African orchestra. Drums of all shapes and sizes lined up like mischievous kids against every vertical space, from which hung gongs, hand harps, and instruments with trumpetlike bells at the end but way too many curves in the middle to go by that name. Anything you could get a halfway decent tune from had been crammed into the souk.

Sterling couldn't stop grinning. He cocked his head at Ahmed, who he'd taken charge of again. "What a shame you're such a creep. Otherwise we could've been buds, man."

We spread out, Vayl taking the upper floor while Cole, Kyphas, and I each chose a different turn and Sterling led Ahmed straight toward the back. Within thirty seconds we'd each called, "Clear."

With nothing spectacular to report in my section, I wandered over to Cole's, where I found him admiring a drum. Shaped like a wine goblet, it came almost to his thigh. "Check this out." He rubbed the head, which, according to the tag, was covered in goat-skin. "It's an antique."

"You should come back and buy it," Kyphas said as she joined us. Cole, looking over her shoulder, gave a short laugh.

"Not on my salary."

Sterling called to us from a back corner of the store, "We need to have a family meeting!"

Vayl joined the three of us, and together we found Sterling and Ahmed standing beside a concrete pedestal. Instead of a statue, it held a wide china bowl painted with blue flowers and green vining leaves. The mage had filled it with blue-stained water. And in the middle of the bowl, floating on a spun-glass rose, was the round, marblelike ball from an Enkyklios.

Cole reached for it. "Don't!" I said. "What, did you totally ditch the class on germ warfare?"

"I might've been surfing that day," he admitted. "Aw, come on, Madame B., don't rake your fingers into your hair like that. You'll give yourself curly red horns and then I'll be forced to go buy a matador costume."

I pulled my hands free, clenching my jaws together as I said, "Well, you're not playing in the ocean today. So assume anything you haven't identified is laced with smallpox until proven otherwise."

"Okay." He looked around until he found a couple of mallets. "Can I pick it up with these?"

"Maybe," I allowed, "but I don't want to take the chance of a booby trap blowing us all to smithereens. Sterling?" I pointed to the Enkyklios ball. "Is this rigged?"

He shoved Ahmed back to Vayl. From the look on his face, the mage didn't appreciate being handled like a basketball, but with his wrists firmly bound all he could do was scowl as Sterling muttered some words over what should be a small treasure trove of information. He got no response. "It's clear. And by that I mean it's not trapped. And it's empty. Whatever was recorded on here is long gone."

I watched Vayl study it, hoping it might trigger a memory as I said to him, "Okay, so we're in Ahmed's shop, and we know he's the mage Roldan hired to mess you up. But we've just found an Enkyklios ball. And we also know that Sister Yalida had an Enkyklios with her before she and the Rocenz disappeared over eighty years ago. Coincidence?"

Vayl said, "I have very little idea what you are talking about. However I do not believe in coincidences."

I nodded. "I guess some things never change. So we have to ask, why is it here?"

"Symbol?" Cole guessed. "Maybe Ahmed is part of some guild and this is where they meet. But to keep it secret from everybody else they use the Enkyklios ball." Now he was really warming up to the idea. "Maybe the balls are in shops all over the city, you know, to mark where their hidden tunnels come out."

"Mages are the most solitary of all the Wielders," Sterling said. "No way is Ahmed part of a guild. Right, buddy?" He shook the mage's arm, but the only response was a dark red flush that rushed up Ahmed's neck and didn't stop until it reached his forehead. My stomach twisted at the thought of how much we were pissing this guy off. The same guy who'd managed to wipe centuries out of Vayl's mind. And who'd attracted the notice of the most powerful werewolf in Europe. I decided then and there that he could never go free. Not if any one of us wanted to survive to see the following dawn.

"Maybe you want to take him to the office," I suggested. "You know, so we can talk a little more freely?"

Sterling nodded and jerked the mage back toward the front of the store.

Kyphas said, "I think Sterling's right. Wouldn't displaying the Enkyklios ball defeat the purpose of keeping whatever it's hiding secret?"

Cole's shoulders dropped. I smacked him on the back. "It's okay. You're still a badass sniper and one hell of a linguist."

"What do *you* think it is?" he asked me.

Before I could answer, Kyphas said, "Maybe it's a trophy."

"That sounds plausible," said Cole, gaining a look of adoration that explained just how far she'd fallen for him.

I glared at her, demanding that my inner crowd think up something cutting to say about what was probably hanging on the walls at *her* place. But they seemed to be off their game, because none of them came up with a great retort before the perfect moment had passed. Instead Vayl said, "I believe Miss Kendrick may be right. However, if Ahmed does take trophies, I have seen several items in this shop that lead me to believe he has a practical purpose for them. And that he puts them to that use before he displays them."

"What do you mean?" Cole asked.

He pointed to a wooden instrument hanging on the wall. Shaped like a viper's head that's been smashed by a passing truck, its "fangs" were stretched so far to the front that they had to be connected at the tips by a wooden peg. Ten ivory strings ran from the peg, over the hole between the "fangs," back to the head of the instrument.

Vayl took care not to touch the strings as he said, "The vampire who ripped me had spent his humanity as a pirate. Part of the booty he tore from the last ship he took included a lyre just like that one. He loved to tell the story of the battle he waged just to kill the siren who guarded it." His eyes locked on Cole's. "Like the Enkyklios ball, it had carried within it special powers. I can tell you similar stories about that flute and those castanets." His workman's fingers brought our attention to simple, everyday products that were only made unique by the way they were displayed. The flute stood on end, held aloft by a hand carved out of mahogany. The castanets hung from a glittering silver chain that had been secured to the ceiling by four white cup hooks.

"Sterling touched that flute," I said. "He would've picked up anything out of the ordinary on it—if it still held magic, I mean."

Vayl nodded and started expounding on his idea that Ahmed had stolen the items primarily so he could drain the magic from them. Old story, really. Lazy bum oozing with talent but zero work ethic doesn't want to put in the practice and study time despite the fact that it could lead him onto new paths that no one has ever walked before. Instead he puts his small store of energy into making off with other people's treasures.

Teen Me had stopped listening almost after Vayl's first word. In fact, for the past thirty seconds she'd been running up Granny May's back porch steps, pausing at the top to jump off, and then running back up them again to repeat the whole process. The entire time she kept repeating, *Vayl was ripped! Holy shit! No wonder he never talks about it. It must've hurt like a muther not to take a whole year to turn, like every other Vampere. And his, what do you call it? Sire? Was a pirate? Is that cool, or what?*

Or what, I told her. *Ripping isn't something you do out of kindness. It's harsh, and usually lethal for both sides. Considering that the vamp turned Vayl's wife first, we can pretty much bet Vayl's Sire was psycho.*

Was? Or is?

What do you say we never find out?

Vayl had stopped talking. Had come so close to me I could feel his power brushing against mine, a sweet friction I could hardly bear without touching him. I closed my eyes. "Madame? Are you quite all right?"

I stared at him, my mind a complete blank. Cole came to my rescue. "Now that we've scouted the shop, we'd better secure the whole building before we question Ahmed. You know, in case his buddies come back before we're ready to deal with them. And, uh, our boss is still bleeding."

Work. Right. That'll get me through this. Or kill me. Sad, right now, that I don't know which would be worse. I said, "Let's go old-school and barricade all the doors and windows."

"I'm on it." Without even a glance at Kyphas, Cole went off to secure the second floor before finishing the job below.

Ignoring the demon's pout, I followed him up to Ahmed's living quarters, grabbed a couple of clean T-shirts when I couldn't locate a first-aid kit, and came back down to find that everyone except our sniper had assembled in the office, a small room whose wide door opened to the service counter.

Sterling had dropped the mage into a wooden chair on rollers that creaked like an eighty-year-old man whenever Ahmed shifted his weight. Our warlock had made himself comfortable by sitting on the edge of a battered wooden desk that held a PC, miscellaneous office supplies and, on its other corner, a blood-soaked vampire.

At the opposite end of the room, Kyphas, probably under orders from Sterling, had filled his teapot with water and set it on a hot plate that stood on top of a filing cabinet so old the handles had been replaced with knotted bandanas. While she waited for the water to roll, she leaned against the doorframe and stared unwaveringly at Ahmed.

"Tell her to stop," he finally whispered. "I am a devout man. A Mage of the Seal. I cannot be tempted by feminine flesh."

Kyphas nodded.

I said, "Did you see that, Ahmed? She's making a mental note. That's what hellspawn do. They figure out what you don't want. Then they offer you everything you think you need."

"Huh-huh-hellspawn?" he squeaked. "In my shop? Make her leave!"

I went up to Vayl and motioned for him to lift his pants leg. It was work to keep the holy-shit-you're-missing-a-hunka-yerself! off my face as I began cleaning and bandaging. I managed it by interrogating the asshole who'd made the past few days complete misery for me.

"Ahmed," I said. "Why would I want Kyphas to go when I'm considering asking her to reach down your throat and rip out your kidneys?"

He cringed. *Wow. These pixie-dust types don't have a whole lotta backbone when their wands are pulled out from underneath them.*

"What have you done with Helena?" Vayl demanded.

"What?" Now our prisoner was both scared and bewildered. Good mix? Maybe. You never can tell until it all boils over. Speaking of which, the teapot had begun to whistle. Sterling handed Kyphas a pouch full of, well, it looked (and smelled) like potpourri.

"Dump it all in," he said. Typical. Leave it to the warlock to keep the secret ingredient to himself until it was time to make real magic.

At the same time Vayl was struggling to stand. I could feel his anger and frustration rising.

"Lord Brâncoveanu—Vasil," I said. "You're making this extra hard to—"

"I care only for Helena's welfare!" Vayl snapped.

Cole poked his head into the door, the barricading evidently up to his standards. "I think I can help."

He strolled over to Ahmed's chair, and whispered at length into the mage's ear. It was almost comical to watch the change come over his face. His expression went from confused and scared to piss-your-pants freaked. Then Sterling's fun-mix hit the air and he fell into a happy daze. Naturally we'd all stuffed our nostrils with Sterling's special wax, so it only felt like we'd been congested for a week. Well, all of us but Vayl, who'd flat out refused. Because, as he'd continuously reminded us, warlocks are evil.

When my *sverhamin* began to smile, I mean really show fang, I thought, *Uh-oh*. But Ahmed had hit the confessional and I didn't want to miss a word.

He looked dreamily into Cole's eyes and said, "I just wanted the money, that's all. It takes money to buy components. And more money to experiment with new combinations that will impress the Ardent enough to convince them to bestow upon you the title of Mage of the Scroll. Roldan had money. Sooooo much money." Ahmed rolled his head around to stare at me. "You have lovely hair. It's like curly, red wood shavings."

"Her hair is not red," Vayl said, wagging his finger at Ahmed like the bad boy had forgotten to take out the trash. "Silly."

"Oh you." Ahmed circled his head around and grinned fool-ishly at the vampire, who'd begun shoving his finger forward like he was trying to stab Ahmed with it. Or saw off a piece of butter for his corn on the cob.

Ahmed stared down at his feet. "I think I'm in trouble."

"Why is that?" I asked.

"Look at my little toe. It's stopped dancing. You know what that means?"

I caught Sterling's eyes. He shrugged. "What?" I asked.

His entire face puckered. "I've been a bad, bad boy." He started to cry. Vayl, his forehead crinkling in sympathy, went over to pat him on the shoulder as Ahmed said, "I have scary werewolves liv-ing in my basement. You know what they eat for breakfast? Raw sheep's liver. Liver is supposed to be cooked, you know!"

Cole took my arm and escorted me to the corner of the little office opposite the file cabinet, at which time he asked, "If I laughed out loud, how hard would you kick my ass?"

I shook my head. "This is so not the scene I was imagining. How are we supposed—oh no. They're—Cole. Tell me they're not…"

He nodded, biting his lip to keep it from betraying him. "Yes, Madame B., I'm afraid so. Your loveypoo is hugging the mage who cursed him. Who is hugging him back. It's a total hugfest. Do you want a hug?"

"No!"

Sterling held out his arms and nodded, so Cole and he embraced while giggling idiotically, and then, of course, Kyphas had to stick her big old boobs into it until everybody in the goddamn room was snuggling like a bunch of drunken idiots doing the Closing Time Dance.

I heard a crack, looked down, and realized I'd just broken the pencil sharpener. When I looked up…*huh*. I caught Ahmed in the middle of a crafty expression that didn't fit with his recent behavior. I checked his wrists. "Sterling! Your cuffs are loose! See what happens when you cuddle during an interrogation?"

"Bound to me!" the warlock shouted just as Ahmed, in a single move, sprang from his seated position to a crouch on the same chair.

Instead of tightening, Sterling's wand fell off Ahmed's wrists, dropping to the brown tiled floor as if its two parts held no power at all.

Everyone moved at once.

Sterling dove for the wand, whispering the words that united the halves and twisted them back into a warlock's conduit.

Kyphas grabbed the teapot off the hot plate. She threw it at Ahmed, screaming, "You might as well start burning now!"

Seeing the container with its boiling contents flying his way, Ahmed yelped and jumped off his chair toward the desk. The tea splattered against the wall, at which point he jumped again, this time aiming for the filing cabinet.

What is this guy, half bullfrog?

I lunged to intercept him and caught his feet just as he tried to land. He crashed to the floor, squealing with pain as Vayl and Cole landed on top of him.

Sterling came after, waving his wand over Ahmed's head. As he chanted words under his breath, some of which sounded a lot like curses themselves, I squatted down by the mage so he could see my face. Pulling out Grief, I made it ready to fire. Then I said, "No more pissing around, you little fuck. You cursed my *sverhamin*. Now you reverse it. Or I put a hole in your head."

I pressed Grief against his temple.

"They'll kill me!" he protested. I pressed harder. He squalled, "It's not that easy to do! I need time to prepare!"

"Or maybe you just need to stop breathing," I said. "I'll bet that would do the trick. What do you think, Sterling?"

"That could work," he said easily. "But it makes a helluva mess. We'd appreciate a few seconds to get clear before you pull the trigger."

"Hmm, good point. Okay, I'll count down from five, and then Lord Brâncoveanu, you, Sterling, and Berggia back to the door. Okay?"

Vayl, staring at my gun like he'd never seen me, or a firearm before, nodded so slightly I'd never have caught it if I wasn't clued in to every one of his gestures.

I said, "Five. Four. Three. Two—"

"All right!" Ahmed wiggled his butt back and forth a couple of times, like he thought he could unbalance the men shoving him into the floor. Then he gave up.

And said, "*Legerut.*"

Cole and I snapped our eyes to each other. Still on his knees beside the mage, he mouthed, *Did you feel that?*

I nodded.

Ahmed's spell had slid over me like a mint-scented shiver. But it had moved past me. I looked at Sterling, whose wand hand had risen sharply. For a moment a sparkling blue shield burned around him like a second skin, revealed only by the presence of magic that ran counter to his. Kyphas didn't act nearly as concerned. I figured she'd only transformed her scarf into the flyssa on the off chance that we'd allow her to impale Ahmed if this latest move turned out to be another ploy.

I expected Vayl to react least, as usual.

He'd pulled away from Ahmed, managed to stand before the spell hit. At first he just stared off into the distance, his jaw clenching at whatever played out on that invisible horizon. Then his head jerked back, like something massive had him by the throat.

"Vayl!" I lunged for him, but Cole wrapped his arms around my waist and whispered, "You can't interfere now," as Vayl's hand shot out, the fist that he'd clenched around his cane trembling from the force of his muscles straining, resisting. His other hand went to the wall, *through* it, and found a beam to brace himself with as his lips sheared back from his teeth in a look of such grinding pain that I moaned his name again.

His eyes came to mine. Locked on. And I swallowed my fear. Instead I poured all the love I felt for him, every ounce of strength, the last shred of my dreams and plans for us into those bruise-tinted eyes, and only when their orange flecks began to fade to honey gold did I remember to breathe. First his hands dropped. Then his head. No one spoke. Or even looked around. We just waited.

Finally Vayl stepped away from the wall and looked down at Ahmed. Only my position allowed me to see the colors changing in his irises. Like the storm clouds that tell you it's time to run to the basement, now black framed them, and in the centers, a deep, bloody red.

"Vayl," I whispered.

"I remember." His voice, so low none of us should have heard it, permeated the room like the rumble of a tsunami. He lifted Ahmed by the collar of his jellaba, rising slowly so we could see the mage begin to choke inside his own clothing, observe Vayl grab him by the hair and turn him so he had no choice. He must face the vampire he'd cursed.

"I remember everything you did to me. What you made me relive." He fastened his hand around Ahmed's neck, lifted and shoved so that the mage moved on the tips of his toes, holding on to Vayl's wrists to prevent a fall. His eyes were so wide I half expected them to pop out and roll down his cheeks as he stared into the blizzard of cold fury he'd unleashed. Though Cole and I were mostly immune to Vayl's powers, we still shivered as icicles began to form in Ahmed's nose hairs and every exhalation pasted another layer of frost around the rim of his mouth.

"It wasn't me!" he insisted. "Roldan—"

"I will see to him in due course," Vayl said. "But you had a choice. You took your pay. You wound your spell." They'd moved into the shop now, and what could we do but follow? We watched, silent witnesses as Vayl slammed Ahmed against a wall, sending brass instruments of all shapes and sizes crashing to the floor. The dissonant shriek of sound accompanied the mage's moan.

Vayl said, "You shoved me back into a hell I thought I had escaped. You tore me from the woman I cannot survive without. This will not stand." His free hand went to Ahmed's chest.

Holy Christ, is he gonna rip out his heart? I stepped forward.

Ahmed blubbered, "Wait! Please! The redhead said you needed information on the bauble in my back room. The Enkyklios ball? It's part of Roldan's payment! I can tell you why he had it in the first—ulp!"

Vayl shook his head. "No. You are done." He covered Ahmed's open mouth, still wagging with suggestions and excuses, with the hand that had threatened his heart. And suddenly all of the bells in the shop began to clang. The breeze, focused by his *cantrantia* so that only the mage felt the full effect of Vayl's power as a Wraith, came cold as an Arctic storm, splintered into his eyeballs, iced his veins, turned his skin blue. Before Vayl had finished even Ahmed's fingernails had frozen solid.

Vayl turned, looked at us silently.

I knew the moment required something immense from me. But before I could dredge up the right response the front door flew open, Cole's cabinet barricade splintering like rotten wood under the onslaught of two massive werewolves. The platinum streaks in the larger wolf along with his big-eared rider proved that he and his Luureken would have to be put down the old-fashioned way. The second wolf's dark brown fur marked him as the one we'd seen hip-deep in oranges with no partner in sight. Now we knew his rider was a dimpled blonde with hate burning like hellfire in her eyes.

The Luureken each brandished a raes in one hand and a fury so deep it seemed to paint the doorway black. We only hesitated a beat or two, but in that time Vayl had already moved to meet them. He left Ahmed to fall like a block of glacial ice behind him and sent the gale of his rage ahead of him, knowing we had our own ways of dealing with his fallout.

The Luureken didn't. They froze in their seats, the spittle from their furious shrieks beading like pearls on their cheeks. Their Weres, whose wounds had taken on the pink of new tissue from the outside, evidently still hadn't fully pulled together on the inside. Because I could hear those torn and shattered tissues crackle and break like thin ice. Their mouths opened, fearsome howls cut off instantly by the rime building inside their throats. And that was all the time we needed.

I hauled Grief out of its holster like a gunfighter in a ten-step standoff. Pumped every bit of ammo I had left into the bodies of those two wolves. And watched them fall with about as much satisfaction as I felt when I witnessed my towels spinning in the dryer.

Cole shot a single round into the leader's Luureken, sending it tumbling out of the doorway in a shower of destroyed wood and blood splatter.

The female berserker just sat where she'd rolled when her mount had gone down, still paralyzed by Vayl's attack.

We gathered around it. Kyphas nudged it with her toe. It blinked so slowly we could hear the frost on its eyelids crackle.

"Now what?" asked Cole.

We all jumped as the other Luureken came flying back through the door and slammed into a huge gong that Ahmed had erected, making such a racket that everybody with the exception of Vayl covered their ears. I wanted to assume the body-thrower was an ally, but the crouch I took reminded me not to hesitate too long because bad guys had ways of putting you off your guard too. Then Raoul followed the body through the door, his face such a dark shade of red I'd have suspected imminent heart attack if he hadn't already, you know, gone over.

"Pick up your trash!" he thundered as he glared at the five of us, giving the rest of the dead only a brief glance. He slammed his fist against the doorframe and all the shattered door pieces pulled back together, closing the shop behind him. "And while you're at it, dump this in the garbage too!" He shoved Astral into my arms.

She looked up at me, her eyes crossing slightly as they met mine. "Hello!"

"Hey, kittybot." I gave her a brief inspection, did the same for Raoul, and took a wild guess at the problem. "Astral, tell me you didn't freak out Raoul's girl."

Raoul waved me off. "Astral was fine," he snapped, his accent thicker than I'd ever heard it. "Better than that. She was so charming I was surprised little birds didn't appear and start singing as they flew tiny circles around her head."

I felt the knot in my chest loosen. If my cat had ruined Raoul's chance at romance I wasn't sure I could forgive her.

Cole decided to be daring and ask, "What happened?"

"Nia spent our entire date cooing over that dratted half animal." He threw up his arms. "How was I supposed to know she was a cat lady?"

I holstered Grief and tried desperately to make the transition from Were-killer to Spirit Guide confidant. *"What?"*

"She told me she had twenty-four cats when she was human. Liked them better than people!" He nodded to assure me I hadn't heard him wrong. "How can you like a cat better than a person? They don't even talk!"

"Hello." Was it my imagination, or did Astral sound offended?

I looked at Cole and shrugged. "I got nothing."

Cole murmured, "I could tell him there are other fish in the sea, but he's not going to want to hear that for at least a couple of weeks."

Vayl stepped forward. "Raoul, I have just remembered that you and I barely get along. Would you agree?"

"I suppose so," Raoul said carefully.

"I think, in this case, that is to your advantage. As is the fact that I am older and, therefore, a great deal more experienced in these matters than you."

Raoul's mouth dropped slightly, but he nodded like he was willing to hear Vayl out.

"You will feel better if you kill something evil. And we seem to have happened on a generous supply." He motioned to the wolves, all of which would recover to attack us again. Unless Raoul wanted to send them into the next world—which he could pretty much do with a word and a tap on the head.

I knew he was giving the idea serious consideration when he took a look around the place, his eyes resting on broken displays, the casualties, our diverse array of weaponry.

"You people need your own cleanup crew, you know that?"

I said, "Does that mean you're staying?"

"What's the upside for you?" my Spirit Guide asked.

I pointed at the surviving Luureken. "They seem to have some Rocenz-related information."

Vayl asked, "Do you recognize this breed?"

Raoul nodded, suddenly sober. "How do you intend to get them to talk? I've never seen a berserker articulate enough to get past a scream."

We all looked at Sterling as Vayl said, "You have never seen the greatest warlock on earth in action either."

"Then I'll dispatch these Weres for you, shall I?" Raoul asked.

We nodded, except for Sterling, who pointed to the frozen female and said, "Leave her to me."

Chapter Nineteen

"A re you sure you want to do this?" asked Raoul. It was the third time he'd said it, confirming his unease with our plan, which was, I'll admit, one of our most grisly. My Spirit Guide leaned against the desk in Ahmed's office with his arms crossed, the extra creases in his uniform reflecting his agitation as a framed picture of King Mohammed VI grinned over his shoulder.

I looked up from the corpse whose forearm skin I was carving off with my bolo and was glad for once that Vayl wasn't there to see me despite the fact that Sterling's spell, and this particular component of it, had all been his idea. Which was, maybe, why he'd volunteered to keep watch over the one Were Raoul hadn't sent to the netherworld—the female Luureken who was still mostly an ice pop with rage filling lying beside the front door.

She was alone at the front now, because at Sterling's direction we'd dragged all the dead back to the office. Then Cole and Kyphas had gone out to find the bodies of the other Luureken. Their job was to bring back pieces of at least two of them, which were also necessary for his spell. Impossible? Maybe for anyone else. I gave them even odds.

I glanced at Raoul, whose grimace told me he was less grossed out, but more offended, than me. I said, "What is it?"

"Mutilating corpses is a crime," Raoul informed me.

"So is trying to kill us." I finished slicing off a patch about three inches square and threw it in the middle of the floor. The slap of dead flesh against cold tile made my teeth ache. I hit the bathroom to clean up, and by the time I came out Cole and Kyphas had returned, pale but triumphant. Predictably, the demon was the one who presented Sterling with their prizes.

"On the floor with the other one," he told them, pointing to where he'd be working.

Cole sank onto the chair, not even protesting when Kyphas began to rub his shoulders. He just stared at the two flaps of skin they'd retrieved as Raoul asked, "What is the purpose of this ceremony?"

I stood in the doorway, unable to let Vayl out of my sight for long, and said, "We're raising the ghosts of the Luureken we killed."

Sterling knelt over the skins, adding his own mix of herbs and powders. He hummed under his breath, the lightning-trapped sphere of his amulet swinging in wide circles as he moved.

Raoul asked, "How is that possible? Sterling's no medium."

"Nope. But then, they won't be real ghosts, so it's a good balance."

He nodded. "Ah, illusory spirits?"

"The best kind. Of course, our little berserker in there will think they're real ghosts. And that's all we need."

He glanced up. Muttered something I couldn't understand.

Cole asked, "Getting a text from the saint patrol, Raoul?"

"They're out of their comfort zone again." His eyes glittered as he glanced at me. "It should please you to know they've actually come up with their own phrase for the danger you put me in, which doubles as their order for me to return to base."

"What is it?" Cole demanded.

"DEFCON Parks."

I moaned. "That's just lame."

Raoul chuckled. "And now you've described half the Eldhayr."

I cocked my head, realizing suddenly the risk Raoul had taken saving my life. Vouching for me with the bigwigs upstairs. Showing when I called despite the fact that my closest relationship was with a creature who'd all but trashed his soul. "How much trouble do you get into hanging out with me?"

A sudden, rare smile. "Only enough to make it worth my while."

I walked over to stand beside him. He stiffened a little when my shoulder brushed his, but relaxed almost immediately. "I think they'll clear you for this deal. It looks nasty from the outside, but Sterling's got tight control of the situation. We know whatever we can find out about the Weres and the Enkyklios ball could get us a lot closer to the Rocenz. All we're gonna do is some creative information gathering."

Vayl said, "And if that does not work, you should leave. Because I will not relent until the Luureken has told me what I need to know in order to free Jasmine." He'd come to the doorway, his fierce expression reminding me more of Lord Brâncoveanu than my *sverhamin*. I felt a heavy weight settle on my chest, but before it could sink in he said, "She has suffered long enough. I will have an end to it."

I hadn't realized how much I'd missed having Vayl in my corner until that moment, when it was all I could do not to run sobbing into his arms like some spineless airhead. I turned to Sterling. "How's it going?"

"Give me some room," he replied.

We shuffled into the open space behind the counter, each of us taking turns watching him work and gauging the mood of the thawing Luureken that still sprawled in the blood of her comrades. Cole pulled out his Beretta and stepped away from Kyphas's full-body lean, making her plant both feet wide to keep from stumbling. She nearly stepped on Astral, who sat quietly at Raoul's feet like he'd found her off switch. He crouched down and ran a finger along her forehead and back between her ears, making them twitch to the side. The other hand reached down and pressed into the heel of his boot. When his thumb jerked back, the hilt of a knife came with it. He pulled it free and stood, holding it comfortably at his side, a shining blade just long enough to pierce a Luureken's heart.

Sterling ignored our preparations because he was still busy with his own. He added a few more dried leaves to the pile, whispered over it, "Shades of shades, rise and speak, mouth my words."

His amulet seemed to be moving on its own now, drawing a circle around the pile on the floor. He hesitated another second. Then he brought his left hand up to the chain, pulled the necklace straight and still. A bolt of shiny silver light shot from its glittering center down onto the concoction. It caught fire, burned white-hot, and then stopped, leaving nothing but ash behind.

He leaned over again, only this time he drove his fist into the pile. Sparks flew from his ring as the ash exploded into the air. It reminded me of a volcanic eruption, only in miniature. When Sterling stepped back, however, not a single speck of the material had settled on him.

"Where'd it go?" I whispered.

"Around," he assured me.

"Uh-huh." I looked at the ceiling doubtfully. "Nothing seems different to me."

Sterling's jaw worked itself long enough that I realized I'd just insulted him. I sighed. Why did I always land the brilliant, sensitive types? "I'm just asking you what the Luureken is going to see that I'm not," I said.

"Oh." He glanced at Vayl, who raised an eyebrow.

"Her words often take more than a single meaning," my *sverhamin* explained. "Perhaps this would be a good rule for you to remember before the two of you end up destroying another building."

I stared up at him, thinking, *Oh, so he knew all along. Yeah, Pete probably trotted out all the gory details of my solo exploits for him. And still he demanded to bring me on as his assistant. Which is kind of how I feel right now. Back to square one, before he'd even looked at me sideways. Which isn't fair. Maybe he feels just as confused as I do. Who's ever going to know with a guy who signals his deepest emotions with a twitch?*

Save it for later, I answered myself as I turned away from him and locked my hands behind my back. *We're working, so let's work. And if we're going to ignore the fact that we both decided to gloss over what should've been a major reunion moment, then fine. It would've been weird with an audience anyway. Especially considering the fact that Vayl's first reaction to becoming uncursed was to kill the guy.*

Then I felt his hands slide over mine. Cirilai had ridden up my finger. He pushed it back down, then raised my arms just enough so he could push forward, press his hips into my back. The rumble of his voice worked like a bell, ringing through my body as he said, "I am curious as well, Sterling. Will the illusions only be visible to the Luureken?"

Sterling's smile seemed to acknowledge more than the question as he looked down at the original spot of his spell. "You'll see the illusions. She'll see ghosts. And hear them, in whatever language they were in the habit of speaking. I'd rate the freak-out factor at about a nine and a half."

I felt a grin play at the corner of my lips, now that I understood. And especially now that Vayl's thumbs were rubbing my palms while his fingers wrapped my wrists so tight it felt like he never planned to let go.

Less than fifteen seconds later the two Luureken whose remains Cole and Kyphas had salvaged rose out of the floor. Even though Sterling had only created echoes of their spirits, I felt their rage like needles rolling along the length of my exposed skin, an acid-green hatred that spewed on everything it touched.

How such ordinary-looking people could contain all that madness I couldn't guess. At first glance they resembled a couple of child-sized grown-ups dressed in street clothes. But you can't hide real evil. The man who'd masqueraded as the snake-photo seller's son had come, the scar crawling along his face and down to his neck like an active disease. Joining him was the flame-eyed girl that Sterling and Kyphas had originally marked. Her scars, which had been even deeper in life than her partner's, pulsed as if she still had a heartbeat.

"I'm going to fuck somebody up," she said to her partner, her voice high as a child's as they paused by Ahmed's desk.

"We're dead, Cleahd," said the man. "You don't get more fucked up than this." It was supposed to be a joke, but neither of them laughed. They just stared at each other with eyes the color of burning logs that kept getting brighter, and hotter, until I began to be amazed one of them didn't burst out screaming.

Finally Cleahd shoved the knuckles of her first two fingers against her lips and said, "Wrull, one of us is still alive. Don't you feel it? She's waiting.'"

Sterling caressed the ring on his pinkie and whispered, mouthing the words Wrull spoke moments later.

"We have to talk to her," he said. "Come on."

Ignoring us as if we were just a set of drums Ahmed had decided to use as doorstops until he had time to price us, they drifted into the hall and toward the surviving Luureken, who was just beginning to sit up. They sat across from her, staring into her confused face as they tucked their knees under their chins and wrapped their arms around them like schoolgirls preparing to play a good game.

At nearly the same time the third illusion walked through the front door. It was the leader's rider, looking so real that I reached for Grief before my brain reminded my hand that Sterling was just that good.

The first two berserkers looked at the new arrival and whispered his name, "Nedo," worshipfully. Then they waited for him to speak, like it was his job to ask the questions they wanted answered. Weird how the rules of life follow into the afterlife, and then even into the magical faking of it.

I glanced at Sterling. He'd closed his eyes. I thought I heard him chanting as Nedo leaned over the wild-eyed survivor, grinning with huge enjoyment when she yelped and crab walked straight back into a bin full of maracas, knocking it over and spilling them with a clash that officially made Ahmed's the loudest scene I'd ever lingered at after the killings were over. I hoped the neighbors wore earplugs to bed.

Nedo glared at the single surviving Luureken like he was insulted she hadn't been decapitated as he inquired, "The Enkyklios ball. Tell us we didn't die for an empty bauble."

Cleahd shrieked, "Tell us we didn't die in vain!"

Wrull crawled up beside the survivor's shoulder and breathed in her ear. "We died for a fucking marble, Eishel. You can't burn enough incense to comfort our spirits in that knowledge."

Eishel reached back, wrapped her hands around a guembri like ones I'd seen musicians strumming in the Djemaa el Fna for the past few days, and stuttered, "N-n-n-n-ooo. You've forgotten already. I-i-i-it's not about the ball. That was just a clue, remember? Sister Yalida left her map inside it. The map that leads to the Rocenz. Roldan made it our solemn duty to guard it—"

"Aaaahhhh!" screeched Nedo.

"In vain!" screamed Cleahd.

"Do you think those CIA fuckers haven't figured all this out already? They're probably halfway to the map right now," Wrull hissed.

Eishel shook her head. "Impossible! The Enkyklios map hasn't been disturbed in decades. We've seen to that." She pulled the guitarlike instrument to her chest.

"No!" wailed Wrull. "The map! You've put the map at risk!"

"Wasted lives!" screamed Nedo. "Empty deaths!"

"Wait!" Eishel cried before Wrull could wrap his claws around her neck. "It's still at the Musee de Marrakech. Think! I'm sure you'll remember if you just try! The rest of our pack is still there, still guarding it. And even if they failed like..." She nearly swallowed her tongue as Cleahd screeched and began tearing out her hair.

"No! I didn't mean that!" Eishel scrambled to her feet, holding the guembri out in front of her like a shield. "I'm only saying, even if our enemies did, somehow, find a way to steal it they could never interpret it. The tannery is as much a labyrinth as a warlock's maze."

"Too late!" wailed Cleahd.

"The vampire and his Trust have already gone!" bellowed Wrull.

"The map! The map!" chanted Nedo, over and over again, punching his head forward with every other word so that Eishel finally hid her face behind the instrument.

They pressed so close to her they could've walked through her if they'd taken another step. "I'll warn the pack, all right?" she cried. "They'll ambush the Trust before they can even crack the door to the storage room."

"Go!" demanded Cleahd.

"Go!" "Leave now!" the other two chimed in, waving their hands like geese herders.

Eishel ran toward the door, working up such a head of steam I half expected the hoot of a train whistle to toot out of her ass as her arms worked up and down like little pistons. It seemed nothing could stop her from leaping into the street now that the entrance had been destroyed. Instead? She slammed into Raoul's replacement full force.

Thunk.

For a second she reminded me of a cartoon cat, foiled in its endless mouse chase by one of those sudden, unexpected impacts that flattens it, tail to whiskers, before it slides to the floor with a long squeak of surrender. I pressed my lips together.

This is not funny.

Then she fell straight back.

Thud.

Cole's strangled whisper broke the silence. "The only way this could get better is if the trapdoor opened underneath that rug she's lying on and she tumbled down to the basement."

Collective intake of breath. Then Cole said, "I barricaded that door shut."

Exchange of guilty looks as we realized what we'd been considering. And then Cole said, "Oh. Wait." One well-aimed kick and we all sighed happily as the floor groaned and Ahmed's basement access door gave underneath what had been a colossal battle followed by the final insult of Eishel's fall. She disappeared with a whisper of windswept clothing and a final, satisfying *clonk.*

We all grinned happily. Except for Raoul, who'd risen above such petty humor. And Vayl, who just didn't get us.

They looked at each other while we shook our heads and wiped our eyes—and shrugged.

Vayl held out his arms. "Do I look like a man who is prepared to steal a map?"

Raoul gave him a critical once-over. "No. You look like you were just mauled by a lion." He motioned to the slashes healing on Vayl's arms and his half-digested calf. "If it makes you feel any better, I'm assuming you won."

"It does." Vayl glanced at us, his eyes lingering on mine just long enough to make sure I understood. "But if that is the impression *I* leave, *you* lot would frighten a well-armed street gang. In which case, I suggest we go back to the riad to change before the authorities decide we look too interesting not to question—"

"Was that our next step?" Cole asked me.

"Yup," I replied, staring hard at him, willing him to read my mind. "Right after Raoul sends the Luureken to the great beyond so she can't warn the pack we're coming."

Raoul scowled at me. "Don't get used to this. I'm not here to help you start your own morgue."

"Don't be ridiculous," I said. "Ahmed's fridge is way too small for that." I took off for the back room and the Enkyklios ball it still held while Raoul tied up our loose thread. Cole followed me.

As I reached for the ball he whispered, "Are we doing what I think we're doing?"

I looked over his shoulder. Kyphas was crouched at the edge of the hole, staring greedily down at Eishel, probably trying to figure a way to take credit for her eventual trip to the pit. That didn't mean she wasn't paying some sort of attention. So I said, "Yeah. We're taking the ball with us."

When he saw where I was looking he didn't argue. Just watched me reach for it, think again, and then call for Astral. Who appeared like she'd been waiting for the summons.

"See the ball? I need you to carry that home for me, okay, girl?"

Astral leaped to the table, stretched out her neck, and delicately nipped the Enkyklios ball off its flowery stand. Then she swallowed it.

"You are such a good girl!" I said.

She didn't grace me with a reply. Maybe she'd figured out how I'd just risked her little hide, because her attitude seemed haughtier than usual as she walked out the front door, as if she assumed the rest of us were ready to follow her.

CHAPTER TWENTY

W e made it all the way back to the square before anyone even took a second look at us. And even then their eyes barely hesitated before skipping on to a lone musician who was strolling along singing quietly as he accompanied himself on a guembri similar to the one Eishel had shielded herself with. In the time we'd spent away most of the crowd had cleared out. The food carts had rolled off to their garages or were shutting down. The Djemaa el Fna had finally decided it was time for bed.

As happened with me anytime I saw a city yawn and set the alarm, I felt the adrenaline surge. Now was when our real work usually began, and tonight was no exception. I walked beside Vayl, every sense maxed out, most of them centered on him. Though I'd worked with him nearly every day for the past eleven months, I'd never been so aware of the confident set of his jaw. The impossible broadness of his shoulders. The predatory smoothness in his step. The temptation to claim him by walking inside the circle of his arm while his fingers brushed the curve of my hip locked my teeth together. I wanted to grab him by the front of his shirt, drag him to the center of the square, and scream, "MINE!"

I knew it was a delayed reaction. Seeing him come back to himself had been too huge for my heart to handle all at once. It might be weeks before I came down from this fierce joy at having a part of my heart returned to me.

How is this different than what Kyphas wants with Cole? asked my Inner Librarian. *You act as if Vayl is a part of you. Isn't that a sort of possession?*

I answered because she wasn't judging. Just asking so she'd know where to file the records. *Maybe the line is so thin in places you'd need a microscope to find it. But you and I both know it exists. All we have to do is take a peek at the Domytr we've got locked up in my head. The difference is love. Not the use-it-till-you-suck-the-life-out-of-it word you hear on soap operas and talk shows every day. Real love. Unending. Unconditional. Unselfish. That's why it's not possession.*

What would you call it, then?

I didn't even have to think. *I'd call it bliss.*

I looked up at my vampire, breathed in his scent like it was filled with miracles. Smiled into his warm brown eyes. And held back. His touch had reassured me. Now I could wait until we had real time. But I still took advantage of walking close to him, brushing against his arm as everyone else pressed close too, so we could use his power of camouflage to hide our blood-stained, fist-bruised bodies from the people who would be most likely to call the police if they saw us.

Sterling and Cole took the lead. My *sverhamin* and I walked behind them with Kyphas trailing at the back. I kept an eye on her, but there was really no need. She stayed quiet and thoughtful, though she did keep an eye to our backs so nothing could sneak up on us. She was, in fact, an ideal rear guard. That alone told me something was up. For once, I was glad to know it.

I elbowed Vayl, tracked my eyes to her, and got his acknowledgment that he'd noticed too. But he didn't say anything. Just explained what he expected to go down at the museum after we'd all spiffed up for the robbery.

"With two Sensitives and a warlock on our side, we should easily be able to locate and eliminate the pack guarding the map," he said. "Eishel said it was in a storage room. Leave the lead Were alive so it can tell us which one. After that, Bergman—"

Cole asked, "What about Bergman?"

Vayl looked at me. "I assumed he was waiting for us back at the riad?"

"No." I felt that fist in my stomach again. "He's hurt. It's not life-threatening, but he's at the hospital." Now the guilt descended. What the hell had I been thinking letting some punch-loving stalker guard my little buddy until the cavalry came? It was worse than leaving him alone!

"I have to call him." I fished out my phone.

"Push the speaker button thingy!" Cole demanded.

"Oh, you're so technical. Remind me not to let you touch any more of Bergman's stuff," I said. But I did activate the group-hear function.

Miles answered immediately. "Jaz! I'm going to have a scar! Actually, three of them. Isn't that great?"

"Uh. Yeah?"

"Monique's with me. She hovers like a Jewish mother, only she's pretty sensitive about her age, so don't tell her I said that. She just left to find me something to eat because I'm starving! I could probably eat a whole pot of spaghetti right now! Did everything go okay?"

Bergman on painkillers. Um, God? Let's not do this too often, 'kay? "Yeah. I mean, great. Just like we'd hoped."

"That's so cool it's like...empirical!"

Cole's shoulders started to shake. Sterling looked back at me and mouthed, *Empirical?*

I said, "...Definitely. So. What kind of medication did they give you, dude?"

"Stuff for pain. And antibiotics. And painkillers. Have I told you lately how much I love you?"

"Nope. But, uh, I figured you..."

Cole was gesturing wildly like he either wanted to talk or climb the Atlas Mountains before we left the region. I kept waving him off. Finally Vayl pointed at him then pointed to the ground. The message was clear. *Down, boy!* He subsided.

I said, "So, Miles, how long are you in for?"

"Overnight. Monique's going to stay with me the whole time. She says she's worried about me. But I think she might be one of those cougars. You know what I mean? *Rrrrrow.*"

When Bergman actually tried to pull off a growl I nearly dropped the phone. Cole had started to slap himself, but it wasn't working. He covered his entire head with his shirt while Sterling buried his face in Cole's shoulder and they both shook uncontrollably. Behind us, even Kyphas began to snort.

Finally I managed to say, "Gee, Miles, are you sure? Maybe she's just being nice."

Bergman said, "Naw, I think she's hot for my bod. I'll tell you one thing. I'm not going to put out on the first date. That's for sure. I'll definitely make her wait until at least date number two."

Cole and Sterling fell to the ground and began to roll around helplessly. Beside me I could see the glint of Vayl's fangs. If I didn't end this conversation right now I would probably rupture something vital from the supreme effort it was taking not to laugh out loud. I said, "That's a sound plan, Miles. You do that. So I'll pick you up in the morning."

"Okay! Have fun boffing your vampire!"

I hung up. Three beats of silence. And then we all roared.

The riad seemed smaller without Monique and Bergman there to brighten the corners. I said so to Vayl as we stood outside his door. Everyone else had gone off to their rooms to clean up. I should be on my way too. But it was hard to separate, even temporarily. So I found another excuse to stay by adding, "It's great that you booked a riad so close to the medina. Makes for a short walk to, well, pretty much anywhere." Then I grinned like a lottery winner as I realized this was the first time he'd heard my compliment as "himself."

I realized he was thinking along the same lines when he said, "It seems that it was my last lucid move for some time."

I said, "I don't know how long this is going to eat at you. I guess it would bother me for longer than twenty minutes too. But Sterling believes the only reason Ahmed could curse you was because you'd already cursed my mother. And you only did that to protect me. If that's wrong, you can wallow in guilt for the next hundred years and I won't fault you."

"I know how miserable I made you."

I smiled up at him. "You were kind of a dick back in the day, weren't you?"

His face went taut and for a second I knew how Ahmed had felt to face his rage. "Yes." Terse, get-the-hell-out-if-that's-your-intention tone.

"But you're not now," I noted.

He pulled a long breath in through his nose. "No."

"That's a helluva feat. I'll bet I can name fifty men who could live three hundred years and never improve on their dickness."

Twitch of the lip. "Is that a word now?"

"Absolutely. Here, I'll use it in another sentence. 'His dickness was so far beyond help they decided to amputate.' I think that's— Vayl? Are you . . . laughing? About the serious malady of dickness? Geez, that's pretty insensitive of you, considering you beat it yourself."

I leaned against the wall, savoring the sound of his pleasure. Then I realized I was leaving a red splotch on the tile. "Ick. I really gotta get a shower. And try to get this shirt clean."

"Yes," Vayl said doubtfully as he viewed it through the stains. "It is so . . . charming."

"I like it. Cole gave it to me for my birthday." Oops. All that work to stomp out the doomsdays and one slip of the tongue had relit the fire.

"I missed your birthday."

"Not really," I said. "We had cake."

"Do I remember Kyphas being there?"

I tried to shrug it off. "Yeah."

"Then you did not have a true celebration."

Wow. He really knew me. Which was probably why he decided to stop with the self-torture and focus on more important matters. "I have a present for you."

"You do?"

"Oh, yes."

"Is it here?"

"In fact, it is. Well, it should be. I meant to check if everything had worked out as planned before I—"

"Oh, baby! Okay, okay, this is great!" I realized I was jumping up and down and clapping my hands. And that Vayl really liked the extra bouncing that caused.

I stopped when he said, "I will need to make a call. But you should be able to open it"—he motioned to our general nastiness—"as soon as we have changed."

I rewarded him with another round of bouncing and, since his clothes were ruined anyway, a bone-cracking hug. No, not his, mine. But damn, did my back feel great afterward!

I said, "I have to go. Shower. Dress. Clean up. You too. Fast, okay?" I kissed him, hard, on the lips. "Oh, did I say? I love you."

There was a hint of gold in his emerald eyes when he said, "I do not suppose you would ever have to tell me again. But I am glad to hear the words."

"Great. Okay. I'm outta here!" And I was off to the showers. Because, hey, it was my first birthday with a boyfriend whose idea of fun was to whisk me off to an exotic island for weeks at a time. Who knew what his idea of a great gift would be?

All the way through my shower I tried to guess. Because surprises tend to gut me. And then I'm left standing, or sometimes lying there, looking like a candy-assed fool. So what could it be? He definitely liked the threads, so maybe a whole new wardrobe. Oh! What about another trip? That would be pretty boss. Like maybe sailing around the world. Or backpacking through Alaska.

By the time I'd washed the last spot of blood from myself and my clothes, I'd made up my mind. Unfortunately, due to the surprise nature of the surprise, the decision had fallen into direness. Vayl was about to present me with another piece of jewelry. Probably something along the lines of a five-tier diamond necklace that I could wear, yeah, nowhere. Gack.

I practiced my thankful face in the mirror as I brushed my teeth. It didn't work until I pasted on the Lucille persona. "No, really, Vayl, you shouldn't have." Spit. "Are you kidding? It's gorgeous!" Rinse, swish, and...spit again. How much did safety-deposit boxes cost? And if I hung on to it until E.J. graduated from high school, would it bring enough at auction to put her through college?

I shoved my legs into a pair of olive-green khakis and told myself not to be disappointed. On top went a sleeveless white tee over which I threw a green cotton button-down and my white jacket. Black boots. Grief. Bolo. And the forearm shield. I filled my pockets with extra clips, pasted a smile on my face, and went to knock on Vayl's door.

"Come in, Jasmine."

I'll admit my heart did a happy flip when he said my name. But when I entered the room to find him lounging in the chair by his empty fireplace, reading the note I'd written him while he was throwback Vayl, I nearly left again. His eyes stopped me. They were like liquid copper. The walk past his bed to the chair opposite his felt like a marathon because those eyes never left me. By the time I sat down I was breathless. So I waited for him to talk.

He laid his hand, with the note in it, across my legs. "You must have been furious with me. And yet you wrote me this."

I shook my head. "I don't even think there's a word for how fast Cole had to talk me down. But even in the middle of feeling like my head was going to explode I knew it wasn't your fault. And later, when you saw my picture and you wanted me?" I looked down at the glass-topped table that sat between us. Wanted to grab one of the mints that sat in an elegant little bowl in its center, just to give my hands something to do besides clutch each other as if they'd never feel his fingers lace through mine again. I said, "It helped a lot."

Vayl folded the note and slipped it into the pocket of his black silk shirt. He rose so fast that I had to move my head to keep him in focus. His cane slammed against the tile as he walked to the balcony door and stared through the glass. "What you must think of me."

I watched him. Waited for him to turn around. He just glared into the night, his jaw tight with emotions he couldn't unleash. Unless he wanted more people to die tonight.

This is a big moment, said Granny May from her sewing chair. Her needle moved so furiously it might've been electrified, except clearly it was being powered by her nimble old fingers. *It would be excellent if you could think of something deeply profound and moving to say that will both reassure him and give him something to remember for the rest of his days.* She peered up at me. Shook her head. *Never mind.*

I opened my mouth. What came out was this: "I'm thinking you're a huge tease. Knowing how hard up I am and just hanging that sweet tush of yours out there for me to ogle when you really oughtta be—"

The rest of my sentence was lost in the rush of his return to me.

My chair tipped backward as his body covered mine, but he caught us, and with a growl of laughter that made my toes curl, rolled us away from the hearth before it could cause any lasting damage.

Hard to return every one of his kisses. Hundreds of them, hot and so sweet that I felt tears prick my eyelids as I finally let myself admit how much I'd missed them. I'd thrown my arms around his shoulders when we'd begun to fall. Now I let my hands roam the hard planes of his back, run up his sides and down his thighs, remind me that he was real and here and—

"Mine," I whispered.

"Yes," he murmured, his lips brushing down my bare stomach and back up the curve of my ribs as he pushed my shirt out of his way.

"Always?" I didn't mean to make it a question. Pulling his hips closer as I wrapped my legs around him, I felt him shudder.

His eyes were full of green fire when they met mine. "Until the end of time."

"Then..." I lifted his shirt so I could watch my fingers slide down the length of his broad chest, covered with lovely black curls, to his flat belly with its arrow of soft hair leading my hands where they'd been aching to go for days. When he drew in a breath and then let it out slowly, hissing through his teeth like a sore athlete lowering himself into a hot bath, I nearly shouted with triumph. That I could make a man like Vayl, who had seen and felt everything, drop his head against mine and moan with desire—yes! This was how I wanted to use my time. Loving this man—no, this vampire—eternally.

I whispered, "Would it be okay if I got you a ring?" He went still under my fingers. But I could still feel his skin, hot with excitement, leaning in to my touch. I said, "I have Cirilai. And I hope you know by now what that means to me. But you don't have anything of mine. So, you know, would you—"

"Yes."

He covered my hands with his, lifted them both to his lips, and kissed my fingers, one by one. "How ever did I find you?"

"I was that skinny redhead killing your leftovers."

He chuckled. "Oh. Right." He cupped my face in his hands. I clutched his shoulders as he began to nibble my lower lip. Then every control I'd had to snap on since Vayl had forgotten my name broke. With a groan that shook me head to toe, I rolled over on top of my vampire and reminded him of exactly what we'd been missing.

Chapter Twenty-One

W hen I came back to my senses I was sprawled across the coffee table with guest mints scattered around my head like confetti. My T-shirt was bunched up around my neck, Vayl was wrapped around my torso, and I won't even mention what tangled around my ankles.

"Uh, now that I can breathe again?" I said.

Muffled sound from somewhere near my collarbone. I interpreted it as, "Yoof?"

"I kinda need to move. I think I'm getting goosed by your cane."

"So that is where it went." Low chuckle. Gawd I'd missed that sound! I felt myself bodily lifted from the scene of my latest indiscretion. But, realizing how deeply my dad would disapprove, I decided the guilt could wait, like, forever. Because Vayl was back. In a bold and reckless sorta way.

I began pulling myself together. Realized I had an audience and slowed down. "You're ... watching?"

He'd dressed faster than me. A gift both of guys and vamps, I guess. He was sitting on the edge of the bed, eyeing my wounds, checking out his own. "It has been ... quite a night."

"Yuh-huh. And if we're smart we'll get the hell outta

here before the cops catch up to us and cause a delay we *can't* afford."

He stood, nodding decisively. "Yes, we should go." He hesitated, cocking his head like he'd just thought of something. "Of course, you could open your present first. If you like."

Yikes! Birthday present! Gaudy diamonds! Where are you, Lucille?

Shit!

She didn't want to come out for him. Because it wasn't right. He'd only just gotten back from the 1700s. And after the most incredible moments of passion we'd shared yet, how could I fake anything now?

I said, "Of course. A present would be fabulous."

Oh crap. He can tell I'm not psyched about this. It'll be our first fight since he got back and it's only been, what, an hour? This is going to be some kind of record!

He reached into his pocket and pulled out a black velvet box. It wasn't big enough to hold a massive necklace. Maybe it was just one gigantic stone. Maybe it was earrings. I could probably deal with that.

I opened the box, trying my best to smile.

It was a key.

An unmarked key.

I took it out. Held it up for him to see. "What does it open?" I asked.

He grinned again. I should probably tell him to stop that. If he did it in front of kids there would be screaming.

He picked me up and carried me to the top of the stairs, where he set me down. Grasping his cane in one hand and the rail with the other, he looked at me with—holy crap, was that actual mischief in his sky-blue eyes?—and said, "I will race you to the street."

I bolted down the steps like the riad was on fire. He tried to pass me, but I snagged his arm and yanked him backward. He laughed out loud. "Cheater!" he called as he grasped me around the middle and carried me down to the first landing.

I managed to wrap my legs around his waist and grab his shoulders, so that I did the next flight riding him piggyback. And then I pulled out my secret weapon. I blew in his ear. He stopped. Then came the tongue, right around the rim of his earlobe and, just lightly, into the center. He shivered.

I jumped off and sprinted to the door.

"Vixen!" he called, following so close I could feel his fingers flicking my curls.

"All's fair in love and birthday pres—" I skidded to a stop. Clapped both hands to my mouth, which did nothing to keep the tears from leaping into my eyes. "Vayl," I whispered. "How..."

He leaned around to look into my face. He must've liked what he saw, because again with those fearsome fangs. A couple of pedestrians shrieked and bolted. I hardly noticed them. I felt like I'd hurtled into a dream.

He stepped to the curb and ran his hand along the hood of the gleaming black car that had not been parked there when we'd walked into the riad half an hour before. He said, "It is a—"

I interrupted him, "1963 Ford Galaxie 500XL Convertible 406 CID 385 horsepower with a V8."

Vayl nodded. "It also has a four-speed manual transmission."

I blinked. I might've been crying by now. But I really didn't care. "It's just like the one Granny May used to have. She drove us to church in it. To the store. Everywhere."

Vayl waited until I'd torn my eyes from the beauty on the street to look at him again before he said, "It *is* the one your grandmother used to drive."

I lost it. Right then and there, I just, well, I kind of hate to say this, but I sat down on my ass and bawled on the sidewalk in Marrakech, Morocco. During which time I had to assure Vayl this was a good thing. And also during which he had to explain to me how Gramps Lew had sold the car to a neighbor of theirs, a farmer who'd always meant to restore it but never had. So it had stayed in the old guy's barn until his son had opened his front door to find Vayl there with a shitload of cash in his hand and a trailer hooked to his rental truck.

When I finally pulled myself together I said, "But, Vayl, she's mint. I mean, I don't see any rust. The interior is the same shiny red I remember. If I pop the hood—"

"It will sparkle," he assured me.

I shook my head. "That kind of work takes time. A lot more than we've been a couple."

He had sat down on the sidewalk beside me, laying his arms across his upraised knees in that way he has of making himself comfortable in any position. Now he looked at the classic parked on the street and admitted, "I bought it soon after we met. I...had hoped someday I might have this chance."

I pointed to the Galaxie. "You can't possibly have felt like that for me then!"

He turned to gaze into my eyes, laying his chin on my shoulder as he said softly, "I have loved you with everything in me from the moment I saw you."

I wrapped my arm around his leg, carefully avoiding his wound. "Damn," I whispered.

He leaned forward, his lips like the breath of life itself, bringing my soul back into the dance every time they touched mine. He took his time, his tongue brushing against mine so gently it was like a second declaration. When he pulled back he said, "Every moment with you has been a revelation. I would not trade a second. Come, my *pretera*." His eyes glittered as my inner girls screamed ecstatically while they threw paper airplanes at each other to celebrate hearing him call me Yaz-mee-na and his little wildcat both in the same day.

I managed a breathless, "Yeah?"

He said, "Let us gather the crew. It is time to *ride*."

Morocco's medina is full of streets so narrow sometimes you're lucky to get a couple of donkey carts past each other. But the new city is full of wide, well-lit boulevards just made for a bunch of cruising assassins. I drove my Granny's car with the top down and the radio blasting, my hair flying out behind me like a kid's kite.

It was fucking awesome.

Vayl sat beside me, never taking his eyes off my face, his lips stuck in that semi-smile that let me know he was perfectly satisfied with the world and everything in it. If we had been living a movie, that's where it would've ended. Happily ever after, baby. Which, of course, is why it lasted less than fifteen minutes.

We pulled up just down the street from the Musee de Marrakech and just sat, listening to the engine purr.

"I can't believe you did this for me," I said, rubbing the steering wheel like it was the soft fur of my malamute.

Sometime during our drive he'd dropped his arm behind my back. Now he touched my neck with his fingertips, sending shivers up and down my spine as he slid closer to me. Though he couldn't hypnotize me, I felt captivated by the facets in his glittering emerald eyes as they caught mine and said exactly what my heart needed to hear.

"We will take it with us everywhere," he said. "No more shabby rentals." He smirked. "No more mopeds."

"I liked those mopeds," Cole objected from the backseat. He sat next to Raoul, who rubbed elbows with Sterling, who'd slid down so he could let his head fall back and stare up into the star-studded sky.

Sterling rolled his head to gaze on Cole. "Somehow I saw you more as a Camaro kind of guy. But whatever pops your clutch. I guess you liked your runaway demon too?"

Raoul huffed, like he found that impossible to believe.

Cole drummed his fingers on the armrest. At least he remembered not to drop Kyphas's name—and therefore give her a clue as to our whereabouts—when he said, "She had her good points. Somewhere deep...deep at her core. Anyway, I'm still willing to give her the benefit of the doubt."

"Oh. So that's why she fell for Vayl's trap like a catfish jonesing for chicken liver?" I asked.

He shrugged. "It was pretty juicily baited." When we all made sounds of doubt he added, "Come on. What demon isn't going to try for the Enkyklios map on her own when you dangle the exact location in front of her like that?"

"*We* didn't, the Luureken did," I reminded him. "She was just conceited enough to think *we* were dumb enough to believe nobody but us good guys would act on it."

"She did steal the cat," Raoul reminded him, like that should be his last straw.

"You're really fixated on the robokitty, you know that?" Cole told him.

I wouldn't have thought it possible, but Raoul straightened even more as he said, "Astral sang to me after Nia left. The perfect song, in fact. I don't think she's fully mechanical. She seems to have... insight."

Since I knew the guys wanted to know but would never ask, I did. "What tune did she pick out for you?"

"She sang 'Always Look on the Bright Side of Life,' from the musical *Spamalot*," Raoul said.

Cole immediately launched into song, with the rest of us providing the whistling where appropriate. "Always look on the bright side of life. Always look on the right side of life."

"It's not funny," said Raoul.

"I believe it is supposed to be," Vayl informed him helpfully.

He sat back and crossed his arms.

Cole scooted forward. "Our demon's taking her sweet time in there. Do you think she's onto us? Maybe she snuck out the back."

"Nope."

"How can you be so sure?"

"Astral's sending me pictures." I turned in my seat, fluttering the fake lashes that received Astral's signals. On top of Cole's slumped form I could see the superimposed image of Kyphas as viewed from the ground up, sneaking through the museum. Just watching her face hover over Cole's made me want to swear. Instead I said, "I can't believe you even flirted with her, much less... She's such a *skank*!"

He never took his eyes off the museum's entrance. "Absolutely. A skank with evil intentions and a shiny gold nugget at the center of her pitch-black heart."

I made gagging sounds while Raoul said, "Share with the other children, Jaz. What's Astral showing you?"

I rolled my eyes at Sterling, who said, "You might as well give us some narration. Otherwise we're just going to start punching each other back here. And you know what that will lead to."

Gawd. With a warlock, an Eldhayr, and an assassin squished into the backseat, everything I imagined went from bad to nuclear. I started talking.

"It's just what you'd expect. Boring little trek through the touristy part of the museum. Human-formed Weres in front, demon following. They're passing priceless paintings and cases full of old crap." I glanced at Vayl. "No offense. I know that stuff must be more meaningful to you than it is to me—"

He shrugged. "Considering where I have been living the past few days, I find I much prefer the present."

"How do you figure she got the Weres to cooperate?" Cole wondered.

Raoul raised an eyebrow. "She's a demon. Just because you people are immune to her powers doesn't mean they're not vast."

Vayl shifted in his seat. Like he was uncomfortable. Which he never is.

I said, "What is it?"

"If Roldan has truly given himself to a Gorgon, and I believe that he has, Kyphas could easily have wormed her way into the deal using that connection. Spawn stick together. That is their first rule."

"But she has a deal with us. What about that?"

"She is a demon. They are masters at playing both sides to their advantage."

"Well, she's got these guys believing they're on her team." I looked back at the scene Astral was beaming to me. "Now they're in a storeroom on the first floor. It's the size of a comfy office. There's a vertical shelf, no, make that three shelves running down its center. I thought it was one because they were all pushed together, but it looks like they run on ceiling and floor tracks like the ones you find in college libraries. The lead Were, who looks a lot like Chris Rock, has separated the shelves. One other Were, who looks slick enough to sell cars for a living, and two stringy-haired Luureken are just standing by the edge of the shelves, waiting."

"Does it seem like they have any idea where to look for the map?" asked Cole.

"Yup. The Chris Rock look-alike has gone straight to the middle shelf. He's being careful not to disturb anything else while he shuffles through some leather scrolls. He's not unwrapping them. Just shining a light on one corner." I took a breath to acknowledge the doubling of my heartbeat and the sudden stinging behind one eye. "He's found it."

The atmosphere inside the Galaxie went from restless and slightly bored to tense and electric. Game faces fell into place. I went on, feeling the anticipation build in the pit of my stomach as I watched the Were hold the map to my salvation over his head.

I said, "Our demon is snarling like she's never heard of wrinkles. She's crouching by the door. She's transforming her *tahruyt* into the flyssa. But it's different. It's... The blade is glowing red. I think whoever's on the receiving end of that swing is going to get cut *and* burned."

"Have the Weres realized her plan yet?" asked Vayl.

I shook my head. "They're partying. So psyched to have the treasure in their hands and be done with guard duty they've forgotten she's there." I turned my eyes to Cole. "I wish you could see her now. It's her eyes. They're so... hungry. And happy."

"Hungry people are never happy," Cole told me.

"There's your basic mistake," Raoul pointed out. "Because she's not 'people' at all."

I said, "She's creeping up on the car salesman. Holy crap, that sword's just as sharp as my bolo!"

"What has she done?" Vayl asked.

"Decapitation," I said, trying to keep my voice level and dry. "One, two, just like that, and he's dead. The second Were is morphing. The Luureken are shrieking. Pulling out their weapons. Naw."

"What?" Sterling demanded.

"The lead berserker is trying to use his raes. That's just stupid. It's a cavalry weapon, you know?"

"O-kay. And who's side are you on?"

"I'm just saying, the demon's gonna—yup, there she goes. She's whipped that sword of hers around so fast he barely has time to block, much less pull off an aggressive move. But the Luureken behind him has a hand axe and she's screaming like a trophy wife who's just found hubby with her replacement. Oooh."

"What?" Barbershop chorus from the four listening guys.

"Axe blade in the demon's chest. She's screaming even louder than her attacker. Damned if she doesn't remind me of Black-beard's wives at the JayCees Haunted House in Granny May's hometown."

Cole leaned forward. "We gotta go there next Halloween."

"Sure."

If we're still around.

I said, "I'm thinking the Luureken shouldn't have buried that axe so deep. Now she's got no weapon and the demon is coming back at her with that flaming flyssa."

"What exactly do you mean by flaming?" asked Raoul, the pro-fessional curiosity in his voice telling me he was trying to figure out if he had the right weapons to combat it should he ever need to.

"When we met her in Australia and she turned her hat into a boomerang, it burned bluish orange. Which I thought was a reac-tion to the prayers we'd protected all the entrances with. This is more like a cherry red that seems hot and..." I swallowed involun-tarily as I watched the sword sing through the air, the flames leap-ing toward the Luureken's throat. "Yeah, starving would be the word I'm looking for." They licked into her neck just before the sword sliced into her skin. And then, as quickly as she cut the life out of the Luureken, Kyphas met the leader's charge. Now fully transformed, its lean form giving it fearsome speed, it still couldn't match the demon's reflexes.

She stood, unblinking, in the face of its heart-stopping growls. Let it see how easily it could tear her throat out. And then, as it leaped, moved with eye-blurring speed. Shoved its head to one side. Chopped into the vulnerable opening she'd made, then stepped forward as his body and half-severed head went crashing into the floor. She grabbed the map before it—or she—could be drenched in arterial spray, turned back, and finished the job.

I told the guys, "I don't think we're going to be battling any more Weres this trip. And I hope whoever cleans the storeroom at the Musee de Marrakech skips breakfast tomorrow."

Astral took one last look at the bodies lying sprawled and lifeless on the floor, their blood crawling toward Kyphas as if begging her to put it back, make the last moments please, please go away. And then, like she knew my wishes, the robokitty looked up into Kyphas's face. Since I'd stopped talking, I could at least admit to myself that her beauty still had the power to stun me, even from a distance. But it seemed different now than it had the first time I'd seen her, stalking Cassandra down the streets of Wirdilling, destroying everyone and everything in her path.

In Australia she'd had the perfection of an ice sculpture. Nice to look at, but you knew you'd better keep your distance unless you wanted freezer burn. Now she seemed to have the ancient sadness of one of Lucifer's groupies. *She never Fell*, my Inner Librarian corrected me, giving her bun a twitch to keep a stray curl from running amok. *Kyphas was born in hell. That makes her spawn, not angel.*

Now you're just playing with semantics, I told her. *Spawn are the children of fallen angels.*

And other things! noted the Librarian.

I'll give you that. Sometimes. I couldn't take my eyes off Kyphas's face, almost grieving as she absorbed the information on the map she'd unrolled. *But maybe Cole was right about her after all.* Now wasn't the time for theorizing though. I whispered, "Astral. Copy that map."

The cat set her recorders to key to the Enkyklios map. I felt my chest tighten as I realized I was about to find out where the Rocenz was located. When my shoulders slumped Vayl said, "What is wrong?"

"The map. It's just a bunch of colored circles surrounded by rectangles. There's some writing I can't see at the top and bottom of the map. But no X to mark the spot where the tool is hidden."

He said, "Then we will take the demoness and the map as

soon as she exits the building." Vayl's tone didn't change, which, of course, it wouldn't. He took shit like this in stride. I guess after overcoming a million or so setbacks you learn how to keep on keeping on. But damn, you've gotta live a long time to get to that place.

Chapter Twenty-Two

We were waiting on the steps of the palace when Kyphas emerged, holding Astral in one hand and the map in the other. She looked only mildly surprised to see us. This, I was discovering, was the drawback of working with old souls. They'd seen so much they were tough to startle.

Vayl held out his hand. "Give me the map, Kyphas."

She hugged it closer to her chest. "I don't think so."

"Remember your contract? You vowed to help us find the Rocenz."

She nodded exactly one time. "I did." Her eyes never wavered from Vayl, but she seemed to tighten, as if some invisible machine had surrounded her with shrink-wrap. I'd already drawn Grief. Now I aimed the barrel right between her eyes.

"You also promised to fight with us," he reminded her.

"The fighting's over," she said. She jerked her head back toward the museum. "I've killed the rest of your enemies."

She may be right, said Granny May, who'd put aside her sewing to set up another game of bridge.

Who's side are you on anyway? And does Winston Churchill really need that big a bowl of Doritos?

Cole had also drawn. But his Beretta remained pointed at the ground as he said, "Kyphas. I thought we were…friends. What the hell?"

"Exactly," she replied. When she looked at him, the longing in her eyes actually churned up some sympathy from somewhere deep inside me. She tore her gaze away from him and pinned it back on Vayl. "Here's your map." She launched Astral, not at him, but at me, fouling my shot as she threw herself behind a huge white pillar.

I dropped my arm and stepped out of the way as robokitty came flying through the air like a claw-laced torpedo. She landed on her paws on the street beside me with the harsh clunk of granite hitting brick. I checked her out, relieved to find her in one piece, but pissed off as well. Now, by handing Astral back, Kyphas had kept her end of the deal. As far as she was concerned our contract was complete.

"Raoul!" I yelled. "Tell me you brought your sword!" He couldn't kill her with it here, of course. But if we could get her through one of the fire-framed plane portals, then the sword would destroy her. I knew one had to be close. They tended to follow me, though neither one of us had figured out why.

Raoul gave his cap a frustrated jerk. "I just came from the worst date of my life. Why would I bring a weapon along?"

Cole and I both said, "People do it all the time!"

We looked at each other. Cole slapped his hand against his chest. "Not me, though. I'm just saying, there was this girl once who got really pissed and—"

"I'd never suggest something like that about you," I assured him. Then I realized all the guys were staring at me with that slightly stressed look that suggested they suddenly weren't quite sure they were safe. "Aw, come on! Really?"

Still keeping an eye on Kyphas, who'd emerged from hiding when we stopped trying to splat her, Cole slid over and patted me on the shoulder. "Forgive us, Jaz. You're right, it's silly to think you'd ever *shoot* an ex when you already know twelve ways to kill him with your bare hands."

"More like thirty, but that's okay. I think."

Vayl stepped forward. "Kyphas, come with us. Whoever called you to recover the map, whatever deal you have made with them cannot technically supersede our contract. You could still be our ally. We would even offer you more if you cared to take it."

"Like what?" she asked.

"Bergman is starting a new business that could use people with exactly your sorts of skills. Jasmine and I are considering becoming his partners. If, as time passed, we all seemed agreeable to the notion, you might even consider joining our Trust."

Like hell! I nearly squeezed the trigger just to prove how opposed I was to his last statement. But Vayl had given me the signal for play-along-with-me-on-this-one, two crossed fingers tapping the hip. So I dropped my gun arm, giving it the rest it needed while I waited for the demon's reply. Her expression surprised me. Was she really considering his offer? And that yearning glance toward Cole. I wasn't imagining the wish in her eyes, was I? Hard to say when seconds later they were filled with yellow fire.

"Our deal is finished, vampire. And as soon as I have the Rocenz, *your* people will be joining *me*." I wouldn't have put it past her to belt out a cheesy cartoon-villain laugh because, really, lines like that belonged in dinner theaters. But she didn't take the time. Instead she dove behind a second pillar. This one was so big you could park an entire camel behind it.

I took off after her, Vayl already five steps ahead, Raoul right behind him, Cole at my heels, and Sterling loping easily at the back. If we'd been on wheels there would've been a lot of screeching and honking of horns as we came to abrupt halts at the top of the steps. Because she wasn't there. I mean, not anywhere we could even chase her. What we did find hidden behind the pillar was a plane portal, still open to her destination.

We stared into the pit, each of us seeing our own version of hell's torturous landscape. Mine was pretty much the same as the last time I'd seen it, when Raoul and I had taken a trip there to get the goods on Edward "The Raptor" Samos. I saw a flaming sky covering an eternity of rock-strewn ground peopled by an endless crowd of shambling, self-abusing citizens. Even though I knew what to expect I still wanted to puke. I peeked at Raoul from under my eyelashes, knowing his view was no better. It made me feel tons less wussified to see that the POW camp in his vision still turned his skin slightly green. He said a few quiet words and the door went as blank as his eyes.

I took his arm and pulled him aside. "Raoul, is that how you died?" I whispered, jerking my head back toward the door. "Because I can still try to make it right for you. The sons of bitches who captured you are probably still alive. I could—"

He shook his head. "It wasn't me. Maybe it should've been." He looked bleakly at the door. "But it wasn't." And that was all he'd say.

We both stood staring at his shiny black boots, until Cole's steady swearing sank into our brains.

I said, "Cole, you're offending Vayl. Plus you never swear, so you're probably upsetting yourself at some level."

"That's just dumb. Plus, Vayl? Am I?"

"I simply believe other words are more effective," Vayl said dryly.

"Like what?" Cole demanded, throwing his hands into the air. Luckily, he'd holstered his gun, otherwise we'd have all been ducking at random moments while he gestured wildly to match his mood. "Oh, phooey, the demon has absconded with our map! Shuckey darn, she's so irritating, because I *fucking* thought she had some *fucking* good in her!"

"Cole?" I went over to put my hand against his forehead. Nope, pretty cool despite our recent run.

"I'm not sick!" he bellowed.

I dropped my hand. "You're betrayed."

"Yeah!"

"By a demon."

"Well, yeah!"

"Who's been lying, cheating, and stealing since the day she was born."

He took a second to check his nails. "She's a pro, isn't she?"

"Um, yeah. The miracle is that Cassandra ducked her for so long." I turned to Vayl. "So what does this mean? Is our psychic off the hook, or what?"

"I believe so," he said. "The demon obviously feels she has fulfilled her end of the bargain, which means Cassandra's soul should be safe."

"I don't like that word 'should.' We need to be one hundred percent on this one."

"There's a test she can do," Sterling said. He sat in the middle of the doorway, his legs in the lotus position, his palms lifted upward above his shoulders like he was checking for rain.

"What are you doing?" I demanded.

"Absorbing the power inherent in this doorway. It's great. Kind of like lying on a magic-fingers bed, only this gets you everywhere." He wiggled his eyebrows at me. "And I mean everywhere, Chill. You should try it."

I yanked my hair over my eyes. "I am surrounded by perverts." I crouched down in front of my warlock. "Sterling. What about the test? Do you think she knows which one you mean?"

"Maybe. She's pretty well-read, right?"

"Maybe? Should? You guys are driving me nuts!" I pulled my phone out of my pocket and tossed it to the warlock. "Call her. Tell her what it is. Tell her I said to do it now. And if she comes up with a bad result, I want to know instantly. Because I will go straight into hell after that bitch and tear her head off her shoulders if that's what it takes to make Cassandra safe."

Sterling gazed up at me. "I'm glad we made up."

"Me too. Now make the call." Only when he opened my phone did I turn to Vayl. He'd picked up Astral and was giving her such a close once-over he could've been mistaken for a vet. "What do you think?" I asked.

"She does not seem to have been tampered with," Vayl said. "Though, of course, Bergman is the only one who can tell us for sure."

"So you think the map in her head..."

He nodded. "It is the one she recorded from Kyphas's hand."

"We're not being very careful about the demon's name now," Cole snapped. "Don't we care if she can spy on us anymore?"

"No," Vayl and I chorused. "Later for sure," I added. "But right now she's so busy trying to get her ducks in a row she doesn't have time to worry about us."

"Would you care to describe her ducks?" Raoul asked.

"We figure she's organizing a raiding party to help her retrieve the Rocenz before we can get to it," I said.

"Yes," Vayl agreed. "But remember, since no demon has the power to move from its world to ours at will, she and her people must be summoned for another purpose as well. That gives us at least some time to find the Rocenz before she does."

"And you're sure the location is locked inside Astral's mind?" Raoul asked.

"Absolutely," I said. "We just need to get her somewhere safe so we can pull a copy out of her and figure out how to interpret it."

"Somewhere safe...are you talking about the riad?" Cole asked.

"That is where we left the equipment," Vayl said.

I held up a finger. "Except Bergman knows how to work it better than anyone else. Especially when it comes to Astral. He was only just starting to train me. This would go a lot faster if we had him on board."

"Are you certain?" Vayl asked, his eyebrows at full lift. "He is recuperating, after all."

"What a nice way to say he's newly stitched and out of his mind on painkillers," said Cole.

"Even bandaged and half-blitzed, Bergman's still better than any four regular people. What do you say?" I asked the guys. "Should we go break him out of the hospital?"

Vayl smirked. "While I enjoy your sense of the dramatic, I think all that is required is the proper paperwork. This should only take a few minutes."

Half an hour later Monique was wheeling Bergman out the front door while he bounced the IT'S A GIRL balloon we'd tied to his wrist and giggled hysterically at the balled-up towel we'd stuffed under his sweater to signify still-to-be-lost baby weight. We hadn't even had to bother with makeup. Just wrapped his head in my new black scarf and shoved Astral wrapped in a blanket into his free arm.

I leaned over so Bergman could see my face as I said, "Miles, most moms don't squish their babies so hard that they squeak. Relax your hold. No, don't cover her whole face with your hand. Pretend she has to breathe, okay?"

God? This guy doesn't need kids anytime soon. Or even a fish. I'll get him a stuffed animal next time I'm home. We'll see how that goes and then I'll be in touch.

"This rocks!" he said in a stage whisper as Cole pushed him toward the Galaxie.

"I can't believe you need Miles this desperately," Monique said again, more doubtfully than ever.

"Earthquakes are no laughing matter," Cole told her gravely. "Only he can tell us if the data we've picked up points to a big one."

I jumped in. "Would you like somebody to ride back to the riad with you, Monique? Maybe Sterling? Or"—I pulled Raoul up beside me so she could get an eyeful of the muscular chest and thighs even his camo couldn't hide—"my friend Raoul could ride with you. He's very protective. Better than a bodyguard."

Nothing. Her glance skittered off him like he was holding a mirror and went straight back to Bergman. "Thank you, no," she said. "I drove Miles by myself, and I can get back the same way." She leaned over him as we reached the car, giving him such a great view of her cleavage that he settled back in the chair like he was in it for the long haul. "You will be all right?" she asked, her voice dropping into that velvet purr only French women can seem to pull off.

He grinned, his eyes rising to her lips as he licked his own. "You should probably ask me in the morning," he said.

"All right, then, I will." She kissed her fingertips, laid them on his cheek, and then went off to find her car. The guys watched her go. All except Vayl, who was unlocking the doors and pulling a blanket out of the trunk so we could make Miles comfortable.

As we began to help him into the car Bergman looked up at me and said, "That woman is after my body."

"Yes," I agreed as Olivia Newton-John's voice suddenly hooted out of Astral's mouth. While she sang, "Let's get physical, physical," he looked down at himself in utter bafflement.

"Do you have any idea why?" he asked.

I eased his feet inside the car and said, "As far as she's concerned you're the total package. Twenty years younger, skinny enough to relish good food, with one of the finest minds on earth. Just, uh"— I motioned to his side, which was so heavily bandaged it looked like he was hiding a bomb under his shirt—"don't let her hurt you, okay?"

"Okay."

I slid in beside him and Astral jumped into the back with Sterling, Raoul, and Cole. We'd put the top up, which meant Bergman's balloon kept knocking everybody in the head but him. In fact, "Where's my balloon?" he demanded as soon as Vayl slid the Galaxie into the street. We'd agreed he should drive so I could look after the patient. Who was starting to panic. "My balloon disappeared!"

"It's on your wrist!" I held his hand up to his face. Just barely thought better of slapping him with it.

"Oh."

Silence. Not just golden. Jewel-encrusted and brimming with stardust. Vayl drove while the rest of us zipped it. We didn't even move for fear we'd set Bergman off and make him undo all the work the doctor had put in on him. The tension had just begun to seep out of my toes and fingertips when Bergman said, "Jaz!"

"What?"

"I am so horny!"

I dropped my forehead into my hand as Cole and Sterling broke into laughter. Maybe even Raoul added a chuckle or two, though I couldn't tell because the other two were honking so loud.

Bergman asked, "Do you know how long it's been since I've been with a woman?"

"I don't—"

"Five years! And then I had to pay for it. Which is so humiliating. Although I really shelled out the cash so she was supergreat. Like Cleopatra. Only not dead." He turned completely around to face me, a feat only somebody as heavily drugged as he was could accomplish, considering he was both injured and seat belted. If we crashed he'd probably shoot straight out the top of the thing and smash into the roof. But no way would I worry about him now because he wasn't even close to done grossing me out. In fact, he was asking me earnestly, "Is it so wrong to want a woman I don't have to become a criminal to make love to?"

I shook my head, wishing I was anywhere but here. Yes, even chasing Kyphas through hell would've been a more attractive option.

What are the chances that he'll totally blank on this conversation in the morning? "That's reasonable," I said.

Bergman had clearly thought this out. He pointed to me, which made me gulp loudly, but he said, "Monique would be nice."

"Okay."

"Except she scares the shit out of me."

"Also reasonable."

"She's very experienced."

"And that's a problem for you?"

"Yup. I've done a lot of reading. But, uh, theory is not at all like practice in these cases. I don't think."

"I see. So what do you want to do?"

"I have no idea."

Silence. This time not even close to a precious metal.

Cole leaned forward, began to rub Bergman's shoulders like he was getting ready for a big boxing match. "So, uh"—he stopped to clear the laughter out of his voice—"you want some advice from somebody who's been there, buddy?"

Of course he's been there. This was my Inner Bimbo, sizing Cole up like he was a big old cheesecake and she hadn't had dessert in a year. Then her eyes strayed to Vayl. *Hmm, I wonder if . . .*

Shut up. This is about Miles. Getting with a cougar. Oh crap, I'm imagining it now. I think I'm gonna puke.

Bergman said, "Yeah, okay. What do I need to know?"

"You think too much," said Cole.

Sterling spoke up. "Waaay too much is my guess."

I looked over my shoulder in time to catch Cole winking at the warlock and nodding.

"Just relax and see what happens, all right?"

"Okay."

"Great! Now that Bergman's love life is back on track can we talk about Astral?" I asked.

"What about Astral?" Bergman frowned, picking up first one foot, then the other, like he thought he might find her flattened form underneath one of them. "Here, kitty!"

"No!" I pointed back at the cat, who'd taken her favorite spot on the ledge beneath the back window. "You stay right there, missy." Thankfully she was programmed to obey my voice above all others, so all she did was flick her tail and half close her eyes at me, as if to say, "I'm too comfortable to move anyway."

I leaned forward so I could catch Vayl's eye. *Okay, I'm about to give the tech-head here another reason to be in the hospital. Are you sure this is going to be worth it?* I asked him silently. He gave me a short nod.

So I told Miles what had happened in the smallest words I could manage. I ended with, "We need to get that map out of Astral. Your equipment—"

"Should do the job," Miles said, suddenly, remarkably, business-like. "How far are we from the riad?"

"Perhaps ten minutes," Vayl said.

"I think I'll catch a nap then. I should try to be as alert as possible when it's time to do the transfer." And he promptly passed out.

I watched him slide about five inches down the seat until the belt finally caught him just below the armpits. "Wow. He is so weird."

"Yes." Vayl patted him on the head. "I am finally beginning to see why you like him."

Chapter Twenty-Three

With only an hour until dawn and Kyphas an entire printed map ahead of us, we couldn't waste a second babying our wounded, morphine-dazed comrade. That's what I told myself, using Albert's stern, no-arguments bark to make my point as I watched Vayl carry him upstairs to his equipment-packed room. But as soon as Bergman sat back in the orange cushioned chair he'd drawn up to the desk he'd transformed into computer central in the seating area of his suite, I checked his bandages. No blood had seeped through, so I felt sure the stitches had held.

"You're the best friend a guy ever had, you know that, Jaz?" Miles said, beaming up at me.

"Yup. You want some water or something?"

"Not around all these electronics. How about a root beer?"

I turned away so he wouldn't see me smile. "I'll see what I can do. Astral? Get your butt up on the desk. Bergman needs to do some work on you."

The cat leaped up as ordered, landing lightly between two monitors, and then ruining the effect by sitting squarely on a keyboard, making Bergman say something like, "Gah!"

I moved to grab her but Vayl was quicker. He murmured, "Raoul needs to speak to you."

My Spirit Guide hadn't ever fully come into the room. He stood outside the door, a party guest who'd realized he couldn't stay after all. I joined him in the hall.

"I have to go," he said.

"But...this is *it*."

"I understand. However, you don't need me for it. And I've been called away."

I realized I might be dangerously close to pouting and pulled my face as close to neutral as I could manage. "Oh."

Raoul reached out, like he meant to lay his hand on my shoulder. But he wasn't that type. If I'd been feeling nasty I'd have told him Nia probably sensed that and that's why she'd preferred the cat to him. Then he said, "Others like you are in this fight as well. They rarely use your colorful language when they call, but they do occasionally ask for my assistance."

His smile reminded me that one of those was my twin, so maybe it would be good if I stepped back, took a look at the big picture, and stopped being so damn selfish every once in a while. "Oh! Well, yeah, then you have to go."

"Wait!" Bergman tried to get up, winced in pain, and let Vayl haul him to his feet. "Raoul. Before you leave, I have to ask you something." He hobbled to the door, holding his side like he thought the support might help him move a little faster. When he got there, he looked at me for a full five seconds before I got the message that I wasn't welcome in the conversation.

I said, "Uh, yeah, well, see you later, Raoul. Uh, Sterling's probably got questions about this whole mission that I still haven't had time to answer."

Just before I could turn away Raoul grabbed me and gave me a lung-squishing hug. "Good luck," he whispered. "If anyone can crush Brude forever, I know it's you."

When he let me go I staggered a little, not so much because I was off balance, but because he'd known, probably all along, that

I'd been fighting the Domytr's possession. And he'd let me deal with it the way I wanted. He hadn't pushed, ordered, or manipulated. He'd just...been there. I swallowed.

"Thanks." I nodded, blinking so the damn tears that kept surfacing when I least wanted them to would get the hell out of my way. Then I went to talk to the warlock. And by God, if he made me want to cry, I was going to grab his wand and wave it around until I was surrounded by toads and lizards. Because that's one thing you can count on with reptiles. They're just not into tender moments.

Bergman found just enough lucid brain cells to connect Astral to a computer, access her latest entry, and print the map. While he typed short phrases into the computer and poked green and yellow buttons on his multi-machine, which, at the moment, was acting as a printer, we took turns making sure he stayed conscious and ducking out to arm ourselves for demon fighting. Hopefully we'd beat Kyphas to the Rocenz and be long gone before she ever showed up. But we hadn't survived this long crossing our fingers and scrunching our eyes shut.

When we'd first encountered the demon in Australia, only Cassandra had been carrying the kind of double-bladed weapon that can easily slice hellspawn's hide. And none of us owned anything that could cause permanent damage. Raoul had raided his own supply to provide us with swords that had been forged by demon-fighters from way back. These are the folks you want smithing your steel when regular weapons take twice as long to cause even a minor injury. Raoul had built himself up quite a collection, and I still couldn't quite believe he'd shared it with us, telling us we could keep the blades until our deal with Kyphas was done. Well, she might be finished with us, but we weren't sure we felt the same.

So each of us took a run to our rooms and belted on the gear Raoul had loaned us. Cole's blade, long and heavy as a shovel, still sparkled like raindrops on a lake when he swung it. His strangely flexible shield fit snugly over one shoulder until he needed to bring it into action.

Vayl's cane-sword had evidently been crafted by a true master, because it damaged demon and wielder alike.

My blade, which rode in a sheath at my back, felt like it had been custom-made for me, it carried so light and swung so smooth. That didn't make it any less lethal. Maybe I'd have the chance to prove that tonight.

When I got back to Bergman's lair, he'd finished translating some writing on the map that had stumped Cole, despite his extensive knowledge of languages.

"This cat's amazing, you know that?" he asked me as I settled down on one of his cushy red chairs while Astral gave us both her inscrutable stare from the middle of his coffee table. It struck me then that she might be a frustrated centerpiece. But I was distracted from the thought when he shoved a copy of the map into my hands. "Look what she came up with."

I nodded over the paper, which had English written in place of the words we hadn't been able to translate before. The paragraph at the top of the page read:

Cursed and thrice cursed be ye who raise the Rocenz without offering proper dues or sacrifice. For Cryrise's hammer and Frempreyn's chisel may spell your salvation, or your doom.

I found it harder to understand the words at the bottom:

Who holds the hammer still must find the keys to the triple-locked door.

"Wow, aren't we all creepy and cryptic," Cole said when Vayl had read out the entire translation.

Bergman slumped farther down in his chair. "This is ridiculous," he said, his words beginning to slur as his fight to stay awake began to fail. "Hammers? Chisels? And now keys? Ya know, whoever made this map doesn't know squat about real treasure." He shook his finger in the air, like he was lecturing a bunch of unruly fourth graders. "Diamonds, man! Silver crowns embedded with rubies the size of my fist! That's what we're supposed to be searching for!" He'd raised his hand to emphasize the point. Now he dropped it, plop, in his lap, like it weighed too much to bother with anymore. "I'm tired."

"Why don't you go to bed, Miles? We've got it from here," I said.

Without waiting for his reply, Vayl picked him up and moved him to the bed, not even bothering to turn down the shimmering green spread before laying him gently on it. Bergman struggled to his elbows. "Where's Astral? Jaz? Can Astral stay and, you know, keep me company?"

"Of course." I gave the cat her order and she trotted over to Miles, who was already snoring. After patting his face experimentally with one paw, she decided he wasn't going to issue any commands in the near future, and curled up under his chin.

I looked back at the guys, who were sitting on Bergman's sofa, poring over the map.

"So does anybody know what all these colored squares and circles are supposed to represent?" asked Cole.

"Maybe it's like a code," said Sterling. "One color, or one sequence of colors, actually means a word."

Cole stared at them for a while. "I don't see a pattern."

"Maybe it's an actual map of someplace," I suggested. They looked up at me.

"Where?" asked Sterling. "There's no reference to it. There's not even a key on the map to tell you which square or circle is which landmark."

I held up my hand. "I know how we can find out."

I skipped downstairs and out the front door. "Yousef? I hope you're not dragging poor Kamal along with you, because at four twenty in the morning I'd really think you were a lowlife." I waited. "Yousef! Get out of the damn bushes!"

Yousef stepped out from behind the thick growth of palm trees the original owner had planted at the front corner of Riad Almoravid. Sucker didn't even have the decency to look embarrassed.

I grabbed his hand. "Come on."

He wouldn't budge. Just stood there staring stupidly into my face, like he'd just heard the world was about to end. I slapped him and he came alive, his eyes sparkling as he spoke rapidly. I looked around for Kamal, but the kid had finally found the backbone to send his friend out solo. So I beckoned for Yousef to follow me into the riad, which he did so eagerly I almost felt guilty. Until I reminded myself exactly what he was hoping to find on the other side of my bedroom door.

We trotted up to Bergman's. "This is Yousef," I said, yanking my hand out of his once I'd finally gotten him through the door. "He's my stalker. Yousef? These are my friends. Cole, could you translate?"

Cole stood up, speaking quickly so our newest party guest wouldn't run off before we could take advantage of his native knowledge. When it seemed like he'd run out of words I said, "Tell him we want to show him a picture and I want to know where in the city he thinks it's located. Tell him I'd be very grateful if he'd think hard about what it could be before he says anything."

I nodded to Sterling, who handed Yousef the map. He glanced so casually at the writing that I decided he couldn't read it. But the drawing he seemed to recognize right away, because he began speaking almost immediately.

"Of course!" Cole translated. "This is the tannery! It has been here for centuries! You should come see. I will give you a tour." He slapped himself on the chest proudly. "I give the skins second life."

Big *aha!* moment when I suddenly realized why Yousef and Kamal had smelled so rank and looked so—mustardy—the first time Cole and I had run into them. And why they'd been holding bath supplies. When you work at a place that makes you wish for a gas mask, you're definitely going to hit the hammam after work so you can dip yourself in scented soap and aftershave.

As Yousef chattered Cole explained. "Tanning is not just turning hides into leather for them. It's mystical, watching the skin of a dead creature be reborn under their hands. These guys are also considered lords of fertility so, uh"—Cole started to grin—"if you're having some problems in the baby-making department he says he'd be more than happy to lend you a hand."

"I'm set," I said. And I meant it. So why had Vayl gone so still all of a sudden?

Cole went on. "He also says the tannery is considered to be the entrance to the world of the dead. And that some of the men who work there, even today, know how to open and close the doorway."

I looked at my *sverhamin*. "What do you suppose that means?" I asked.

He arched an eyebrow. "It means our map is genuine." He stepped forward, pulling out his wallet. By the way Yousef's eyes bugged at the handful of euros he pulled out, it probably amounted to more than he made in six months.

I watched them—a dark, childless Rom who'd taken two centuries to master his craving for blood leaning over the sun-baked tanner with the caterpillar mustache—and couldn't imagine more different men. Yet here they stood, bound by their connection to Marrakech and me.

As Vayl said, "We need a guide," and Yousef pocketed the bills, I let myself wonder if the tanner could help him in another way. Vayl had been savaged by his sons' murders, but his grief hadn't kept him from adopting Helena. And despite his medieval attitudes at the time, he'd still managed to be a good dad to her. To me, that said he still wanted the role. Needed it maybe. What if Yousef really was a fertility guru? What if he—and I—could make Vayl's dream come true?

I shook my head. Shoved the thoughts into the Miracle Basket at the back of my brain, which, as far as I knew, was directly connected to an incinerator. Because crazy thoughts could not be tolerated inside my skull. Especially not when they had to share space with a Domytr.

Besides, I had to keep up with Yousef, who'd brought bewildering passion to his new job. In fact, he shot out of the room like the cops were on his tail. Didn't even look back, just assumed we wanted to get there as bad as he wanted to earn his money.

We ran after him, only barely avoiding an embarrassing body jam at the door because I beat the guys out and Vayl clapped Sterling and Cole's shoulders together before shoving them forward. Somehow we all kept our feet and raced down the stairs after our guide, hoping his slap-happy sandals didn't attract Monique. Unfortunately, she was waiting for us at the bottom, cell phone in hand.

"I have many friends," she called as we swept past her. "If it's an earthquake, I need to know who to call!"

"We think we can stop it from here!" I shouted over my shoulder. "Hunker down and wait for more news. We'll be back soon!" *I hope.*

"What about Miles?" she cried as Yousef slammed out the front door.

Cole answered for me. "Take care of him for us, will ya?"

Though I expected Yousef to be three blocks ahead of us, he

was beside the Galaxie when we reached the street. As we piled in, Vayl shoved Yousef to the backseat with Cole and Sterling so he couldn't cuddle next to me. I grinned at my *sverhamin*, loving that hint of possessiveness that I returned with interest. Starting the car felt like loading a gun. I felt my hands begin to shake. I was going to drive my baby to the big showdown!

Vayl put his lips to my ear. "Are you ready to annihilate some demons?"

I thought about Kyphas. And Brude. No more than the grit between my foot and the accelerator. And knew my shiver had as much to do with wasting them as it did Vayl's hot breath tickling one of my most sensitive spots. When I turned my head his lips hovered next to mine. I stole my smile from his repertoire, just a twitch to show how hard I was working to master my passion as I let my eyelids drop. "I'm up for it," I said. Glancing over my shoulder I added, "Best route, Yousef?"

Cole gave me his reply. "I'll show you. We'll come to the tannery from outside the city, taking the Route Des Remparts to the Bab ed-Debbagh."

I knew the gate, an arched break in the impressive ochre wall that stretched for miles around the old city, proving that even in the thirteenth century they knew how to turn towns into fortresses.

As I swung the Galaxie into motion I said, "Vayl, do you remember the gate from the last time you were here?"

His nod went more up than down. "Helena and I toured the city one day and we saw it then. Legends say that an evil djinn named Malik Gharub is trapped within the gate, so I suggest none of you rub anything that resembles a lamp."

I glanced over my shoulder, making sure Sterling could see my expression.

"Fine!" he said. "I won't go after the djinn! Although just a touch could probably fuel me for a year without even sleeping."

"Why does he want to skip sleep?" Vayl asked me.

"He's studying to be a Bard," I said. "Takes time, you know? He'd get there twice as fast if he could skip the Z's."

"Ah."

"Speaking of skipping," Cole interrupted, "Yousef says there's a pothole coming up that's big enough to swallow us whole. Stay in the middle of the road."

"Will do," I replied. For the rest of the trip I paid attention to the tanner and his interpreter, who continued pointing out the turns and the axle-breakers. I didn't much mind the backseat driving because, dayum, my new wheels could put the power down! I suddenly wondered . . . was that all? It'd be just like Vayl, having trotted out the big surprise, to hold off on a little one like, "Oh, by the way, I had Bergman make a few modifications," until he decided it was time to pop the details on me. I vowed to give the girl a good going over as soon as I had a free minute.

Which wasn't now. Because we'd arrived at the Bab ed-Debbagh, a gray archway topped with a simple array of vertical stones. We parked in a lot outside the gate, piled out, and secured the car, following Yousef onto cobbled streets that turned and twisted so many times before they released us into the city proper we had to wonder how anybody had ever conquered it. This close to dawn we only met a few farmers carting their wares to the souks to be sold later that morning. Otherwise, all we saw were feral cats nosing through piles of trash that had blown against the walls of neglected red-walled homes that might once have housed rich merchants. Now they held the poorest citizens of Marrakech.

We ducked into lanes so narrow I could stretch out both arms and touch the walls that fenced them. We bounded up staircases whose steps were so chipped and worn I could easily imagine the steady succession of invaders who had pounded up and down them in their quest to be the next great conquerors of a shining Moroccan city. And I wondered if it could possibly have stunk as bad back then as it did now.

Yousef stopped beside a doorway with a large pot of some dark green plant growing beside it. He broke off a piece for each of us and gestured for us to hold it under our noses. When we did, we inhaled the refreshing scent of mint, strong enough that the other smell barely got through. Then he led us into an abandoned building whose windows might never have held glass, up stairs that had been formed of the same rough material as the walls, and onto a roof that groaned occasionally, making me wonder just how much weight it could hold beyond the rusty metalwork railing that divided it into thirds. He took us to the edge, gestured below, and spoke.

Cole said, "We're here."

We looked down, our extra visual capabilities showing us a large open space, its uneven border shaped by the tall, windowless buildings just like ours that surrounded it. In the middle sat cement tubs that would shine so white in the sun I suspected looking at them without sunglasses could give you headaches. Some stood alone. Some were connected circles or squares, like Tetris blocks where the line is nearly finished, or where one in the shape of a backward L has fallen randomly next to another shaped like an I. Of the individual vats, a few looked to be a much darker color. Those had high rims that wouldn't allow accidental slippage, but many were dug so deeply into the ground that they worked as actual pools, and they were filled with a brew that looked certain to kill whatever touched it. Animal hides in various stages of tanning stretched across maybe a third of the vats and, gawd, the stench! Even with the mint stuffed against my nostrils I couldn't get past it.

Yeah, I could believe the legends about this place. And that the Weres had decided to hide a demon's tool here seemed like a stroke of genius. If Roldan could see us now he'd be howling as he regarded us from his comfy little beanbag throne in one of Valencia's posher villas.

"Go ahead, you pitiful schmucks," he'd say. "Just try and find my needle in Marrakech's nauseating little haystack."

To which I'd have to reply (after kicking him square in the teeth, of course), "We've got the map, ya douche. It's not gonna be that hard." If that was true, of course, some hellspawn or other would've retrieved the Rocenz a long time ago. But I didn't need to be that honest with myself today.

We've got the map. We've got a tanner. How hard can it be? I assured myself as we crowded around the clue page Bergman had printed from Astral's visual memory. I should've known better than to ask myself that question.

Vayl turned the map so the shapes on it matched the vats twenty feet below us. Most of us could see them without the aid of the two or three pole lights that worked so poorly they left the majority of the tannery in shadow. But Yousef, with his nose nearly brushing the paper, still had to squint to make the images stand apart from one another.

Vayl said, "We need a light for our guide."

Sterling reached into one of his pants pockets and pulled out a yellow yo-yo that I recalled from our last mission together. Its string, a thin black line that looked like it would tangle if you even looked at it funny, fit around his middle finger and then clipped into a groove on his left bracelet. Holding the toy as if he meant to "walk the dog," he tossed it toward the ground. As soon as it jerked to the end of its line it began to glow. By the time it had rolled back up to where he could snag it, our warlock was holding a glow-globe.

He trained it on the map while Vayl said, "Cole, ask Yousef if any of this looks familiar to him."

Cole translated quickly, but his eyes weren't on the prize. He was peering into the darkness, his expression so close to bitter he might've just swallowed a glass full of cranberry juice. He didn't seem to concentrate on Yousef's reply, but his words were steady.

"Of course the dyes we use are different than the ones shown in the map. But otherwise it looks right."

Sterling's light wavered, and an odd image caught my eye.

"Hey." I pointed to his hand. "Hold that underneath the page, wouldja?"

Sterling moved the yo-yo beneath the paper. In one spot it seemed to reveal a second picture.

I'd been bending as close to it as I could manage considering I was shoulder to shoulder with four other people. Now I glanced up at Vayl. "There's definitely something else here. I think the original map wasn't just drawn, it was built, like those old paintings that have a second portrait hidden underneath. The real map is lying under a thin layer of material that's got to be removed before we can figure out where the Rocenz is."

"So we still have to get the treasure scroll from the demon," Cole said flatly.

"Yeah." I watched him closely. Finally I said, "You don't have to do this, you know."

Even lit by the distant glow of Sterling's light and detailed by my night vision, I could barely read Cole's expression. If I had to guess I'd have said he was feeling about as much self-loathing as a young girl who's mowed her way through an entire package of Chips Ahoy. But instead of saying, "I've been naive," he said, "I'll kill her myself."

Which was when I realized she'd gotten to him. Somehow that bitch had wriggled through the cracks in his heart and set down roots. And I had no idea how to respond to the anger snapping in his eyes now. Except to be honest. "You can't get that done on this plane."

"I know."

"You shouldn't kill her at all."

He glared at me. "Why not?"

"Because you're mad at her." I didn't have to remind him of

the first rule. I could see he remembered that we don't kill when we're angry, because that's when we stop being assassins and become something else entirely. He was just standing in a place I'd been too many times myself. And he really didn't give a shit.

CHAPTER TWENTY-FOUR

So we waited. Dawn approached. Vayl drove back to the riad. Yousef went down to work. But Kyphas never showed. We began a watch, two on, one sleeping in the room nearest the roof access, all of us with our noses so deep in the mint we began to forget what real air smelled like.

The room we picked felt like the rest of the tannery, stripped of everything beautiful, its bones dry and cracking, but still of practical use. I'd been in worse places. Then I realized the brown stained walls, the dirt-choked floors, the single hanging bulb that hadn't felt a charge in decades weren't depressing me. It was Cole, nursing an anger that fit him about as well as a judge's robes. And Sterling, ill at ease enclosed in a space that sucked in the heat while it rejected light, air, and worst of all, music. He'd start to hum a tune and then trail off, like he'd forgotten the melody. Until he finally just stopped.

Yousef brought us meals, for which we paid him so well that he nearly wept. And I tried not to develop an attachment to him. I liked his loyalty. It was just that I knew he hoped I'd reward him with a hearty slap on the cheek followed by a kick to the shin. And I couldn't wrap my mind around that. Didn't even want to try.

At dusk Vayl returned. He took one look at us and said, "We are going to the roof."

As soon as we stepped into the open we felt better. I wondered how entire families survived in rooms like the ones we'd left, how they shielded their souls from the crushing hopelessness walls and ceilings like those brought down on them. And I thought, looking sideways at Yousef and Kamal, who'd come to join us after their visit to the hammam, that some of them didn't.

"Kamal," I said, "tell Yousef that we're expecting violence tonight. And if it comes, the two of you have to stay on the roof."

When Kamal translated and I saw the excitement brighten Yousef's face I nearly shook him. But I knew he'd enjoy it too much, so I just said, "It won't be the kind of pain Yousef enjoys. You have to make him understand that. You could both die."

Kamal half turned, like he wanted to bolt but his feet had somehow stuck to the floor. He whispered, "Who are you?"

"It's better that you don't know, okay? We need Yousef to read the map after we get it, but only when it's safe." I handed them both more euros than they'd ever seen. "We'll give you twice that when this is over. Just hang out here. That's all you have to do. Okay?"

Kamal nodded until Yousef pinched him and demanded some translating, dammit! Then he seemed even happier to cooperate than his buddy. To the point that they found us all rickety folding chairs to sit in while we watched and waited some more. My work is way exciting. Except for the times when it bores me out of my mind.

I couldn't have been asleep long. My dreams had only begun to take on the detail of real life when Vayl shook me awake. I checked my watch. Three a.m. He motioned for me to join the rest of the crew at the edge of the roof, all squatting in a neat row like marksmen waiting for the bank robbers to come riding into town. Yousef and Kamal huddled on one end, whispering to each other. Next to them Sterling crouched, watchful as a stalking lion. Cole knelt to his left, grasping the hilt of his sword like he meant to pull and charge within the next couple of seconds. Vayl went to sit at his shoulder, waiting patiently until Cole turned to meet his eyes.

"Remember why we do this," Vayl said. I'd sunk to my heels on the other side of him. Now he tilted his head toward me. "Jasmine cannot be free without the Rocenz."

"I know that," Cole snapped.

"Did you know she has been experiencing nosebleeds and headaches?"

We both stared. "Little escapes my attention when I am fully attuned," Vayl said.

"It's nothing—" I began.

"He is killing you!" Vayl let me see the flecks of orange starting to paint over the stormy blue of his eyes before he turned them back to Cole. "Saving Jasmine is your priority tonight. All else pales."

He turned back to the scene unfolding below us, and though I could feel Cole's troubled gaze on me, I concentrated on the action in the tannery as well. Because nothing could come of significant looks, no matter how mopey we made them.

The creatures who'd appeared below us kept to the tannery's dark corners at first. But as their search went on and it became obvious that they couldn't figure out their map, they lost the patience stealth requires and became a lot easier to count.

"She sucks at recruiting," Cole said.

"How many do you see?" Vayl asked.

"Three so far."

"Add the two who have remained by the plane portal door and, of course, the demon," Vayl reminded him.

"She's not with them?"

"No." He turned and stood in one smooth motion, raising his cane in such a way that I knew instantly we were in trouble. Without fully understanding why I needed to, I came to my feet and pulled steel. Then I caught sight of Kyphas standing across the roof from us, her flyssa hanging at her side.

"You will never win this fight," Vayl said, pointing the cane at her like he was already seeing the sword it contained carving through her flesh.

"I'm not here to battle," Kyphas said, glancing down at the figures slithering among the vats like she thought they might overhear us. She held out—what the hell?

"That's the map," said Cole, unnecessarily, because we could all see the raggedy-edged scroll rolled tightly in her fist.

"She can't decode it," I said. "She's brought it to us so we can find the tool and then she's taking it back with her."

"No, of course not. Well, I mean yes to part of that. We can't decode it. But I'm here because—" Her eyes lit on Cole like a butterfly lands on a flower, so lightly he never felt their touch, before moving on to Sterling's, mine, Vayl's, even Kamal's. She ignored Yousef so completely he might as well have been a roof vent, standing completely still, shocked to immobility in the face of her absolute beauty. "We have a contract," she finished.

"You said it was finished," Vayl reminded her.

She took a step forward.

Vayl's hand tightened on the jewel that would release the spring-loaded sheath. I raised my sword. Cole wrapped his hand around the hilt of his. Sterling—relaxed. Only Vayl and I knew he was now at his most dangerous, with his hands resting in his lap, one crossed over the other so that his bracelets were touching.

"Kyphas." Vayl made her name a warning even she could understand.

She responded by tossing him the map, her eyes flashing yellow as she said, "Did you think your little scheme would go unnoticed in hell? That Torledge hasn't been aware of every move you've made since you landed in Marrakech? He knows this is his best chance to retrieve the Rocenz and he wants *me* to be the dog that fetches it for him. I may be the laughingstock of Lucifer's court after letting your Seer slip through my fingers, but I will not bow down to that rabbit fucker."

Vayl and I raised our eyebrows at each other. Either she was one badass actress or—

"I knew it!" said Cole.

I wanted to slap myself on the forehead. But that would just hurt me. And Kyphas was the one I wanted to mutilate. Physical violence would only make Cole do the white knight act, however. So I appealed to him one last time. "Dude, you did hear what she just said, yeah? That the contract still holds? Think back. What was her upside in that deal?"

He actually had to take a second. Then he said, "Oh. Souls. She's going to get Brude. And the Oversight Committee."

I nodded. *Good boy, maybe I should give you a sticker. Positive reinforcement so you'll remember your damn lesson.* "She's still in the biz. Always will be. And that face, that incredible face that makes you long for her to reform and become Little Bo Peep, is what makes her so good at what she does."

"What are you saying?" Cole asked.

My sigh came out more like a huff. "Quit thinking with your dick for, like, ten seconds. I think that's all you need to save your life here."

He grimaced at her. "Are you going to take those souls when Jaz gets the Rocenz?"

She shrugged. "Of course." When she saw his face tighten she held her hands out to him. "Look at it this way. It'll make Jasmine's life so much easier. Brude will never be able to hurt her again. Those senators won't be able to manipulate the Agency to make themselves look better. Which means your jobs will be secure and your country will be safer. Where is the disadvantage in that?"

My hand crept to my chest, pressing against the pain in my heart as I watched Cole accept defeat. He seemed to age every second as he said, "Souls, Kyphas. You'll never get it because you see them as, I don't know, purses to be snatched and stacked in your closet because you're like some kind of crazed klepto. But they're way more than that." She tried to speak, but he held up his hand and, amazingly, she let him go on. "Yeah, some of them belong in hell. I've only worked with Jaz for a few months and I believe that to my bones. Maybe even the ones you bargained for should be there. But I can't be with the kind of person who yanks them out of people's bodies, throws them into the pit, and doesn't even understand the kind of misery she's causing."

"Cole—"

He turned his back to her. And I understood, just like she did, that it was the ultimate insult. *So you think you're a dangerous beeyotch? You don't scare me. After what you've done? You don't even rate a glance over the shoulder.*

Kyphas stood there for a second. And then her eyes flared to bright yellow. No telling what she'd have done if we hadn't been there with him. I stepped in front of him. Sterling jammed his bracelets together.

"Begone, demon," said Vayl.

Her nostrils flared, as if she was trying to scent the future. Could she take all of us? Or at least hold us off until her minions appeared to even up the odds?

I smiled at her. Not like Lucille, who can be sweet in even the direst of situations. Like Jaz. Head tilted down, so you could barely see the thin stretch of the lips accompanied by narrowed bring-it-on eyes.

You want a fight? Here I am. You just broke my best friend's heart. I don't need any other excuse to fuck you over.

She hesitated. Another breath. Two. And then she wheeled around, ran to the access door, shoved it so hard it embedded itself into the wall. A moment later she was gone.

"Quickly," Vayl said, tucking his cane under his arm so he could unroll the map. He motioned for Sterling to hold his light underneath it as I searched for weaknesses in its structure.

"Here," I said, pointing to a slight bubble in the bottom corner. "Does anyone have a knife?" The guys eyed each other's swords. "Seriously? We don't have, even, a pair of nail clippers between the four of us?"

Kamal stepped forward, bowing a little as he offered me the handle of a sturdy work knife, which, had I been forced to guess, he probably used on a daily basis to cut the scrap pieces off of the hides.

"You rock," I told him as I sheathed my sword and took the tool from his hand.

He frowned. "I am a rock?"

"No. It means, you're cool like a rock star. You know, like Beyoncé." When his eyes went wide, I quickly added, "Or a guy rocker would be, maybe, a better comparison, sure, I can see that. So, you rock like Usher."

The whole time I was talking I was also working Kamal's knife into the bubble and slicing the top layer of leather free of the map. I did glance up once. Kamal was smiling, so he must've appreciated my final comparison. Sterling and Vayl held the edges of the map to keep it taut. Yousef was checking out the broken door and muttering to himself, no doubt about the amount of force necessary to drive it into the wall in the first place and whether or not he could survive blows like that if he decided to switch his obsession from me to Kyphas midstream, so to speak. Cole still had his back to us, only now he seemed to be watching the activity below. Hopefully that meant he'd focused at least half his mind on the job.

I went back to work. Frankly I'd have much preferred staking out some dirtbag's hotel room or following the trail of our latest national security threat. Both might require the same sort of speed and finesse I now had to bring against the old scroll, but neither would've held the fate of my soul in their hands at the end of the mission. I felt sweat trickle down the small of my back as I slipped the blade gently between the layers, trying to keep it even, to see where one page left off and the other began. I was almost glad when the headache began. I took it as an omen that I was succeeding, moving closer to freedom, while Brude could only pound helplessly against the walls of his prison while he watched his hopes slip farther away.

"Okay, Kamal, I want you to take the cut edge and start pulling up on it. Firm but gentle, got that?" I asked, looking up to make sure he understood what I meant. He nodded. I blinked, waited for the two of him to meld back into one. My head pounded in time with my pulse, painful enough now to make me want to lean over and puke. So maybe it was the source of my double vision. But maybe not. I closed my eyes again.

"Jasmine?" Vayl's voice, soothing as a cool cloth to my forehead, allowed me to take a full breath for the first time since we'd begun the operation.

"I'm okay," I said.

As I'd asked him to do, Kamal lifted the top layer of the map, giving me a better view of my work, allowing me to cut quicker and more decisively. Less than a minute later I was done. I handed the knife back to him and continued to lean over while Vayl, Sterling, and the tanners glued themselves to the new picture, muttering to each other like a bunch of scholars who've just found an attic full of never-before-seen Lincoln letters.

"The demon's got them all back in a group," Cole reported from his perch by the wall. "It won't be long before they make a move."

I walked my hands up my thighs. *Nope, no puking yet. Okay, let's try taking the head a little higher. Ow! Can a brain actually explode? Maybe I should wrap it in something just in case. Do they have compression bandages in badass black?*

I felt a hand on my shoulder. Since it was easier to look down, I identified its owner by the red high-tops toed up with my shoes.

I reached out, grabbed a handful of T-shirt, and climbed myself a little higher. "Cole," I whispered. "I feel terrible."

"Me too."

My chuckle came out more like a sigh because anything else would've shaken me up too much. When I finally met his eyes, stark and sad in a face made for joy, I tried to smile and hoped it came out real. "Let's just get each other through this. We can do that. Right?"

Doubt dropped his eyes. But they came right back up to mine and didn't waver when he said, "Yeah. You and me, Vayl and Sterling, Bergman and Cassandra." He stopped. Nodded. "We can do this."

We locked arms, and though I was the one with spears shoving themselves through my skull, it seemed like the give-and-take was mutual as we helped each other shuffle toward the bowed backs of Vayl, Sterling, Yousef, and Kamal.

CHAPTER TWENTY-FIVE

I kept telling myself Vayl had lived nearly three hundred years now. And it would take me longer than that to know him well. Still, even though his broad back was turned to me I would bet my savings his eyes were the clear blue of a Nordic sailor. The kind who sees past the waves and beyond the horizon, which is why he's still on the ocean long after his neighbors have given up and taken factory jobs.

Though we made no noise as we came up behind him and the rest of the map readers, he didn't even turn his head. Just said, "Sterling, would you check for activity below?"

As our warlock strode to the roof's edge, Cole and I moved to take his place, all of us treading lightly around one of the weak spots near the roof's center that we'd identified when we'd first come up. Vayl held the yo-yo light while Yousef explained through Kamal what he was seeing.

Yousef pointed a brown-stained finger at one of the squares. "These are empty now. And this one"—he joined a second finger to the first and tapped them against a large circle in the bottom corner that seemed to have been drawn with a bolder outline than the others and filled with squiggly red lines. "It was capped long ago."

"Why?" Vayl asked.

"My great-grandfather used to tell the story of how one morning the men came to work to find all of the liquid in the vats boiling. They stood around, trying to decide what had happened, fearful that the tannery would be closed forever. Then, one by one, the vats cracked, pouring out their contents onto the ground. All except for this one." Yousef peered closely at the map. "Yes, this is the one that had to be capped because the dyes thickened and began to spurt into the air at random times. Whoever was hit by even a drop was burned to the bone. Not just anyone could cap it, either. Only the men I told you about earlier—those who can open and close the doors to the world of the dead—were strong enough to come near."

Vayl ran the light around the extra-black edge. At one section Cole said, "Stop. Go back. See that?"

We were so quiet for a moment that we could hear each other take in a couple of extra breaths. Then Yousef said, "It is the holy sign."

"It's a bird," said Cole.

Yousef shook his head. "The tail and the beak are singular—it is a dove."

"He's right," I told Cole. "It's one of the few symbols that can drain the mojo right out of a demon."

"I didn't know that. Why didn't I know that?"

"Because until you started working with us, you never needed to, am I right?"

He paused to take a mental hike into his last career. "You're right. I dealt with some funky stuff, but never demons."

Vayl nodded. "We all seem to have to face them eventually. And when that happens, we learn that dove symbols carry with them great power. As Jasmine said, they can weaken a demon's defenses. And they can lock any hellspawn out of a protected area."

"Which would explain why Kyphas needs us to unlock the vat," I said.

Cole spoke in a near monotone. "But that doesn't explain what Roldan has to do with it."

"No," Vayl agreed. "But do not discount his hatred for me. I am the reason Helena slipped through his grasp. If the demon promised him revenge for that, he would agree to anything."

"I'm a little busy at the moment," I said. "But as soon as my schedule clears, I am so going to kick Roldan's ass."

"Not if I get to him first," said Vayl.

"Nice words," said Sterling. "But they won't do you much good if those hellspawn grind you into assassin burgers in the meantime." He was leaning one elbow against the roof's edge, like he was about to pose for a picture.

"What're they doing down there?" asked Cole.

Sterling said, "They've set up a defensive line. Probably because they know we have to come down within the next couple of hours."

We joined him, let him point out Kyphas and her three active minions. We were still assuming another two hung back to guard their retreat.

"It shouldn't be that hard," noted Cole. "If the door guards stay in place, our numbers are even. We can take them."

"Have you ever fought *kloricht* before?"

"Oh, so that's what they are." He scratched his chin like he actually had a mental index to thumb through before he could give us a truthful answer. "No. But I assume they have asses?"

Vayl's lips twitched. "Yes."

"Then they're kickable."

Vayl's smile widened ever so slightly. For once it looked like he and Cole agreed, even though Vayl, at least, knew the *kloricht* were famous for their fighting ferocity. Because if they killed enough of Lucifer's enemies they could use the souls as a ladder to climb right out of the pit. The standing theory on the Great Taker's strange generosity was that he felt loyalty should be rewarded. And these pups were true. Most of them had been soldiers. The kind who'd followed orders to the letter. Even if that meant herding train cars full of innocent Jews into the gas chamber.

I suddenly wondered where the *kloricht* went when they escaped hell. No way would they be allowed entry into paradise. So what was left to them? *The Thin?* Deep in my mind's prison, Brude's howling laughter confirmed my guess. He'd built the foundation of his army on Satan's escapees.

I spoke up. "Yousef. How close are the *kloricht* to the vat we need to uncap?"

"Halfway across the tannery," he said through Kamal, who'd started to bite his fingernails between sentences.

Sterling said, "Even with all our skills combined, they'll be on us before we can move the lid and lift the tool to the top of whatever muck is still inside the vat. Not to mention the danger we might still be facing from the liquid itself. If it burned men fifty or sixty years ago it still could today."

"So we fight," said Vayl. He gave me his slow smile. I felt my whole body respond.

Kamal sniffed. "Are you people actually excited about this?"

Cole drew his sword. I knew the vibration that ran through him had nothing to do with fear as he and Sterling bumped fists for good luck. "It's like asking a pro football player if he's ready for the game, dude. This is what we *do*."

Chapter Twenty-Six

S ince Sterling could provide air support and use the Party Line to update us on the demons' movements, we decided to leave him on the roof. Alone. Because we still needed Yousef to guide us to ground zero. And Kamal...

When we turned to leave him with the warlock he made a please-don't-abandon-me sound. I stopped and looked up at Vayl, who asked, "How old are you, son?"

"Sixteen."

Shit.

So his next question was for Sterling. "Can you protect him?"

Sterling's hair seemed to whisper spells of its own as it brushed against his collar with the shaking of his head. "I can't make any guarantees. The boy should leave."

"Yeah, and if they grab him right outside the gate and use him as a bargaining tool?" asked Cole. "What are we gonna do then?"

"We will leave the decision to him," Vayl said firmly. "It is his life, after all."

Kamal slapped his hand over his chest like Vayl had threatened to carve out a piece of it. "I want to go home," he said.

Vayl nodded. "Of course. Sterling?" He turned to the warlock. "Do you have any sort of charm this boy can carry for extra protection?"

Our warlock reached into his back pocket, pulled out his wallet, and from it lifted a card. Kamal took it, studied it, looked up incredulously. "You want me to trust my neck to...a library card?"

"It's special," Sterling assured him. "Just put it in your pocket and say these words as soon as you leave the building." He whispered in Kamal's ear. "It will make you seem harmless to all who lay eyes on you for the following five minutes."

"That's not long."

I raised an eyebrow at him. "For chrissake, Kamal, how long is it gonna take you to run away from here?"

"All right." He pocketed the card. Followed us downstairs.

By the time we reached the center of the tannery I figured he was shutting the door of his house behind him. But he'd be back tomorrow. Which boggled my mind. I couldn't imagine how anybody could work here for more than a few minutes, much less the years Yousef had obviously put in.

I crumpled the new bouquet of mint that he'd picked for me earlier and held it to my nose. It wasn't working as well as it had before. Maybe I was getting used to its smell. Or maybe I was just too close to the piles of animal skins, still wearing their layers of rotting flesh and feasting insects. Either way, the stench made me want to hurl the last thing I'd eaten into the nearest pool of bloody-looking liquid.

I decided it would help if I concentrated on holding my sword safely at my side so that neither one of its razor-sharp edges could slice into Yousef or Vayl as I followed them. Cole walked close behind me, hugging the walls of the tannery's outer edges like the rest of us while he tried not to make any noise that would attract Kyphas and her gang.

We'd come into the tannery from the north. The vat we needed was in the southeast corner. That meant a careful hike between grunge-soaked walls and ancient pools that contained everything from lime water to pomegranate juice to watered-down pigeon dung.

What would this place have been back in the States? Maybe a succession of clear blue pools edged by lush greenery with fountains set every twenty feet or so to draw the eye on to some new pleasure. Or maybe a fish farm, its tanks heaving with healthy bass, the purity of its H_2O so closely regulated that most countries would willingly run it through their taps. Here the vats crammed against each other like shackled prisoners, their contents reminding me of bottomless pits. I imagined if any of us fell in we'd drift downward forever while the chemicals ate the skin off our bones until all that was left was an eternally sinking skeleton.

Sterling's voice yanked me back to the job. "The *kloricht* are holding steady," he said.

"Where is the plane portal in relation to us?" Vayl asked.

"If you're at one o'clock, it's at four."

Yousef kept up a steady, creeping motion, though I could see him shaking as he led us toward our goal. He looked over his shoulder once, to make sure we were still following. And the gleam in his eyes told the whole story. He couldn't have been happier if I'd just cracked a dictionary over his head.

Behind him Vayl moved with the stealth of a born predator. I would've complimented his skill, but the headache was knocking harder now, and if I had to say anything I might puke. I glanced back to see if Cole felt the same. Uh, considering that he was winding a long purple string of gum between his teeth and fingers like taffy, probably not.

I nearly turned back to Vayl and said, "I can't work under these circumstances. I need peace before a kill, man." But then I imagined myself meditating and maybe downing a cup of chamomile tea before pulling off my next hit. And that was so ludicrous that I nearly slapped myself across the face. *Pull it together. You can do this.*

And afterward, free margaritas for everyone! shouted my Inner Bimbo from her favorite barstool. Which she promptly fell off of. I glared at her.

This is why nobody listens to you, ya lush.

Teen Me was waving frantically from the second-story window of Granny May's house. Now why would she be up there? That wasn't even the room I usually stayed in. I looked around for somebody to ask, but my Librarian was sprinting down the road like she'd just heard there was a two-for-one sale at Borders. And Granny May's bridge table? Deserted.

I stopped. "Something's wrong." *Hey, no vomiting! Two points for me!*

Vayl murmured to Yousef and we stopped at the edge of a small alcove formed by the side of yet another deserted building, part of the medina's outer wall, and a third structure that the tannery seemed to be using as a warehouse. Inside this capital U was lowercase U formed by one large tub. *Our* tub. But all I saw was a white blur as I pulled back and ducked inside the abandoned home with Vayl, Cole, and Yousef. We huddled beside the open door, discussing our options.

Sterling spoke into our ears. "Demons are holding steady," he reported.

"Why would that be?" I wondered aloud. "Why didn't they ream us up on the roof? Why retrieve the map and then hand it back to us? What are they waiting for?"

"They're demons," Cole said bitterly. "Playing games like this is their favorite pastime."

I didn't reply. Vayl had been watching me like if he just held still and stared hard enough he could see right into the workings of my brain. The thought scared me less than it would have a few months before. Until he said, "Jasmine? Are you thinking that they already have the Rocenz?"

"Yeah," I whispered. *I'd* only just realized that's where my thoughts were taking me. How had he figured it out?

Cole said, "That's ridiculous."

"Not really," Vayl said. "In fact, it makes a great deal of sense to hand a treasure map over when you have already retrieved the loot."

"But we've been watching the place. Kyphas hasn't been here since she got the map."

"No," I said. "Because she's had the Rocenz for a lot longer. The whole bit about getting the map? That was to fulfill her contract with us. She agreed to help us find the tool. And we're about to. In fact, she's leading us right to the spot where it's been held since Roldan and his Gorgon rider took it from Sister Yalida over eighty years ago."

Sterling spoke up. "What are you saying, Chill?"

I replied, "You guys know about the canals?"

Cole had been quietly translating all this time. Now Yousef tugged on my sleeve, shaking his head in confusion. I said, "Thousands of years ago demons could travel to our realm a lot easier than they can now. Part of the reason was because the Great Taker had built all these canals between his world and ours. And no, they're nothing like those placid little rivers you see every time Denmark advertises for tourists. Anyway, small teams usually made up of a couple of fighter types and a Seer or holy man eventually sealed the majority of them. Except the ones that were well disguised." I paused, to wave my hands around the tannery.

"But the map," Cole protested. "The dove!"

"Yeah," I agreed. "Probably taken from the dead hands of just such a crew. I don't think the holy mark was meant to show where they'd completed their work. I think it was their guide, leading them to the place where they needed to make that seal real. I'll even go further. I think Sister Yalida was a member of that crew. And the story about her possessing the Rocenz was just part of a bigger tale, one in which she probably used the tool to find the canal that she and her comrades needed to lock. But they were killed in the process. Then their murderer, Roldan, hid the Rocenz in that very canal."

"Why?" Vayl asked.

"You said the Gorgon eats his death. I'm guessing the Rocenz can somehow separate the two of them again. Maybe the same way it can split me and Brude. If that happened, wouldn't they both die?"

Vayl stared at me thoughtfully. "I cannot be certain without researching the matter, but yes, I would think so."

"Why keep the map, then?" Cole asked. "Why not destroy it?"

I shrugged. "Maybe the Rocenz's other powers are just too tempting to give up."

"What about the writing on the map?" Sterling asked doubtfully.

"Temptation again," I replied. "It's hell's stock-in-trade, and here we are, risking our souls to get the Rocenz for ourselves."

Vayl sent a piercing look out the door, scanning the tannery as if sight alone could force it to reveal how much of my theory tracked true. He said, "Much of what you say makes sense. The tannery legend, that it adjoins the land of the dead, could have its basis in fact. And then, there is the smell."

"Exactly," I agreed.

Through Cole, Yousef said, "I do not understand."

I explained, "The canals run below places that hide the odor of hell. Where the people who live or work around the site die earlier than usual for explainable reasons, so that the life-sucking characteristics of the canals aren't ever pinpointed."

Yousef began to talk rapidly and grabbed at his own arm. Cole translated. "Then, when the boiling began in all the vats during my grandfather's time, and the vat outside this house began to burn people to the bone, was that substance shooting into the air hellfire?"

"Yeah," I said. "Demons ride it straight from their world to ours in petrified bone ships they call Rin-Chaen. If we looked around the tannery long enough, we'd probably find theirs. It explains why none of us have seen the plane portal we assumed they came through and left guards beside—because they didn't use one. Of course they had to close the canal behind them, because they were called here, and that's part of the deal. But if *we* opened the canal, it's a different story."

Yousef's skin had begun to look a little gray where it met his beard. "What happens then?" he asked.

I counted off the possibilities on my fingers. "All kinds of hell dwellers could escape without finding themselves beholden to anyone. We could be looking at a potential invasion from hell. Or, we might succeed in our mission and retrieve the Rocenz. In which case the other half of the demon's contract is met."

Yousef was nearly bouncing on the balls of his feet now. "What does that—I have no idea what that means!"

Vayl had barely blinked during my explanation. Now his unwavering gaze broke and he moved it to Yousef. "We promised the demon the chance to snatch souls in exchange for her cooperation, four specific ones. She has promised to harm no one in the Trust. But that does not mean the *kloricht* standing with her, or perhaps crouching on the other side of that lid, have our best interests at heart. His eyes cut to Cole. "And you are no longer in the Trust, which makes you doubly vulnerable."

I snapped, "Cole! Say you want to be back in the Trust."

When he gave me a look his mom must've seen every time she demanded obedience from him and he ran right into the street instead, I suddenly felt like I had a lot in common with her. He said, "No."

"Why *not*!"

"A Trust is like a family, which I have. And yours is headed by Vayl, who I don't like." He turned to my *sverhamin*, adding, "No offense."

"None taken," Vayl replied smoothly.

Cole went on. "So don't think by yelling at me you're going to make me cave. I'll find my own way. And I'll be in charge the *whole* time."

"Yeah!" I fumed. "Until some mucus-dripping ball-ripper ganks your soul and feeds it to the family for dinner. *Then* guess who'll be in control!"

Cole crossed his arms and refused to talk anymore. Which was fine, because if he had I probably would've punched him.

Typically, Vayl had moved beyond our petty bickering and decided scouting was in order. Which meant during our argument he'd been inching toward the corner of the building. Now he leaned around to take a long, hard look. When he got back he didn't seem any happier.

"What did you see?" I whispered.

"It is just an innocent-looking circle of concrete covering a vat standing no higher than your knees," he said.

"Are you telling me my theory's crap?" I asked hopefully.

He shook his head. "We must get in closer. The sign, if it is present, could be on the other side."

My stomach rolled. He meant hellsign, which could work as a lock to seal nearly any portal. Because it was painted with the blood of an infant.

Without even looking back to check that we were following, Vayl led us into the open. This time I came second, with Cole at my shoulder and Yousef bringing up the rear. I watched the shadows for signs of movement, the windows for the surge of bodies that signaled ambush. Every muscle in my back clenched, waiting for a bullet, or more likely an arrow, to split my spine.

Would you pull yourself together? You're out of range, rabbit. Granny May looked up irritably from a hand she and Amelia Earhart were clearly winning. *And even if you weren't, you'd still have to do this. So pull your head out of your ass before you let one of these fine boys down!*

I nodded, just like I'd really heard her, and kept moving, pretending the dye pools to my left were just buckets of dirty water. We moved completely into the alcove this time, not touching the smooth-walled tank as we spread out, taking turns watching for Kyphas's charge and scanning the vat for graffiti. The top was unmarked, but grimy enough to support a healthy layer of moss. Instead I saw it had become a graveyard for the skeletons of small creatures that had made the unfortunate decision to rest on it temporarily or use it as a transbuilding highway.

Yousef said something to Cole, speaking so quickly now that he had to ask him to repeat himself. "What'd he say?" I asked.

"He wants to know if he can stand guard. Preferably from the car."

Staring at the tiny bleached skulls, I could hardly blame him.

Vayl said, "Tell him to go back around the corner of the building and to call out if he sees anything moving."

As soon as Cole started translating Yousef began to shake his hand gratefully. He waved goodbye to us and ran out of sight. Back to his house if he had any sense.

Vayl said, "You must tell me how you and Yousef came to meet sometime, Jasmine." Mild. Slightly amused. Except for the gold flecks in his dark green eyes that told me just what he planned to do to the tanner if he stepped over the line.

"Don't slam his face into anything," I warned him. "He'll just start stalking you too and then we'll never—shit. I found it."

Silence as we stared at the lip of the lid, where the fresh outline of a raven had been drawn with its beak buried in the entrails of a screaming child. The blood Kyphas's summoner had used wasn't even dry enough yet to flake.

"Fuck." I don't know if I reached for Vayl's hand, or he grabbed for mine, but our fingers interlaced like we each felt the need for rescue.

"Exactly," Vayl said with such feeling that his voice seemed to rumble inside my chest.

Sterling's voice sang into the silence, lifting our shoulders, bringing our eyes to the sky like we could really see him looking down on us as he said, "If you break that seal, I can throw down a net that will only let the Rocenz through."

I'd known he was the best. But to wield that kind of power? Even with all his stores available to him he'd still probably have to sleep for a week afterward.

Vayl might've been impressed too, but he never hesitated. "Do it," he said.

Cole looked down at the sword in his hand. Took some time to adjust his grip and, maybe, his attitude. Because his voice sounded different, more businesslike, when he asked, "So how do we break the lock?"

I said, "We hit the raven with our blades. Not like we mean to plow through rock, but like we're trying to kill an actual bird. The fact that we're attacking with Raoul's weapons should be enough to split it, but we may have to strike it several times before it gives, okay?"

"Okay."

"And when it starts to go? Have the sense to get back."

"No problem."

I looked up, barely able to see the roof of our lookout building from ground zero. "Sterling? Have you got us covered?"

"Three cooks about to spoil the broth," he confirmed. "All of you bust it back behind a wall as soon as the lid splits. I'm going to light the place up."

I felt Vayl's powers like icy fingers tickling the back of my neck and knew our warlock wouldn't be the only *other* throwing sparks tonight. "You're beautiful when you're about to kick ass," I told him.

His dimple appeared briefly and then dashed away. "I think that was my line."

"Naw, 'cause I'm the sexy one." I pointed back and forth

between us. "Beautiful, sexy. Sexy, beautiful. We need to get this straight now, you know, so after we get blown to bits they'll know how to tell the difference between us."

"It will still be no problem," said Vayl. "Your bits will be jumping up and down, madly demanding revenge. While mine will be wafting through the air like a misguided balloon."

"See," I said. "Even your bits are beautiful. They waft."

"Jumping up and down is definitely sexy," Vayl assured me. "Would you like to do it two or three times right now before we get down to business?"

Sterling and Cole groaned at the same time. "Ewww!"

And then we couldn't think of a single new delaying tactic. So Vayl unsheathed his sword while Cole and I raised ours.

We took turns swinging, the metal of our blades clanging against the wings of the raven like hammers against an anvil. No way could the demons not hear us. We'd have to hurry. A rumbling from somewhere so far below us it felt like the other side of the earth made us look down and reset our stances.

"Again," Vayl said.

We swung. The bird took three more slices to its wings. I whispered, "Vayl, it's giving! Armor yourself!"

He said, "If I could, we would all be encased in ice by now. But I have lost the abilities I gained after 1770." Including the one he'd taken from a Chinese vampire during our mission to Corpus Christi that had given him the power to shield himself and others in a blanket of ice.

I took a moment to glance at him, amazed that his expression was as relaxed as if he was waiting for his evening paper to be delivered. Wow. *I* would've been bitching so loud the complaint departments in every company on the continent could've heard me. *He* hadn't even thought to mention that his curse had permanent side effects.

I gritted my teeth and got back to work, more determined than ever to beat the bastards who'd set us up so neatly.

Cole delivered a blow that cut the raven's head at the neck. The lid cracked in a dozen places as the ground beneath our feet shifted, hard, to the left. Both of us stumbled backward.

"I can see red between the cracks!" Sterling told us. "Is it getting warm down there?"

I wiped the sweat off my face. "Feels like a furnace."

"It's going faster than I expected. Take cover!"

Vayl hustled us back toward Yousef's hiding place. He wasn't there. We made it just in time for the lid to fail. The sound of it shattering worked like a bugle call for Kyphas's crew.

"Demons on the move!" Sterling said. "Coming at you from multiple directions. I suggest you keep a wall at your backs. Or better yet, run!"

"To where?" Vayl asked.

"I'll cast a Hand on the roof of that building," Sterling said. "Stand inside the palm and only one of them can attack you at a time."

"Done."

We charged through the doorway, but as soon as we were inside Vayl paused, causing a major traffic jam. He spun around. "Jasmine, you must stay behind."

"What?" I was so shocked I didn't even care that I sounded like a strangled chicken.

"The Rocenz is somewhere in that rubble. We can give you the time you need to find it. And I am concerned about the *kloricht* receiving reinforcements. We know a human had to call this group. Nothing and no one but you can stop them from repeating the summons."

"They could be in an entirely different city, you *know* that!"

"I think not. In fact, to call demons from a canal, I believe our human must be very near the spot. Practically standing on top of it, in fact."

"That's right, I'd forgotten. But we didn't see anybody on the way—" *Shit. Yousef and Kamal!* I wished my guys good luck and sprinted out the door, understanding that their lives depended on me doing my best work tonight.

A second explosion knocked me to the ground. It had begun.

CHAPTER TWENTY-SEVEN

I stood up and peered back through the new gap in Vayl and Cole's building where a huge chunk of the wall had blown away. Through it I could see the canal spouting a geyser of bluish orange flames twenty feet high. If I looked harder I could see faces in the flames, screaming in ecstasy as they swam toward freedom. And then, falling from the sky like a net of stars, came Sterling's reply. As soon as the connected balls of shimmering light hit the fire they exploded, sending my butt back to the ground and my hands over my head. As if my frail little arm bones could really protect me from flying timber.

When I looked again Sterling's spell had reduced the geyser to a fountain and the faces inside it were screaming.

"Demons closing on your building," Sterling said, sounding out of breath and slightly gleeful.

"Nice shot," I heard Vayl say. "How soon can we expect them?"

"Three minutes."

"Sterling," I said. "Can you see any other movement in or around the tannery? I'm looking for humans now."

"So I heard. I've got nothing but soul-snorters—wait a minute. Some idiot just came out of the building east of the canal. Dressed like a man. He's moving toward the rubble. Can you see him?"

"Not from here. Which is a bad spot anyway, considering. I'm changing positions."

I couldn't slip around behind the man. There just wasn't enough room between the rampart wall and the vat for the shadows to hide me. So I moved past him on the north side, crouching low enough for a long line of hide-covered tanks to disguise my scuttling outline. I ended up in front of the building he'd just left. I still couldn't see him. But I caught sight of the *kloricht* and Kyphas, moving quickly from vat to vat, closing in on Cole and Vayl like a fatal disease. And the worst part? We'd been right. They'd had two extra guards, maybe standing with the ship they'd sailed in on. But now, with so much at stake, they'd put all their forces into one concentrated attack. Sun Tzu would not approve.

My quarry had to have heard the demons, but he didn't seem to care. He was bent over the lid's remains, avoiding random droplets from its fountaining fire, ignoring the howling faces and scrabbling claws of the demon host straining to be free as he searched through the debris. The depth of the alcove partially blocked my view, and I didn't dare twitch now that the *kloricht* were close enough to sense my movements. So I tracked Kyphas's summoner as long as I could, and when he strayed out of view I watched the demons he'd invited into our world.

Though they'd taken basic human forms, they still managed to look comfortable walking on all fours. Probably because it allowed them to jut their chin barbs out as far as physically possible. Their silver mohawks shone in the moonlight as they turned to talk to one another, their whispers sounding like the hiss of steam escaping an overpressured valve.

I opened my mouth to tell Vayl he had company, but Sterling was on the ball. "Okay, you two, visitors entering the ground floor. I count five plus the demoness. You're standing right in the center of the Hand now. As long as you're there, you won't be outnumbered. So stay cool. And I'll see if I've got something up my sleeve that can zap them without frying you guys at the same time."

"Thank you, Sterling," said Vayl, his tone nearly as calm as our warlock's. "We appreciate it."

I wanted to rush the dude still rifling through the broken lid pieces and bits of building rubble, but I knew I had to wait until the demons were committed. Three minutes later I heard the clash of steel and Cole yelling. My whole upper body twitched against the wall.

"Jaz, don't move," said Sterling. "Somebody else just walked into the ruins."

"What are you doing here?" asked Kamal. In English.

"What do you think?" answered Yousef. Also in English.

What the fu—

"I think you're never going to keep it without a fight," said Kamal.

"Come on, then." I imagined Yousef flicking his fingers toward himself, probably hoping Kamal would beat him badly enough that he'd at least get some fun out of it.

Then I heard the hollow slap of knuckles on flesh.

I spun around the corner, hoping a better view would help me figure out what the hell was going on.

Yousef had Kamal by the shirt collar. He was pounding him so hard that sweat droplets flew off the boy's face. But Kamal had grown up in the streets, and he'd learned a few tricks of his own. Including the flailing leg move that eventually connects somewhere tender.

Yousef went to one knee. But he didn't let go. In fact, he buried his fingers in Kamal's neck. "You little perversion," he gasped. "The world is going to be a better place without you."

I snuck in closer, trading my sword for a weapon more appropriate to the moment. But I kept Grief pointed toward the ground, because I was listening to the debate raging in my head.

Yousef is the bad guy! Granny May screeched. *He's clearly bent, or he wouldn't get such a thrill when you slap him around!*

Maybe not! argued Teen Me. *Kamal might not be as innocent as he seems. I'm going to date plenty of guys who'll be perfect gentlemen until they "run out of gas" in the middle of nowhere. And then it'll be like they've gone deaf and grown four extra pairs of hands!*

Kamal swung wildly and managed to slam his fist into Yousef's eye. Suddenly their positions were reversed. Yousef lay on the cracked cobblestones while Kamal straddled him, delivering punishing blows that would've knocked out anyone with less resistance. Yousef smiled through the blood and his missing front tooth.

"You hit like my great-grandmother!" he taunted, not even trying to block the blows. One hand crawled up Kamal's chest, reaching for a choke hold, while the other felt beneath his back. "Ha!" he shouted in triumph as his hand came free, and in his grip he held . . . *the Rocenz.*

"Stop!" I yelled as he started to swing. The hammer made it to Kamal's ear before Yousef managed to halt it. Good thing too, because I was that close to blowing his brains out.

"Get up, Kamal," I said.

He grabbed the Rocenz and got to his feet, backing away from Yousef, who slowly dragged himself upright, coughing and spitting pink phlegm as he rose.

Kamal murmured something. "What'd you say?" I asked.

"Thanks for saving me."

I nodded, turned back to Yousef. "You can speak English. What's that about?"

"Kamal taught me," he said. "What else is there to do to pass time here every day?"

"But you never told us your secret," I said.

"No. I like knowing what the ladies say when they think I'm ignorant. It's like peeking into their diaries."

"You are such a freak."

"Yes," he agreed, holding up a finger to keep me from continuing my train of thought. "But not evil."

"Are you trying to tell me you didn't summon the demons that are fighting Cole and Vayl on the roof right now?"

He glanced at the flames full of enraged demonic faces, gnashing their teeth at Sterling's net, and the expression on his face sent a chill through me. He pointed at Kamal. "He did it."

I glanced at Yousef's young translator. Who seemed sort of... smug.

I watched him flip the Rocenz in his hand, throwing it up high enough so that it did a full 360 before he caught the handle. "What are you doing, Kamal?" I asked carefully.

"Deciding not to spend the rest of my life wading in shit," he said. "For the longest time I thought I didn't have any other choice. And then I met the most beautiful woman in the world." He pointed to the hole the explosion had blown in Cole and Vayl's building just as Kyphas stepped through it.

"Good boy," she crooned, giving him such a lusty wink I knew where he thought he was going to be spending the rest of the night. She held her arms out to him.

I swept Grief from Yousef to Kamal and fired. The boy crumpled, screaming as his kneecap shattered. But I was already too late. He'd thrown the Rocenz to Kyphas.

"Your contract," I reminded her.

"You found the tool," she told me. "It's not my fault that you lost it again." She laughed. "If you ever retrieve it, I'll be sure to meet you at the gates of hell to help you with Brude's name-carving party. Until then..." She shrugged. And leaped back into the blackness of the building.

I lunged after her, shooting until my clip was empty. At the same time Yousef ran to Kamal and knelt beside him.

"You stupid, stupid boy. What have I told you about beautiful women?"

Kamal winced. "Let them beat you...but don't let them break you?"

"Exactly." Yousef hauled off and punched Kamal one last time, giving him an instant black eye and, at least, a short nap before he'd have to deal with his new reality.

"I have to go," I said, gesturing to Kyphas's blood trail, shining like silver in the blackness of the building ahead of me.

"Me as well," said Yousef. He leaned down, gathered Kamal, and lifted him up onto his shoulder.

I nodded, and we ran in opposite directions. Yousef flapping his sandals as he hustled toward the exit. Me reloading and chambering a round as I trailed the demon up to the roof.

Chapter Twenty-Eight

When I skidded through the roof's open doorway, I felt like I'd entered a video game. I shook my head, forcing away the need to bounce into fantasy. But the sense remained, reinforced by the minefield of gaping holes that allowed me to see straight into the rooms below. Still smoking around the edges, they showed that Sterling had found a way to help Vayl and Cole out after all.

They stood at the opposite end of the roof, shoulder to shoulder, battling the three surviving *kloricht*. Vayl bled freely from multiple wounds on his chest and shoulders. Cole held his left arm tight to his side. But they both had that determined look that let me know they weren't even close to giving up.

I wanted to run to them. To mow down anything that dared come against them. Starting with Kyphas. She stood halfway between me and my guys as if waiting for me, her flyssa shining like Death's fangs. The Rocenz hung at her belt like it was no more than a handyman's tool.

"Come on, Jasmine," Kyphas said as she glanced back at the men. "Look what I've brought on your pretty boys. Doesn't it make you furious? Don't you want to just—kill me?"

Here's where I should've kept my mouth shut and shot her in the face. She would've healed eventually. But she wouldn't have been able to talk. Which meant she couldn't have needled me into any dumb stunts. But I was more like her than I cared to admit. And I wanted to torture her before I cut her in two.

So I said, "Oh, I'll destroy you, Kyphas. But Cole's already done me one better. Because he's never going to love you. He wants a home. Kids. A future he could never share with a heartless monster who keeps trying to kill his friends."

"Cole has no idea what he wants," she replied. "If he did, he'd have it by now. Lucky for him, I do. And I'm going to give it to him." She patted herself between the breasts, like she was experiencing an actual swelling of feeling for him inside. My instinct was to destroy it before it came out to swallow him. So I squeezed the trigger, nice and easy. Fifteen times.

It's tough to describe the mess I made of her chest. A team of surgeons would've taken hours to dig all the pieces of bone from bloody bits of muscle and organ that I destroyed in a matter of seconds. She didn't die, but damn did she bleed. And the force of the hits sent her stumbling backward into one of the pits Sterling had opened with his missile shots.

I ran to the edge. She lay flat on her back on the floor of the same depressing apartment I'd paced the length of while watching for her arrival not half a day before.

"Maybe I should stop doing that to my targets," I murmured. "It never ends well."

I got the oddest feeling I'd said something prophetic when she sat up and grinned. "Thanks for the assist!" she called. "I couldn't have done this without you!"

Then she reached into the mass of gore Grief had made of her torso and pulled out—

Holy Christ, is that her heart?

But no, it wasn't beating. Wasn't even the right shape. Too smooth, too round. It was a fist-sized, blood-soaked stone. Setting it between her feet, she grabbed the Rocenz and hugged it, anointing it with her own blood as she chanted words I couldn't hear. Then she looked up at me, her grin so malevolent I felt my skin crawl. With a sound like a cannon shot, the pieces of the Rocenz came apart in her hands, the hammer and chisel shining so bright her skin glowed like a lampshade around them.

She set the chisel to the stone and struck it with the hammer. The sound barely carried to me over what I thought was the last cry of Cole's enemy. I glanced back. And realized it hadn't been a *kloricht*'s death-scream at all. In fact, now Vayl was furiously trying to fend off two attackers. Because Cole had hit his knees. I heard the distant sound of Kyphas sinking another mark into the stone, and Cole yelled again, clutching at his heart as if she'd stuck the chisel straight into his body.

Oh, no. No, no, no! I spun around. "What the fuck do you think you're doing!" I screamed to the demon crouching fifteen feet below me.

"Didn't you know?" she called, her dancing eyes telling me how much she was loving my panic. "The Rocenz does special work in our hands. We can make it transform souls just by chiseling"—*chink*—"their"—*chink*—"names"—*chink*. "You thought you could just drag him around the world, let him play lapdog, beg for your affection while you screwed your vampire every chance you got? You think that didn't make him just a little crazy? Make him wish he could find a woman who wanted him with her forever?" *Chink, chink, chink.* "Well, that's me, baby! Cole will be mine in every way just as soon as I finish his name."

I glanced over my shoulder. He was lying prone now, looking at me with horror in his reddening eyes. Blood ran down his forehead because—I shook my head, swallowing bile—horns had begun to rip through his skull. He reached out to me.

Vayl, battling for both their lives, could only say, "Run, Jasmine!"

I pointed to Cole, but the motion was more like throwing him an imaginary rope. "I'll save you. Just...hang on to yourself," I said. I turned and ran, jumping two entire flights of stairs so I could get to—

No surprise. The door to our stakeout room had been closed. Bolted. Probably reinforced with another demonic seal. The thought of which made me so crazy that I actually slammed my body against it five or six times before the pain of my fruitless attempts brought me back to myself. I imagined I could hear the steady metallic beat of Kyphas's chisel spelling out Cole's doom.

What's happening? screamed Teen Me as she clutched at her hair and ran circles around Granny May.

Shut up and concentrate! Gran replied. *Kyphas is turning Cole into a demon. Now think of a way to get us inside quick. Because he* would *have the shortest name ever.*

Even if I'd imagined the chiseling, I wasn't making up the screams I now heard shooting down from the roof. *She was close. Goddammit, I wasn't going to make it!*

I could've dropped into the room the way Kyphas had, but she'd have expected that. Which meant something trappish would've been waiting for me. Think bungee sticks that I wouldn't have seen until I'd impaled myself. That left the windows. None of which had glass or even bars. In a place like this, why bother? So there was no obstacle to slow me down when I ran into the adjoining room and jumped on the sash of the window that looked out onto the tannery just like Kyphas's did. Straight drop and a sure hip-dislocation to the stones below. Nothing above but more cavernous holes signifying other glassless windows. Oh, and a single decorative element. A rectangular bar running the length of the building set about six feet above the window. It wasn't in terrific shape. I could see where parts of the top edge had begun to crumble away. But I had no choice.

So I shucked my boots and turned to face the building. Spreading my feet wide for balance, I gauged the distance and jumped.

I smashed my fingers into the bar on the way up, barking them so badly that I was afraid blood would gush, making handholds so slippery that grip would become impossible. But if I'd cut myself, it wasn't bad enough to make me fall. I caught the bar just like I had when I was a kid on the playground in elementary school. And again in college when I discovered rock climbing. And yet again when the CIA realized I could be trained to kill killers.

I dug my toes into the outer wall of the building, finding small caves in a surface that looked smooth as glass from the ground. And moved, quickly, quietly, to my left. I'd pulled myself up to the edge of Kyphas's window when Bergman blew her door off its hinges. The concussion slammed into me, ripping one hand from its anchor and punching me back into the wall of the building.

It's funny what you recall about people. Granny May always used to say, "You never know what moments are going to stick, so you'd better try to make them all worth the glue." Yeah, I never quite got her either.

I'd lived with Miles all three years that he'd gone to grad school. And what I remembered most about that time was the day he came back to the apartment, soaked to the skin after walking twelve blocks in one of those monsoons you occasionally get in the Midwest in late April. I'd said, "Damn, Bergman, you look miserable."

And he'd replied, "I am. But it's amazing how clearly you think when nothing can get any worse. I know what I want to do with the rest of my life now."

"Does it have anything to do with inventing umbrellas that flip out of your backpack at the first hint of rain?" I'd asked.

"Nope," he'd said. And he hadn't explained, but he'd had the most satisfied look on his face. Not pipe-and-slippers contented. No, this was more I-have-found-the-Grail happy. I hadn't seen that expression on him again. Until now.

I gave myself a second to be grateful I could see at all considering the fact that my eyes still weren't sure they belonged in their sockets, my head felt like it had been laboratory tested by Impact-Wrenches-United, and I'd only now managed to regain enough of a grip to pull myself up Kyphas's window high enough to lock my arms around its edge.

Exhaustion forced me to take a short break before I did the rest of the climb. During which time I noted that Kyphas sat on a prayer mat she'd obviously stolen from a heathen, since she wasn't developing boils by having contact with it. She was still holding the Rocenz, but she'd taken a break from her work to gape at Bergman, who stood in the doorway with Astral at his side. Kittybot's butt was still smoking, which meant instead of convalescing, Miles had been inventing some sort of anti-spawn missile especially tuned to her launching capabilities. Which meant he'd been planning this for a while. Had he programmed that smug expression on Astral's face too, or should I just assume it was a cat thing?

I cursed myself for not ordering her to force Bergman to stay in his room and recover. Because he looked so thin and ethereal standing there that he could've passed for his own shadow. Except for the silver tools flashing in both of his hands. At least, that's what my mind told me they were. It was Bergman after all. Lord of the miniature screwdriver. Why would I assume he'd be carrying a pair of Eldhayr daggers?

Except that I'd seen him take Raoul aside before my Spirit Guide had left for missions unknown. I'd registered the I-have-serious-business look on Bergman's face. I just hadn't gotten nosy about it because Miles was Mr. Secretive. Why ask when you know your pal is never gonna tell?

Now it all came together in the amount of time it took for Bergman to raise those finely crafted knives as if he was about to carve the Thanksgiving turkey. He'd gone to Raoul to demand weapons that could injure a demon. And before that, his contemptuous look at Kyphas should've been my clue. He'd been planning this then, deciding, for all of our sakes, that he had to be the one to kill her.

I pulled myself into the room and ran toward them.

"KYPHAS!" I screamed before she could break him in two like she'd tried to do in Australia. She jerked around, her eyes widening as she saw me lunging toward her, pulling my double-edged blade from its sheath as I shouted, "Me and you! *Right now!*"

Even as I attacked I wanted to swear. Because Bergman wasn't backing off. Out of the corner of my eye I could see the blood spreading through his shirt as he strode forward and drove the right-hand knife deep into her side.

Wait? Why is his chest *bloody?*

But no one had time to answer my questions. Kyphas was screaming, twisting to fight him. She tried to bring the hammer down on his head, but Bergman blocked her easily as he drove the second knife into her shoulder.

"Ridiculous little speck!" Kyphas screeched. "I'm going to beat you until even your own mother won't recognize you!"

He stretched out his arms. "Bring it on!"

She slammed both fists into his chest, throwing him so far back into the hall that all I could see were the soles of his shoes. But then her wailing distracted me. She was kneeling, staring at her hands, which were red with Bergman's blood. They'd begun to steam, as if she'd just stuck them in a bowl of acid.

I dove for the stone, but she grabbed it first and shoved it back inside her chest. Then she slammed the pieces of the Rocenz together, though I could tell it tortured her to grasp anything in her burning hands.

She took a wild swing at me and missed.

I stabbed in and up, but she jumped back just in time to sustain a scratch that would probably heal before the fight was over.

Miles came scrambling back, his shirt flapping open in the breeze he made so we could both see the dove he'd carved on his own chest.

"Those knives I left in you have the blood of my dove on them," he told her. "Just like your hands do. I assume you know what that means."

I did. The contact with a holy symbol had weakened her. No wonder I could fight with her on my own level. But that wasn't all.

Looking as ill as if she'd just ingested poison, she rose to her knees and reached out. "No. Please."

He grabbed her wrists and said, "I'm sending you back to hell with the mark of holiness on you. They'll tear you to pieces. Just like that man did to my friend when we were kids." He began dragging her away from me, toward the hall. He must be heading for the canal. Which meant he'd been keeping tabs on the Party Line, the skunk.

But he looked anything but guilty as he pulled Kyphas down the rickety stairs. He said, "You knew some horrifying details. Which meant you watched that monster torture and kill my friend. You let it all happen so you could snatch his soul and use it for bait to hook mine years later. Did it ever once occur to you to step in?" He glared at her. "Naw. 'Cause you hellspawn with your pretty faces and your demented quotas couldn't care less about the innocent."

Bergman dragged Kyphas closer and closer to the canal while I stalked them like Yousef had been trailing me before, desperate to find my way into the action but certain of the kind of welcome I'd get if I picked the wrong approach. So I followed at a respectful distance and kept my trap shut, knowing that if I threw Bergman off his game now Kyphas would seize the advantage and break every bone in his body.

Cirilai sent wave after wave of warmth up my arm, telling me that Vayl and Cole were on their way. The fact that neither they nor Sterling had said a word meant they thought Bergman had plugged into the Party Line too. Sucked a little that we'd have to communicate using hand signals and instinct, but you took what you got. I could only hope that Sterling had been around us long enough to tune into our vibe.

Which left the robokitty, still trotting at Bergman's feet like she'd been trained to heel. Hard to tell how she could help, especially if Bergman had already used one of her ass grenades to break down Kyphas's door. Too bad we couldn't fit a whole arsenal into that sleek little torso of hers. Then we could back her up to the plane portal and have her lob them right into hell. I'd be willing to bet that just viewing the wreckage would make all of Kyphas's working parts seize up like an oil-starved engine.

Which brought me back to Raoul, who liked engines, especially when they were pulling trains. I nearly called him then. But he'd given Bergman the daggers to start with. He'd known this moment had been brewing. Could probably see it all happening from his penthouse on-high. So what if Cole crapped out in the process? An acceptable loss, maybe. Or maybe he just liked hearing me beg for my loved one's lives.

I did nearly fall to my knees when that thunderous voice of his filled my head, blasting away all doubt as to who was the more powerful of us two, and therefore likely to kick my ass into oblivion.

YOU ARE POISED AT THE EDGE OF YOUR LIFE'S PRECIPICE. YOU CAN CLIMB. OR FALL. BUT YOU MUST MOVE!

Raoul's undertone came clear to me as well. *Stop whining and do what you do best. Not everything is your fault. Cole left the Trust, which made him vulnerable to Kyphas and the Rocenz. Bergman's fury at his helplessness as a child led him to choose the time and moment of his attack. Don't let their actions, and your fear of the consequences, paralyze you.*

I took a deep breath, paused to reload Grief, and moved on.

I caught up to Bergman, Astral, and Kyphas at the edge of the alcove. Leaning against the corner of the building for the few seconds it took to wipe the sweat off my face, I tried to get my bearings.

The vat glowed with a light so alien I wouldn't have been surprised to learn the mother ship was buried just under the tannery's surface. Sterling's net had begun to sag under the weight of dust particles and small rocks, which attached themselves to it like iron filings to a magnet. As soon as they touched, a bright blue flame leaped up and they hardened. Already I could see a new lid forming where the old one had been before.

As if he wanted her to witness the process up close, Bergman had dragged Kyphas right to the tank's edge. She was wailing now. Begging him not to throw her in. Astral, perching on a pillow-sized piece of rubble, seemed to be egging him on. The fire reflected eerily in her black eyes as she sang a tune by Bobby "Boris" Pickett, in such an authentic voice that I felt a smile stretch my lips. "They did the mash. They did the *monster* mash."

Somehow Astral's song cleared the air just enough that I realized I could speak safely. "Bergman," I said softly. "You can't open the canal. Sterling's net is there to keep Kyphas's allies from attacking us. No telling what you'll release if—"

He yelled, "Yousef! Are we set?"

Behind us, my stalker called back happily, "It is done, Mr. Miles! Come and see!" Bergman's smile raised goose bumps on my arms. But nothing had happened to the net. It continued to cover the vat, sparkling like a spiderweb covered in dew. So what—

Miles told me, "I know better than to touch the canal. It's not necessary anyway. I didn't even know about it when I made this plan."

My headache gained strength again, pounding against my temples as I said, "Oh?" Politely. Because he'd changed. When I wasn't looking, he'd become fierce and unpredictable. I gave him my Southern belle *do-tell* nod.

He explained, his tone real gentlemanly as he said, "I knew you'd show. You always do. And Raoul told me that where you are, a portal eventually appears. He doesn't know why, but…see? There it is."

He nodded, glancing over my shoulder as he did, so I looked. He was right, a plane portal stood in the middle of the tannery, just in front of a tank twice as large as the canal. It contained the swamp of chemicals necessary to begin the whole leather-making process. Balancing on the edge of the vat, Yousef stood holding a small, leather-bound book in one hand.

"I make a perfect place to put her!" Yousef said proudly, motioning to the door, the center of which wasn't its usual velvety black. I'd underestimated my stalker again. When he'd told me his workplace was considered the doorway to the land of the dead, I didn't realize that he could open those doors.

"So what's next?" I asked, careful to keep my eyes on Bergman despite the fact that they wanted to dart to Sterling, who'd just dropped off the roof of the building opposite mine. His move reminded me of Mary Poppins. Only instead of holding an umbrella he had a rope that lowered him so gently you'd swear his best friend was standing on the anchored side. All he had to do was stick a sandaled foot through the loop he'd tied to the end and hang on. I glanced at my broken fingernails, my bruised toes, and thought, *Wielders piss me off.*

Which was probably why Bergman knew the warlock had joined us. He could read my expressions better than I could Vayl's. Without turning his head he said, "Hey, Sterling, what's up?"

"Not much. How they hanging, dude?"

"One's a little lower than the other but my doctor says I can still have kids. How about you?"

Sterling was struggling too hard against a sudden urge to laugh to be able to form a coherent reply.

"How about you, Vayl?" Bergman asked, so überaware that he'd detected the vampire's presence even before I had, and I was wearing his ring! I turned to find my *sverhamin* standing just behind me holding Cole in his arms.

"We battled well, Miles. But I am afraid Cole is not himself."

I brushed a hand through our translator's hair. Even it had lost its usual wild spring. "Cole," I whispered. "Your eyes..."

"The world's gone red, Jaz," he said, sounding like a little kid who's gotten lost and knows his mom and dad should've found him by now. "It's like I'm looking at everything through a curtain of blood." His voice sounded like it had crawled over sharpened stones to get to me. "And I like it."

I glared at Kyphas. "You're doing this to him! Changing him into something he was never supposed to be!"

"He was always meant to be mine!" she said, with more spirit than she had a right to, considering her blood had left a pool the size of a dinner plate on the ground beneath her.

"Not in this state!" I said. "Look at him! This isn't the Cole you fell for! This is a crimson-eyed half-man who *still* won't love you once you've completely demonized him!"

She stared at him, her expression so needy I felt embarrassed to witness it. Then her eyes rolled up to Bergman. "Let me go and I'll release your friend," she said.

"You and your deals," Miles said sarcastically. "Where have they gotten us so far? You're still holding the Rocenz. Jasmine's still possessed. We're still not convinced Cassandra's a free bird. And now Cole's soul is halfway to perdition. You want to know what *I* think?"

She shook her head, slowly at first, and then when she caught the look in Bergman's eyes, a whole lot faster. He told her anyway.

"I think you need to die."

"I *can't* let go of the Rocenz!" she cried. "The blood between my fingers and the handle burns like acid, but it won't let go of me until it finishes the job it started! That's how it was crafted! And Cassandra *is* free! I told you the contract was complete!"

He leaned down. "You know what I know about demons?" She shook her head. "Demons lie." He yanked her upright. Whether it was the move or his intentions, I didn't know, but they both began to bleed heavily as he dragged her toward the door.

I turned to my *sverhamin*. "Vayl," I whispered.

He laid Cole down, gently propping his back against the corner I'd been using. "Our Trust, the stone, and the Rocenz," he reminded me. "We care for nothing else."

I stared down at Cole, blinking hard to stop the stinging in my eyes. "What if—"

Vayl pulled me away from the building, nodding for Sterling to join us as he said, "Cole may not be in the Trust. But he is a friend of us all. We protect him as if he was one of our own."

The three of us met at the head of the canal and walked, shoulder to shoulder, after Bergman and Kyphas as they stumbled toward Yousef and the door.

I said, "We've gotta get that stone out of her chest, Miles. Cole can't be okay again while—"

"I know what I'm doing!" he yelled, his eyes blazing as they caught mine.

"What about the Rocenz?" Vayl asked gently. "Jasmine cannot go on much longer without—"

"This demon's gotta die! Look at what she does to people she loves!" he shouted, pointing at Cole, who'd begun to cough something thick and bloody onto the ground between his trembling hands. "What do you think she's going to do to us the second she gets a chance? I've been reading up on spells. It's basic negation. She dies, her shit dies with her!"

"It's not always that simple though," Sterling said, his suggestion so gentle he might've been singing Miles a lullaby.

But our genius hadn't climbed to the top of his field without a hearty helping of thick-skulled stubbornness. He took a beat to stare into the hell Yousef had opened. I didn't know what his eyes revealed, but mine showed an island so tiny you couldn't have stretched out to sleep at night. The water around it was clear enough to reveal the fins and jagged teeth of the sea creatures that circled it as if they'd been called for a feast. Some of them couldn't wait, and those attacked each other, tearing huge hunks of meat from the backs and sides of weaker prey until the water ran red.

Bergman shoved Kyphas toward the door. "You'd better hope you fall on land, bitch. But it won't matter for long. Some of those sharks can walk."

I said, "Bergman! No!"

Vayl sprang forward like a panther leaping into the hunt.

Sterling swung his wand into play as the flames around the portal flared.

Every part of my mind screamed, *Bergman, no! Bergman, stop! You don't know what you're doing!* as I lunged after Vayl.

Sterling's wand shot out a claw of electric-blue bolts that flew between us. Too late. Bergman had pushed Kyphas into the portal's center. Then he stumbled and fell to his knees, pulling Kyphas down with him. He didn't stop there though. He was still moving. Sliding toward the gateway as if he was being...*pulled.*

"Bergman!" I shouted as Sterling's claw hit, raking down Kyphas's body, making her writhe and scream.

Miles began to shake from the echo zapping him through their connection, which now he couldn't seem to break even though he wanted to.

"Let me go!" he yelled. He tried to jerk away, but his hands stayed tight to her wrist and the Rocenz despite the fact that she'd planted her feet in his stomach and was pulling back just as hard as he was.

Astral leaped around their heads as they struggled, her urgency a reflection of the emotion she was recording. But nobody seemed to know what orders to give her.

Kyphas screamed, "Cole! Don't let them take me back!"

Unrecognizable sounds from behind us. I couldn't tell whether our sniper was puking or laughing, but the sound he made let me know he didn't give a shit where she ended up.

Vayl grabbed Bergman around the waist. Dug in his heels and tried to wrench him free.

Bergman screamed, "My arms! Vayl, you're breaking my arms! And my stitches! Ahhh!"

Now all three of them were inching toward the door, as if an invisible rope held them and was pulling them slowly into the pit.

Pissed at myself that I hadn't been able to respond faster, mad at Bergman for his sudden, unexplained bid for superhero status, infuriated with Yousef for helping him and Kyphas for just being herself, I joined the trio edging toward the gateway with the finesse of a tornado. In other words—I fell on them.

It had the effect of a wide receiver jumping onto the top of a pileup. Astral hopped on top of me, which resulted in some grunting, but no observable progress.

I took hold of Kyphas's arms and jerked. Astral sank her teeth into the demon's hand and pulled. Her wrist began to bleed where Bergman's hand would not slip. But even with the added grease and everyone playing tug-of-war, we couldn't break their grips. Because Bergman and Kyphas were no longer in charge. Something from inside that doorway had grabbed them both.

"Sterling! Do something!" I yelled as Vayl looked around for something we could brace ourselves against.

Sterling was emptying his pockets. "No, that won't work," he said and threw a pouch onto a growing pile on the ground. "That'll just burn holes in them," he murmured, and a velvet bag joined the bunch.

"Come on, you good-for-nothing warlock!" I yelled, nearly gagging on my own puke as I swallowed a wave of hell-stench that made my eyes roll back in my head. "Pull a rabbit out of your ass already!"

Bergman was only three feet from the door when I heard Sterling say, "A blessed shield be on you!"

The spell literally blew Vayl off Bergman, slamming him into the ground, leaving him dazed and steaming.

"Vayl!" I screamed as a second explosion of shield-shaped air ripped me off Kyphas. I rolled down a narrow aisle until my thighs hit a vat. "Fuck!" The only advantage of being slammed into a concrete bowl was that it had temporarily taken my mind off the potential loss of the Rocenz, and my life. Oh, and my headache.

I gripped the side of the vat and struggled to my feet, staring as Bergman lunged backward, trying to free himself from the demon's hold. When he got one hand off her wrist, I realized Sterling's spell had worked for him too. Now it was just between him and Kyphas again.

"Bergman!" I yelled. "We have to have that hammer!"

Even though my knees tried to buckle under me with every step, I began walking toward them, moving my eyes between Vayl, Cole, and Bergman. My *sverhamin* looked as sick as I felt, and his clothes were so badly singed they'd be going straight to the dumpster. But he was already rising. Cole—God, I could hardly stand to see his face, drawn taut in a snarl that, along with the finger-length horns, made him look more beast than human. His red eyes flickered on mine but he didn't recognize me.

Kyphas could see him too. But she seemed determined to ignore the devastation she'd brought on him. Instead of giving him a smile, a nod of encouragement, she stared into hell's fishing hole. When she finally turned back toward Bergman the door had begun to swallow her. She'd managed to wedge her heel into its base, but even her superior strength couldn't hold it back for long.

She looked up at him, both hands tight on the Rocenz now. "Save me," she whispered.

He sat on stones so caked with dried droppings, animal hair, and fat that the smell would never come out of his jeans, holding the other end of the only tool that could save my life.

I dropped behind him, wrapped my arms and legs around him like we were about to take the bumpiest sled ride of our lives, and held on tight, his blood soaking into my clothes as I said, "Save yourself, Kyphas." I jerked my head toward Cole. "And start by admitting there's one soul here that means more to you than your own life."

Her eyes went back to Cole, whose groans were becoming harder to tell apart from his growls. I couldn't read the expression on her perfectly formed face. I prayed it leaned toward pity. But before she could confirm or deny my hopes, she lost her grip on our world. Her legs slipped through the door. Water splashed. She jerked to one side.

Her knuckles went white as she clutched the Rocenz and screamed. "Cole!"

He screamed too. As if he could feel her pain.

Her torso was through. Bergman and I jolted forward like we'd come to the end of our roller-coaster ride and it was nearly time to debark. But I had a feeling we were just strapping in.

Shadows towered over us. Sterling dumped all his pockets, hoping to find the one spell that would separate the Rocenz from its operator. Vayl, holding his sword high like he meant to decapitate her, staggered forward.

"Give him up, Kyphas!" Vayl commanded. And again, dropping the sword slightly as if he was willing to make a deal, "Let Cole go. He might even love you for it."

One of her hands released. Reached into her chest and came out, fouled with blood and black stringy gore. But she also held the rock she'd chiseled.

Bergman reached for it. As soon as he touched it, Kyphas was yanked into the air. Bergman and I must've peered into hell at the same time, because we both screamed. Later he described his monster like something off the Sci-Fi channel, skinless and oozing, its hands so perfectly formed into blades that they sliced into Kyphas's muscles like meat hooks. My version wasn't so clear. It was as if the muck of the tannery vat had transferred itself into that ocean, and what rose from it to drag Kyphas under could only be seen in bits.

Algae-green tentacles that wrapped around her thighs, their slime eating into her skin like cure-resistant bacteria. A tuft of blond hair that fell like silk over huge hungry eyes gleaming with wicked humor.

The worst part? Bergman, still holding the rock, also flew upward, bringing me along for the ride. We slammed back down again so hard that I lost my grip and he began to slip through the gateway.

I lunged for his legs, yelling, "Vayl! Something huge is pulling us in!"

I caught Bergman's calves just as his belt disappeared through the gateway.

Screaming. So many voices I couldn't separate them anymore. Some in my mind. Some in hell. At least two in the world I was trying desperately to keep my best friend inside.

Bergman wedged his ankles under my armpits. "Ow! Son of a—"

My own voice was drowned by the sound of Sterling chanting, but the spell that raised the hair on the back of my neck wasn't helping me or Bergman. We kept inching forward. I risked a look, which was when I saw Vayl, outlined in a red glow, jump through the planar door.

"Holy shit! Sterling, what did you do?"

"Don't talk to me," he ordered. "I have to concentrate on him or he's going to get stuck there."

Speaking of which...I got a better grip on Bergman's calves and twisted, trying to roll him out of the gate. We just went sideways. And then we rolled the other way. Great moves if we ever wanted to transform ourselves into burritos. Kinda pointless for escaping a hell hatch.

"Don't let go!" I cried. I wasn't sure whether I was talking about the rock—or me—or hope. But the fear building in me gave me strength to pull even harder, especially when Bergman began to shake. And then it turned into a full-body shudder. He was dying, his soul unable to cope with the pain, the horror of lying poised over a pit whose contents—for him—I could only imagine. He began to pray. I heard him say something about his parents. Was I supposed to contact them? Or leave that job to the Agency? I couldn't understand his directions. And it pissed me off that he thought he needed to give them.

"Astral!" Vayl bellowed. "To me!" The cat, who'd spent the whole conflict singing "We Gotta Get Out of This Place" by the Animals, ran across our backs and leaped into the abyss.

"My cat!" moaned Bergman.

"She's helping!" I yelled.

"She's going to get decimated! We *all* are!"

"Are you seriously giving up when we've almost won?" I shouted. "You do realize if you let them get you that the Great Taker is going to find out every one of your secrets." I felt his legs tighten. Aha! He'd heard! "He'll probably even put you to work inventing some savage torture device that you'll then have to try out first on yourself. Is that really how you want to spend eternity?"

I felt his muscles bunch, and waited. Held my breath.

Vayl and Astral jumped back through the door. His sword dripped with blood and pus. Astral said, "Hello?"

Vayl said, "Now, Jasmine! Pull!"

A huge yank, Bergman backing himself out of the doorway though I could see how it tore at his shirt and gouged his skin. No doubt all his stitches would have to be redone. But it didn't stop me. I put everything I had into tugging him free. Not just muscle but bone and blood and every drop of love I'd ever felt for him. My feet scrabbled against the cobblestones until I felt them grabbed by two different sets of hands.

Don't let go. Just don't let go, I told myself. As the thought ran through my mind I felt my hands, slick with sweat and blood, slip from around Bergman's waist. Just before I lost my grip, I grabbed hold of the back of his belt and locked my fingers around it, wormed them under it until you couldn't have separated me from it without cutting my hands off.

Vayl and Sterling gave one hard yank. I screamed, tears jerking from my eyes as my ankles twanged.

As an explosion rocked the other side.

And Yousef began to read from his little book of gateways.

I sat up, feeling like I'd been bludgeoned by a pair of construction cranes, and not caring. At. All. Because Bergman was safe. Free of hell with Cole's namestone in one hand. And the Rocenz in the other. While Kyphas's severed hands still gripped the handle.

Chapter Twenty-Nine

We stood around Vayl's bed. He'd taken down his sleeping tent so it should've looked normal. Pristine white coverlet that reminded me of how my skin had looked thirty minutes into my after-battle shower. Pillows in the same color. Lamps on glass-topped tables beside the bed, both lit to reveal that which wasn't right at all. Cole, tossing and turning, his eyes glowing like reflectors as he looked around the room aimlessly, like nothing interested him enough to capture his attention for more than a few seconds at a time.

Sterling stood at the head of the bed. He'd set us in specifically appointed spots. Vayl and Bergman at each of Cole's feet. Me at the side that hadn't been bumped up against the wall. Even Astral had her place, sitting regally on Cole's belly, riding the waves of his restlessness.

Sterling held his wand in his right hand. Cole's namestone, rubbed clean to reveal its shining puce exterior, lay in his left palm. His words lilted off his tongue like a hymn as he said, "The demon completed three letters of the carving before she stopped. I can strip them off the stone, but they've been brought to a sort of life, you understand? I can't completely undo them."

"So what is it that you have arranged here?" asked Vayl, gesturing to the stone, to all of us, to the unlit candles he'd set in the window-sills and to robokitty, surfing Cole's unrest like an old pro.

"It's a reclamation," said Sterling. "Kyphas bound a part of Cole into each letter and tried to transform it into pure evil. When I pull the letters off, I'm going to put each one into you. Because you're his closest friends. You know him. You love him. So you have to con-centrate every thought on all your memories of him. And as your bit of him is cleansed by those, it will return to him. Make him whole again."

I raised an eyebrow. "So we're like, what, water filters?"

Sterling smirked. "You could say that."

We all heard the hesitation in his voice, but Bergman was the only one who could bring himself to ask, "Will he be the same? After?"

Sterling turned his wand between his fingers. He sighed. "Of course not. We're all changed, every day, by our experiences. Usu-ally in ways so minute that years will pass before anyone notices. Sometimes it's a little more radical." His voice, lyrically gentle, assured us Cole could survive what was to come even as he said, "Imagine nearly becoming a demon. Vayl, you've probably been closer than any of us. Can you predict what Cole will be like after this?"

From the way Vayl's lips thinned I could tell he didn't like the question. Because he didn't want to go to the place in his head that would give him the memories he'd need to provide an honest answer. I also knew, even before his turning, he'd never been the type to back away.

He looked at each of us in turn. And then he said, "The night-mares will be the worst part. Those, and the urge to come back to this place. To rip away the lid that is growing over Sterling's net and find out what it could have been like to let the hellion in him join with Kyphas forever. But as long as he has us to remind him of who he is, as long as we *need* him, he will hold fast."

We stared at our friend, skirting the edge of what Granny May used to call Satan's Playground, suffering unimaginable torments because the games they played there made everybody scream—and because right now he wanted to be on the team.

"Touch him," said Sterling. "Make sure you have contact with his skin."

I took his hand. Vayl and Bergman each wrapped their fingers around an ankle. Every candle in the room flared. Vayl didn't seem surprised, but Miles and I traded *Wowsa* eye blinks.

The warlock held the stone out over the center of Cole's body, almost directly on top of Astral's head if they'd been sitting perfectly still. He nodded to me.

"Okay, kittybot," I whispered. "Access everything you just downloaded on Cole Bemont."

She jacked her jaws open and out came the Enkyklios spotlight, signaling the playback of a brand-new holofile, one the three of us had made together while Sterling had prepared the reclamation. The movie began with the first time I'd ever met Cole, in the ladies' room at a party thrown by terrorists. Though only a few months had passed, we'd both changed. I looked thinner then, worn down, and so grim that it seemed like I'd forgotten how to smile. Cole looked...younger.

Astral's job was to play every file we'd entered into the Enkyklios that had to do with Cole, what we knew about his family and his work. Sterling said it would help him to see who he'd been when he was fully human. I wasn't so sure. He'd gotten the crap kicked out of him a few times while I'd known him. Maybe he'd see this transition as a way to protect himself from that ever happening again.

Raoul, I whispered. *Where are you? We could really use—*

Sterling began to speak, arcane words I recognized only by the buzz at the base of my brain and the goose bumps rising on my skin. As the rhythm of his spell filled the room, I knew without a doubt that if he really wanted to become a Bard, nothing would stop him. Already his magic felt like music, making us sway slightly from one foot to the other as we held tightly to our friend.

Cole began to convulse. It hurt to watch him, arching his back so high I heard his bones pop in protest a couple of times. When he lay flat again his legs began to tremble, but Vayl and Bergman held on, watching with me as the letters Kyphas had rammed into her heartstone transformed into a black, tarry substance that dripped into Sterling's hand.

I'm not drinking that. Don't even ask. But Sterling had other plans. He took Cole's essence to the candles. Little by little he let the liquid from the stone drip into each flickering flame, until he'd walked the whole course of the room. By the time he was done the place had filled with grayish blue smoke.

Why haven't the detectors gone off? Granny May was back at her tapestry, looking curiously at the sky.

Seriously? I'm inhaling Cole-juice and all you can think about are fire-safety rules?

What's he smell like? asked my Inner Bimbo with an avid look on her face.

How can I take anything you say seriously when your lipstick is always smeared? I replied.

I'd like to know too, said Teen Me.

What, you're all in this together now?

Granny May shrugged. *He's the one who could've been. So... we're interested. Plus, we know who he ends up with, romantically speaking. Which gives us even more of a stake. So to speak.*

We do? Who?

She waved her finger in front of her face and gave me that *tch, tch* noise that makes me want to throw pillows. *Quit changing the subject. We want answers.*

I sighed. *He's like...those french fries you can only get at the county fair. You know the ones I mean? Lick-your-lips salty with some sort of addictive secret flavoring that you know isn't good for you but you don't care because it's so amazing.*

They all nodded. Yup. That was Cole.

"Concentrate!" Sterling said, so sharply that I jumped and nearly lost my grip of Cole's hand. I started to watch Astral's projections but our warlock said, "Think of private conversations with Cole. Think of him at his most honest. His most human."

Almost at the same moment Vayl, Bergman, and I began to laugh. Sterling raised his eyebrows. "Really?"

"He's pretty funny," said Miles.

"Good. Keep that in mind." Sterling stepped away from the bed. I should've guessed what was about to come when he wrapped his arm around the bars that covered the windows. Three quick movements of his wand drew a sparkling white image in the smoke that faded as soon as it appeared. But it seemed to work as a catalyst, raising a wind inside the room that swirled the smoke in a circle, shoving more of it down our throats.

My curls began to dance in the air. Vayl's shirt flapped against his broad chest. Bergman sneezed. Cole went perfectly still as we remembered. His you-should-hug-me-now grin. The way his eyes lit when a woman, any woman, entered the room. And the love that spilled out like concession-stand popcorn when he talked about his family, old girlfriends, the beach, bubblegum...

And then we could see it happening. The smoke clearing as our breath wafted out, looking winter-day frosty. The cleansed air swirling into Cole, relaxing him more and more with each breath. The edges of his eyes fading to pink and then to white before closing. He began to snore.

Sterling left the window. "Astral can stop now," he said.

I gave the cat her order and she closed the Enkyklios down, stepping off Cole's stomach only to curl up beside him. "Good idea," I told her. "Keep watch and let me know as soon as he wakes."

We still hadn't let him go, though. It was like, having brought ourselves so close to the part of our team that brought us the most happiness, we couldn't walk away.

Sterling said, "You did well. I believe he's been completely reclaimed."

We nodded. Vayl stepped back. So did Bergman. I squeezed Cole's hand. Then I placed it gently on the bed and began to turn away. *Wait. What did I—*

"Jasmine?" asked Vayl, coming to slip his arm around my waist. "Are you all right?"

I peered at Cole's eyes. They stayed closed. Maybe I hadn't seen them flutter just slightly. Maybe those two slits of red I thought I'd spied peering out from beneath his lashes had just been a side effect of sniffing soul-smoke.

This is why you never did drugs, right, Jazzy? asked Granny May as she threaded her needle.

Amen. I nodded, and laying my head against Vayl's shoulder, I let him lead me from the room.

CHAPTER THIRTY

I t is nearly dawn," Vayl said. He stood by the window to my room, looking down into the courtyard. Lights came on in a second-floor window, distracting us both.

"Is that Monique's room?" he asked.

"Yeah."

We watched, shameless voyeurs, as Bergman's skinny frame crossed in front of the curtain and stopped. His shadow was joined seconds later by the curvilicious shape of Monique. They stood that way for a long time. And then the distance between them slowly closed, until to our eyes they were a single entity. Moments later the light went out.

Vayl turned to me. "I hope she is gentle." For the first time, his smile made him look old. He stared up into the sky, and I realized how much he was going to miss the sun.

I said, "Won't you be able to stay awake now? I mean, now that you remember what year it is and everything?"

He turned to me. Shrugged like it didn't matter as he said, "No. I have lost..." He paused, looked toward the sky, as if by force of will he could make the sun come out while he was still up so he could see sunshine and clouds again. "As with the ice armor, the ability I had gained to stay awake beyond dawn and dusk has been wiped out by the curse."

"That fucking Roldan."

His nod barely moved air. "Just so. However, we have the Rocenz now." He gestured to the tool sitting on my trunk, looking so innocent I might've guessed the maintenance man had forgotten and left it there after he fixed the air conditioner. If I hadn't known better.

"Yeah. What do you say after we use it to carve Brude's name into the gates of hell, we beat Roldan to death with it?"

He raised an eyebrow. "Feeling violent tonight, my love?"

Though I'd closed the door behind me, I hadn't been able to take my hand off the knob. It was like I thought this one extra step could keep Cole safe if he woke and needed me to come running and— *what? Smother whatever Kyphas left in him? How would you do that without killing the rest, the best part of him now?*

I dropped my hand and walked over to Vayl. Wrapped my arms around him. Breathed in his scent, closed my eyes and pretended that I was lying on a bed of pine needles with him, naked and willing, beside me. I said, "Umm, not as much now. I do want to know some things though."

"All right."

"Back at the tannery, Sterling sent you into hell."

A sigh, so soft I nearly missed it, that told me he'd prefer never, ever to discuss those last hairy moments when neither of us knew if we'd survive to share another moment like this one. He said, "Yes. I knew I could only destroy Kyphas from the inside. But I needed help."

"Astral?"

His arms tightened around me. "You know Bergman. He would never outfit her with one weapon designed to defeat demon defenses when he could as easily equip her with two. Knowing he had already used one of Astral's grenades to destroy Kyphas's door blockade, I brought her through the door so I could direct the second grenade at both her and her...attackers."

I waited for him to tell me what he'd seen in hell. But he wasn't inclined to describe his version. Can't say that I blamed him. So I asked him another question that had been nagging at me.

"What happened to Helena?"

He pulled away long enough for me to wonder why his eyes had gone such a dark, troubled blue. And then he pulled me in even tighter. "We moved several times after that first trip to Marrakech. Finally we settled in Northern Ireland, where she met a boy named John Litton who had brains and ambition but, alas, no money. They were married on my estate in the spring of 1783 and sailed to America with Berggia and his wife shortly after." He paused. "I had many an entertaining letter from her for the next two years. And then a single note from John telling me that she had died in childbirth."

"Oh, Vayl," I whispered. "I'm so sorry." I hesitated, but I just had to know. "Did the ... the baby die too?"

"No, they lived."

"She had twins?"

"Yes."

Wow. Now I felt even closer to her. And more determined than ever to exact some sweet revenge for her. A life that short shouldn't have had to spend so much time with misery in it. I said, "The Berggias?"

"They helped John raise his daughters and died at a very old age, within just a few days of one another."

"That's good, then."

"Yes, they were a devoted couple who deserved some happiness"—his lips brushed my forehead—"like us. I can feel it, almost within our grasp. But first we must go back." He tipped his head toward the tannery, though we both knew he meant deeper. "And it must be soon."

"Yeah. But we need to make detailed, get-in-get-busy-get-out plans. And my head still hurts."

"So let us leave that for tomorrow." He slid his hands up my back, squeezed the tension out of my shoulders. Ran his fingers down to the base of my spine. Parts of my body seemed to wake from a long sleep. To stretch and moan as trickles of pleasure washed through them.

I pressed my breasts against his chest. "Tomorrow's soon enough for me," I whispered as I ran my fingers up into his soft curls, as I left feathery kisses along his cheekbones, the sides of his lips, the base of his jaw.

"Then tonight," he murmured into my ear, moved his lips downward, brushed his fangs against my neck. "In what we have left of it. Jasmine. Give me something to remember."

Acknowledgments

Thanks so much to my agent, Laurie McLean, whose unfailing enthusiasm keeps me feeling optimistic. Orbit is a fab publisher, so I must thank all of my partners there, who include my editor, Devi Pillai, publicity geniuses Alex Lencicki and Jack Womack, and my copy editor, Penina Lopez. Love and gigantic hugs to my readers, Hope Dennis and Katie Rardin. Thanks to Roxanne Montgomery Trahan for introducing me to Jimmy Buffet's great song "Breathe In, Breathe Out, Move On." Anouk Zijlma was a wonderful source of information about Marrakech, so thanks to you, dear lady. I deeply appreciate your help! And to Jazfans everywhere—you rock!

extras

orbit

meet the author

Cindy Pringle

JENNIFER RARDIN began writing at the age of twelve, mostly poems to amuse her classmates and short stories featuring her best friends as the heroines. She lives in an old farmhouse in Illinois with her husband and two children. Find out more about Jennifer Rardin at www.JenniferRardin.com.

introducing

If you enjoyed BITTEN IN TWO,
look out for

THE DEADLIEST BITE

Book 8 of the Jaz Parks series

by Jennifer Rardin

We ran up the main stairs to the third floor, where I found my jeans crumpled beside the cozy brown suede chair where I liked to curl up every afternoon with a book and a can of Diet Coke. I pulled my phone out of the back pocket and stuck it between my ear and shoulder while I shoved my legs into my Levi's.

"Hello?"

"Jaz? Where's Vayl?"

"Hi, Cassandra. He's with me."

"He's all right, then?"

"What?" I felt my fingers go numb. Usually I reacted faster. It was my job to make sure my emotions didn't cloud my judgment. Even for the extra three seconds it took me to realize my psychic friend was freaking out about my lover. "What did you See?"

"There was a mix-up in Australia. I accidentally packed one of your T-shirts in my suitcase. So I was folding it back into my luggage because Dave and I are coming up to visit you and Evie. It was supposed to be a surprise—" She swallowed a sob.

"Tell me now, Cassandra." I tried to keep my voice calm. No sense in shouting at the woman who had already saved my brother's life with one of her visions. But if she'd been in the room I'd have shaken her till her teeth rattled.

"When I touched your shirt I saw you, leaning over Vayl's body. He had a stake through his heart. The blood—oh, Jaz, the blood." She started to cry for real now.

"Anything else? Come on, Cassandra, I need to know everything you Saw." I'd zipped into my pants. Run to the stairs. Managed to make it to the second floor without breaking my neck. Jack was way ahead of me.

"I don't know. There's this explosion, but not like the kind you see in movies. It's more . . . ripply. And at the middle is a young man. Younger than you. Taller, even, than Vayl, with full brown hair that keeps falling onto his forehead. He's snarling, which makes two deep dimples appear on his cheeks. He's standing in front of a tall oak door, above which is hanging—"

"A pike with a gold tassel," I finished.

"Yes!"

"Shit. Cassandra, that's Vayl's front door. And you've just described the kid who was ringing the bell."

"Did Vayl answer?"

"I don't—"

A shot rang out, tearing my heart in two. Too far ahead of me to gauge his location, Jack growled menacingly, already on his way down the final set of steps. I glanced into the well made by the turn of the stairs from second to first floor. Yeah, I could jump it. So I did, landing on Vayl's blue, overstuffed sofa. Rolling into the walnut coffee table fronting it, knocking it across the hall into a case full of antique knives. I raised my arm, protecting my face from the shattering glass.

Not knowing how far the glass had scattered, I protected my bare feet by jumping back onto the couch. Then I took one second to assess the situation.

Twenty feet from me, at the other end of the hall in front of the open door, Vayl lay in a spreading pool of blood, the bloody hole in his forehead a result of the .22 lying on the floor. Two reasons the young man kneeling over him still wasn't holding it: he needed both hands for the hammer and stake he now held poised over Vayl's chest, and Jake's teeth had sunk deep enough into his right wrist that, by now, he'd have been forced to drop it anyway.

Only a guy as big as this one wouldn't have been thrown completely off balance by a full-on attack via 120-pound malamute. His size had kept him off his back, though it hadn't allowed him to recover his balance enough to counter with the stake in his free hand. That would change if I didn't reach the scene in time.

I jumped to the outside of the stairs, holding the rail to keep from falling as I cleared the fallout from the display case. Another jump took me to the floor. Five running steps gave me a good start for a spin kick that should've caught the intruder on the temple. But unless they're drugged, people don't just sit and wait for the blow.

He pulled back, catching my heel on his nose. It broke, spraying blood all over his shirt and Jack. But it didn't take him down. In fact, it seemed to motivate him. Desperation filled his eyes. He ripped his hammer hand out of Jack's grip, though the bloody gashes in his forearm would hurt like a son of a bitch when his adrenaline rush faded. Afraid his next move would be a blow to my dog, I lunged at him. I was wrong. He threw the hammer at me, forcing me to hit the floor. I rolled when I felt his shadow loom over me, knowing the worst scenario had me pinned under all that weight. But it never fell on me. I jumped to my feet and began to unholster Grief, though the last thing I wanted was to kill the bastard before I found out who'd sent him.

Still, I was too late. The intruder had retrieved his .22 and was pointing the business end at my chest. He'd probably hit me too if he held his breath long enough to stop shaking. The only positive I could see was that I stood between him and Vayl. For now.

Jack growled menacingly and began to approach the man, his fur standing on end so he looked like the miniature bear he sounded most like when he vocalized.

The gun wavered as the man said, "You tell that dog to stop, or I will shoot it."

"No, Jack," I said. "Sit."

He came to an unhappy stop beside me. Once again I was looking down the barrel of my ultimate end. Because Raoul had informed me that my body couldn't take another rise to life. If this scumbag capped me, I'd be done. And I *so* wasn't ready.

I said, "I don't know you. And I thought I knew all of our enemies. You're not a werewolf. You're not Vampere. You're definitely not a pro. So what's a human who's never killed anybody in his life doing trying to off the CIA's greatest assassin?"

His eyebrows went up. So. He hadn't been told about our work. Baffling. Still, whoever picked him had chosen well. Amateurs occasionally succeeded where professionals failed because they were unpredictable. And motivated. This one definitely had his reasons for being here. I could see it in the way his eyebrows kept twitching down toward his nose. He was a time bomb ready to blow everybody in the room to bloody bits.

He raised the gun. Uh-oh. While I'd been thinking, so had he. And it looked like he'd made a decision. "You need to walk away from that vampire," he said.

"No."

He pushed the barrel toward me, to make sure I understood he could pull the trigger. "I'm not playing. I will kill you if that's what it takes to smoke him."

"Doesn't matter. I'll die if you do that anyway."

The remark confused him. Upset him. *This isn't a bad man, but damn, something has pushed him way past his limit.* I watched his finger tighten on the trigger. I said, "Don't. Dude, you'll be killing a federal agent. They put you in jail forever for that kind of shit."

"Jail?" He laughed. "I'm already in hell." Which was when I knew there was nothing I could say to divert him. I looked down at Jack, touched the soft fur on the top of his head in farewell. Glanced over my shoulder at Vayl. Only long enough for the pain to lance through my heart.

I could pull on him, make my final moments an epic shootout. But Jack could get hurt in the cross fire. And I'd never forgive myself if that happened. "Get it over with, then."

NOT SO FAST!!

I slammed my hands over my ears, though I was pretty sure the voice came from inside my head until I saw that the intruder was wincing and wiping blood from his earlobes as well.

The floor started to shake. Jack yelped and tried to hide between my legs as the polished pine floorboards between me and the intruder began to splinter and the fiery outline of an arched doorway pushed itself up from the basement below.

"Well," I whispered to my dog. "This is new."

I was pretty sure the intruder couldn't see the plane portal rising to stand between us. Most humans never did. But he did get a load of the five-by-six-foot gap developing in the floor. And when my Spirit Guide, Raoul, seemed to step out of thin air, I didn't blame him for needing to sit down. Which he did. On a plush, round-seated chair that was currently covered with wood chips.

Raoul recovered his weapon so easily I felt a little stupid to have ever been paralyzed by it. Maybe I was getting soft in my old age. Maybe seeing Vayl halfway to dead had freaked me out more than I should've let it.

Raoul reversed the gun and lightly tapped the intruder on the forehead with it. "Wrong choice, Aaron. And here I thought you knew better." He lifted the back of his jungle camouflage jacket and stuck the .22 in the waistband of his matching pants. Then he turned to face me. "Stop trying to get yourself killed. Even the Eminent agreed with me on this one. It isn't your time yet."

"I wasn't *trying*—it's not? Cool." Nice to think that the folks who called the shots upstairs had actually approved of Raoul helping me for once. Especially since it had involved saving my neck. Again.

"So what do you and the other Eldhayr think about this dude? What did you call him, Aaron?" I asked, pointing my chin toward the failed assassin.

Raoul pulled me aside. "I'm not allowed to interfere there." He looked hard into my eyes, trying to communicate information I hadn't known him long enough to decipher. He said, "All I can say is that it's good, really good, that you didn't kill him. Keep doing that."

"What about Vayl?" I asked. "What can you say about him?"

"You really need to hear that he's going to be okay? You already know that, Jaz. A bullet to the head can't kill a vampire as powerful as him."

I shrugged. It's one thing to understand something intellectually. Something completely different to see your lover looking fully dead from a head wound. So I reminded myself again, *He's just been knocked out. If you lifted his head you'd see the back of his skull has probably already re-formed. You shouldn't be trying to figure out how your stomach can manage to clench itself that tight. You should be patting yourself on the back for hooking up with a guy who's that tough to kill.*

"Jasmine? Jaz? Is it over? What happened?"

The voice, small and tinny, could've been mistaken for one of my inner voices. If I hadn't suddenly realized I'd dropped my phone during the fight and now Jack was trying to dial China with his nose.

"Cut it out," I murmured as I picked it up. "You don't even like rice." I put the receiver to my ear. "Cassandra? I can't believe you're still there."

"He's important!"

"Of course he is. But he'll be fine. Vampires are—"

"No! I mean, yes, of course. But I'm talking about the young man."

"WHAT? You can't be on Raoul's side in this. This guy, Aaron, nearly killed us both!" I glared at the would-be killer. He stared straight at me. Raised his chin slightly. Didn't even blink.

Cassandra yelled, "Jasmine Elaine Parks, you listen to your future sister-in-law, dammit! Something is making me tingle like I'm electrified. Let me talk to Aaron!"

I held the phone out to him. "You have a call."

He grimaced. "I'm a little busy right now."

"Either you talk to the nice lady or I punch your lights out." His eyes went to Raoul, so I added, "Oh, don't look to him for help. He's like the UN. He'll bitch and whine about my behavior, but he'll sit back and let me do the dirty work because, in the end, he knows I'm the one who's gonna save the world."

Raoul growled, "That was a low blow."

I shrugged. "I'm sorry. I know the Eminent ties your hands a lot. I just tend to get pissy when people try to kill the guy I love." I looked up at him. "But I do appreciate you coming when you did. Great timing, as usual."

I shoved the phone toward Aaron. "The threat still stands, mainly because I'm highly ticked off and I wanna hit something. It'd be so great if you gave me an excuse."

Aaron took the phone, staring at me suspiciously as he said, "Hello? Yes. No." He listened for a while before his face puckered. But he managed to master the emotion Cassandra had pulled out of him before he said another word. Which was "Thanks."

He handed the phone back to me. "Well?" I asked the woman on the other end who deserved a respectful ear, both because she'd survived nearly a thousand years on this earth, and because she'd chosen to spend the next fifty or so with my brother.

Cassandra took a deep breath. "I can't be sure without touching the boy, but I consulted the tarot while he and I were speaking. It points to the same signs the Enkyklios has been showing me. I have to do more research. But it would be best if I could touch him—"

"What are you trying to tell me?"

"Whatever you do, don't hurt him," she said, unknowingly echoing Raoul's advice. "I believe that, in another life, he was Vayl's son."